NO ONE RETURNS *from the* ENCHANTED FOREST

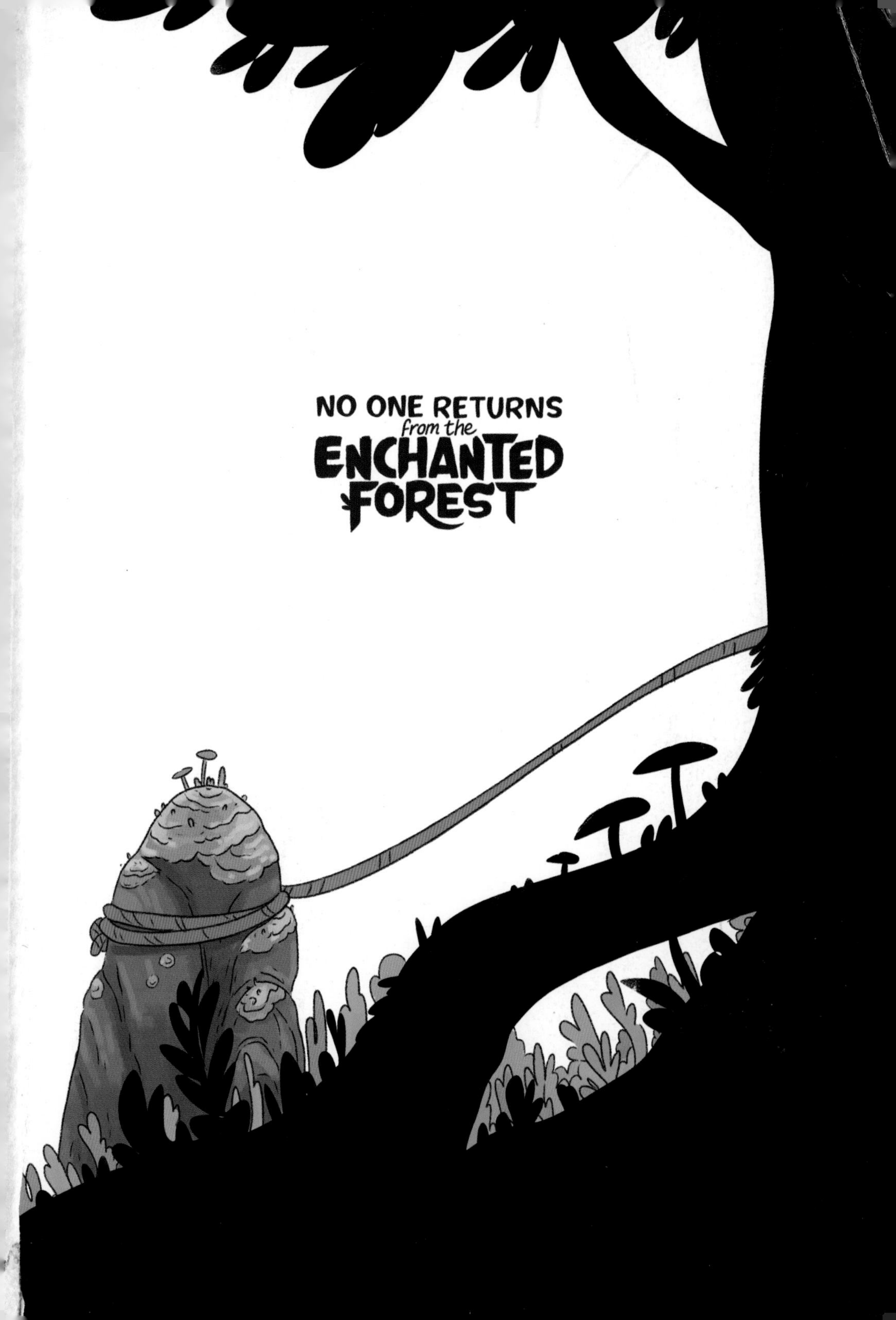

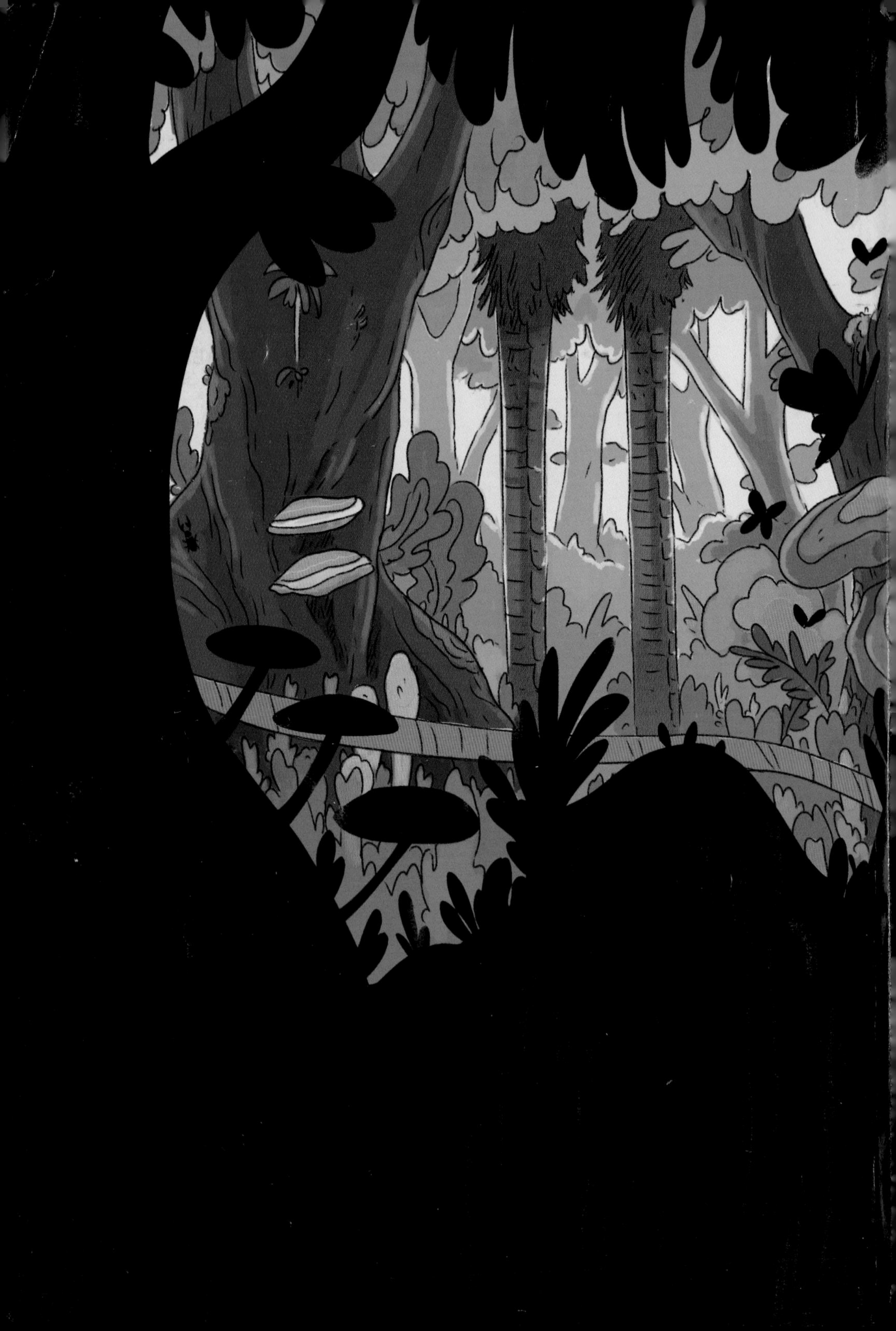

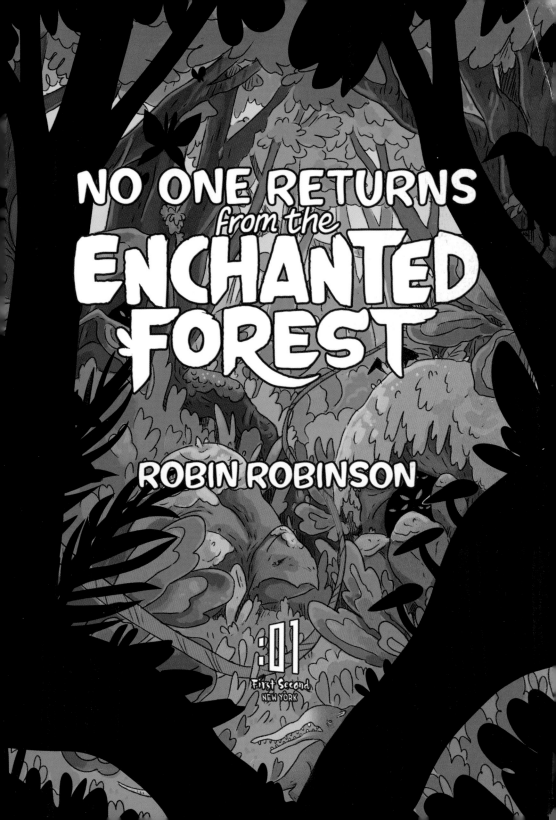

NO ONE RETURNS
from the
ENCHANTED FOREST

ROBIN ROBINSON

:01
First Second
NEW YORK

First Second

Published by First Second
First Second is an imprint of Roaring Brook Press,
a division of Holtzbrinck Publishing Holdings Limited Partnership
120 Broadway, New York, NY 10271
firstsecondbooks.com
mackids.com

Library of Congress Control Number: 2020919818

Our books may be purchased in bulk for promotional, educational, or business use.
Please contact your local bookseller or the Macmillan Corporate and Premium Sales Department
at (800) 221-7945 ext. 5442 or by email at MacmillanSpecialMarkets@macmillan.com.

FIRST
EDITION

First edition, 2021
Edited by Robyn Chapman and Bethany Bryan
Cover design by Kirk Benshoff
Title design by A. L. Kaplan
Interior book design by Molly Johanson and Robin Robinson
Color assistance by Nathan Robison
Printed in China by 1010 Printing International Limited, North Point, Hong Kong

ISBN 978-1-250-21153-8 (paperback)
1 3 5 7 9 10 8 6 4 2

ISBN 978-1-250-21152-1 (hardcover)
1 3 5 7 9 10 8 6 4 2

Digitally penciled and inked in Clip Studio. Colored in Photoshop with custom brushes.

Don't miss your next favorite book from First Second!
For the latest updates go to firstsecondnewsletter.com and sign up for our enewsletter.

THIS BOOK IS FOR MY LITTLE BROTHERS, ALK AND JAK.
I WOULD DEFINITELY VENTURE INTO THE ENCHANTED FOREST FOR YOU.
(BUT PLEASE DON'T MAKE ME--I'M NOT THAT GOOD AT KNITTING!)

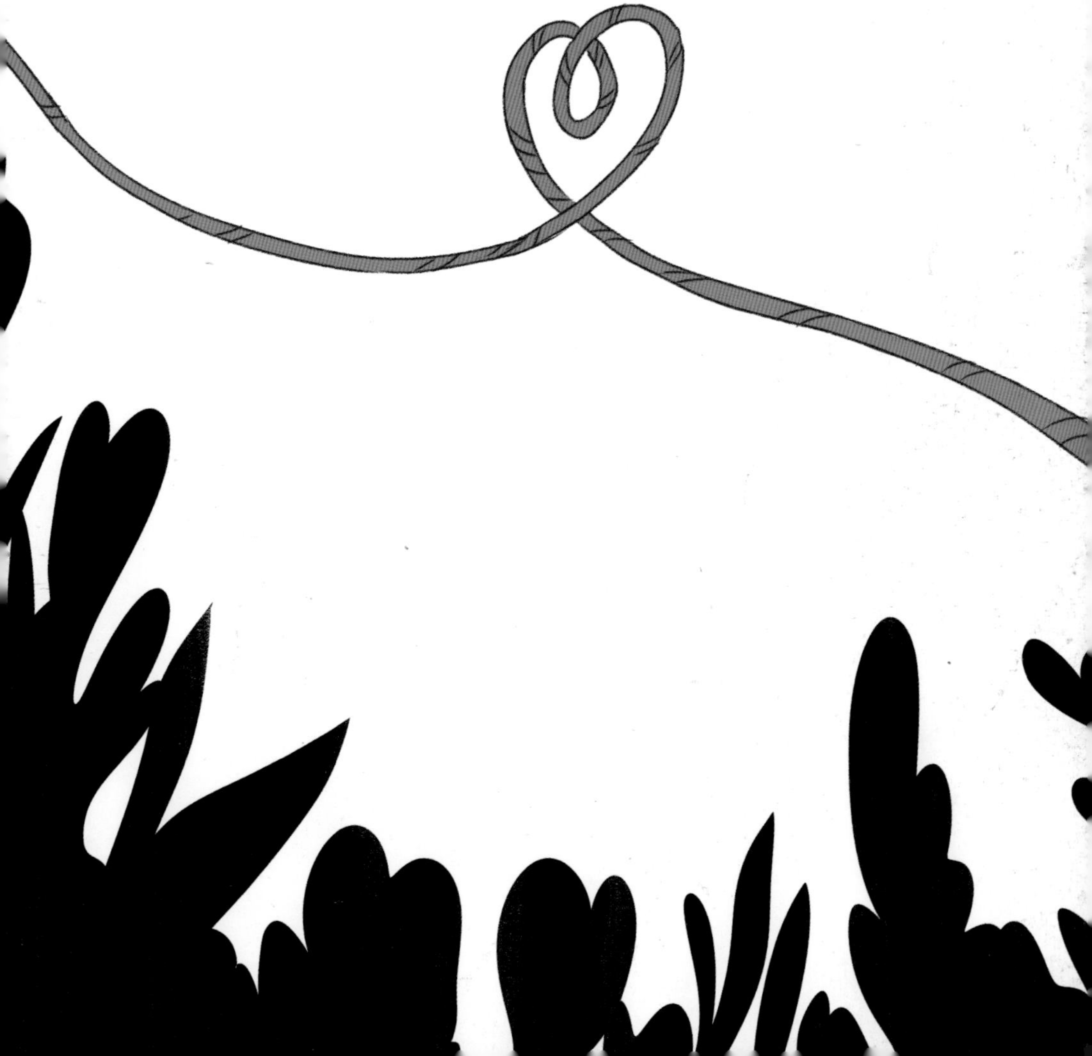

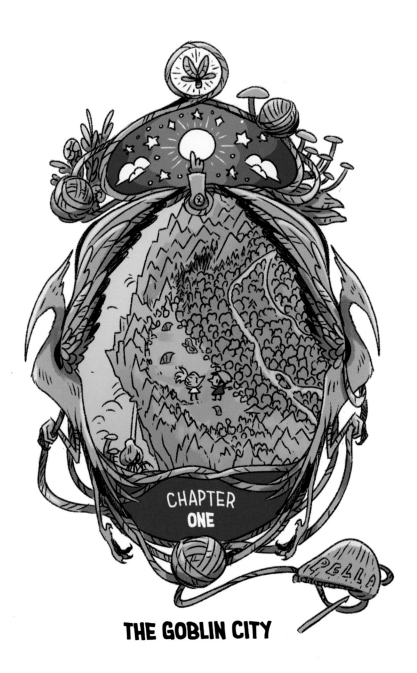

CHAPTER
ONE

THE GOBLIN CITY

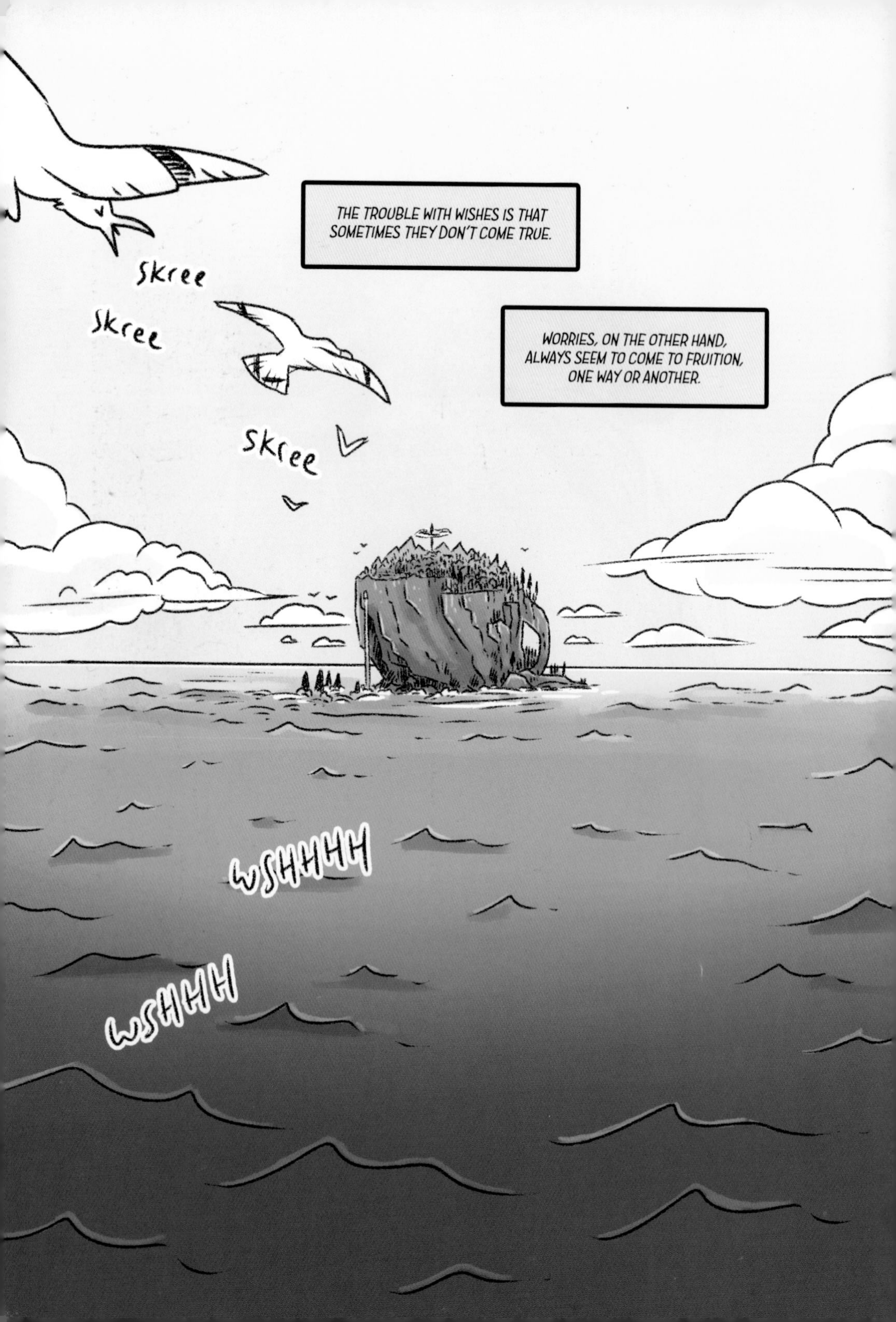
THE TROUBLE WITH WISHES IS THAT SOMETIMES THEY DON'T COME TRUE.
Skree
Skree
WORRIES, ON THE OTHER HAND, ALWAYS SEEM TO COME TO FRUITION, ONE WAY OR ANOTHER.
Skree
WSHHHH
WSHHH

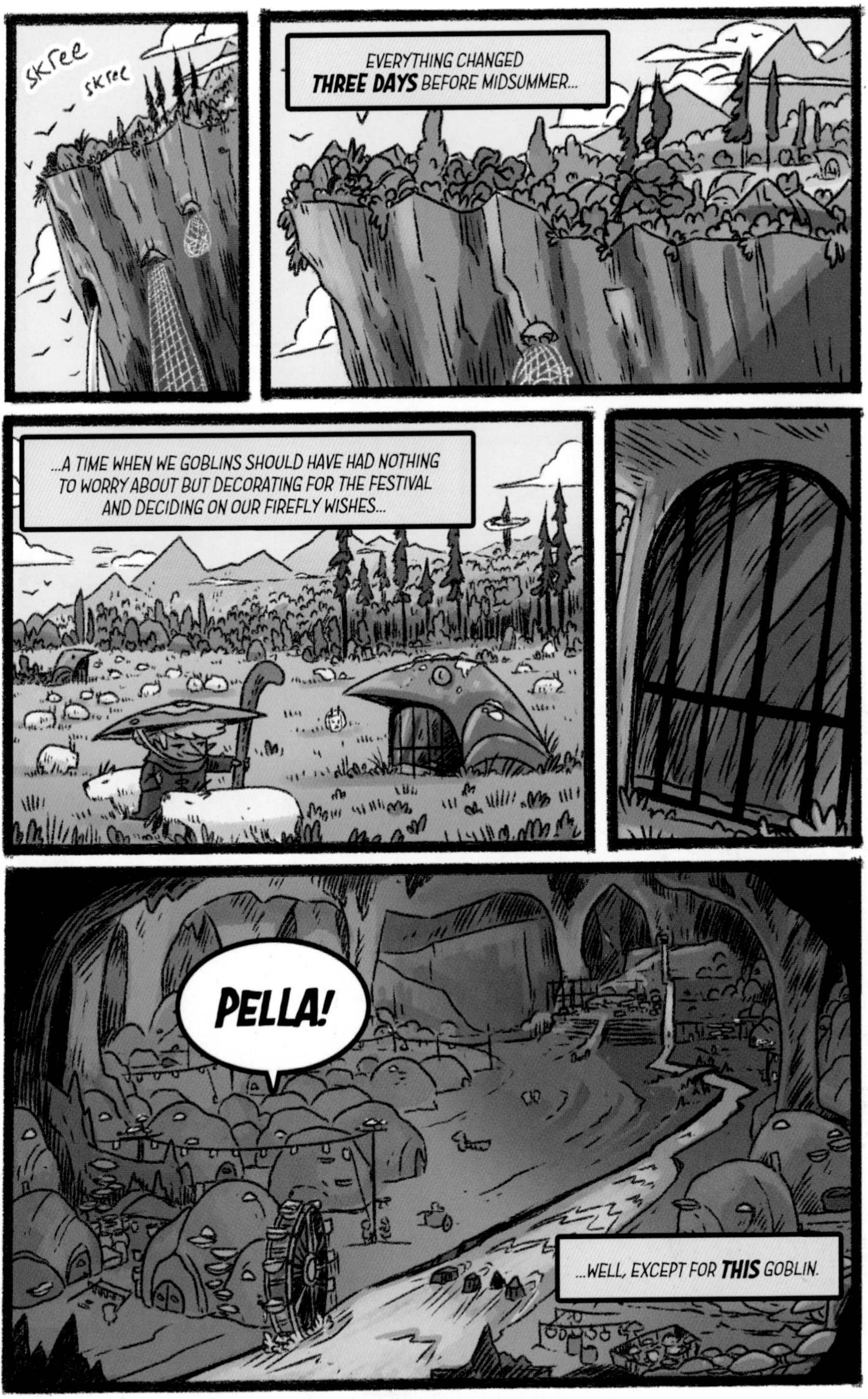
SKREE
SKREE
EVERYTHING CHANGED
THREE DAYS BEFORE MIDSUMMER...
...A TIME WHEN WE GOBLINS SHOULD HAVE HAD NOTHING TO WORRY ABOUT BUT DECORATING FOR THE FESTIVAL AND DECIDING ON OUR FIREFLY WISHES...
PELLA!
...WELL, EXCEPT FOR THIS GOBLIN.

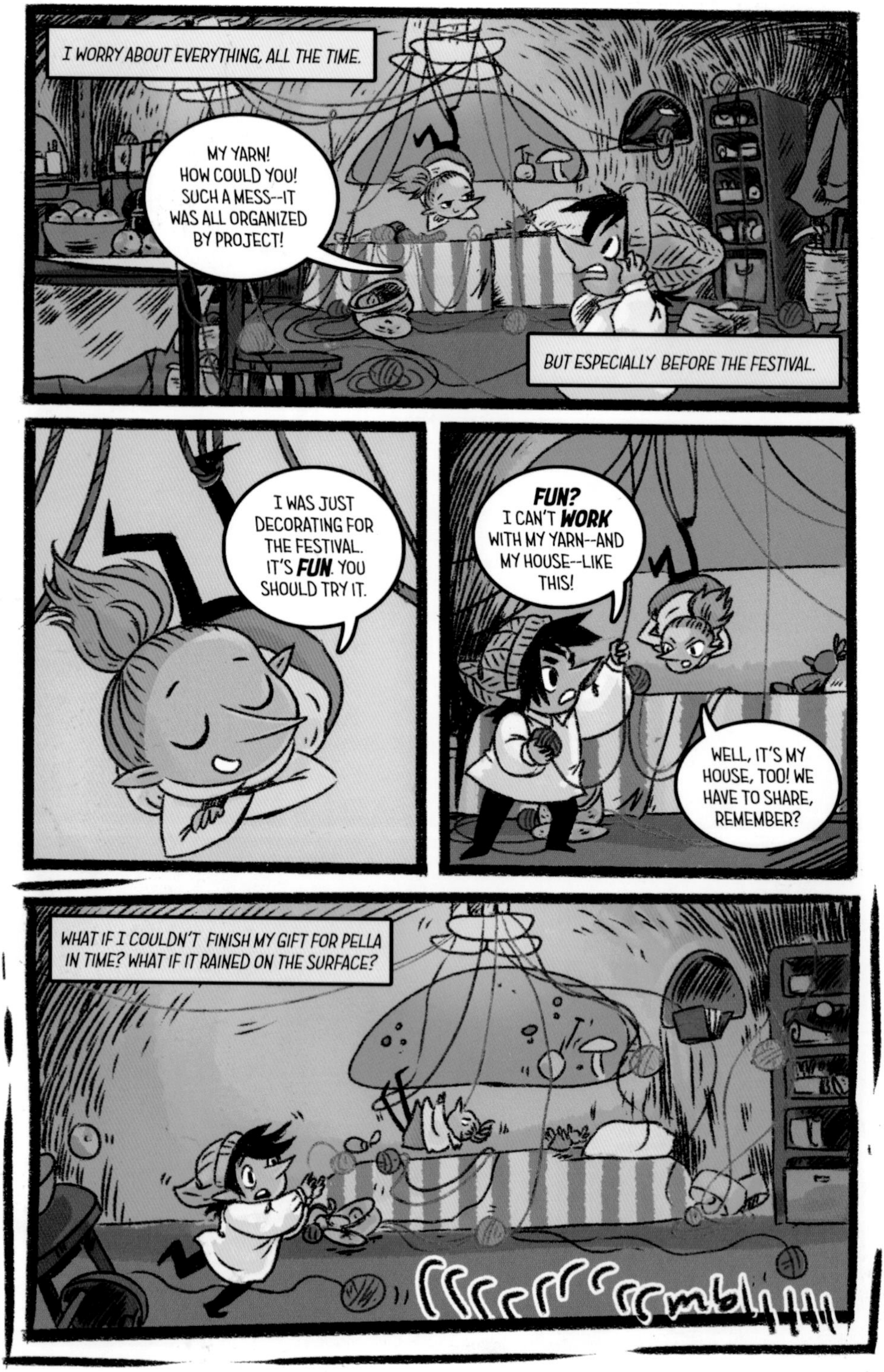
I WORRY ABOUT EVERYTHING, ALL THE TIME.
MY YARN! HOW COULD YOU! SUCH A MESS--IT WAS ALL ORGANIZED BY PROJECT!
BUT ESPECIALLY BEFORE THE FESTIVAL.
I WAS JUST DECORATING FOR THE FESTIVAL. IT'S **FUN**. YOU SHOULD TRY IT.
FUN? I CAN'T **WORK** WITH MY YARN--AND MY HOUSE--LIKE THIS!
WELL, IT'S MY HOUSE, TOO! WE HAVE TO SHARE, REMEMBER?
WHAT IF I COULDN'T FINISH MY GIFT FOR PELLA IN TIME? WHAT IF IT RAINED ON THE SURFACE?
rrrrrrrrrmbl,,,,

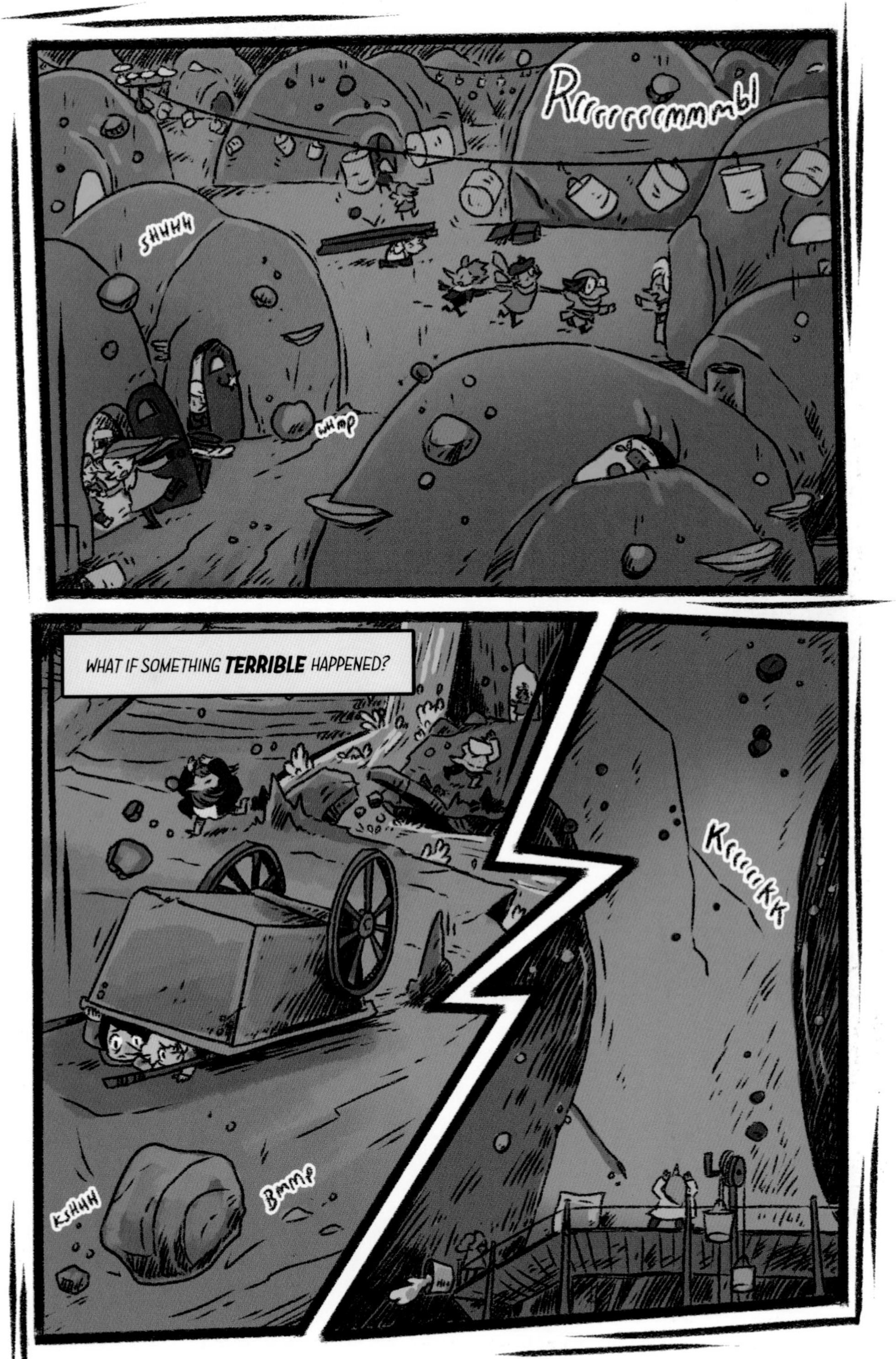
Rrrrrrrrrmmmmbl
SHHHH
WHMP
WHAT IF SOMETHING **TERRIBLE** HAPPENED?
KrrrrrKK
KSHHH
Bmmp

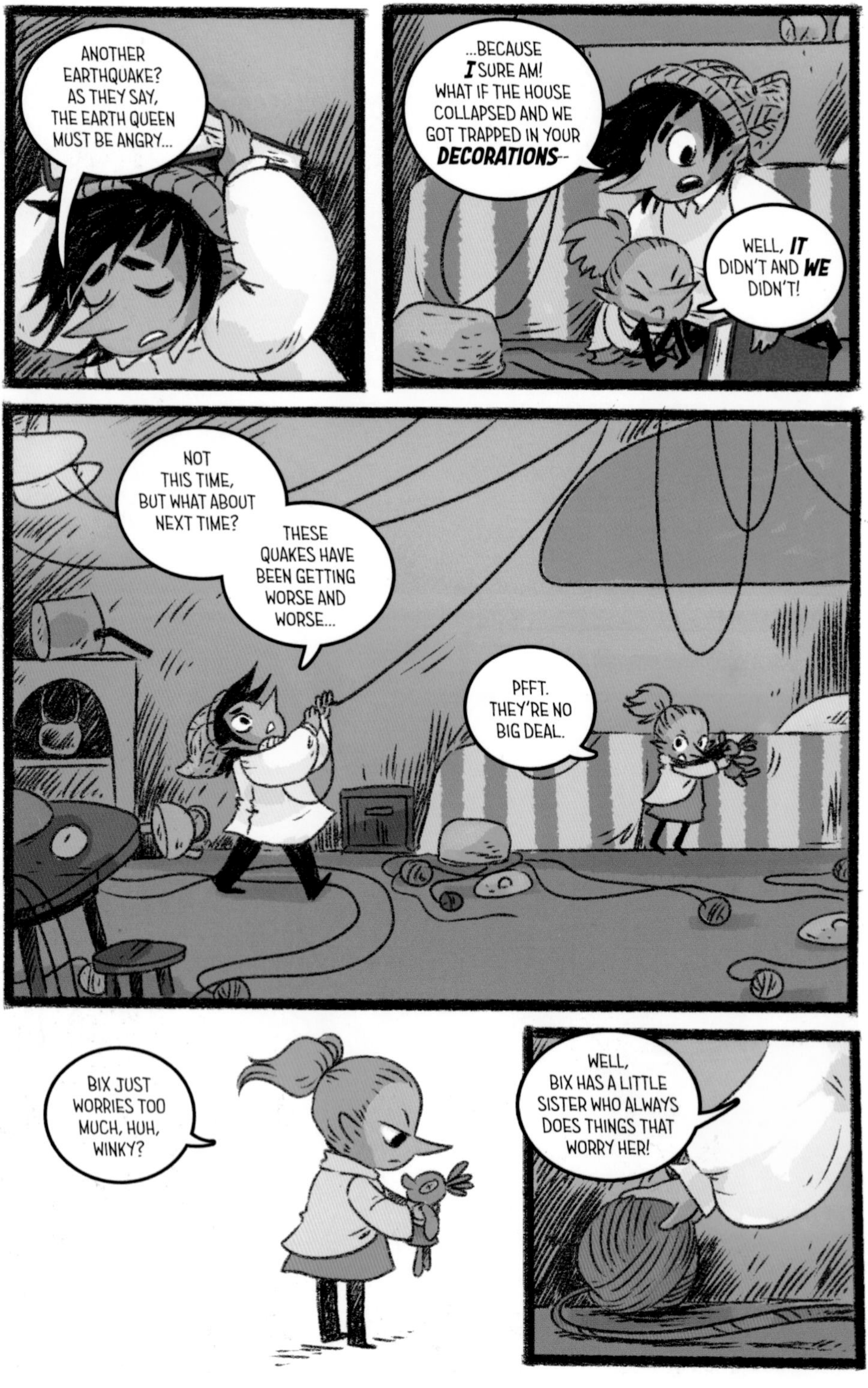
ANOTHER EARTHQUAKE? AS THEY SAY, THE EARTH QUEEN MUST BE ANGRY...
...BECAUSE I SURE AM! WHAT IF THE HOUSE COLLAPSED AND WE GOT TRAPPED IN YOUR DECORATIONS--
WELL, IT DIDN'T AND WE DIDN'T!
NOT THIS TIME, BUT WHAT ABOUT NEXT TIME?
THESE QUAKES HAVE BEEN GETTING WORSE AND WORSE...
PFFT. THEY'RE NO BIG DEAL.
BIX JUST WORRIES TOO MUCH, HUH, WINKY?
WELL, BIX HAS A LITTLE SISTER WHO ALWAYS DOES THINGS THAT WORRY HER!

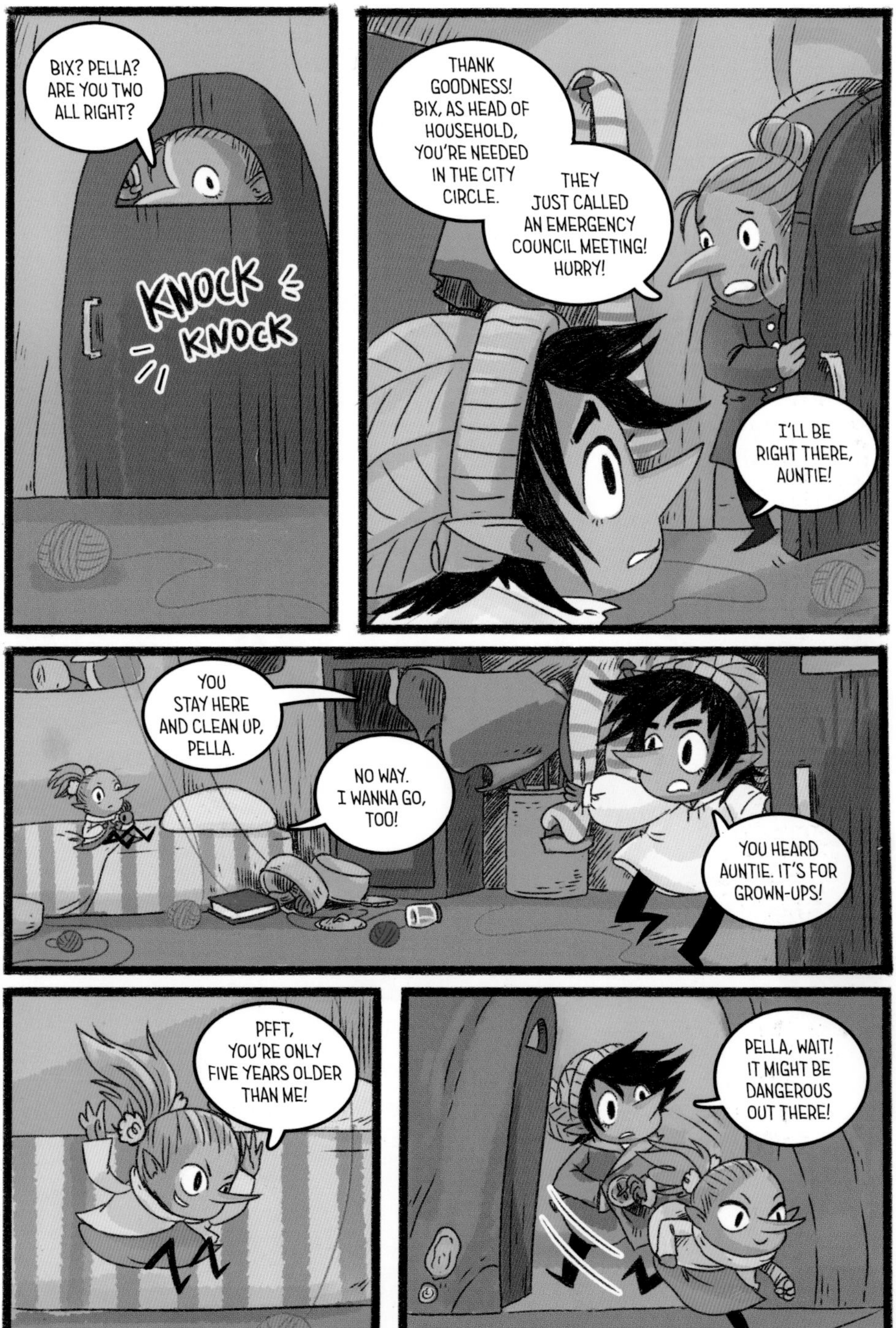

BIX? PELLA? ARE YOU TWO ALL RIGHT?
KNOCK KNOCK
THANK GOODNESS! BIX, AS HEAD OF HOUSEHOLD, YOU'RE NEEDED IN THE CITY CIRCLE.
THEY JUST CALLED AN EMERGENCY COUNCIL MEETING! HURRY!
I'LL BE RIGHT THERE, AUNTIE!
YOU STAY HERE AND CLEAN UP, PELLA.
NO WAY. I WANNA GO, TOO!
YOU HEARD AUNTIE. IT'S FOR GROWN-UPS!
PFFT, YOU'RE ONLY FIVE YEARS OLDER THAN ME!
PELLA, WAIT! IT MIGHT BE DANGEROUS OUT THERE!

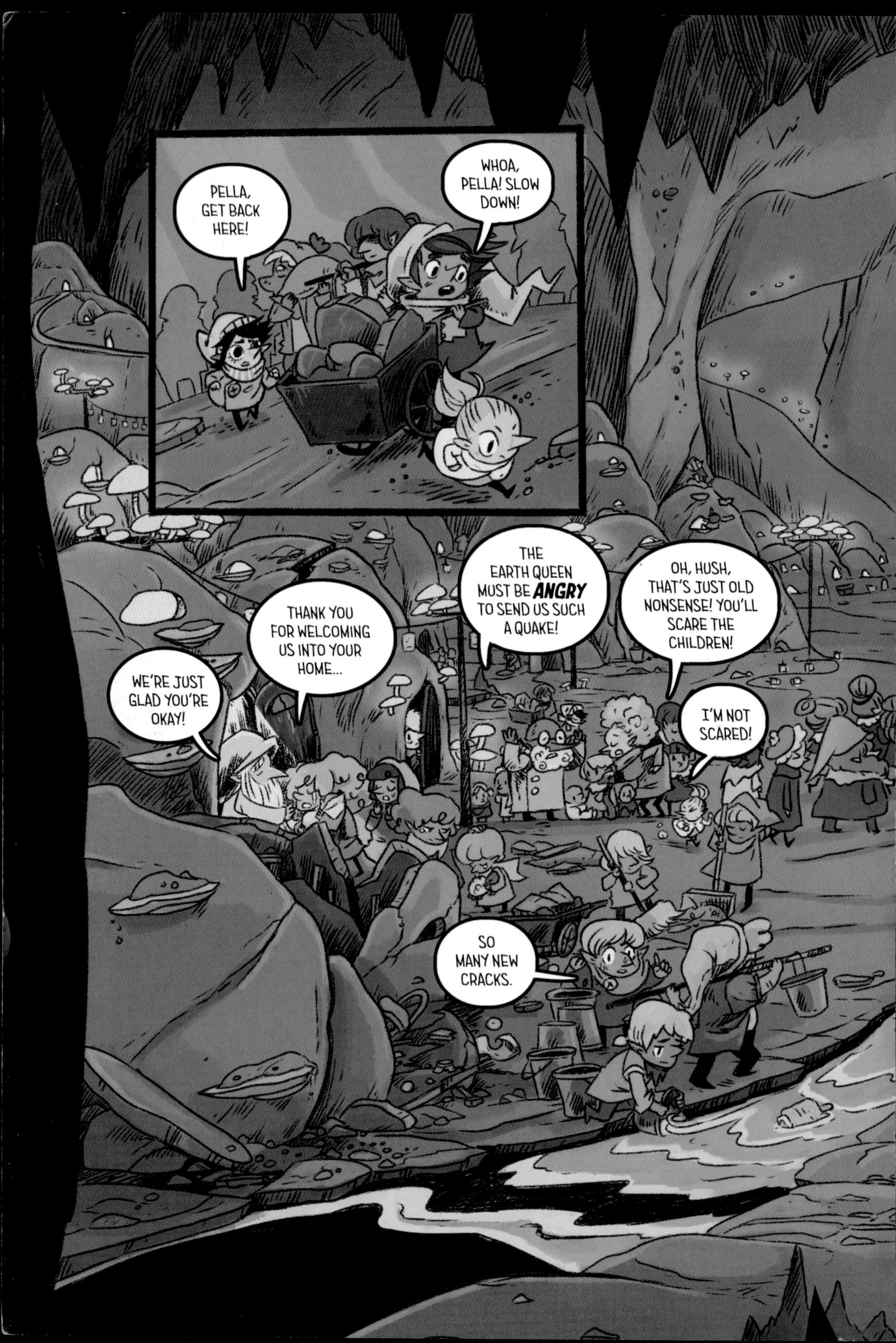
PELLA, GET BACK HERE!
WHOA, PELLA! SLOW DOWN!
WE'RE JUST GLAD YOU'RE OKAY!
THANK YOU FOR WELCOMING US INTO YOUR HOME...
THE EARTH QUEEN MUST BE ANGRY TO SEND US SUCH A QUAKE!
OH, HUSH, THAT'S JUST OLD NONSENSE! YOU'LL SCARE THE CHILDREN!
I'M NOT SCARED!
SO MANY NEW CRACKS.

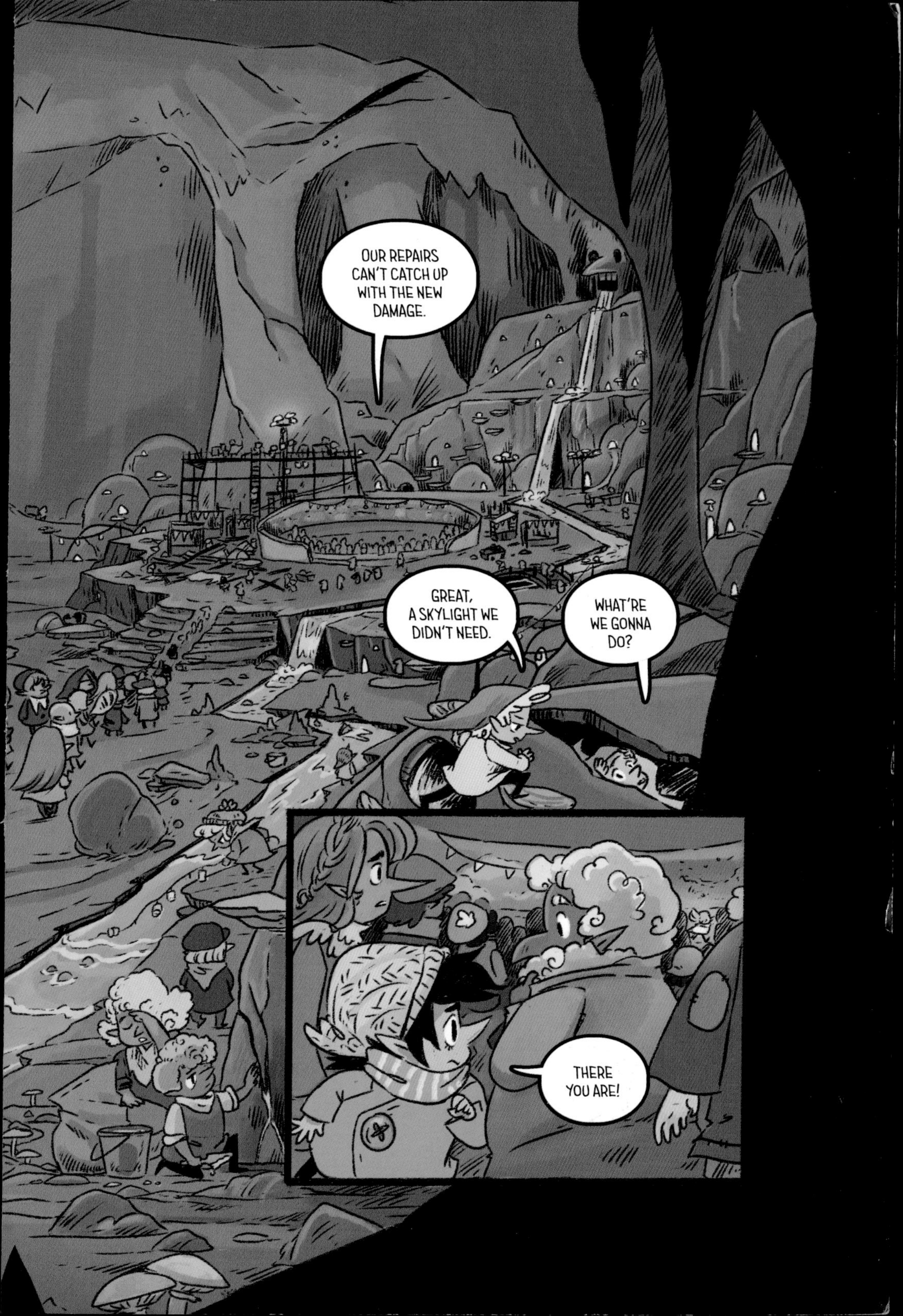
OUR REPAIRS CAN'T CATCH UP WITH THE NEW DAMAGE.
GREAT, A SKYLIGHT WE DIDN'T NEED.
WHAT'RE WE GONNA DO?
THERE YOU ARE!

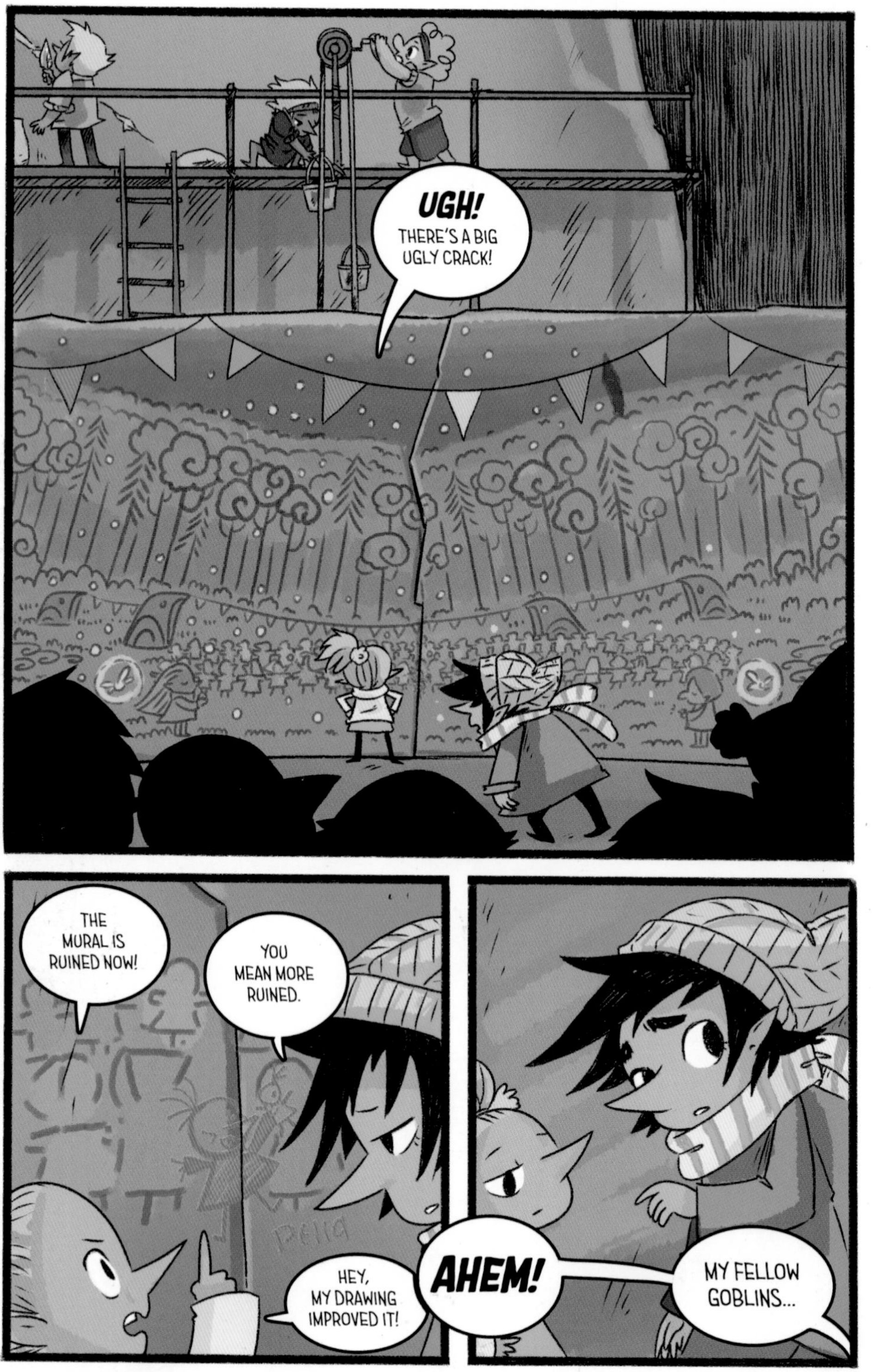
UGH!
THERE'S A BIG UGLY CRACK!
THE MURAL IS RUINED NOW!
YOU MEAN MORE RUINED.
HEY, MY DRAWING IMPROVED IT!
AHEM!
MY FELLOW GOBLINS...

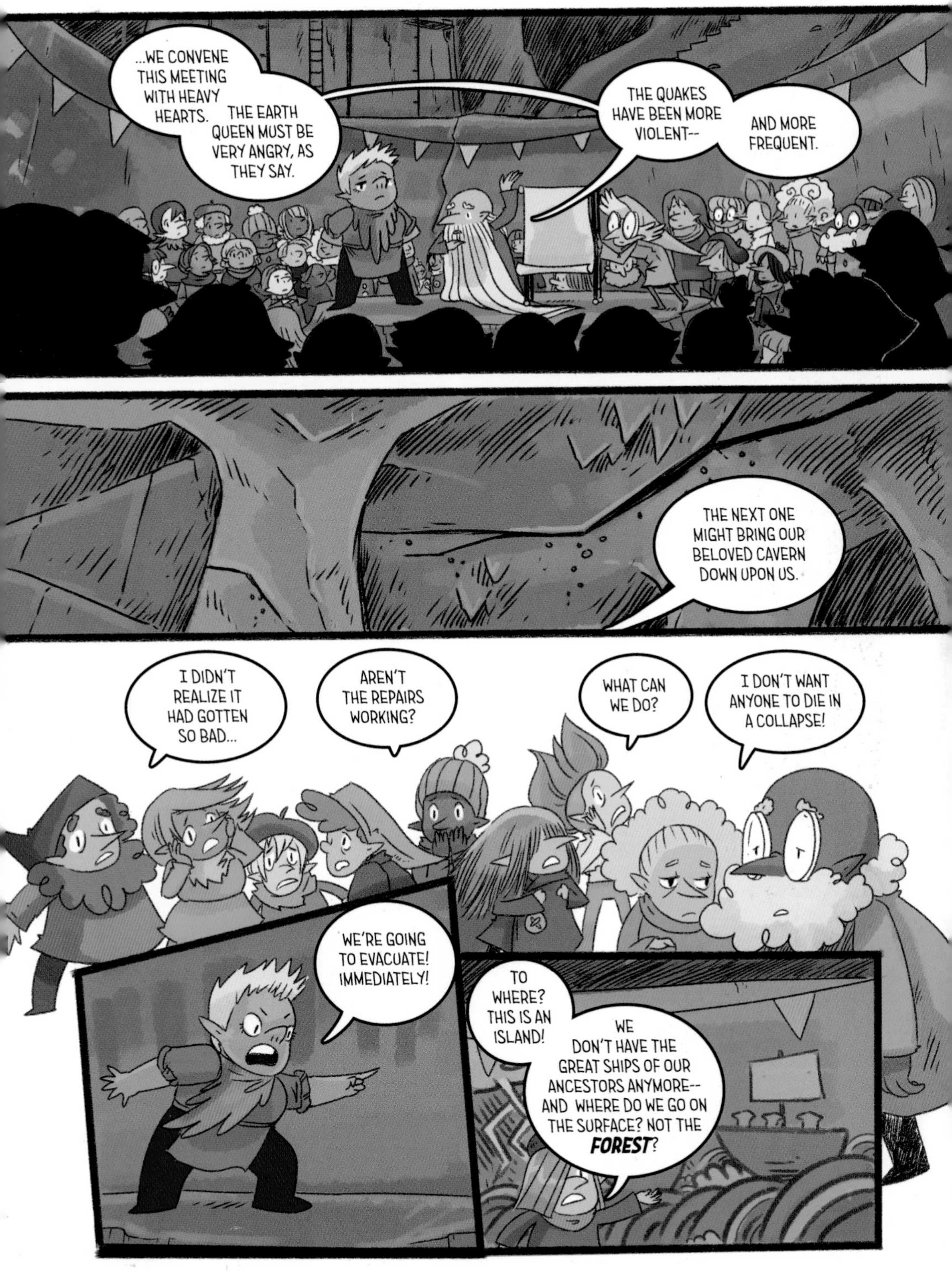
...WE CONVENE THIS MEETING WITH HEAVY HEARTS. THE EARTH QUEEN MUST BE VERY ANGRY, AS THEY SAY.
THE QUAKES HAVE BEEN MORE VIOLENT--
AND MORE FREQUENT.
THE NEXT ONE MIGHT BRING OUR BELOVED CAVERN DOWN UPON US.
I DIDN'T REALIZE IT HAD GOTTEN SO BAD...
AREN'T THE REPAIRS WORKING?
WHAT CAN WE DO?
I DON'T WANT ANYONE TO DIE IN A COLLAPSE!
WE'RE GOING TO EVACUATE! IMMEDIATELY!
TO WHERE? THIS IS AN ISLAND!
WE DON'T HAVE THE GREAT SHIPS OF OUR ANCESTORS ANYMORE-- AND WHERE DO WE GO ON THE SURFACE? NOT THE FOREST?

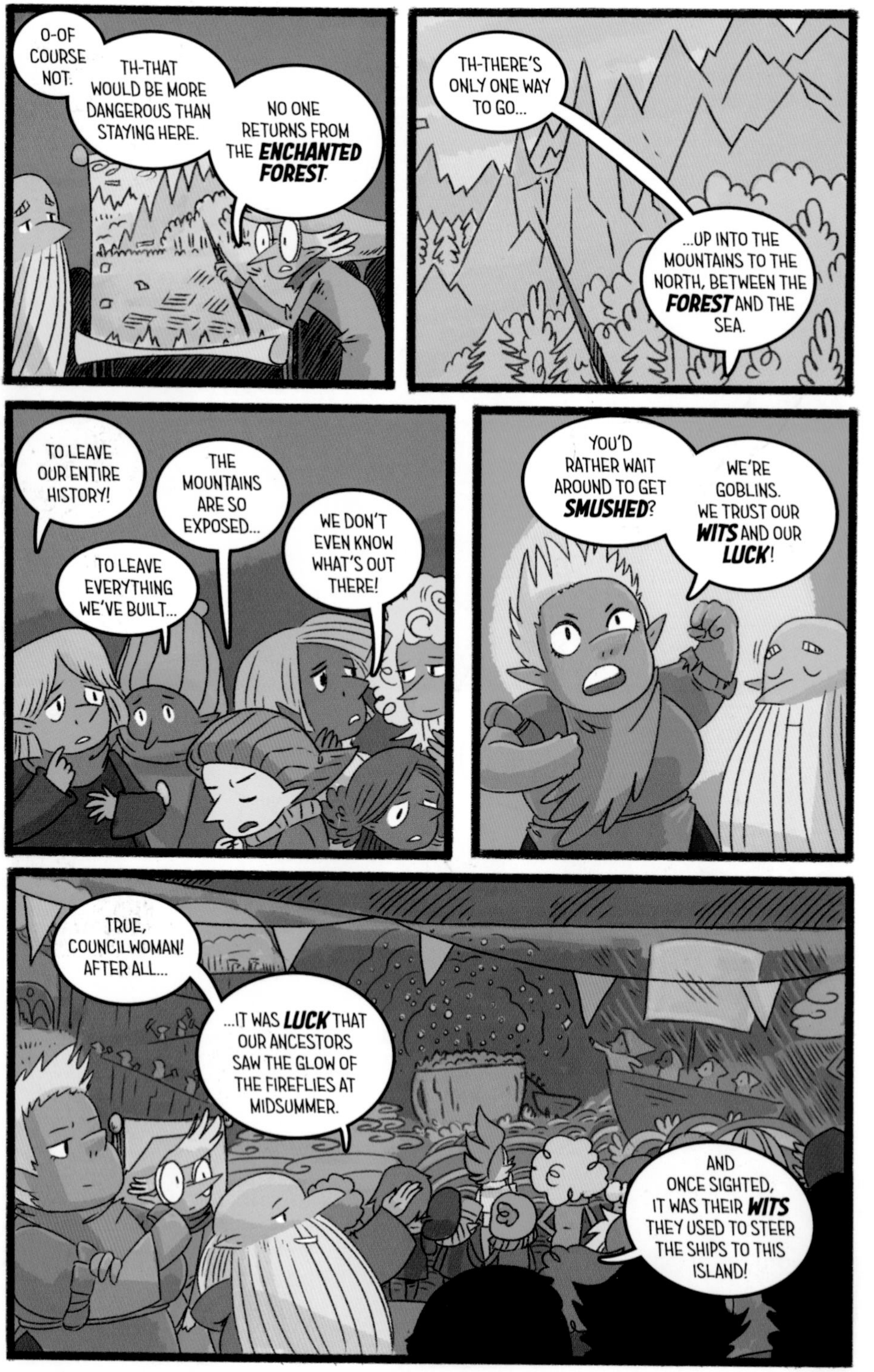
O-OF COURSE NOT.
TH-THAT WOULD BE MORE DANGEROUS THAN STAYING HERE.
NO ONE RETURNS FROM THE **ENCHANTED FOREST**.
TH-THERE'S ONLY ONE WAY TO GO...
...UP INTO THE MOUNTAINS TO THE NORTH, BETWEEN THE **FOREST** AND THE SEA.
TO LEAVE OUR ENTIRE HISTORY!
TO LEAVE EVERYTHING WE'VE BUILT...
THE MOUNTAINS ARE SO EXPOSED...
WE DON'T EVEN KNOW WHAT'S OUT THERE!
YOU'D RATHER WAIT AROUND TO GET **SMUSHED**?
WE'RE GOBLINS. WE TRUST OUR **WITS** AND OUR **LUCK**!
TRUE, COUNCILWOMAN! AFTER ALL...
...IT WAS **LUCK** THAT OUR ANCESTORS SAW THE GLOW OF THE FIREFLIES AT MIDSUMMER.
AND ONCE SIGHTED, IT WAS THEIR **WITS** THEY USED TO STEER THE SHIPS TO THIS ISLAND!

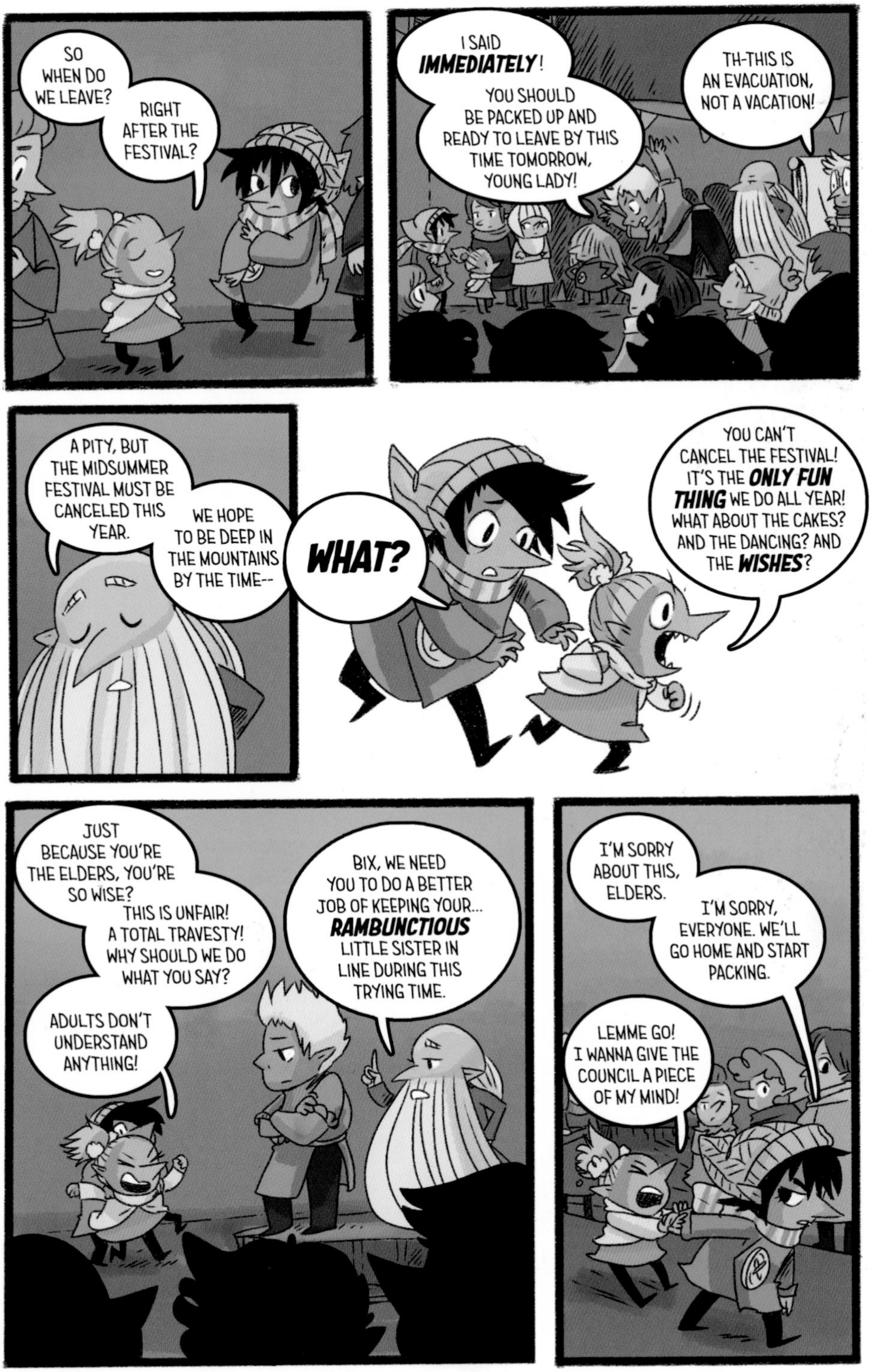
SO WHEN DO WE LEAVE?
RIGHT AFTER THE FESTIVAL?
I SAID **IMMEDIATELY**!
YOU SHOULD BE PACKED UP AND READY TO LEAVE BY THIS TIME TOMORROW, YOUNG LADY!
TH-THIS IS AN EVACUATION, NOT A VACATION!
A PITY, BUT THE MIDSUMMER FESTIVAL MUST BE CANCELED THIS YEAR.
WE HOPE TO BE DEEP IN THE MOUNTAINS BY THE TIME--
WHAT?
YOU CAN'T CANCEL THE FESTIVAL! IT'S THE **ONLY FUN THING** WE DO ALL YEAR! WHAT ABOUT THE CAKES? AND THE DANCING? AND THE **WISHES**?
JUST BECAUSE YOU'RE THE ELDERS, YOU'RE SO WISE?
THIS IS UNFAIR! A TOTAL TRAVESTY! WHY SHOULD WE DO WHAT YOU SAY?
ADULTS DON'T UNDERSTAND ANYTHING!
BIX, WE NEED YOU TO DO A BETTER JOB OF KEEPING YOUR... **RAMBUNCTIOUS** LITTLE SISTER IN LINE DURING THIS TRYING TIME.
I'M SORRY ABOUT THIS, ELDERS.
I'M SORRY, EVERYONE. WE'LL GO HOME AND START PACKING.
LEMME GO! I WANNA GIVE THE COUNCIL A PIECE OF MY MIND!

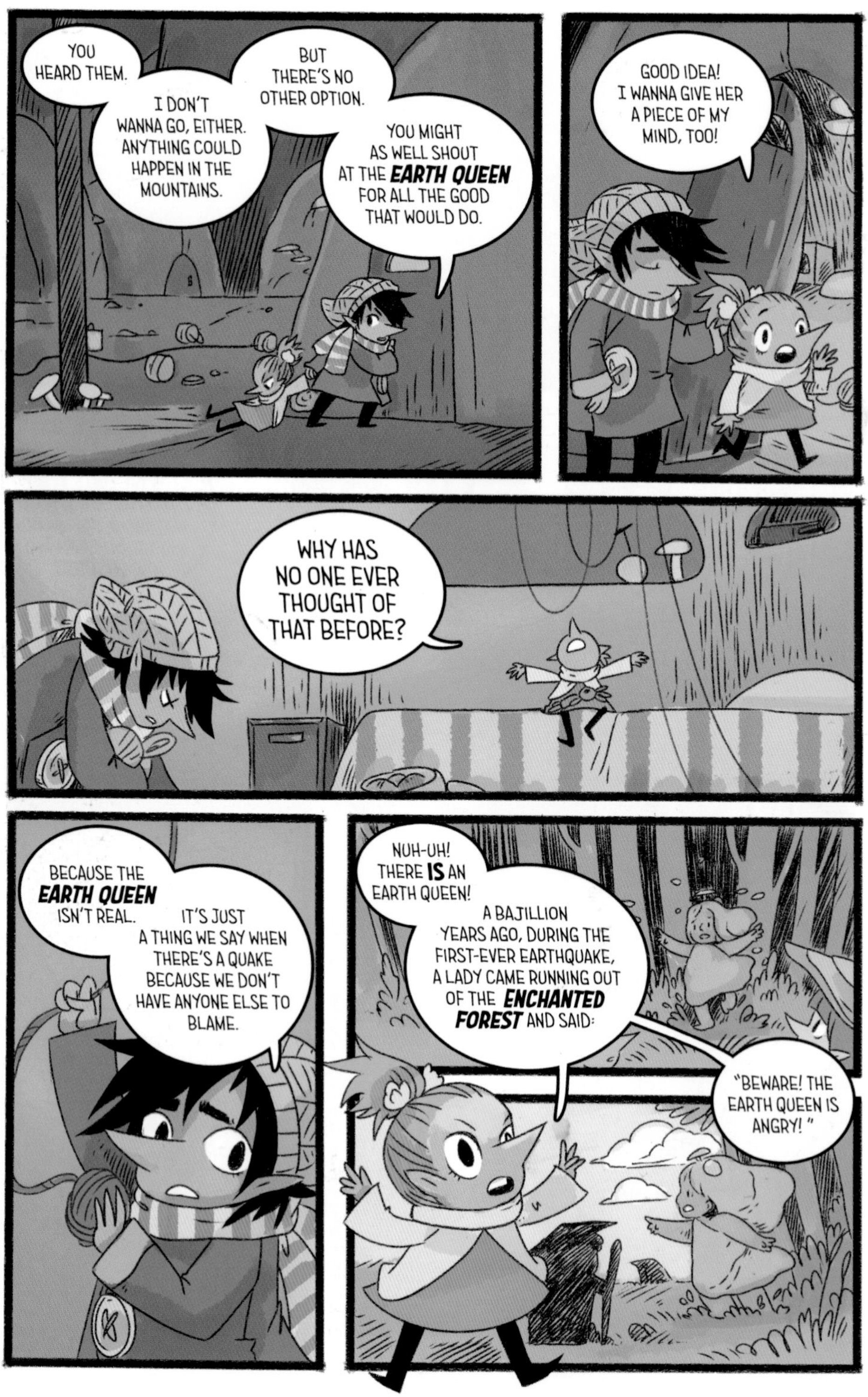

YOU HEARD THEM.
I DON'T WANNA GO, EITHER. ANYTHING COULD HAPPEN IN THE MOUNTAINS.
BUT THERE'S NO OTHER OPTION.
YOU MIGHT AS WELL SHOUT AT THE EARTH QUEEN FOR ALL THE GOOD THAT WOULD DO.
GOOD IDEA! I WANNA GIVE HER A PIECE OF MY MIND, TOO!
WHY HAS NO ONE EVER THOUGHT OF THAT BEFORE?
BECAUSE THE EARTH QUEEN ISN'T REAL.
IT'S JUST A THING WE SAY WHEN THERE'S A QUAKE BECAUSE WE DON'T HAVE ANYONE ELSE TO BLAME.
NUH-UH! THERE IS AN EARTH QUEEN!
A BAJILLION YEARS AGO, DURING THE FIRST-EVER EARTHQUAKE, A LADY CAME RUNNING OUT OF THE ENCHANTED FOREST AND SAID:
"BEWARE! THE EARTH QUEEN IS ANGRY!"

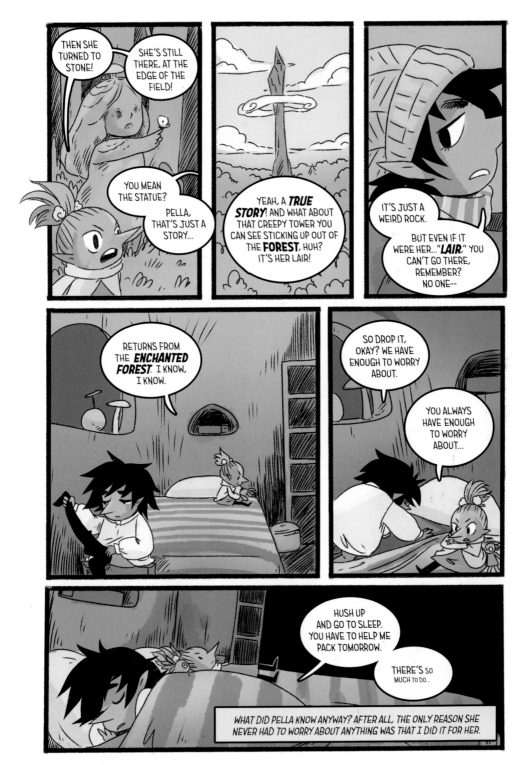

THEN SHE TURNED TO STONE!

SHE'S STILL THERE, AT THE EDGE OF THE FIELD!

YOU MEAN THE STATUE?

PELLA, THAT'S JUST A STORY...

YEAH, A *TRUE STORY*! AND WHAT ABOUT THAT CREEPY TOWER YOU CAN SEE STICKING UP OUT OF THE *FOREST*, HUH? IT'S HER LAIR!

IT'S JUST A WEIRD ROCK.

BUT EVEN IF IT WERE HER..."*LAIR*," YOU CAN'T GO THERE, REMEMBER? NO ONE--

RETURNS FROM THE *ENCHANTED FOREST*. I KNOW, I KNOW.

SO DROP IT, OKAY? WE HAVE ENOUGH TO WORRY ABOUT.

YOU ALWAYS HAVE ENOUGH TO WORRY ABOUT...

HUSH UP AND GO TO SLEEP. YOU HAVE TO HELP ME PACK TOMORROW.

THERE'S SO MUCH TO DO...

WHAT DID PELLA KNOW ANYWAY? AFTER ALL, THE ONLY REASON SHE NEVER HAD TO WORRY ABOUT ANYTHING WAS THAT I DID IT FOR HER.

15

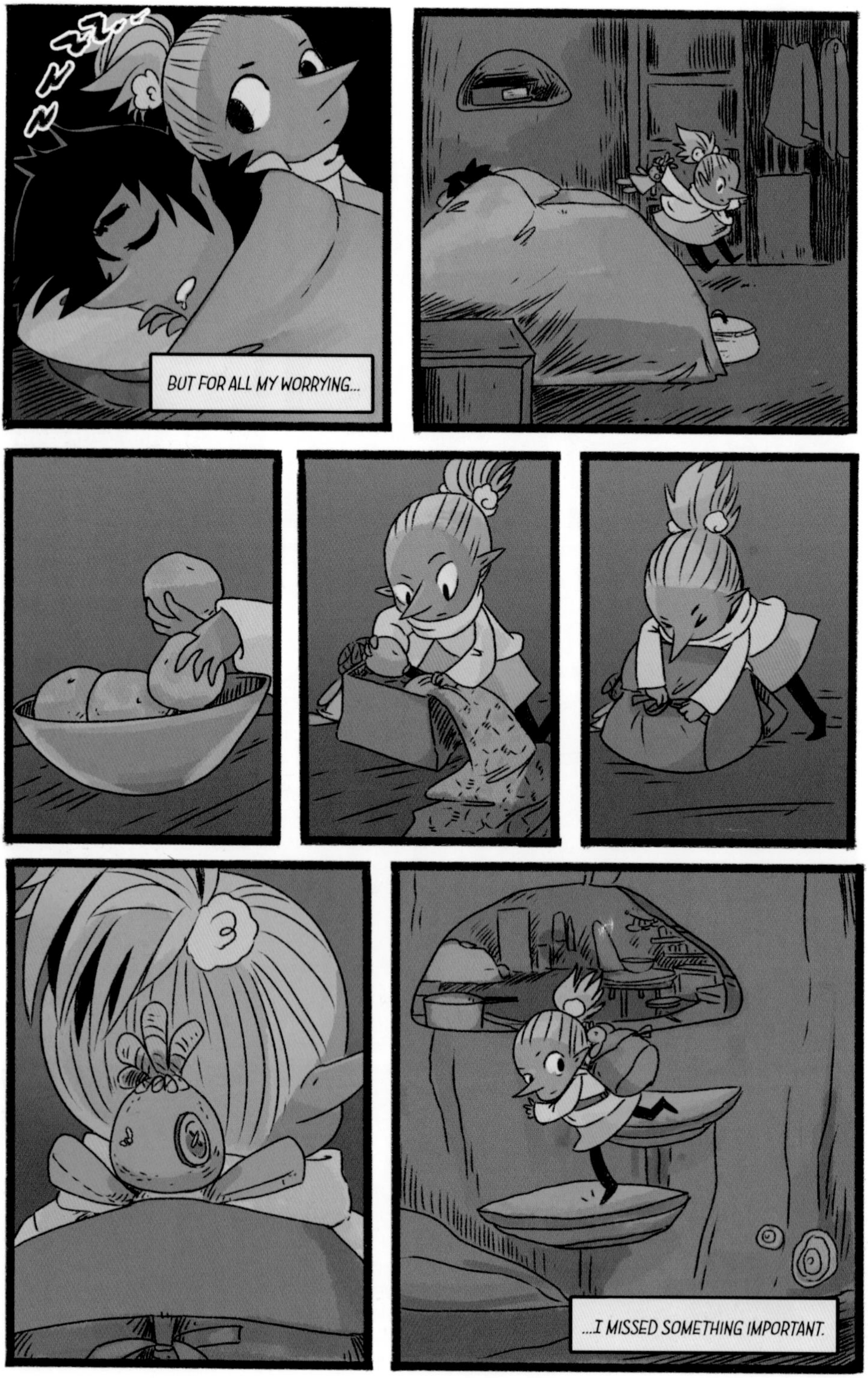

BUT FOR ALL MY WORRYING...
...I MISSED SOMETHING IMPORTANT.

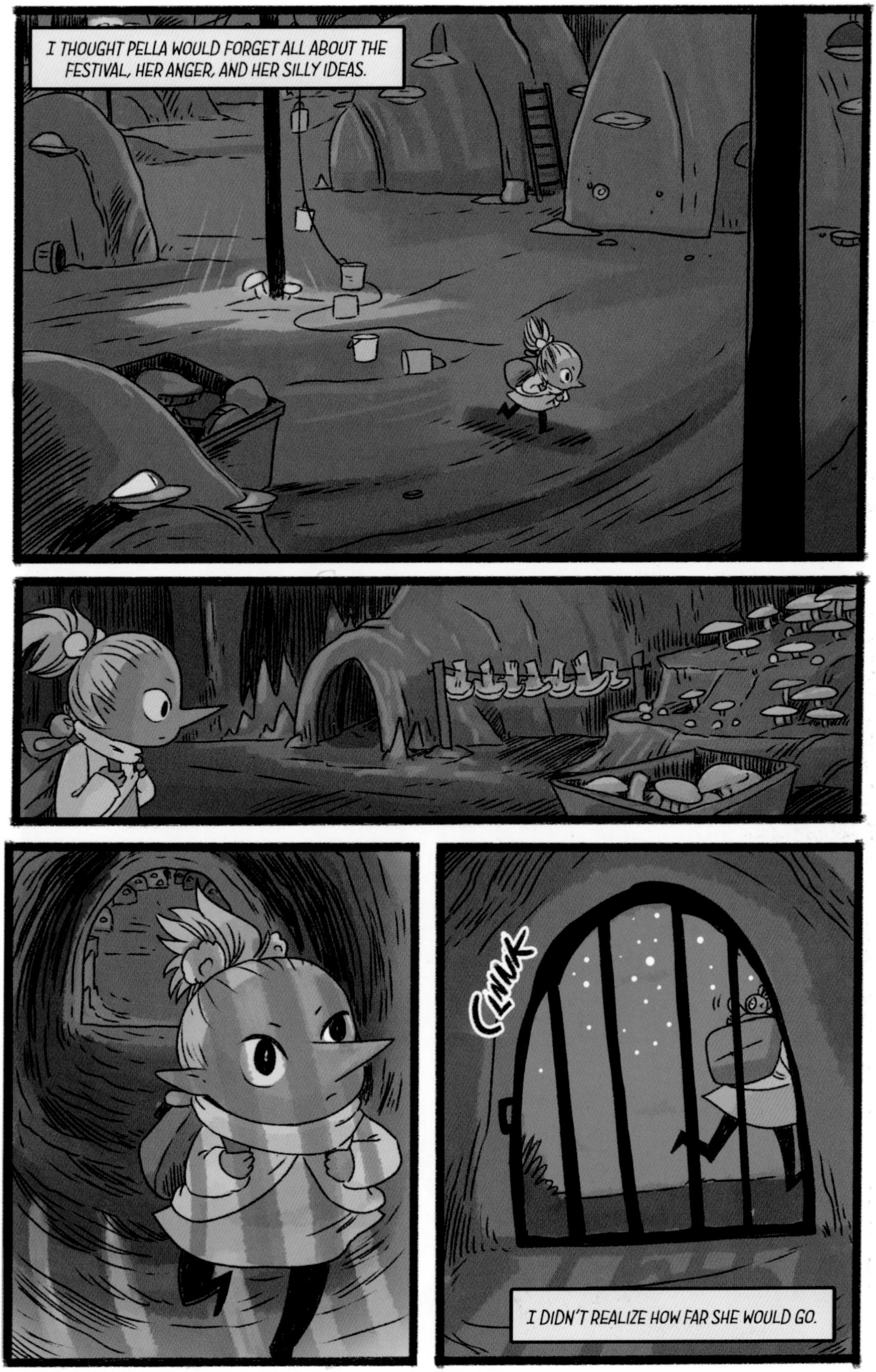

I THOUGHT PELLA WOULD FORGET ALL ABOUT THE FESTIVAL, HER ANGER, AND HER SILLY IDEAS.
CLINK
I DIDN'T REALIZE HOW FAR SHE WOULD GO.

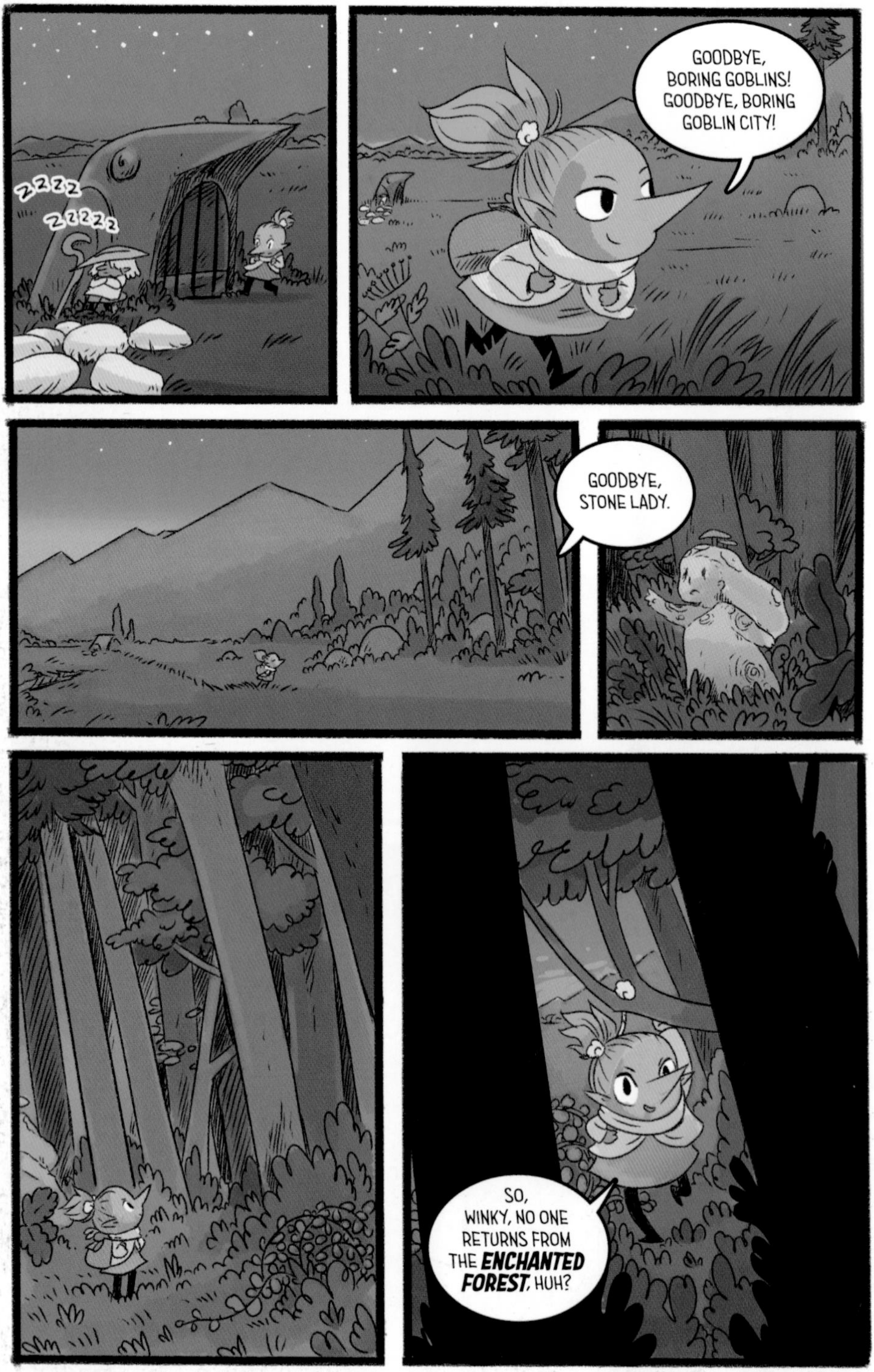
ZZZZ
ZZZZZ
GOODBYE, BORING GOBLINS! GOODBYE, BORING GOBLIN CITY!
GOODBYE, STONE LADY.
SO, WINKY, NO ONE RETURNS FROM THE **ENCHANTED FOREST**, HUH?

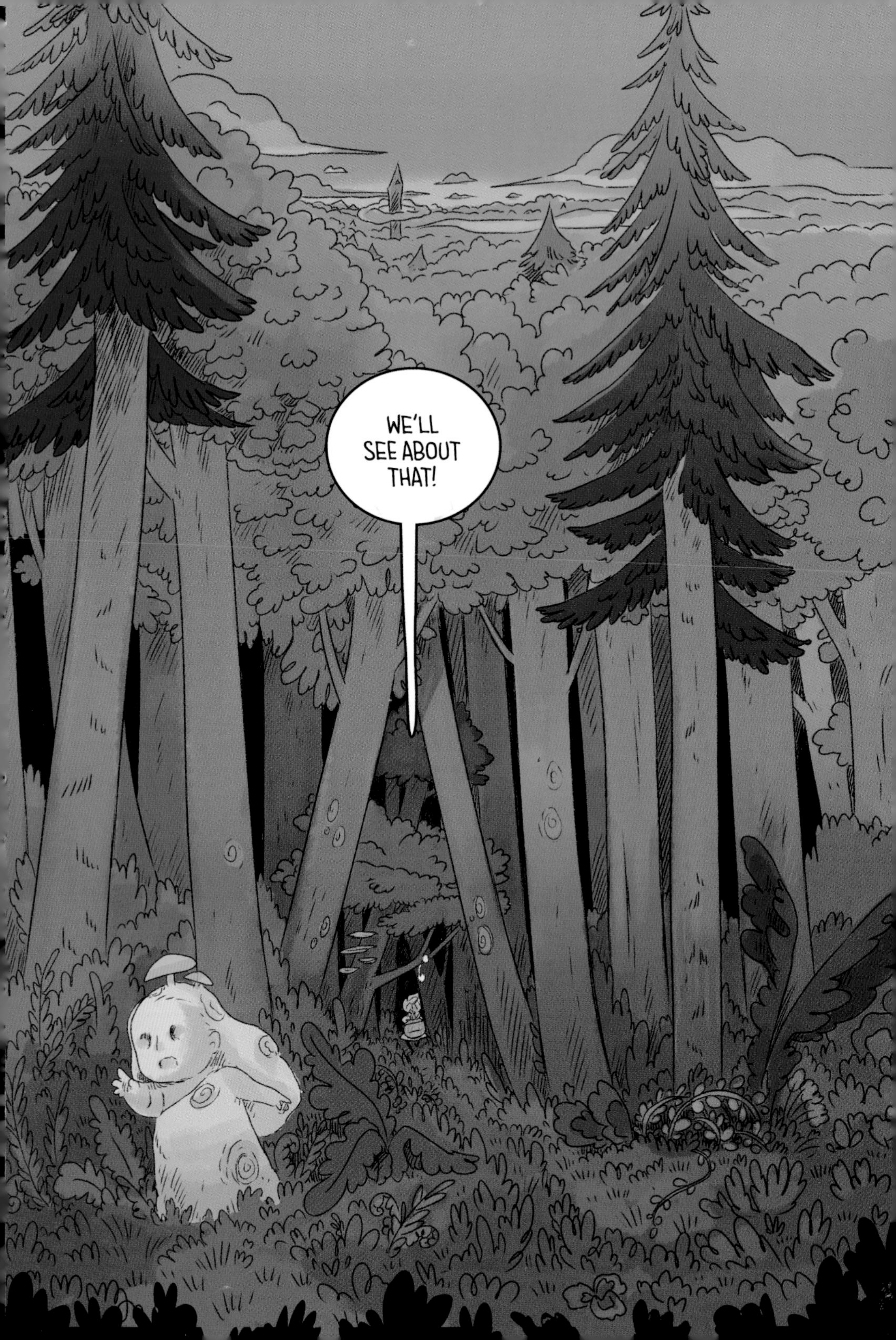
WE'LL SEE ABOUT THAT!

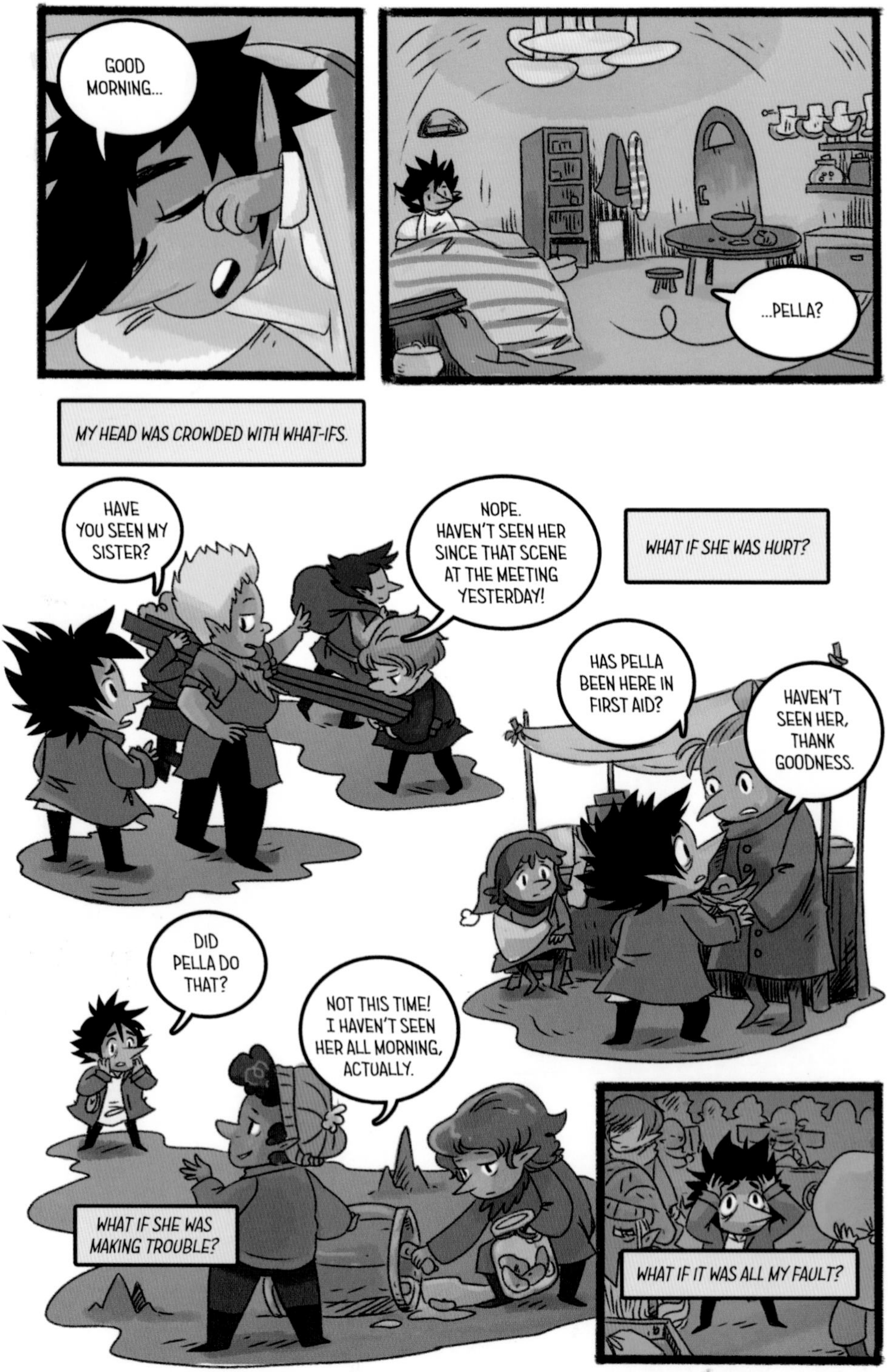
GOOD MORNING...
...PELLA?
MY HEAD WAS CROWDED WITH WHAT-IFS.
HAVE YOU SEEN MY SISTER?
NOPE. HAVEN'T SEEN HER SINCE THAT SCENE AT THE MEETING YESTERDAY!
WHAT IF SHE WAS HURT?
HAS PELLA BEEN HERE IN FIRST AID?
HAVEN'T SEEN HER, THANK GOODNESS.
DID PELLA DO THAT?
NOT THIS TIME! I HAVEN'T SEEN HER ALL MORNING, ACTUALLY.
WHAT IF SHE WAS MAKING TROUBLE?
WHAT IF IT WAS ALL MY FAULT?

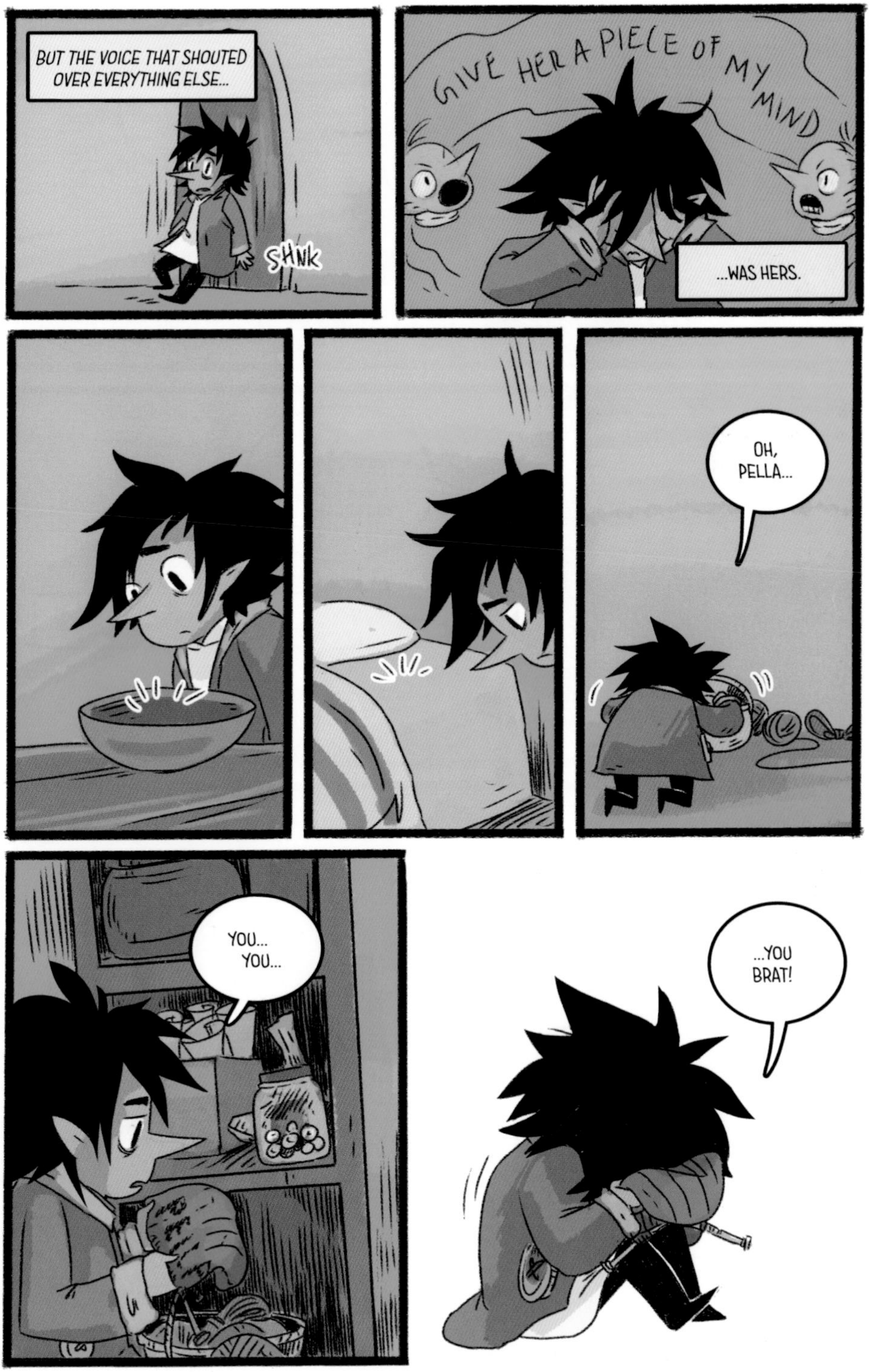

BUT THE VOICE THAT SHOUTED OVER EVERYTHING ELSE...
SHNK
GIVE HER A PIECE OF MY MIND
...WAS HERS.
OH, PELLA...
YOU... YOU...
...YOU BRAT!

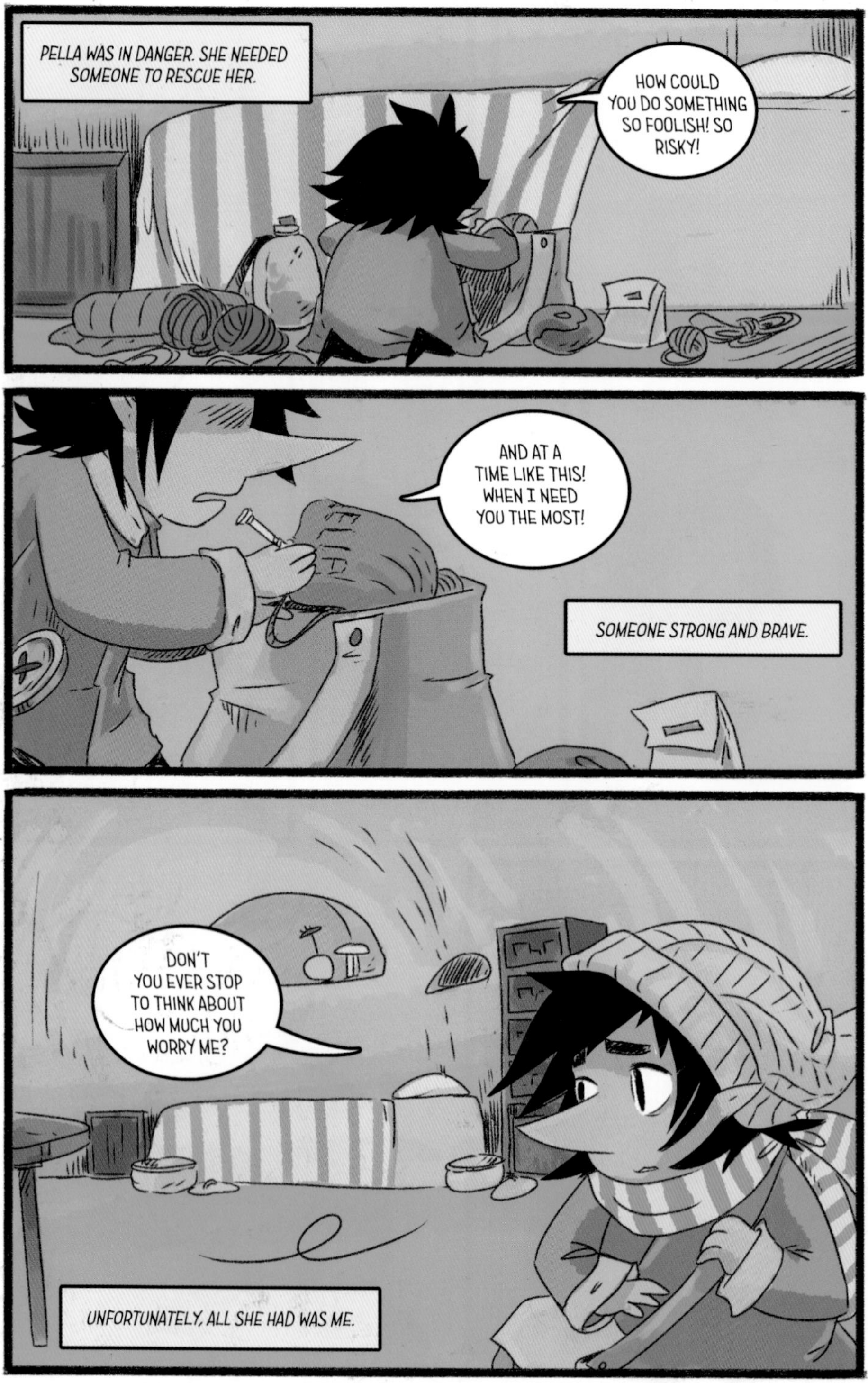

PELLA WAS IN DANGER. SHE NEEDED SOMEONE TO RESCUE HER.
HOW COULD YOU DO SOMETHING SO FOOLISH! SO RISKY!
AND AT A TIME LIKE THIS! WHEN I NEED YOU THE MOST!
SOMEONE STRONG AND BRAVE.
DON'T YOU EVER STOP TO THINK ABOUT HOW MUCH YOU WORRY ME?
UNFORTUNATELY, ALL SHE HAD WAS ME.

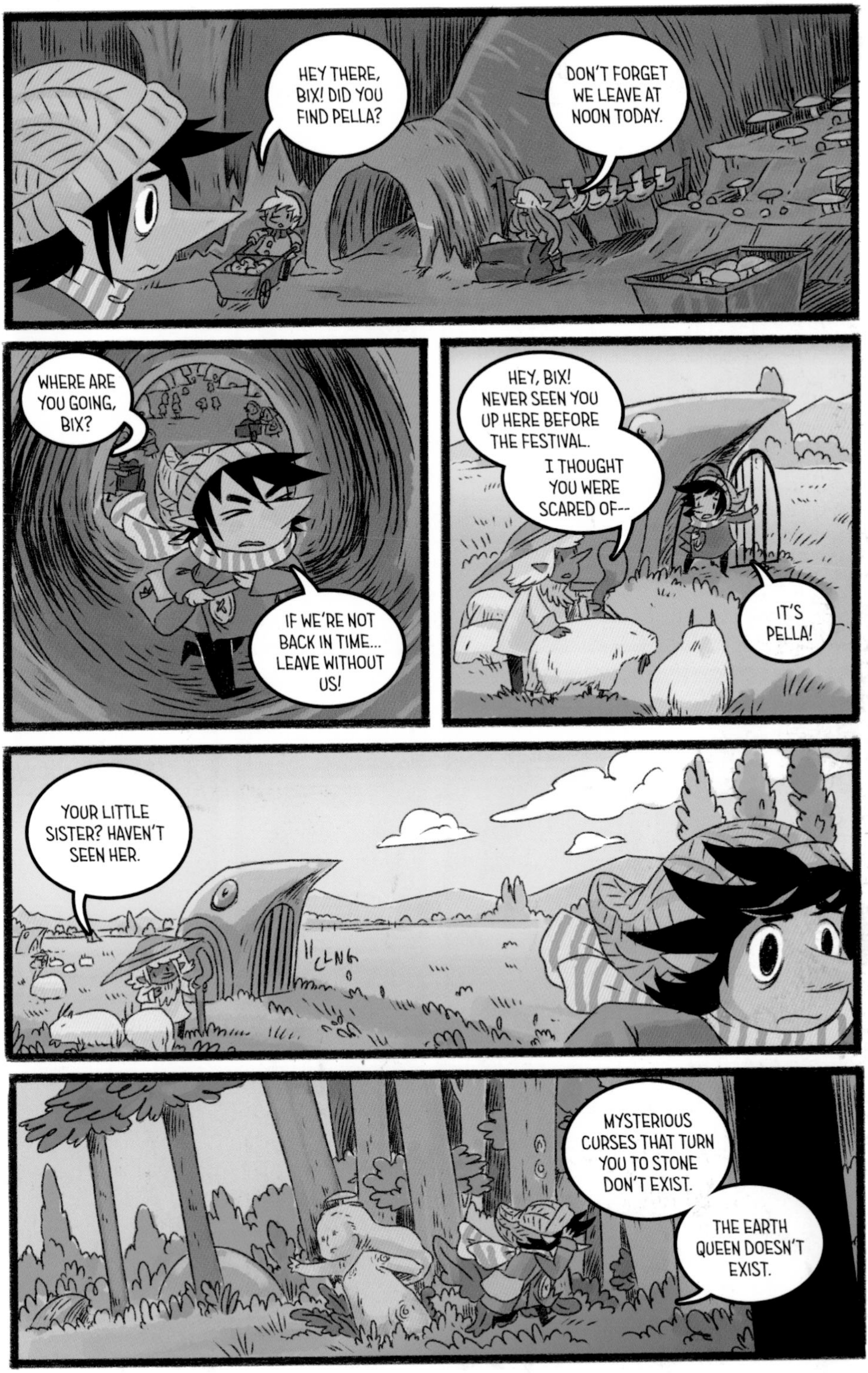
HEY THERE, BIX! DID YOU FIND PELLA?
DON'T FORGET WE LEAVE AT NOON TODAY.
WHERE ARE YOU GOING, BIX?
IF WE'RE NOT BACK IN TIME... LEAVE WITHOUT US!
HEY, BIX! NEVER SEEN YOU UP HERE BEFORE THE FESTIVAL.
I THOUGHT YOU WERE SCARED OF--
IT'S PELLA!
YOUR LITTLE SISTER? HAVEN'T SEEN HER.
CLNG
MYSTERIOUS CURSES THAT TURN YOU TO STONE DON'T EXIST.
THE EARTH QUEEN DOESN'T EXIST.

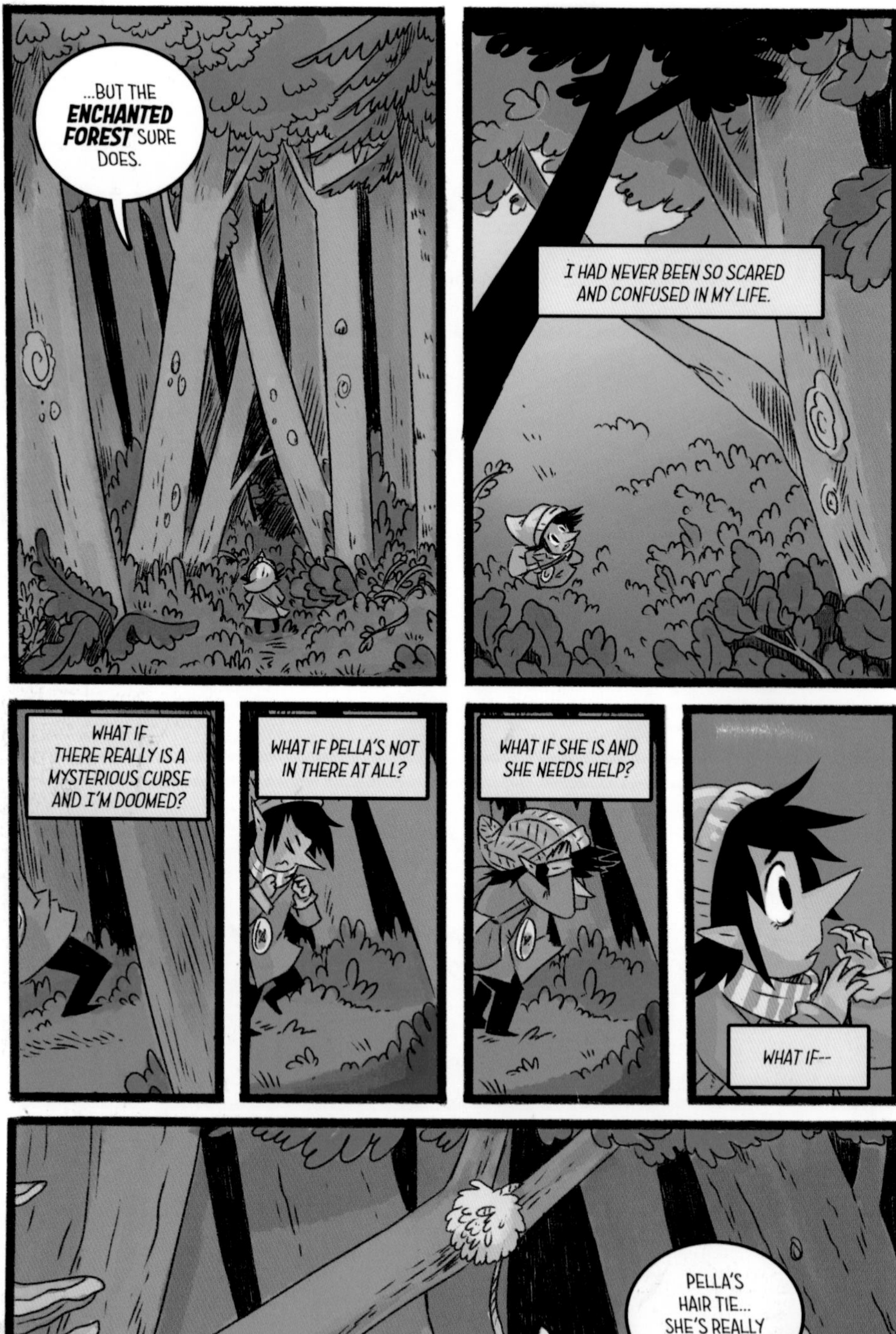

...BUT THE ENCHANTED FOREST SURE DOES.
I HAD NEVER BEEN SO SCARED AND CONFUSED IN MY LIFE.
WHAT IF THERE REALLY IS A MYSTERIOUS CURSE AND I'M DOOMED?
WHAT IF PELLA'S NOT IN THERE AT ALL?
WHAT IF SHE IS AND SHE NEEDS HELP?
WHAT IF--
PELLA'S HAIR TIE... SHE'S REALLY IN THERE.

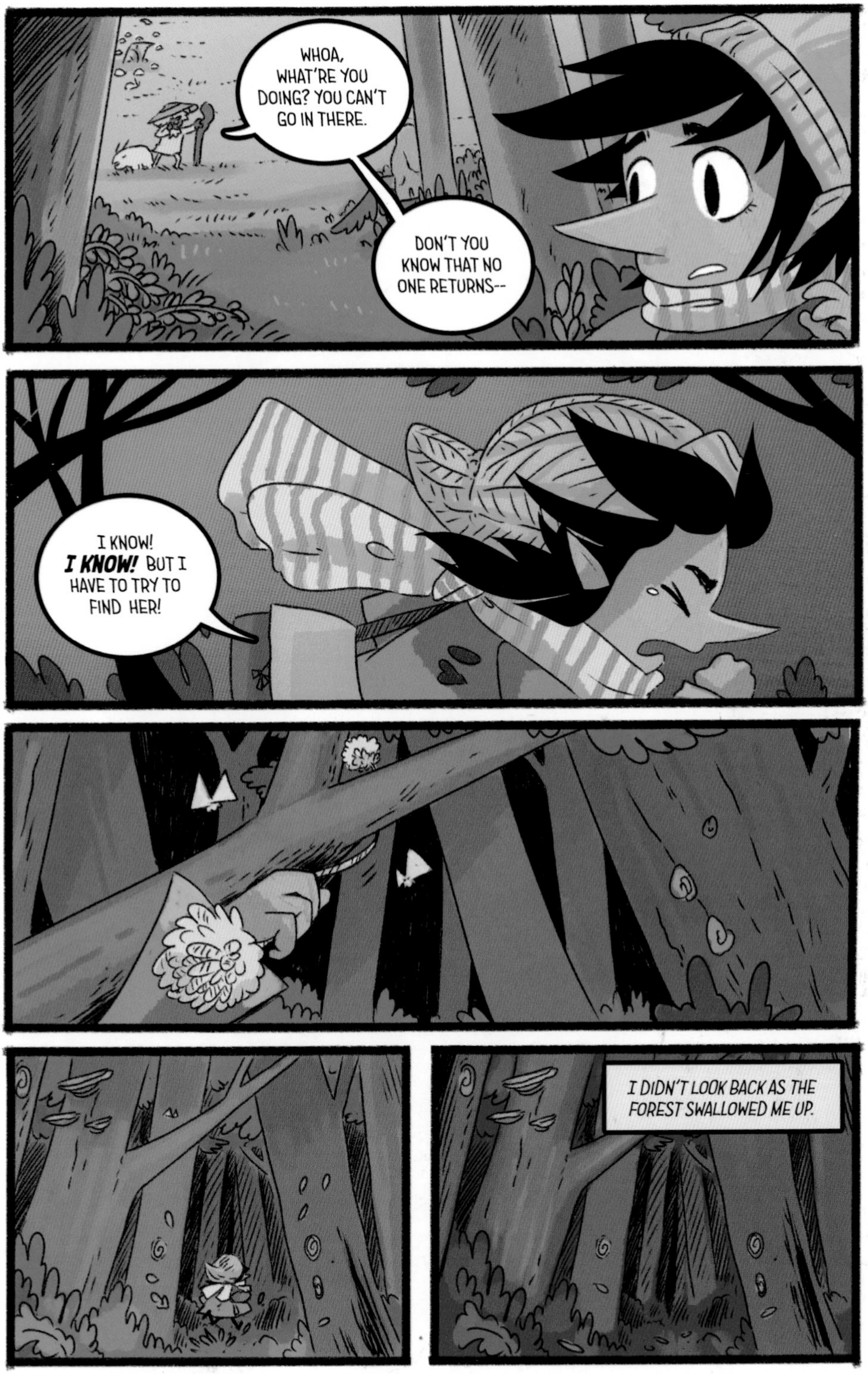
WHOA, WHAT'RE YOU DOING? YOU CAN'T GO IN THERE.
DON'T YOU KNOW THAT NO ONE RETURNS--
I KNOW! **I KNOW!** BUT I HAVE TO TRY TO FIND HER!
I DIDN'T LOOK BACK AS THE FOREST SWALLOWED ME UP.

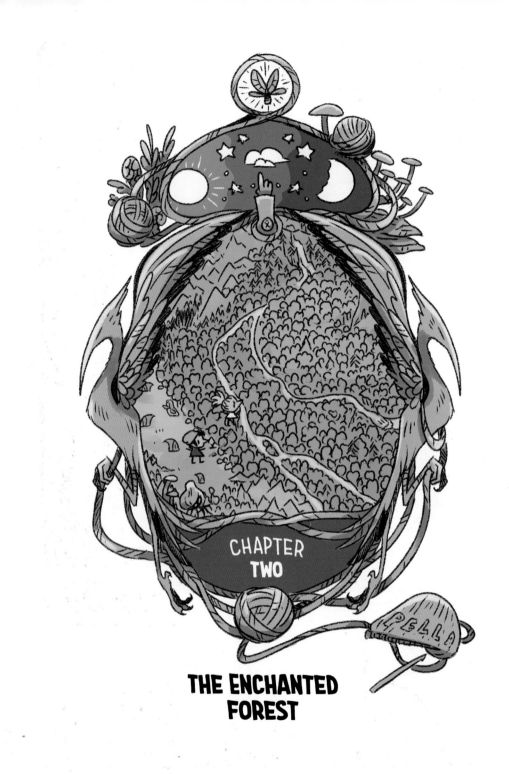

CHAPTER TWO

THE ENCHANTED FOREST

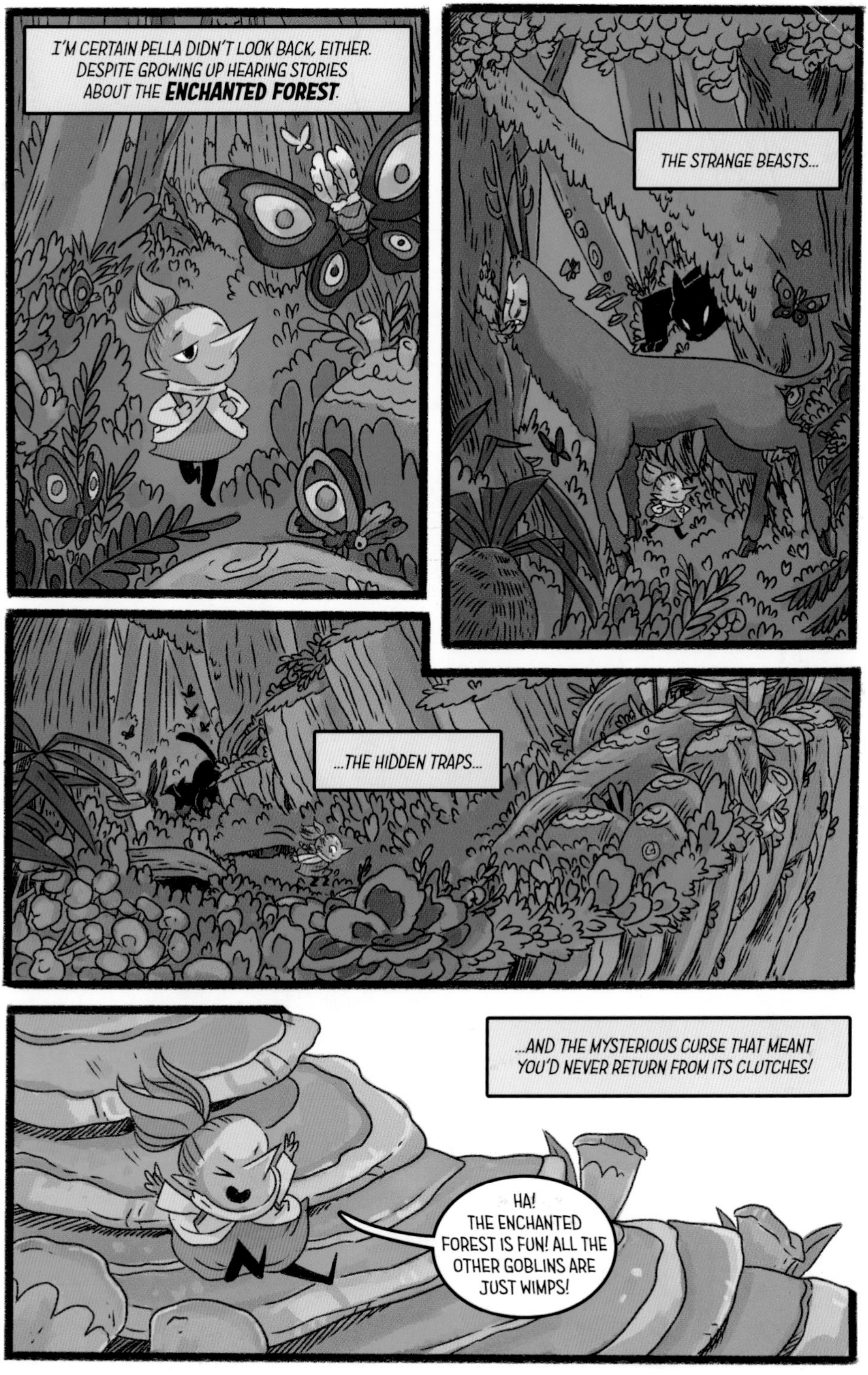
I'M CERTAIN PELLA DIDN'T LOOK BACK, EITHER. DESPITE GROWING UP HEARING STORIES ABOUT THE ENCHANTED FOREST.
THE STRANGE BEASTS...
...THE HIDDEN TRAPS...
...AND THE MYSTERIOUS CURSE THAT MEANT YOU'D NEVER RETURN FROM ITS CLUTCHES!
HA! THE ENCHANTED FOREST IS FUN! ALL THE OTHER GOBLINS ARE JUST WIMPS!

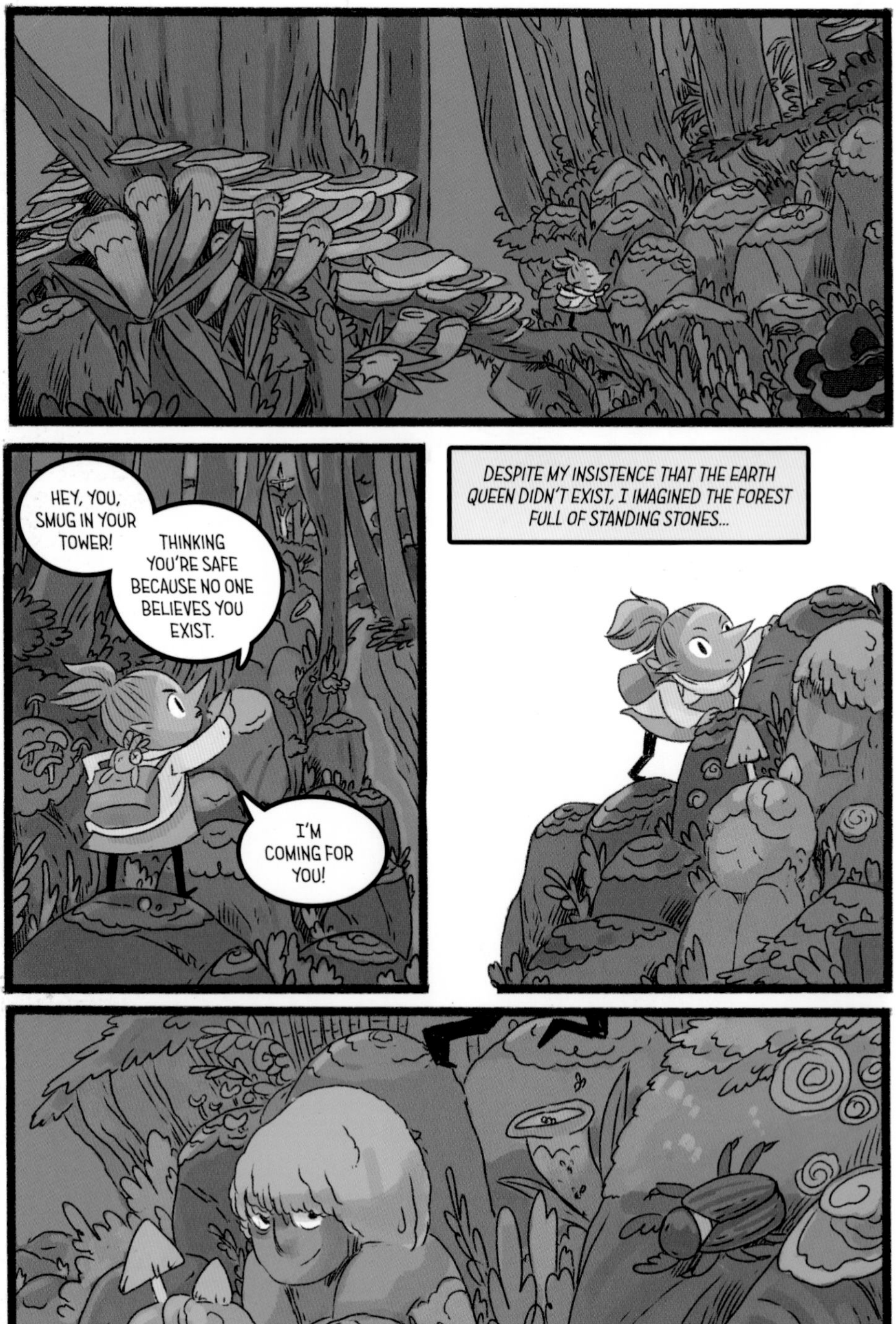
HEY, YOU, SMUG IN YOUR TOWER!
THINKING YOU'RE SAFE BECAUSE NO ONE BELIEVES YOU EXIST.
I'M COMING FOR YOU!
DESPITE MY INSISTENCE THAT THE EARTH QUEEN DIDN'T EXIST, I IMAGINED THE FOREST FULL OF STANDING STONES...
...THAT HAD ONCE BEEN GOBLINS WHO FOOLISHLY DARED TO ENTER.

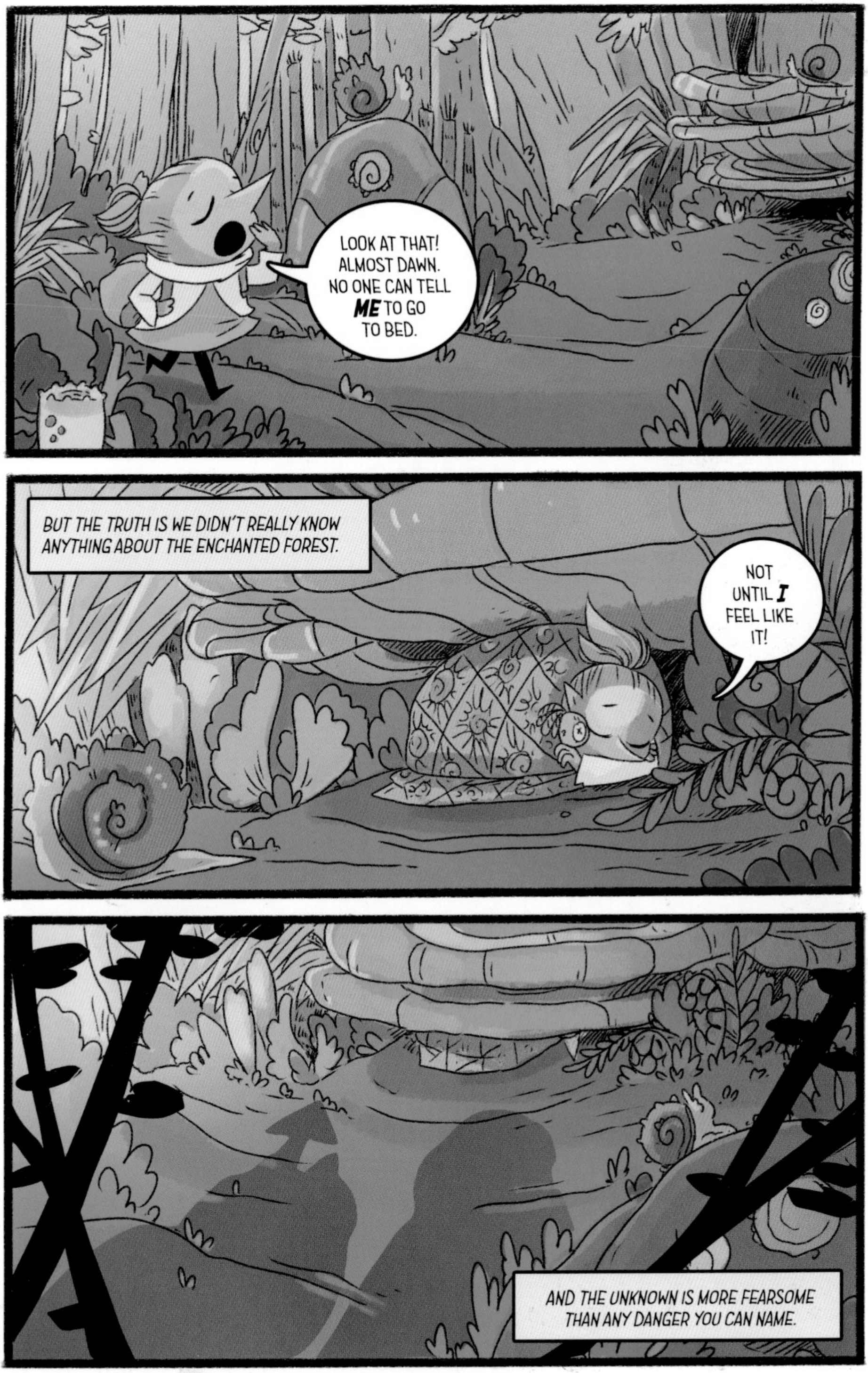

LOOK AT THAT! ALMOST DAWN. NO ONE CAN TELL ME TO GO TO BED.
BUT THE TRUTH IS WE DIDN'T REALLY KNOW ANYTHING ABOUT THE ENCHANTED FOREST.
NOT UNTIL I FEEL LIKE IT!
AND THE UNKNOWN IS MORE FEARSOME THAN ANY DANGER YOU CAN NAME.

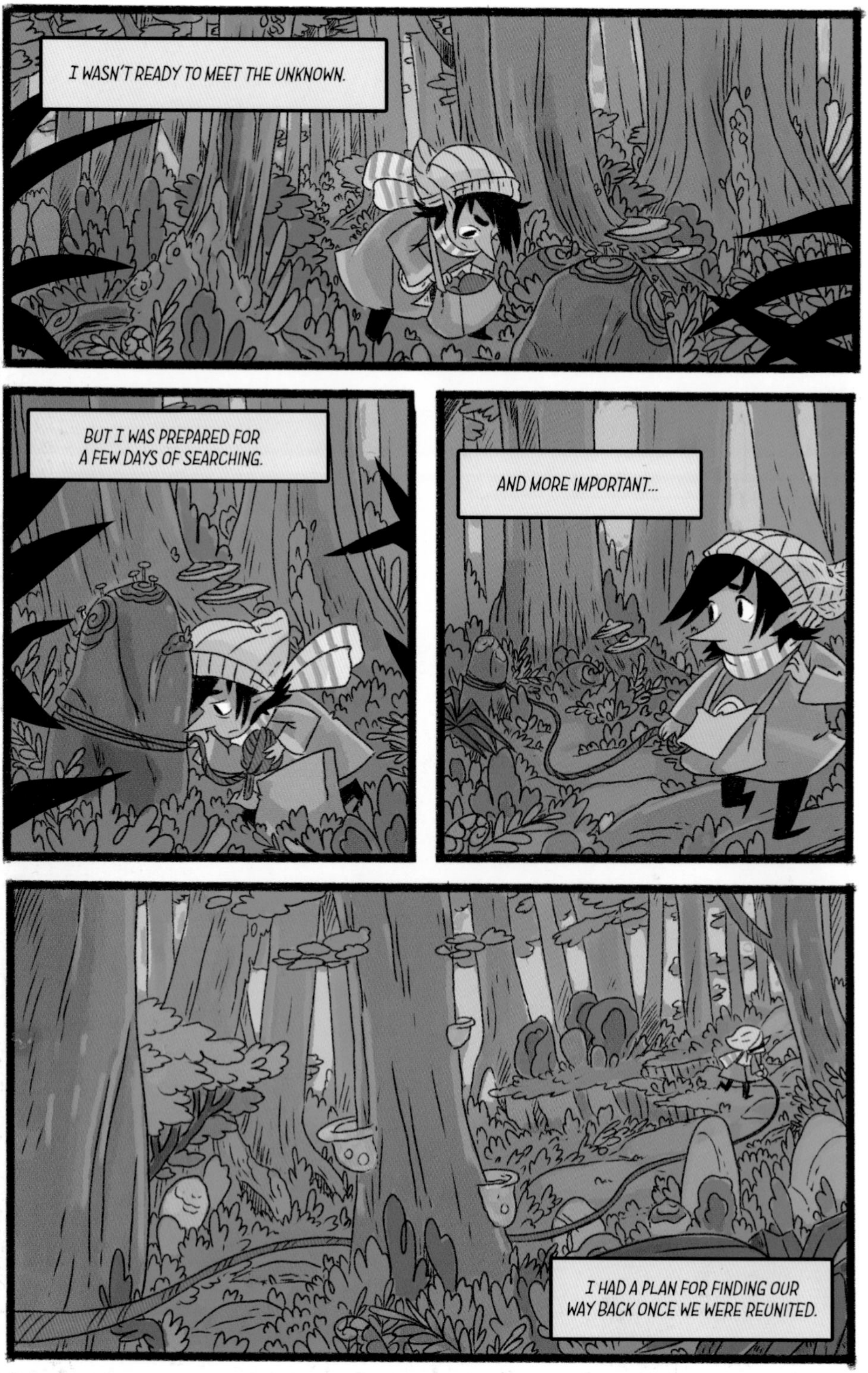
I WASN'T READY TO MEET THE UNKNOWN.
BUT I WAS PREPARED FOR A FEW DAYS OF SEARCHING.
AND MORE IMPORTANT...
I HAD A PLAN FOR FINDING OUR WAY BACK ONCE WE WERE REUNITED.

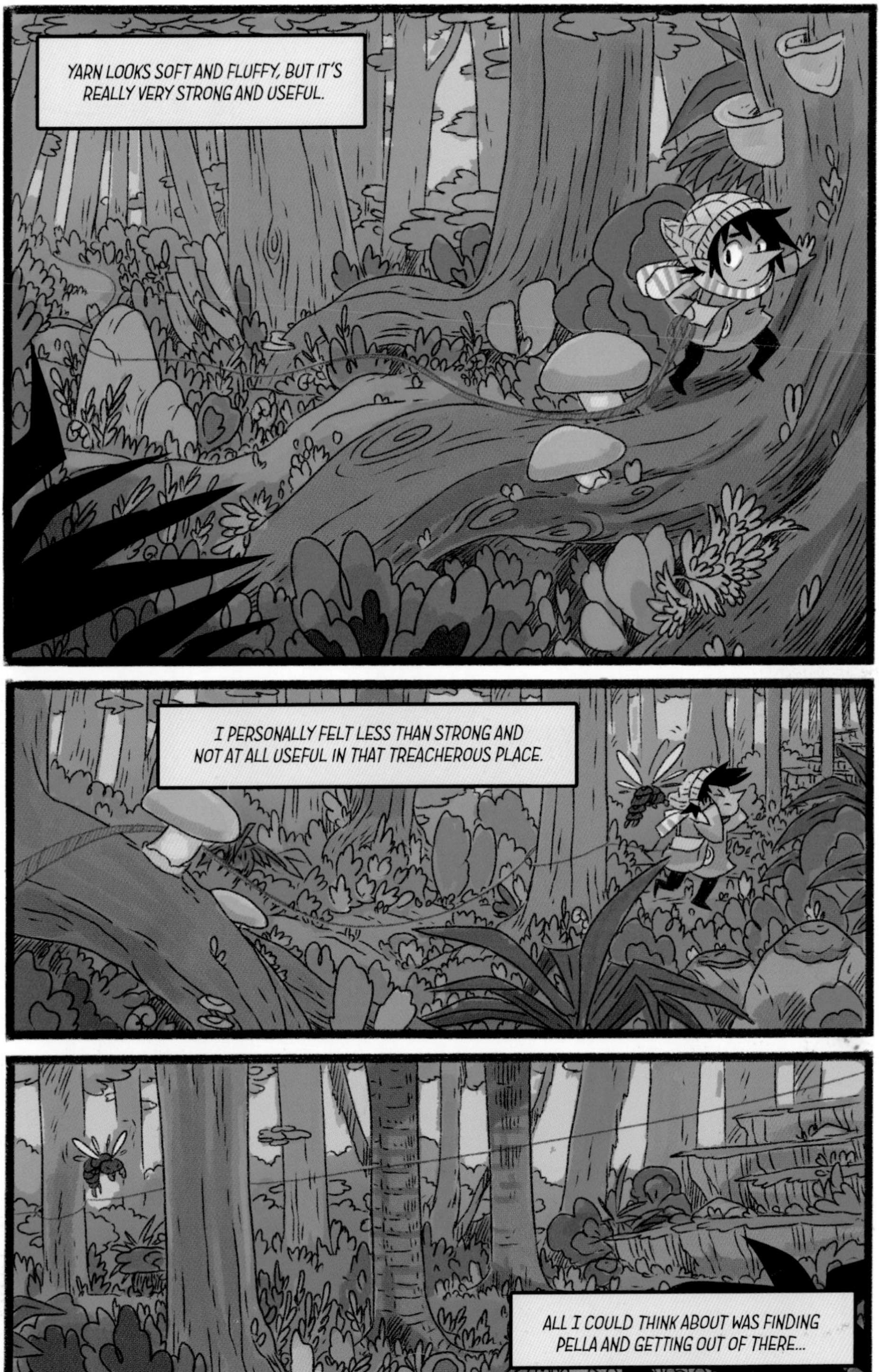
YARN LOOKS SOFT AND FLUFFY, BUT IT'S REALLY VERY STRONG AND USEFUL.
I PERSONALLY FELT LESS THAN STRONG AND NOT AT ALL USEFUL IN THAT TREACHEROUS PLACE.
ALL I COULD THINK ABOUT WAS FINDING PELLA AND GETTING OUT OF THERE...

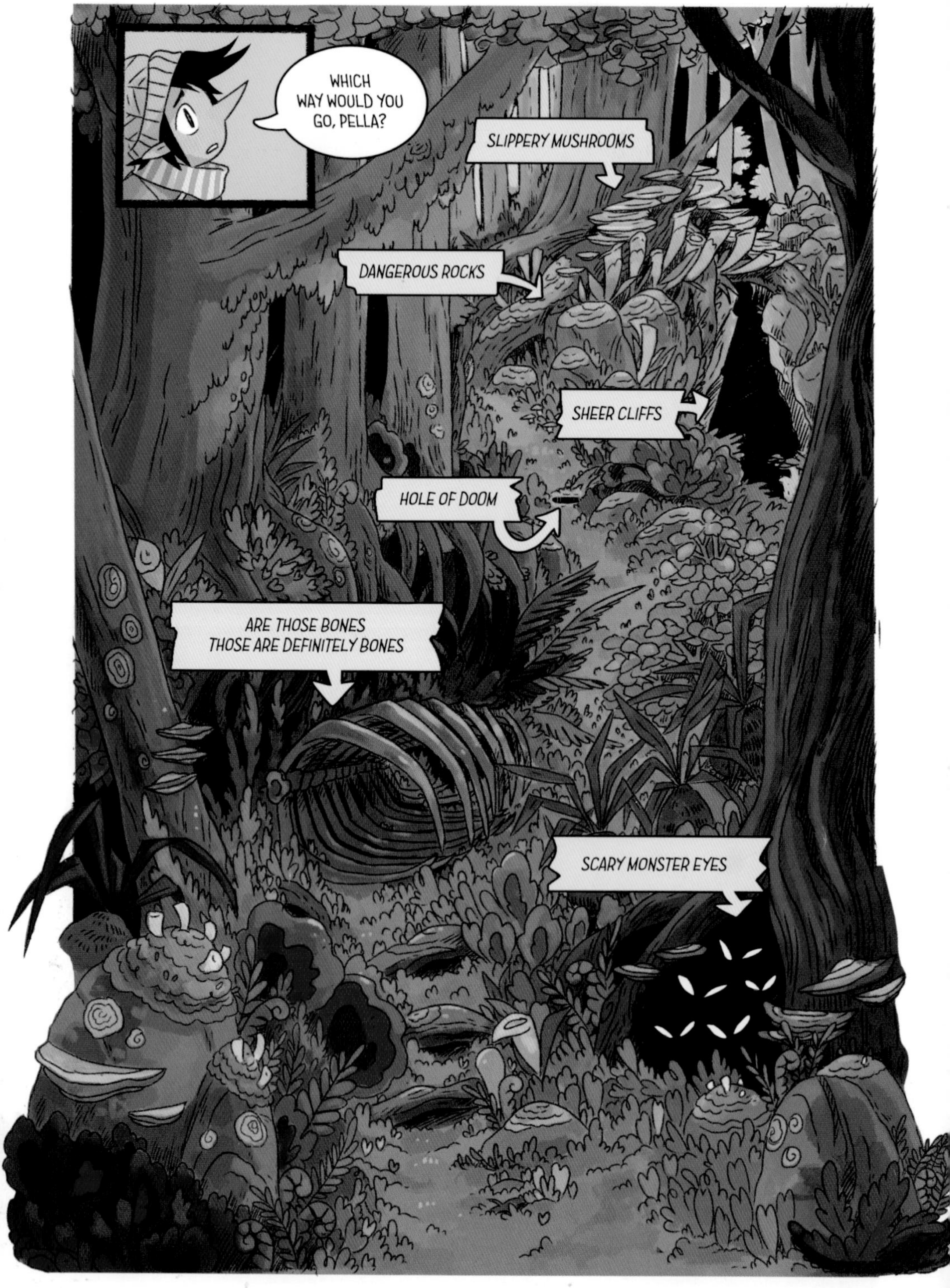
WHICH WAY WOULD YOU GO, PELLA?
SLIPPERY MUSHROOMS
DANGEROUS ROCKS
SHEER CLIFFS
HOLE OF DOOM
ARE THOSE BONES
THOSE ARE DEFINITELY BONES
SCARY MONSTER EYES

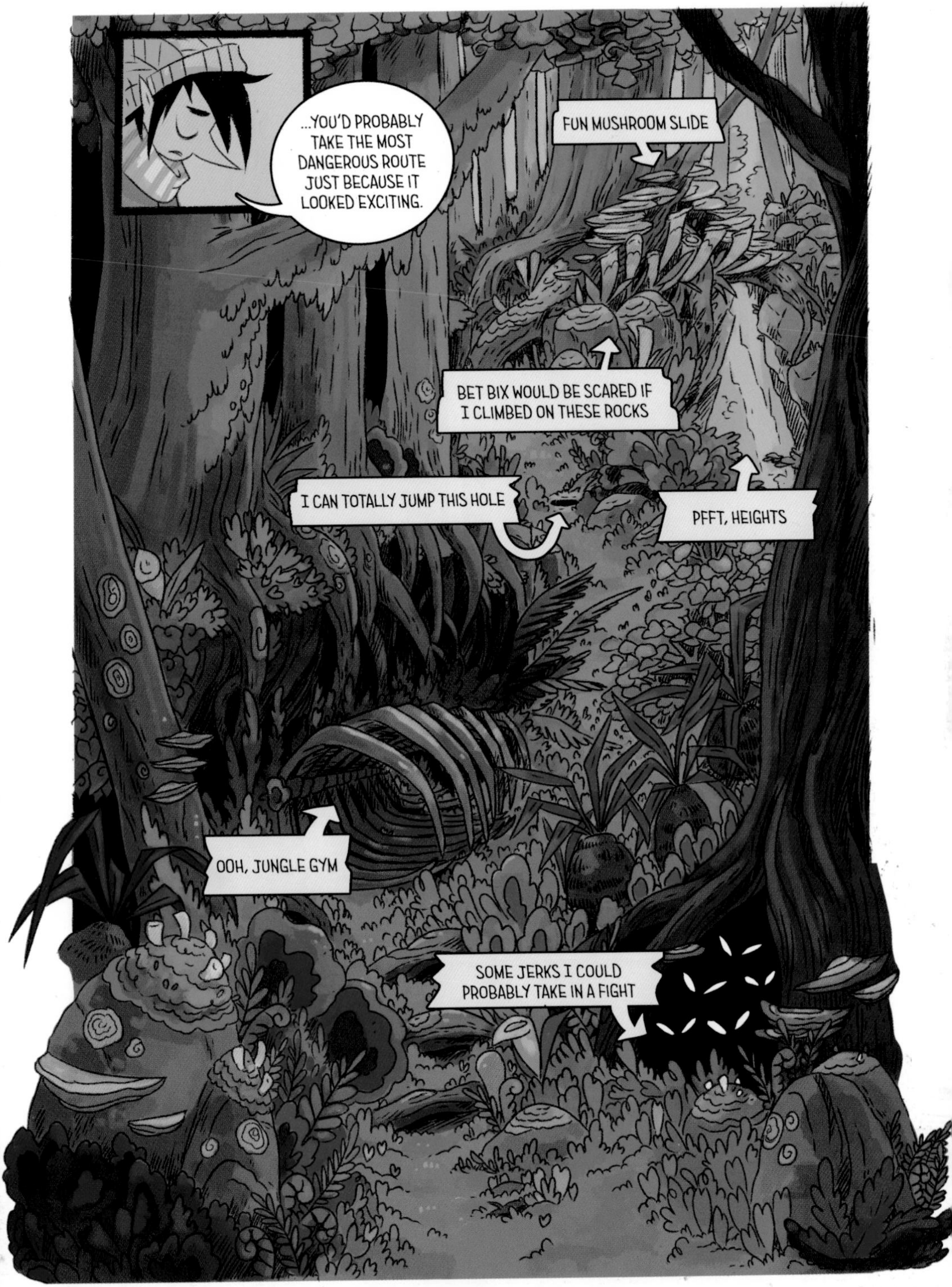
...YOU'D PROBABLY TAKE THE MOST DANGEROUS ROUTE JUST BECAUSE IT LOOKED EXCITING.
FUN MUSHROOM SLIDE
BET BIX WOULD BE SCARED IF I CLIMBED ON THESE ROCKS
I CAN TOTALLY JUMP THIS HOLE
PFFT, HEIGHTS
OOH, JUNGLE GYM
SOME JERKS I COULD PROBABLY TAKE IN A FIGHT

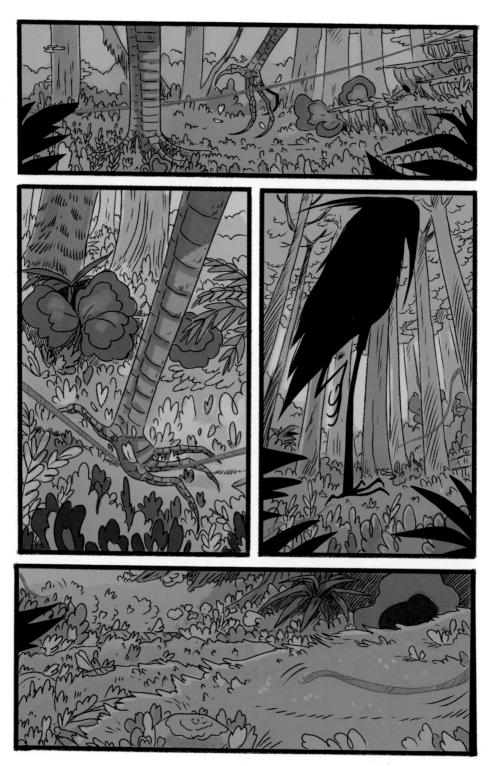

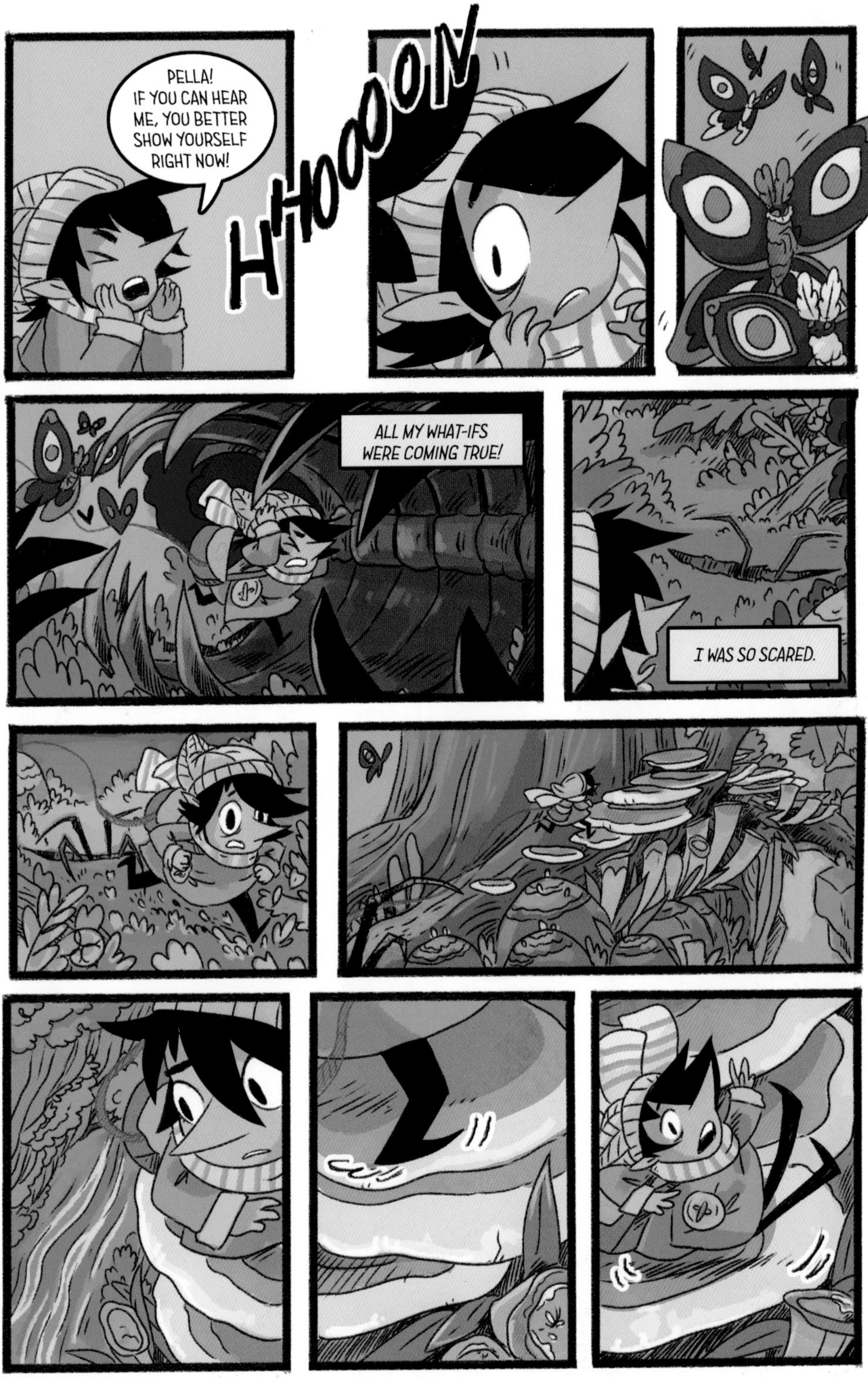
PELLA! IF YOU CAN HEAR ME, YOU BETTER SHOW YOURSELF RIGHT NOW!
HHOOOON
ALL MY WHAT-IFS WERE COMING TRUE!
I WAS SO SCARED.

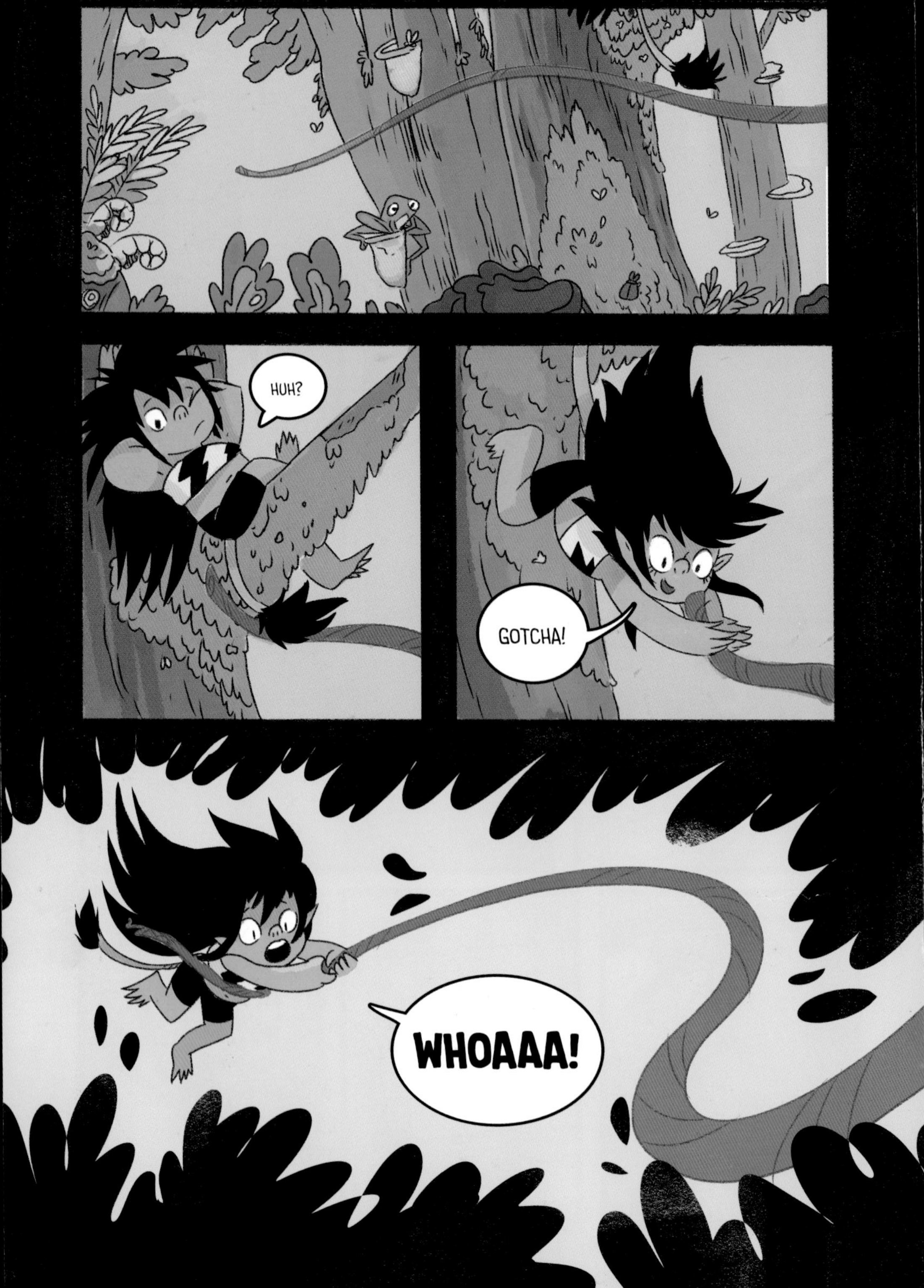
HUH?
GOTCHA!
WHOAAA!

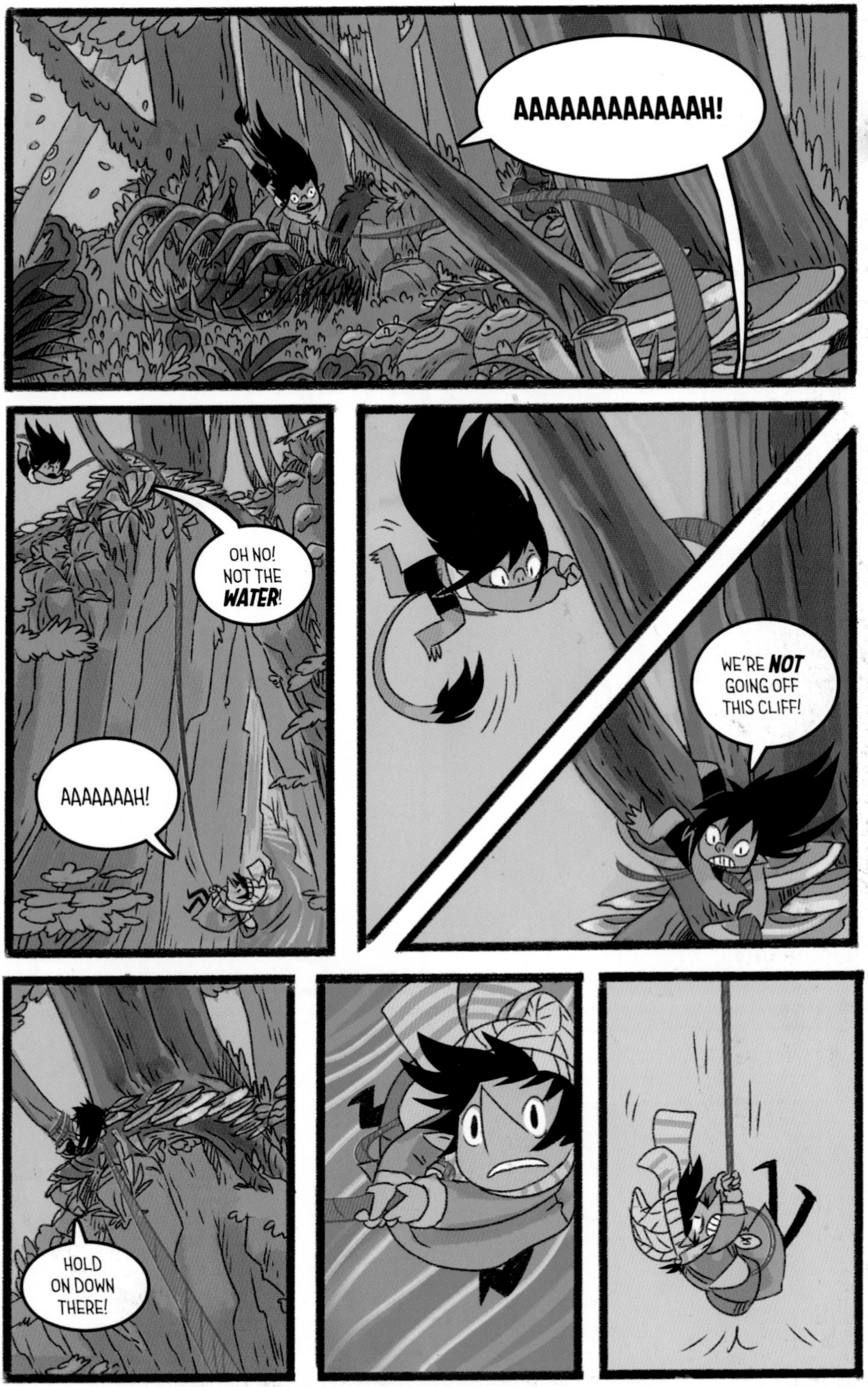
AAAAAAAAAAAAAH!
OH NO! NOT THE WATER!
AAAAAAAH!
WE'RE NOT GOING OFF THIS CLIFF!
HOLD ON DOWN THERE!

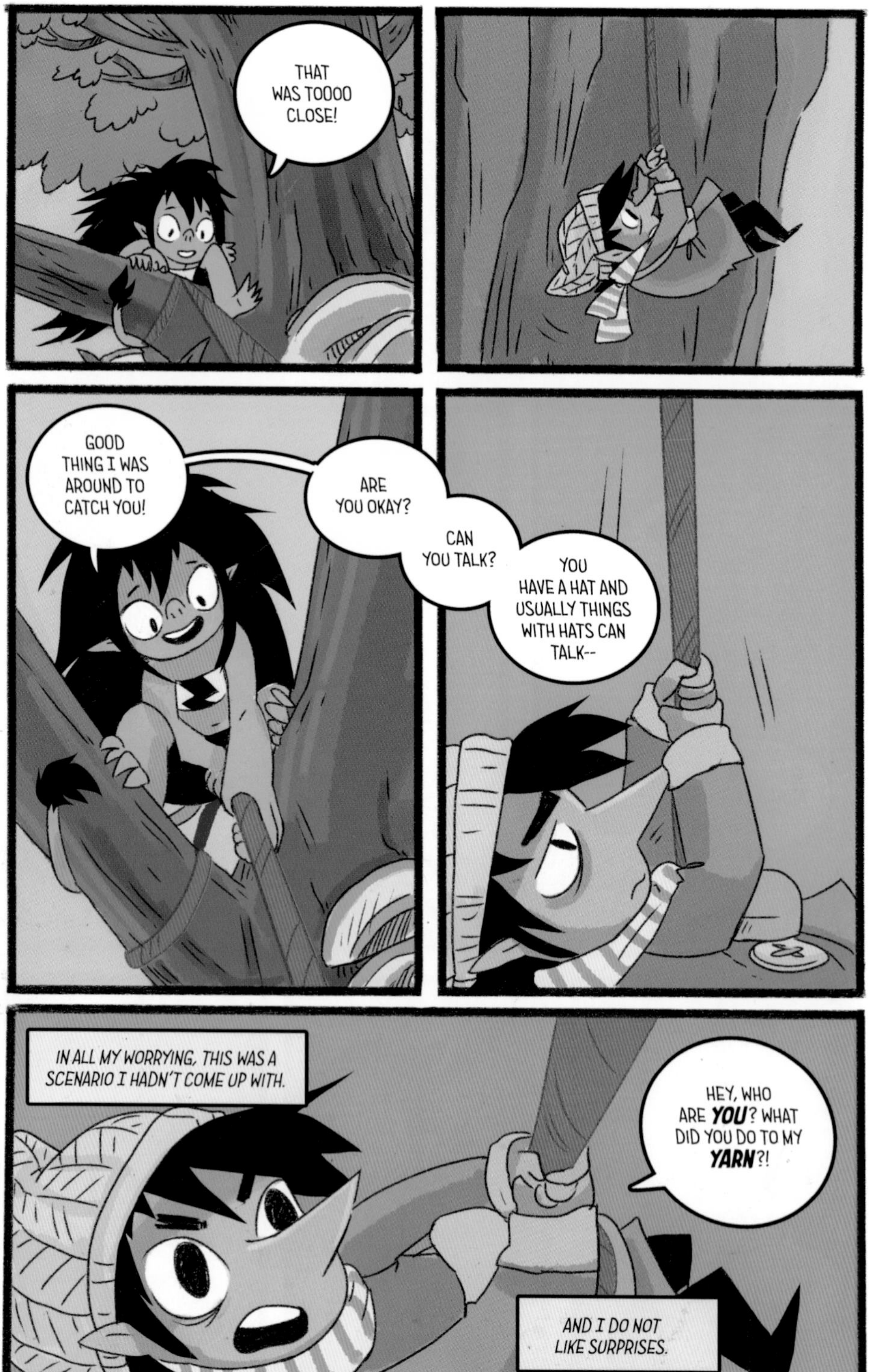
THAT WAS TOOOO CLOSE!
GOOD THING I WAS AROUND TO CATCH YOU!
ARE YOU OKAY?
CAN YOU TALK?
YOU HAVE A HAT AND USUALLY THINGS WITH HATS CAN TALK--
IN ALL MY WORRYING, THIS WAS A SCENARIO I HADN'T COME UP WITH.
HEY, WHO ARE ***YOU***? WHAT DID YOU DO TO MY ***YARN***?!
AND I DO NOT LIKE SURPRISES.

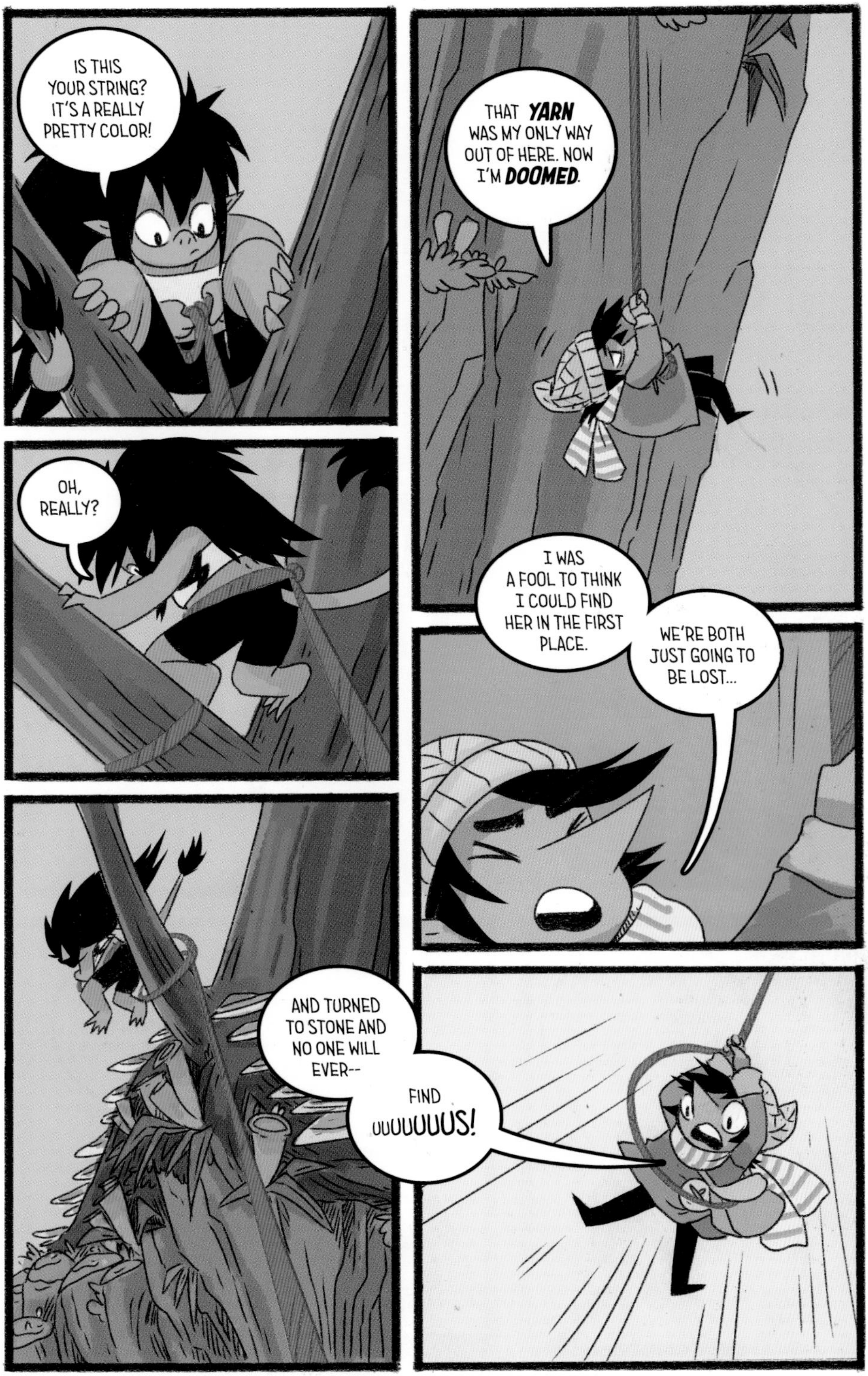
IS THIS YOUR STRING? IT'S A REALLY PRETTY COLOR!
OH, REALLY?
THAT YARN WAS MY ONLY WAY OUT OF HERE. NOW I'M DOOMED.
I WAS A FOOL TO THINK I COULD FIND HER IN THE FIRST PLACE.
WE'RE BOTH JUST GOING TO BE LOST...
AND TURNED TO STONE AND NO ONE WILL EVER--
FIND UUUUUUUS!

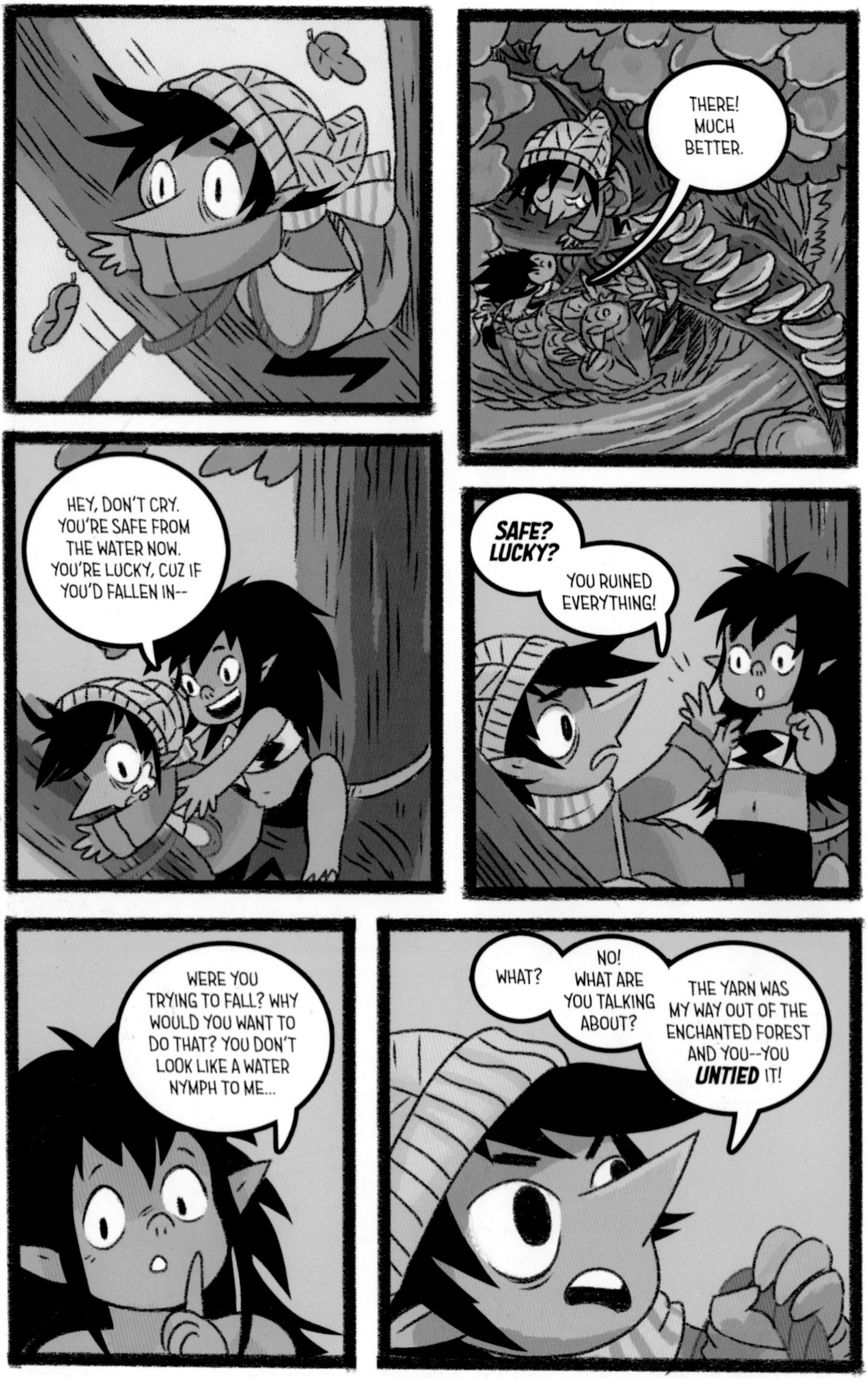
THERE! MUCH BETTER.
HEY, DON'T CRY. YOU'RE SAFE FROM THE WATER NOW. YOU'RE LUCKY, CUZ IF YOU'D FALLEN IN--
SAFE? LUCKY?
YOU RUINED EVERYTHING!
WERE YOU TRYING TO FALL? WHY WOULD YOU WANT TO DO THAT? YOU DON'T LOOK LIKE A WATER NYMPH TO ME...
WHAT?
NO! WHAT ARE YOU TALKING ABOUT?
THE YARN WAS MY WAY OUT OF THE ENCHANTED FOREST AND YOU--YOU UNTIED IT!

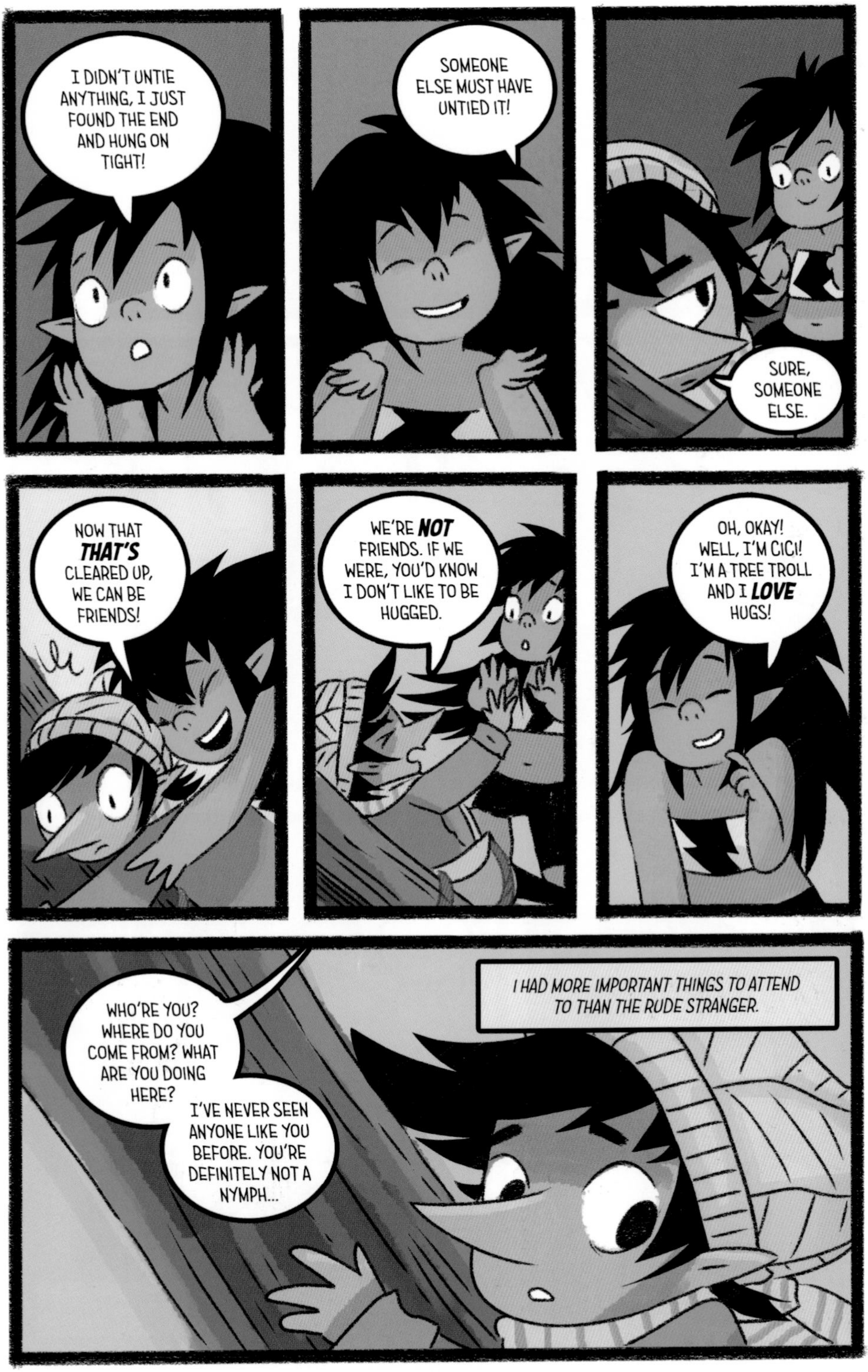
I DIDN'T UNTIE ANYTHING, I JUST FOUND THE END AND HUNG ON TIGHT!
SOMEONE ELSE MUST HAVE UNTIED IT!
SURE, SOMEONE ELSE.
NOW THAT **THAT'S** CLEARED UP, WE CAN BE FRIENDS!
WE'RE **NOT** FRIENDS. IF WE WERE, YOU'D KNOW I DON'T LIKE TO BE HUGGED.
OH, OKAY! WELL, I'M CICI! I'M A TREE TROLL AND I **LOVE** HUGS!
I HAD MORE IMPORTANT THINGS TO ATTEND TO THAN THE RUDE STRANGER.
WHO'RE YOU? WHERE DO YOU COME FROM? WHAT ARE YOU DOING HERE?
I'VE NEVER SEEN ANYONE LIKE YOU BEFORE. YOU'RE DEFINITELY NOT A NYMPH...

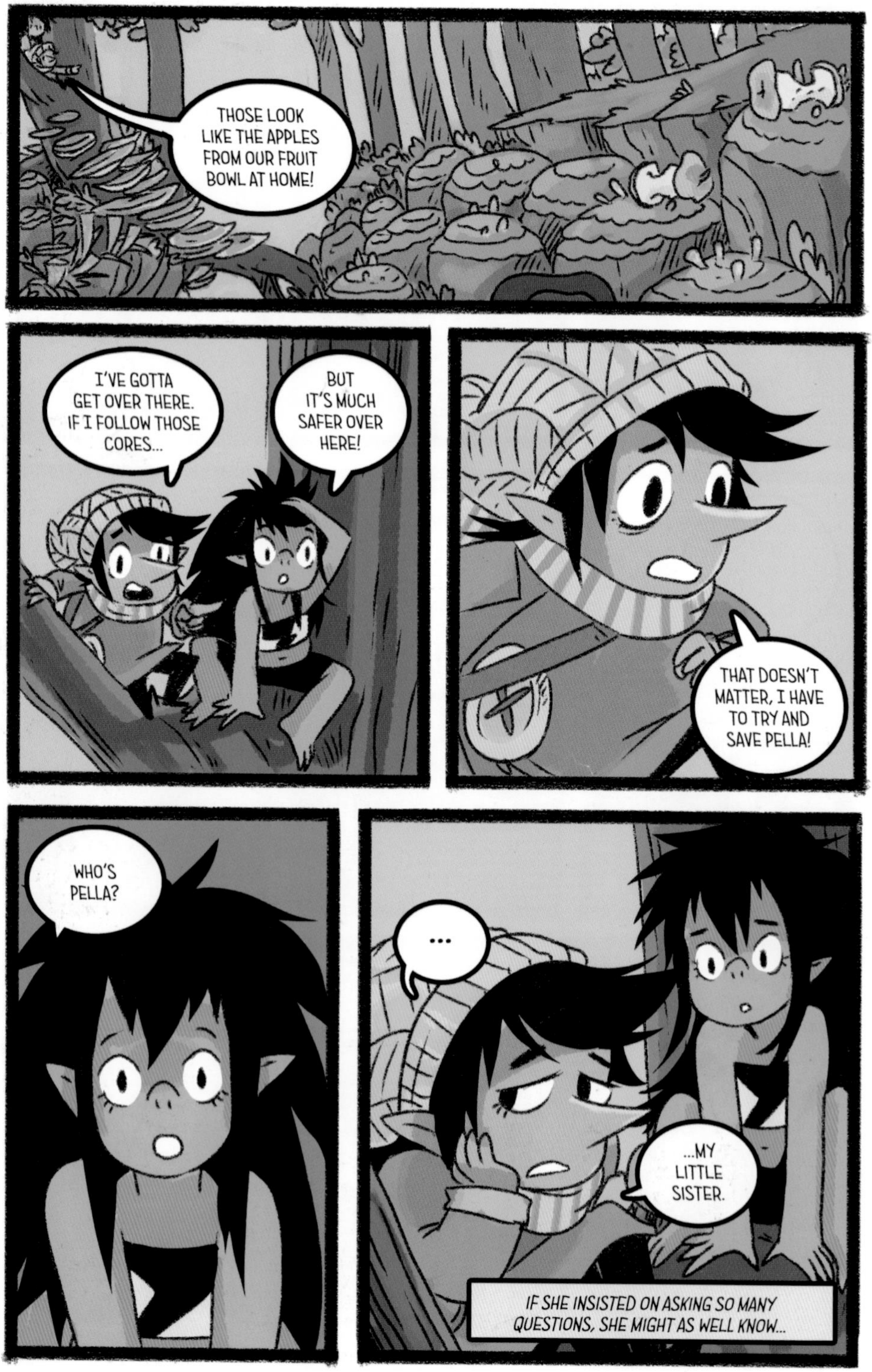
THOSE LOOK LIKE THE APPLES FROM OUR FRUIT BOWL AT HOME!
I'VE GOTTA GET OVER THERE. IF I FOLLOW THOSE CORES...
BUT IT'S MUCH SAFER OVER HERE!
THAT DOESN'T MATTER, I HAVE TO TRY AND SAVE PELLA!
WHO'S PELLA?
...
...MY LITTLE SISTER.
IF SHE INSISTED ON ASKING SO MANY QUESTIONS, SHE MIGHT AS WELL KNOW...

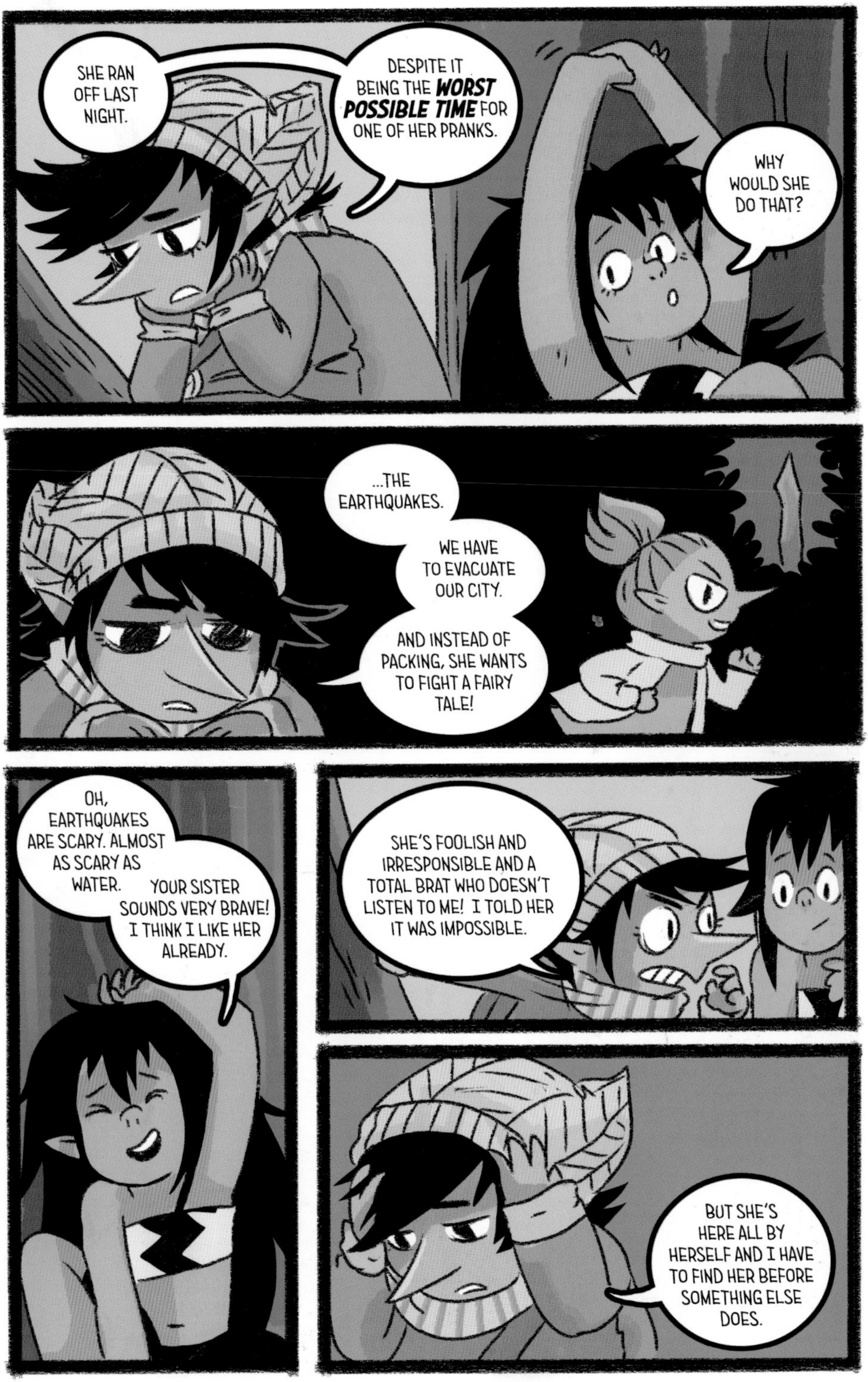
SHE RAN OFF LAST NIGHT.
DESPITE IT BEING THE **WORST POSSIBLE TIME** FOR ONE OF HER PRANKS.
WHY WOULD SHE DO THAT?
...THE EARTHQUAKES.
WE HAVE TO EVACUATE OUR CITY.
AND INSTEAD OF PACKING, SHE WANTS TO FIGHT A FAIRY TALE!
OH, EARTHQUAKES ARE SCARY. ALMOST AS SCARY AS WATER.
YOUR SISTER SOUNDS VERY BRAVE! I THINK I LIKE HER ALREADY.
SHE'S FOOLISH AND IRRESPONSIBLE AND A TOTAL BRAT WHO DOESN'T LISTEN TO ME! I TOLD HER IT WAS IMPOSSIBLE.
BUT SHE'S HERE ALL BY HERSELF AND I HAVE TO FIND HER BEFORE SOMETHING ELSE DOES.

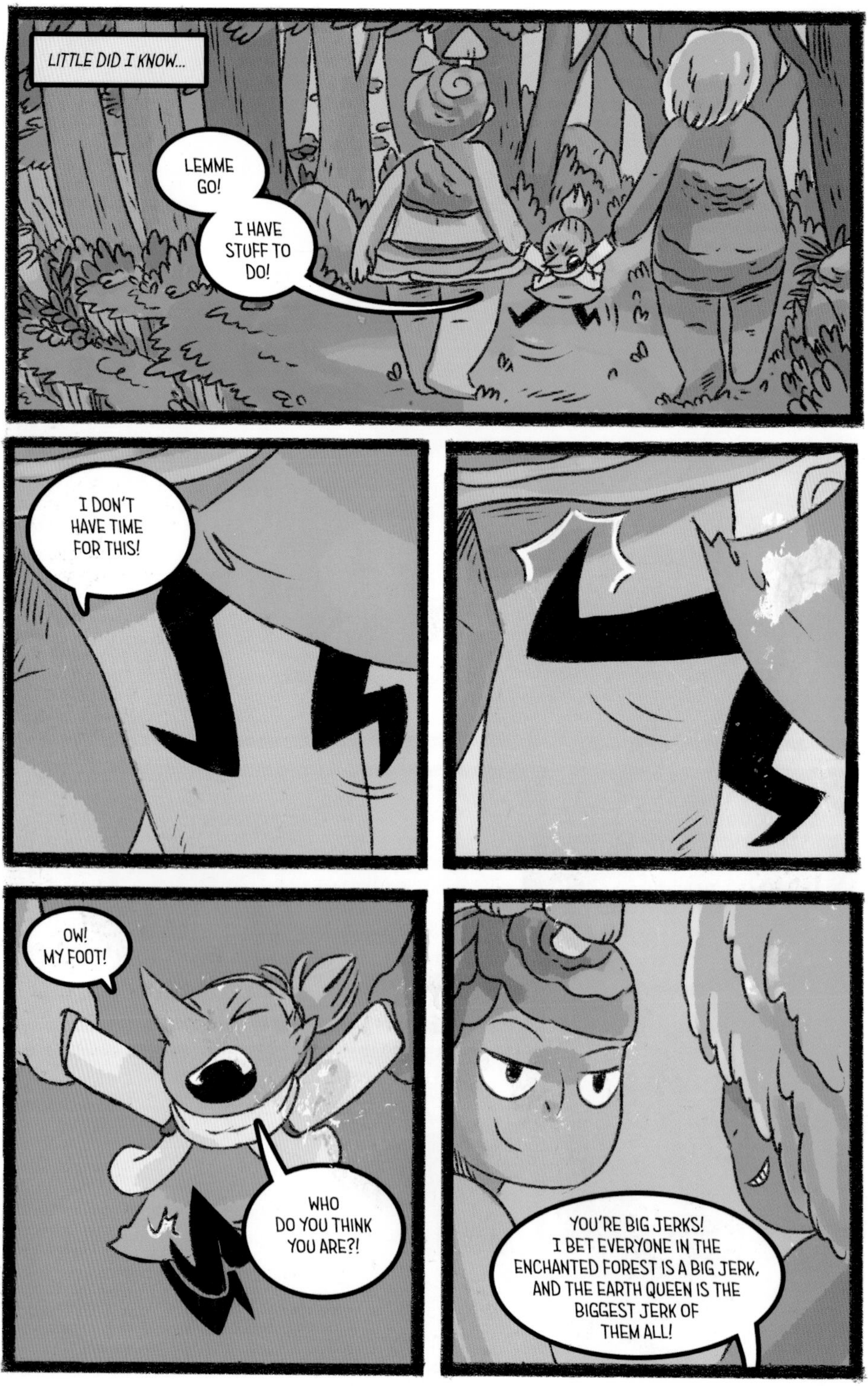
LITTLE DID I KNOW...
LEMME GO!
I HAVE STUFF TO DO!
I DON'T HAVE TIME FOR THIS!
OW! MY FOOT!
WHO DO YOU THINK YOU ARE?!
YOU'RE BIG JERKS! I BET EVERYONE IN THE ENCHANTED FOREST IS A BIG JERK, AND THE EARTH QUEEN IS THE BIGGEST JERK OF THEM ALL!

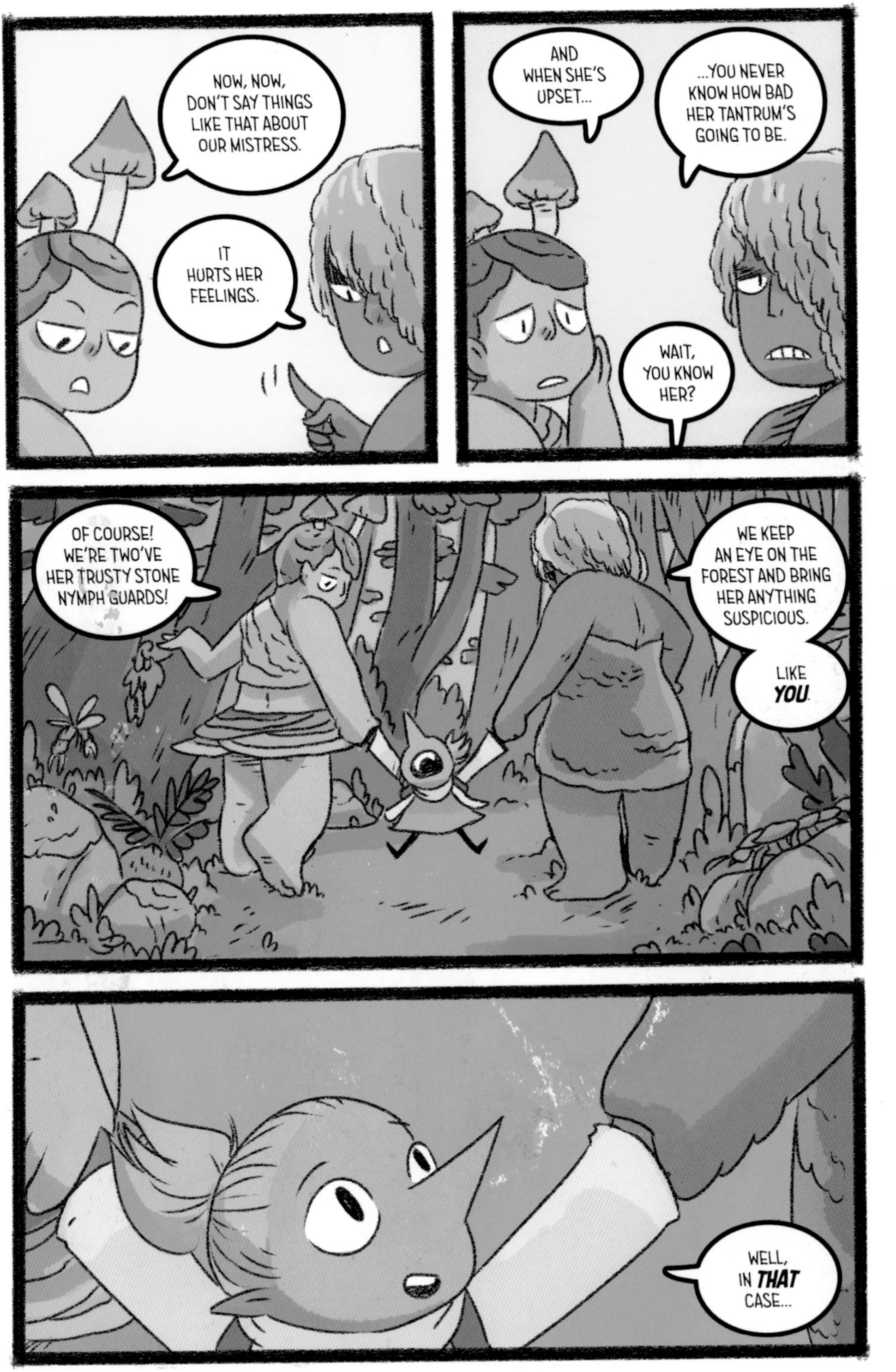
NOW, NOW, DON'T SAY THINGS LIKE THAT ABOUT OUR MISTRESS.
IT HURTS HER FEELINGS.
AND WHEN SHE'S UPSET...
...YOU NEVER KNOW HOW BAD HER TANTRUM'S GOING TO BE.
WAIT, YOU KNOW HER?
OF COURSE! WE'RE TWO'VE HER TRUSTY STONE NYMPH GUARDS!
WE KEEP AN EYE ON THE FOREST AND BRING HER ANYTHING SUSPICIOUS.
LIKE ***YOU***.
WELL, IN ***THAT*** CASE...

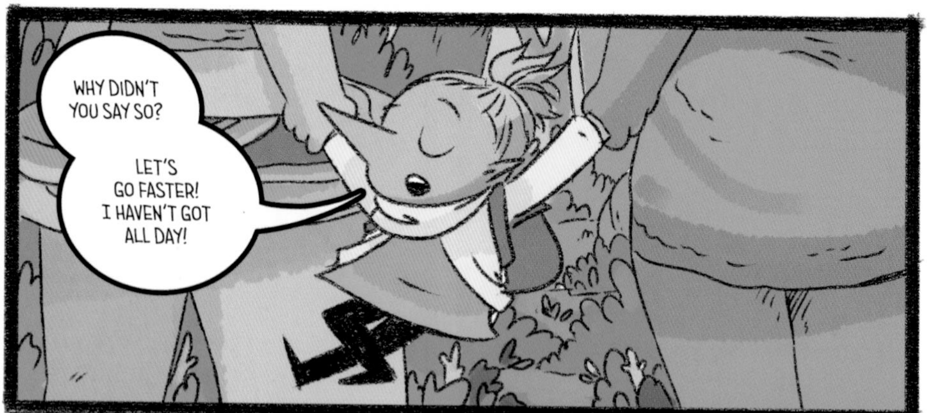
WHY DIDN'T YOU SAY SO?
LET'S GO FASTER! I HAVEN'T GOT ALL DAY!

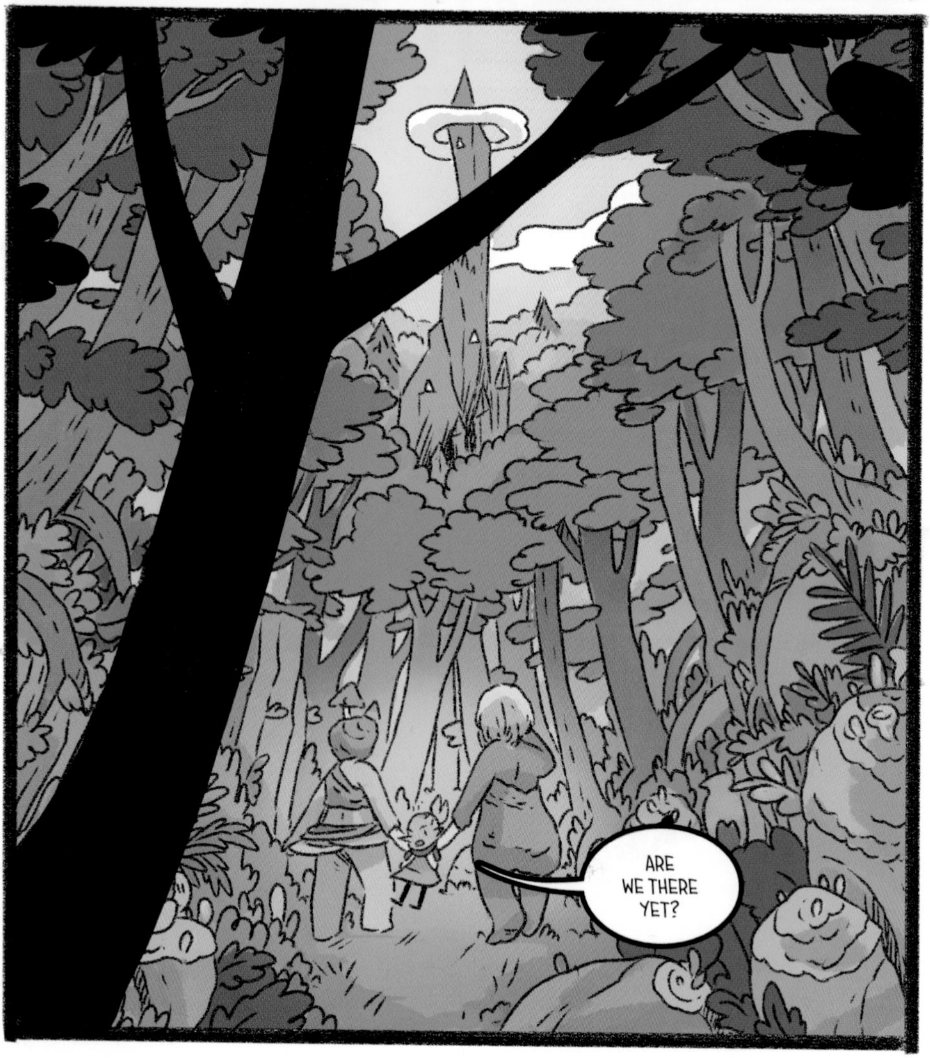
ARE WE THERE YET?

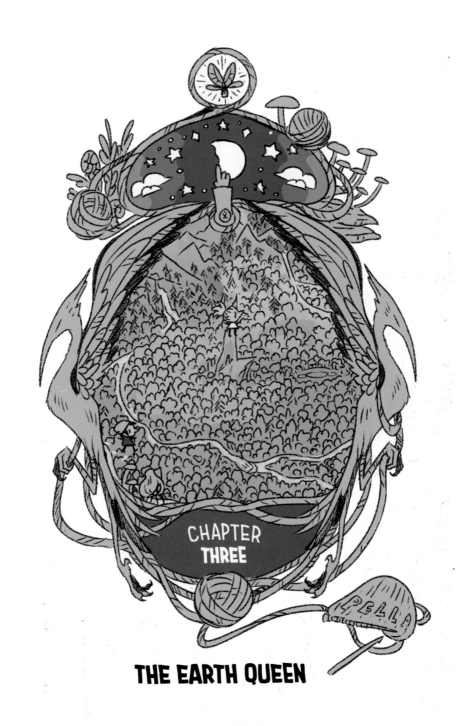

CHAPTER
THREE

THE EARTH QUEEN

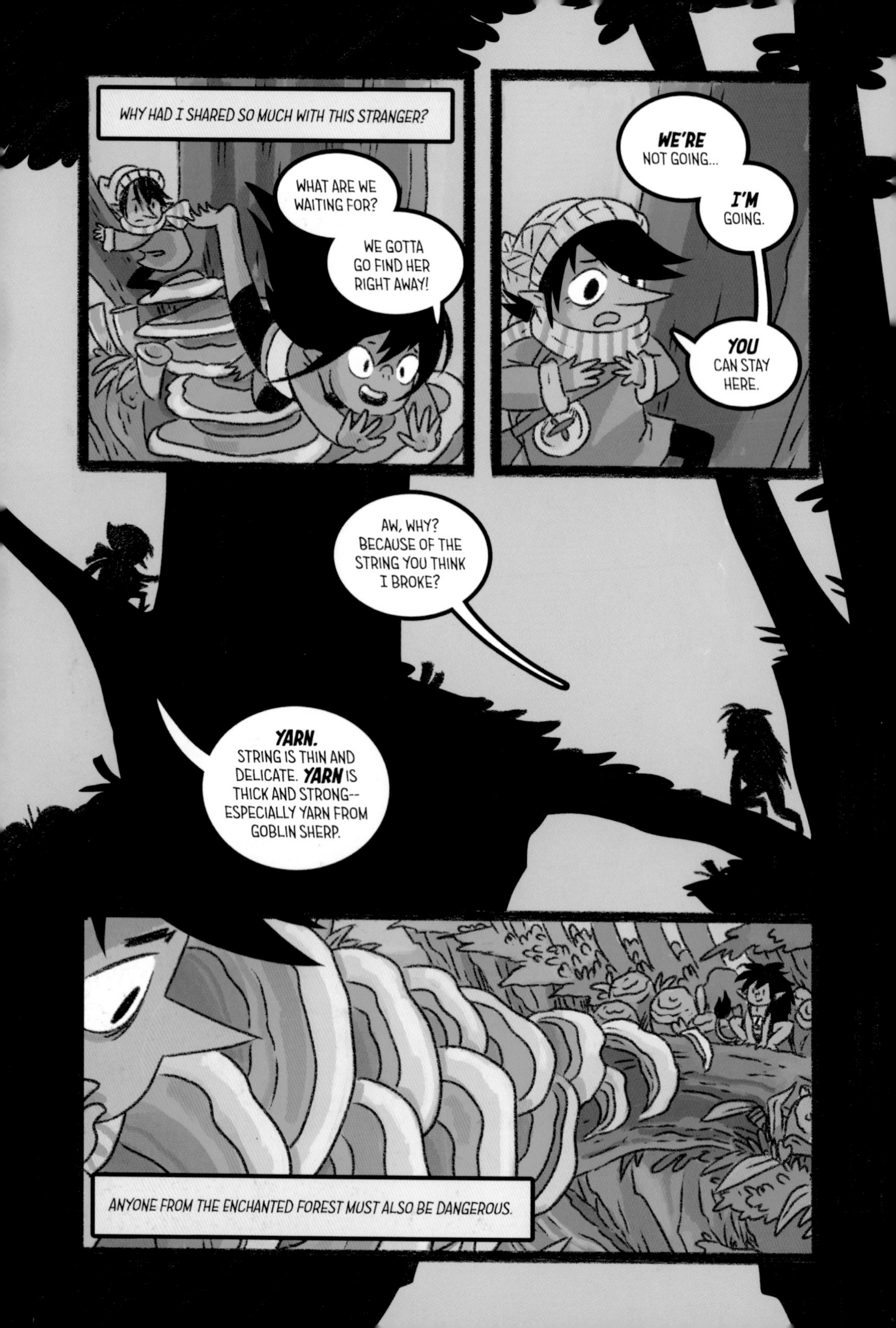
WHY HAD I SHARED SO MUCH WITH THIS STRANGER?
WHAT ARE WE WAITING FOR?
WE GOTTA GO FIND HER RIGHT AWAY!
WE'RE NOT GOING...
I'M GOING.
YOU CAN STAY HERE.
AW, WHY? BECAUSE OF THE STRING YOU THINK I BROKE?
YARN. STRING IS THIN AND DELICATE. YARN IS THICK AND STRONG-- ESPECIALLY YARN FROM GOBLIN SHERP.
ANYONE FROM THE ENCHANTED FOREST MUST ALSO BE DANGEROUS.

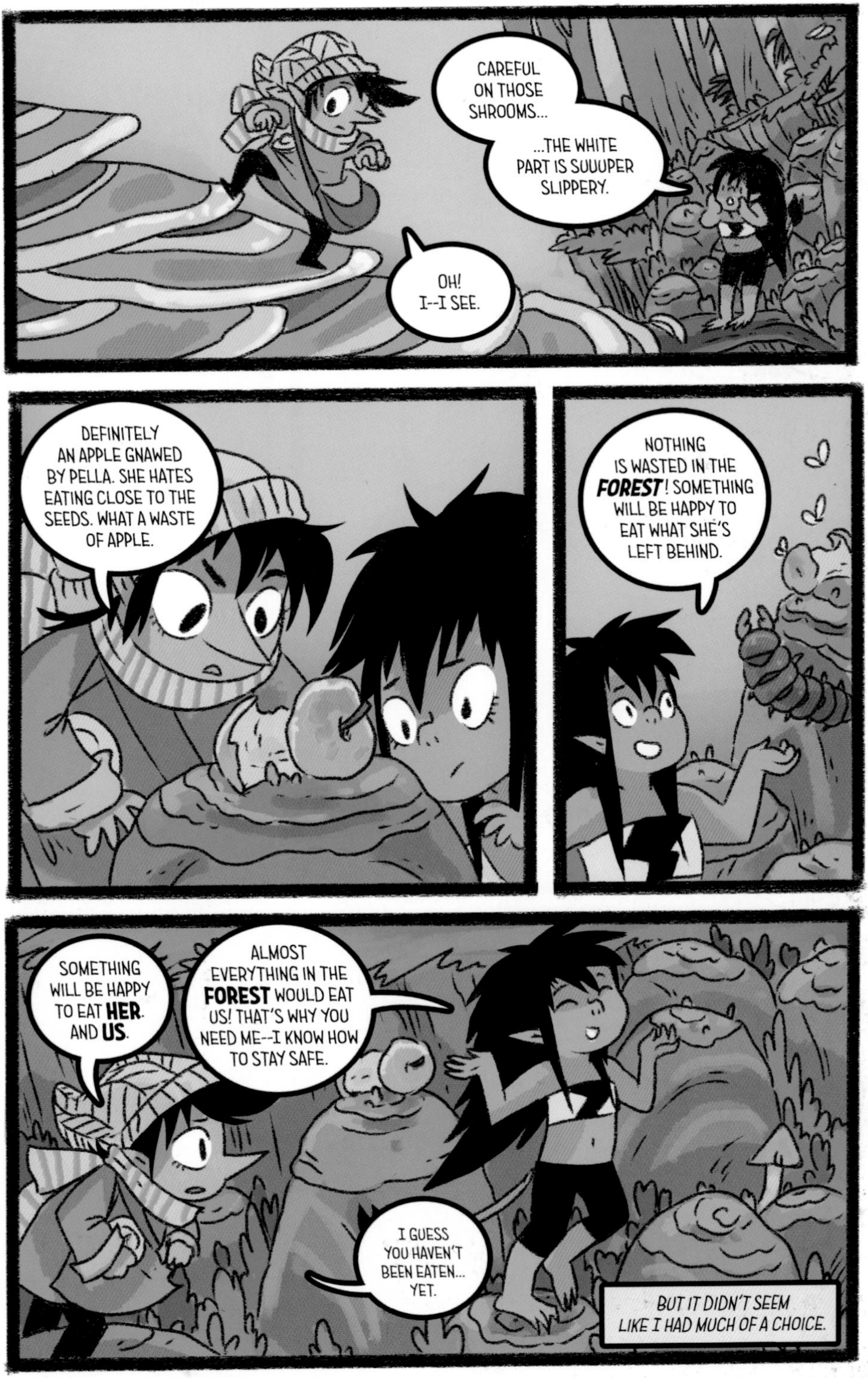
CAREFUL ON THOSE SHROOMS...
...THE WHITE PART IS SUUUPER SLIPPERY.
OH! I--I SEE.
DEFINITELY AN APPLE GNAWED BY PELLA. SHE HATES EATING CLOSE TO THE SEEDS. WHAT A WASTE OF APPLE.
NOTHING IS WASTED IN THE **FOREST**! SOMETHING WILL BE HAPPY TO EAT WHAT SHE'S LEFT BEHIND.
SOMETHING WILL BE HAPPY TO EAT **HER**. AND **US**.
ALMOST EVERYTHING IN THE **FOREST** WOULD EAT US! THAT'S WHY YOU NEED ME--I KNOW HOW TO STAY SAFE.
I GUESS YOU HAVEN'T BEEN EATEN... YET.
BUT IT DIDN'T SEEM LIKE I HAD MUCH OF A CHOICE.

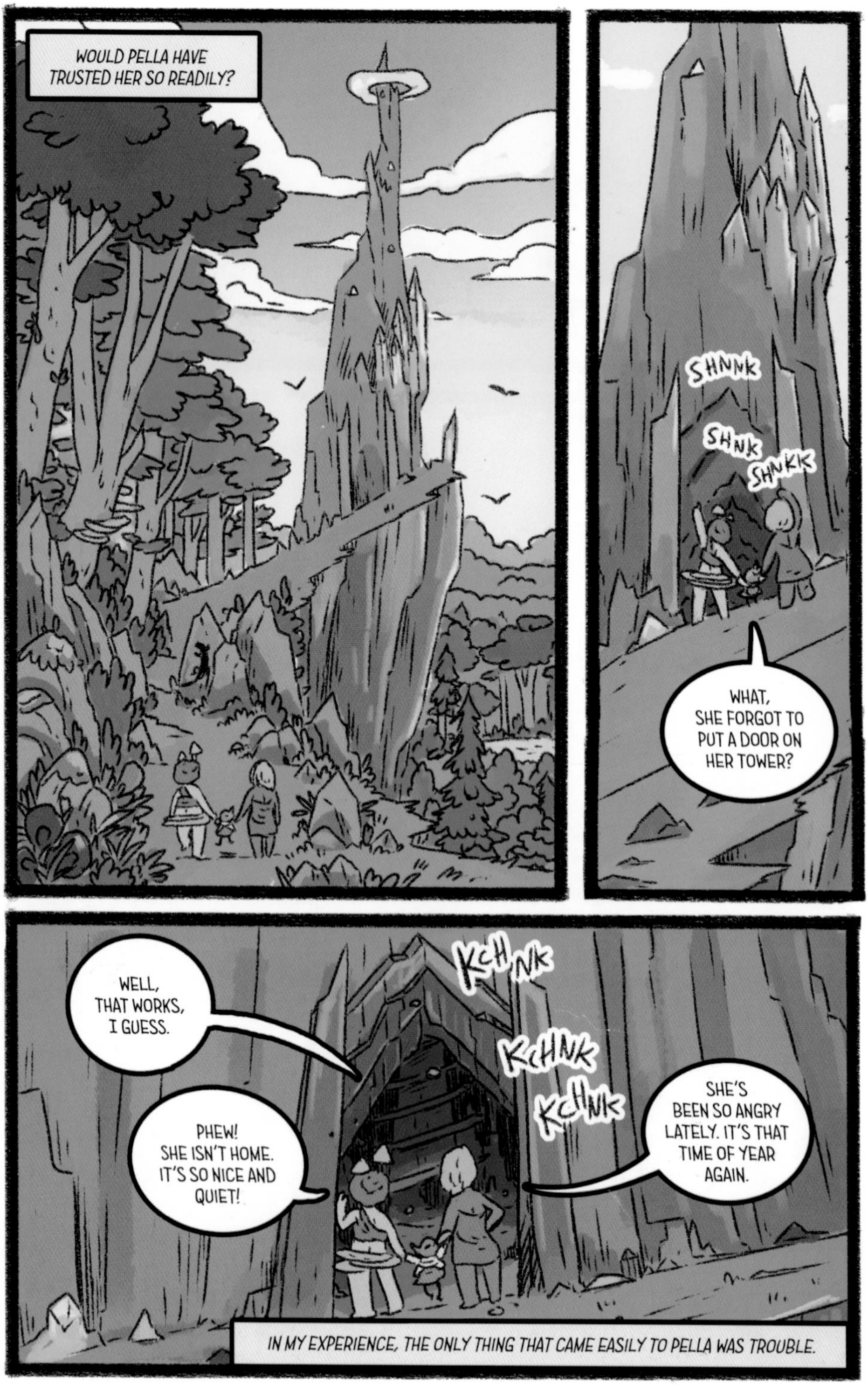
WOULD PELLA HAVE TRUSTED HER SO READILY?
SHNNK
SHNK
SHNKK
WHAT, SHE FORGOT TO PUT A DOOR ON HER TOWER?
KCHNK
WELL, THAT WORKS, I GUESS.
KCHNK
KCHNK
PHEW! SHE ISN'T HOME. IT'S SO NICE AND QUIET!
SHE'S BEEN SO ANGRY LATELY. IT'S THAT TIME OF YEAR AGAIN.
IN MY EXPERIENCE, THE ONLY THING THAT CAME EASILY TO PELLA WAS TROUBLE.

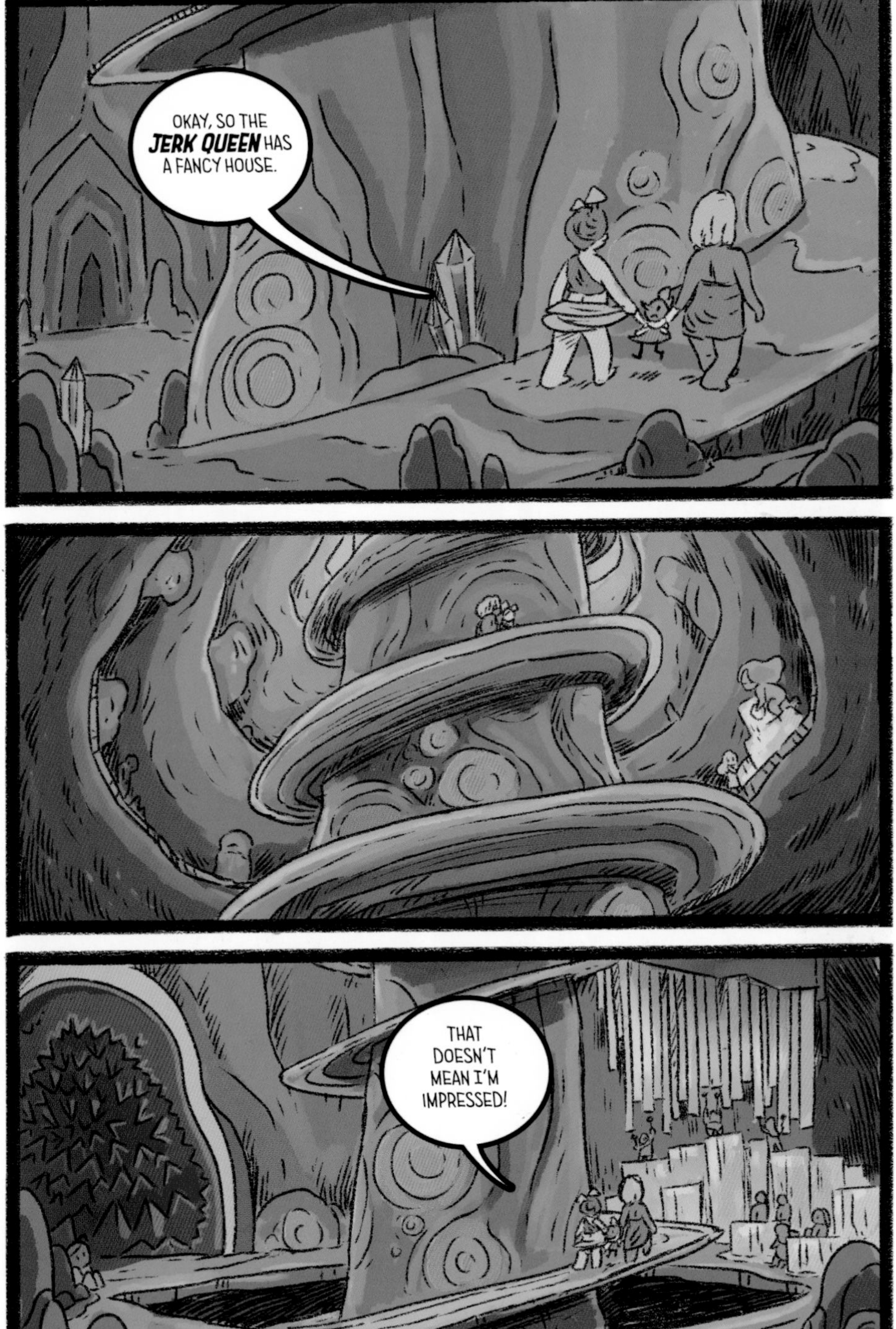
OKAY, SO THE **JERK QUEEN** HAS A FANCY HOUSE.
THAT DOESN'T MEAN I'M IMPRESSED!

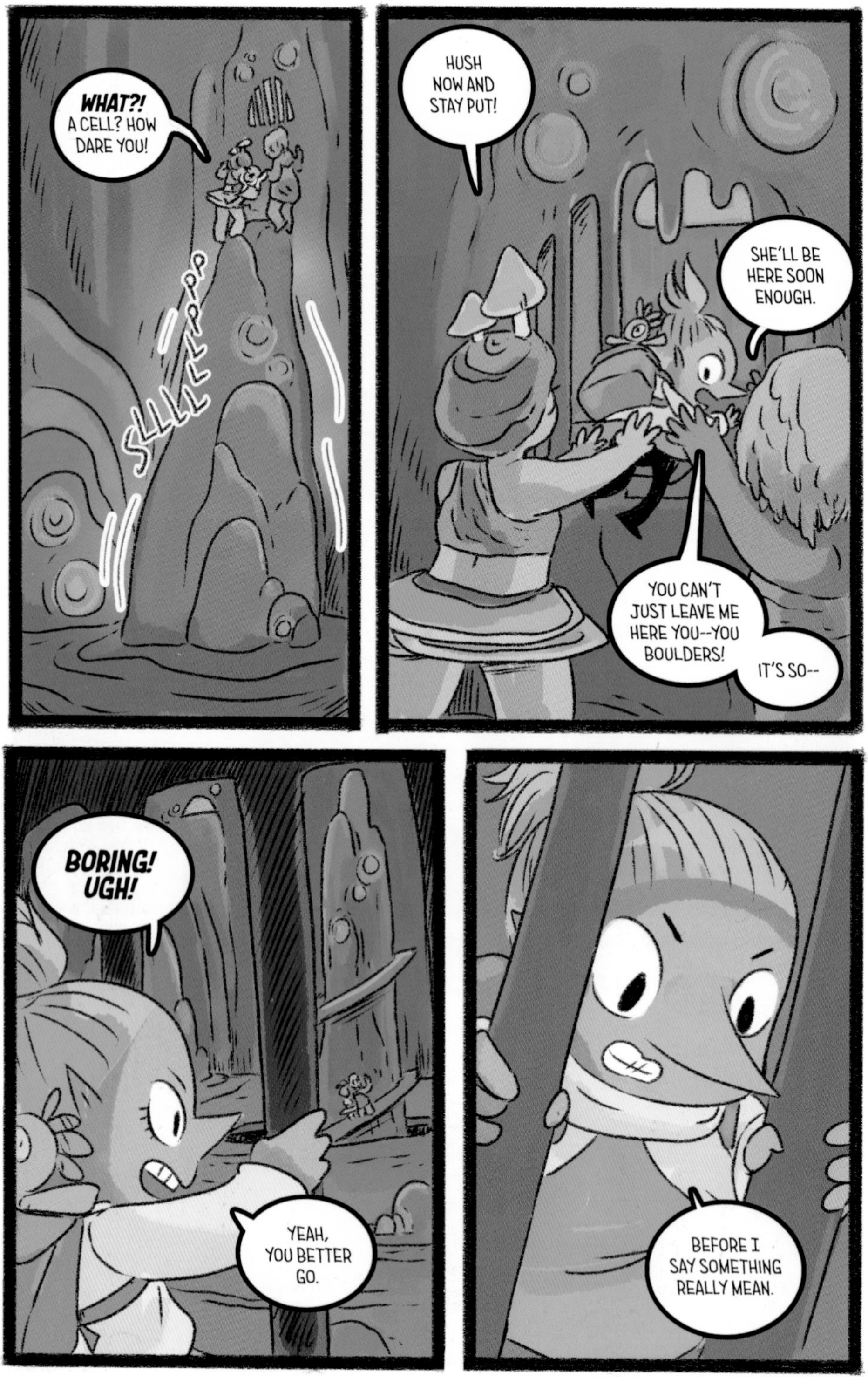
WHAT?! A CELL? HOW DARE YOU!
HUSH NOW AND STAY PUT!
SHE'LL BE HERE SOON ENOUGH.
YOU CAN'T JUST LEAVE ME HERE YOU--YOU BOULDERS!
IT'S SO--
BORING! UGH!
YEAH, YOU BETTER GO.
BEFORE I SAY SOMETHING REALLY MEAN.

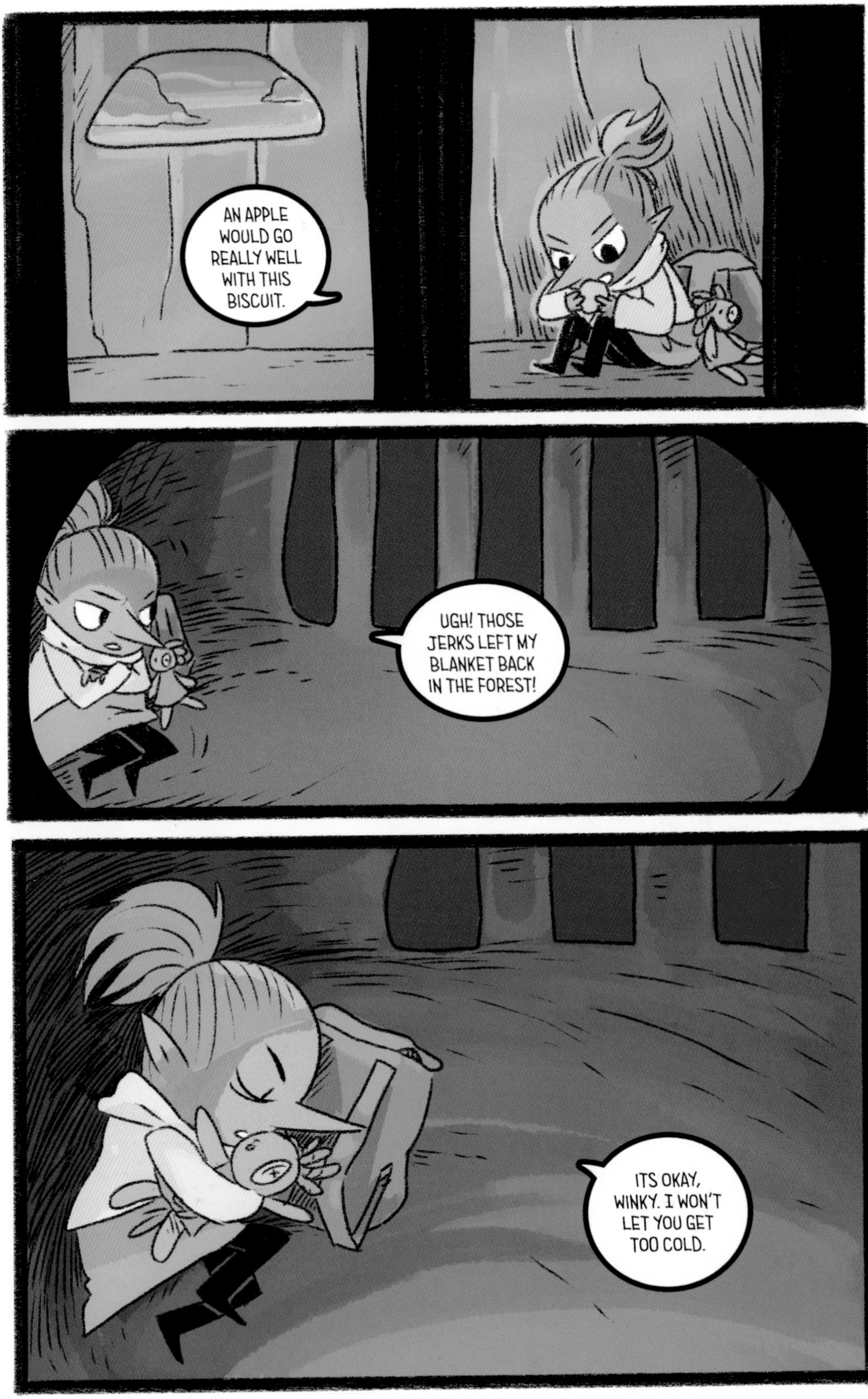
AN APPLE WOULD GO REALLY WELL WITH THIS BISCUIT.
UGH! THOSE JERKS LEFT MY BLANKET BACK IN THE FOREST!
ITS OKAY, WINKY. I WON'T LET YOU GET TOO COLD.

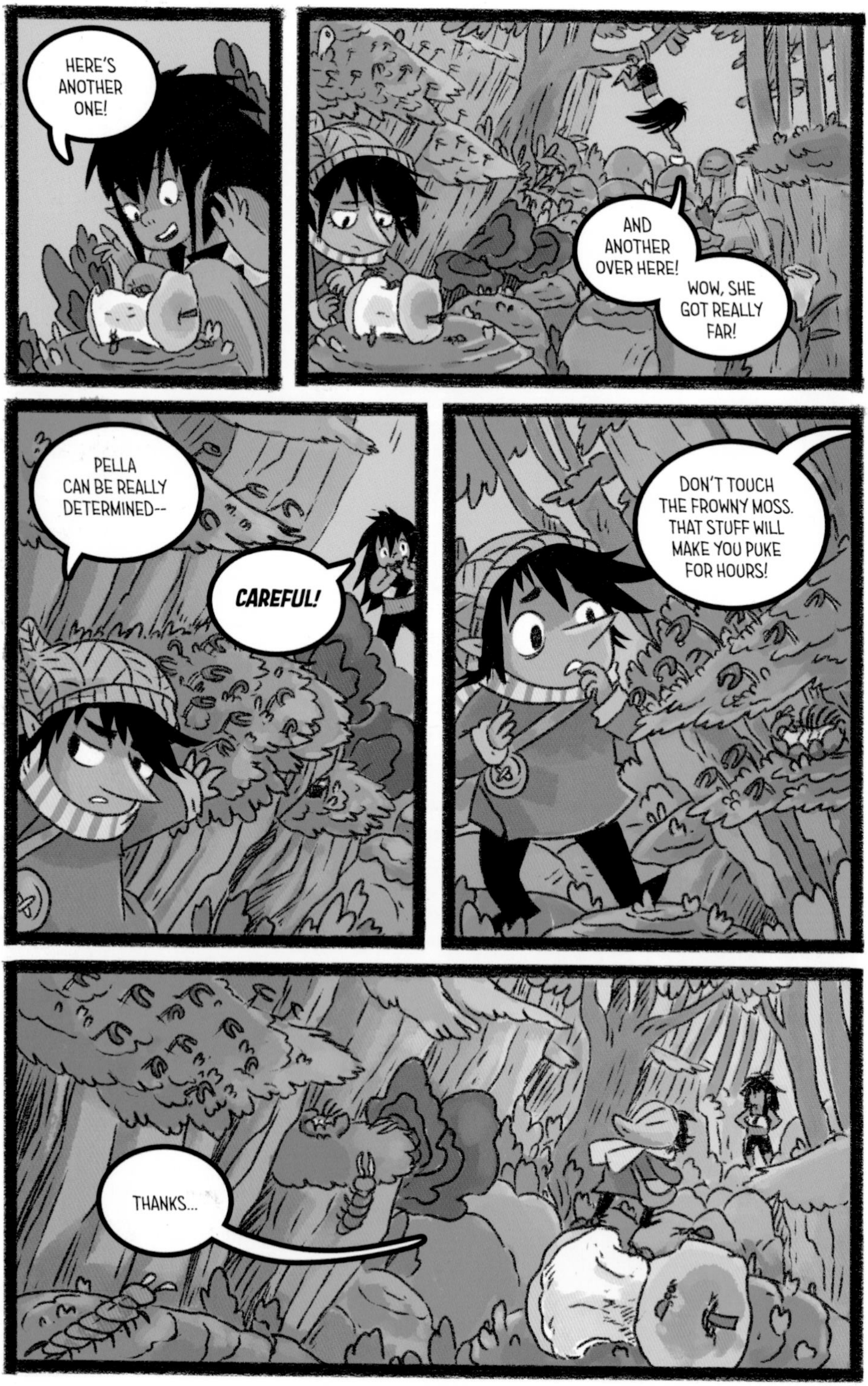
HERE'S ANOTHER ONE!
AND ANOTHER OVER HERE!
WOW, SHE GOT REALLY FAR!
PELLA CAN BE REALLY DETERMINED--
CAREFUL!
DON'T TOUCH THE FROWNY MOSS. THAT STUFF WILL MAKE YOU PUKE FOR HOURS!
THANKS...

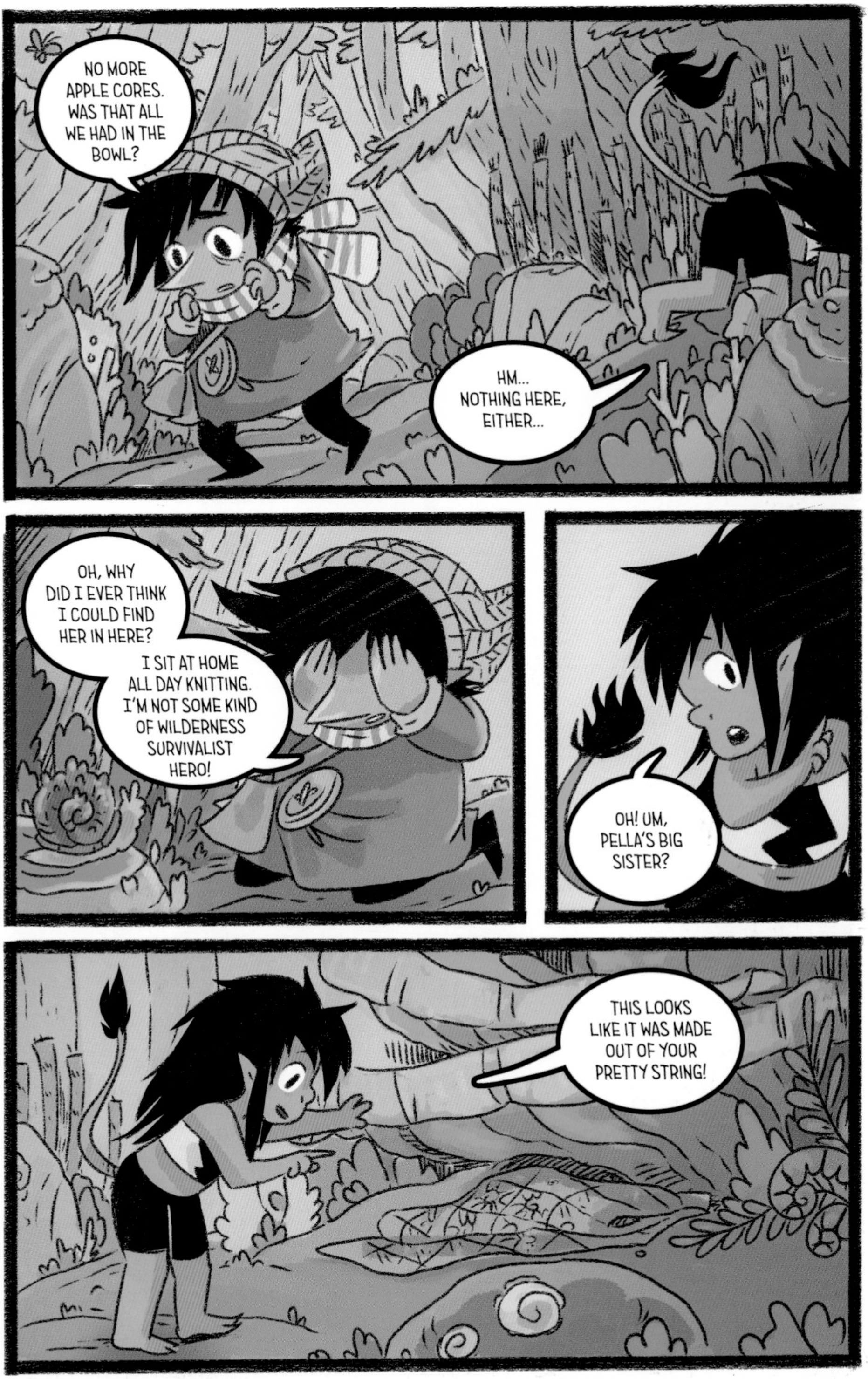
NO MORE APPLE CORES. WAS THAT ALL WE HAD IN THE BOWL?
HM... NOTHING HERE, EITHER...
OH, WHY DID I EVER THINK I COULD FIND HER IN HERE?
I SIT AT HOME ALL DAY KNITTING. I'M NOT SOME KIND OF WILDERNESS SURVIVALIST HERO!
OH! UM, PELLA'S BIG SISTER?
THIS LOOKS LIKE IT WAS MADE OUT OF YOUR PRETTY STRING!

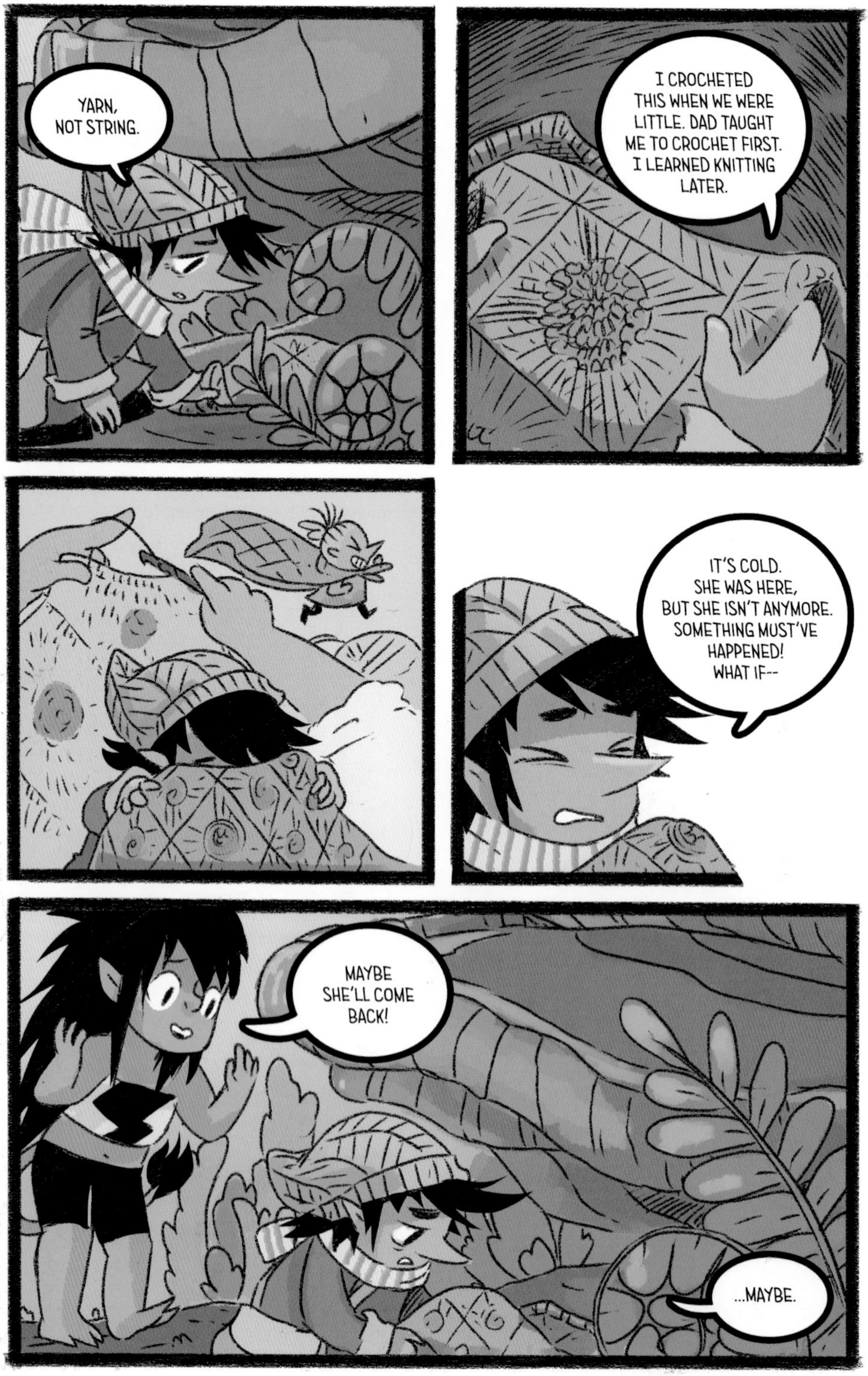
YARN, NOT STRING.
I CROCHETED THIS WHEN WE WERE LITTLE. DAD TAUGHT ME TO CROCHET FIRST. I LEARNED KNITTING LATER.
IT'S COLD. SHE WAS HERE, BUT SHE ISN'T ANYMORE. SOMETHING MUST'VE HAPPENED! WHAT IF--
MAYBE SHE'LL COME BACK!
...MAYBE.

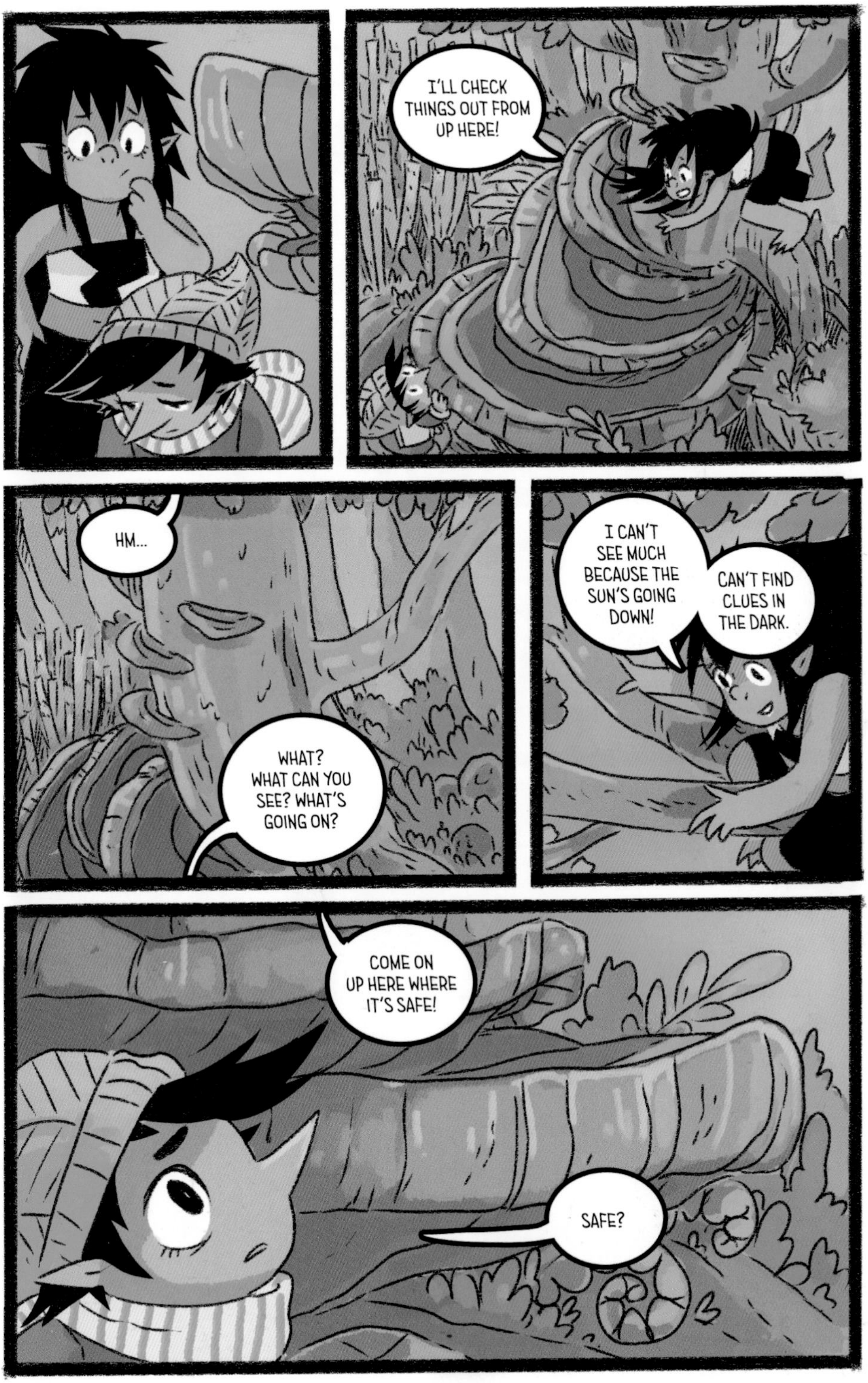
I'LL CHECK THINGS OUT FROM UP HERE!
HM...
WHAT? WHAT CAN YOU SEE? WHAT'S GOING ON?
I CAN'T SEE MUCH BECAUSE THE SUN'S GOING DOWN!
CAN'T FIND CLUES IN THE DARK.
COME ON UP HERE WHERE IT'S SAFE!
SAFE?

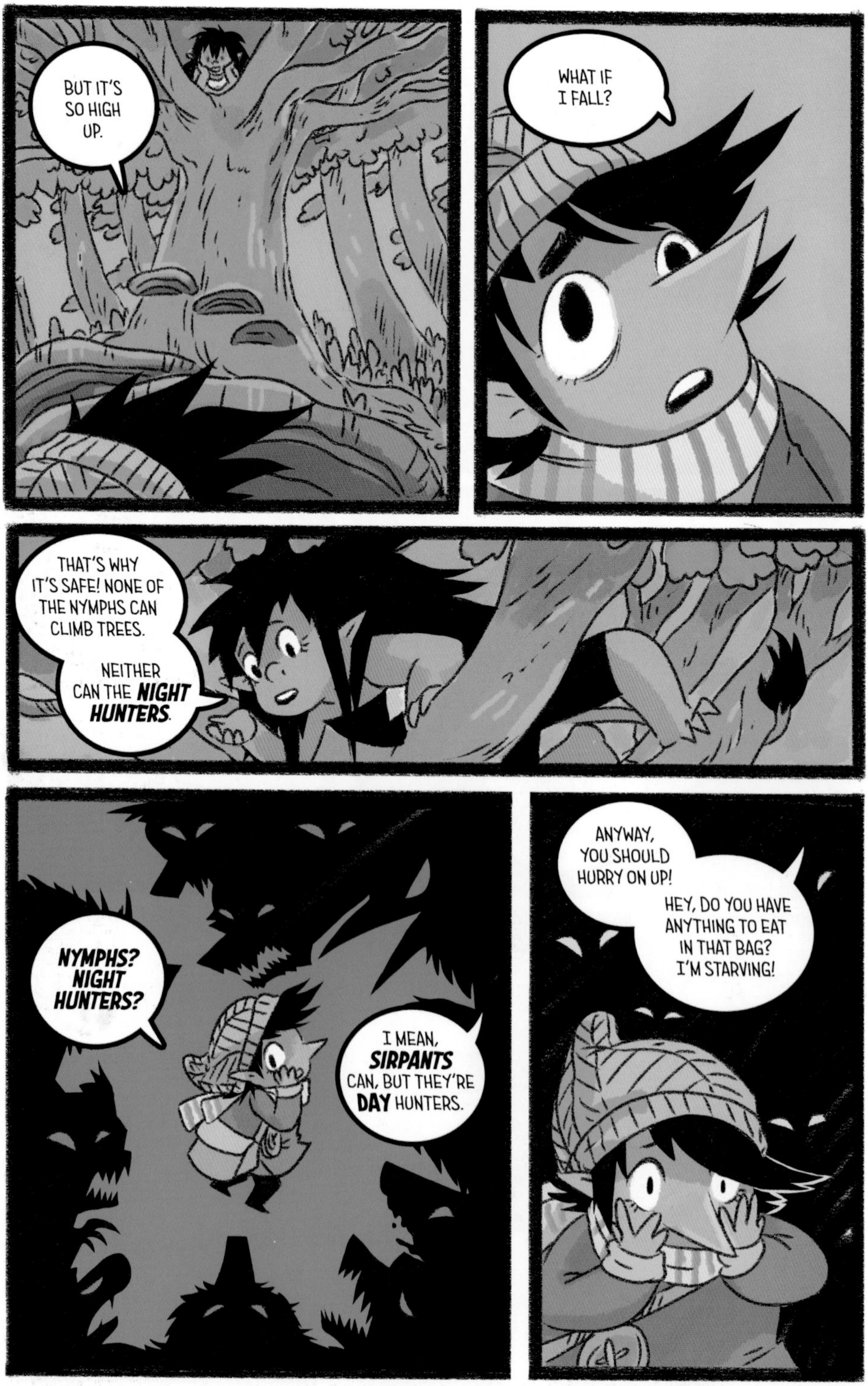
BUT IT'S SO HIGH UP.
WHAT IF I FALL?
THAT'S WHY IT'S SAFE! NONE OF THE NYMPHS CAN CLIMB TREES.
NEITHER CAN THE NIGHT HUNTERS.
NYMPHS? NIGHT HUNTERS?
I MEAN, SIRPANTS CAN, BUT THEY'RE DAY HUNTERS.
ANYWAY, YOU SHOULD HURRY ON UP!
HEY, DO YOU HAVE ANYTHING TO EAT IN THAT BAG? I'M STARVING!

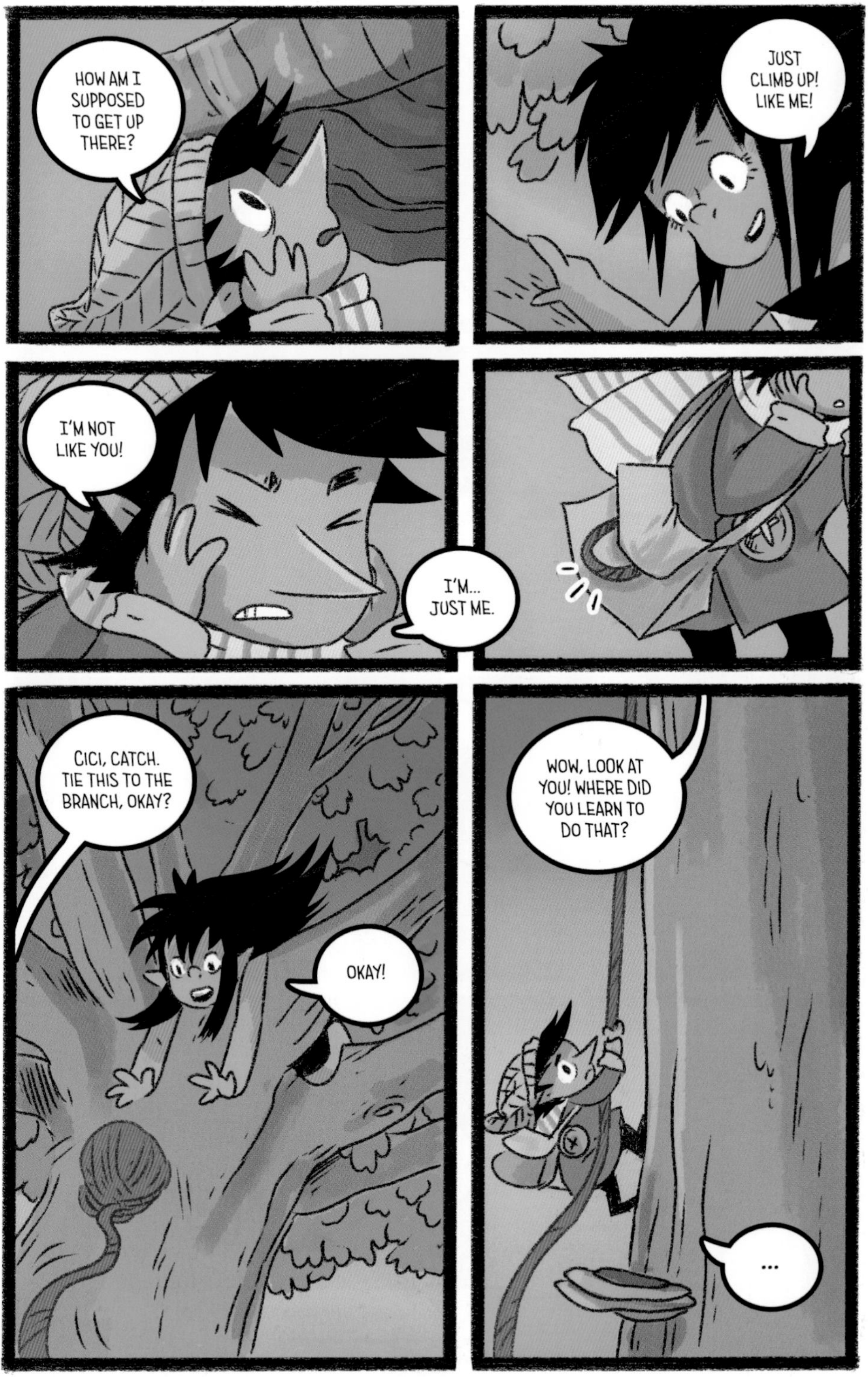
HOW AM I SUPPOSED TO GET UP THERE?
JUST CLIMB UP! LIKE ME!
I'M NOT LIKE YOU!
I'M... JUST ME.
CICI, CATCH. TIE THIS TO THE BRANCH, OKAY?
OKAY!
WOW, LOOK AT YOU! WHERE DID YOU LEARN TO DO THAT?
...

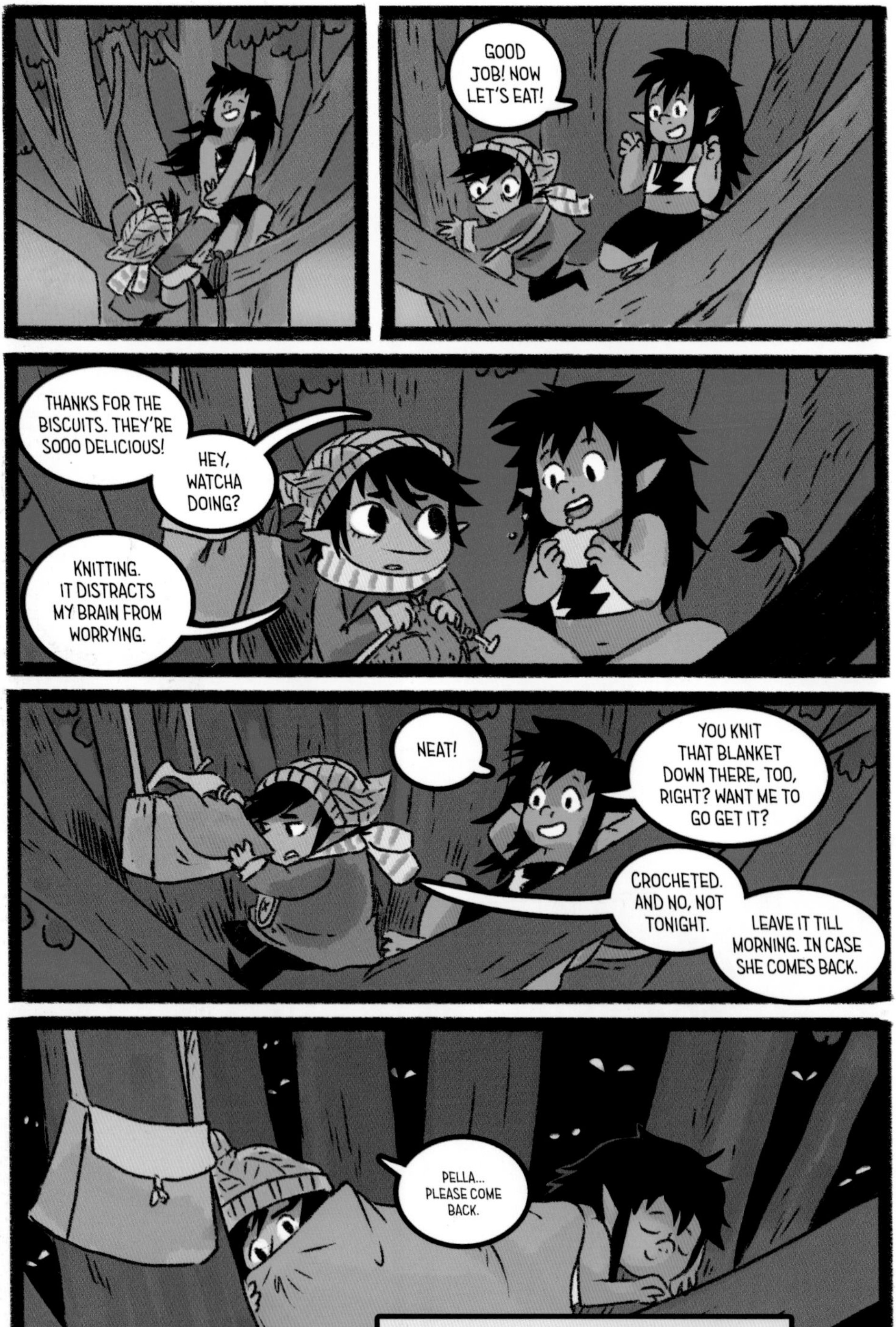
GOOD JOB! NOW LET'S EAT!
THANKS FOR THE BISCUITS. THEY'RE SOOO DELICIOUS!
HEY, WATCHA DOING?
KNITTING. IT DISTRACTS MY BRAIN FROM WORRYING.
NEAT!
YOU KNIT THAT BLANKET DOWN THERE, TOO, RIGHT? WANT ME TO GO GET IT?
CROCHETED. AND NO, NOT TONIGHT.
LEAVE IT TILL MORNING. IN CASE SHE COMES BACK.
PELLA... PLEASE COME BACK.
I COULDN'T STOP THINKING ABOUT PELLA.

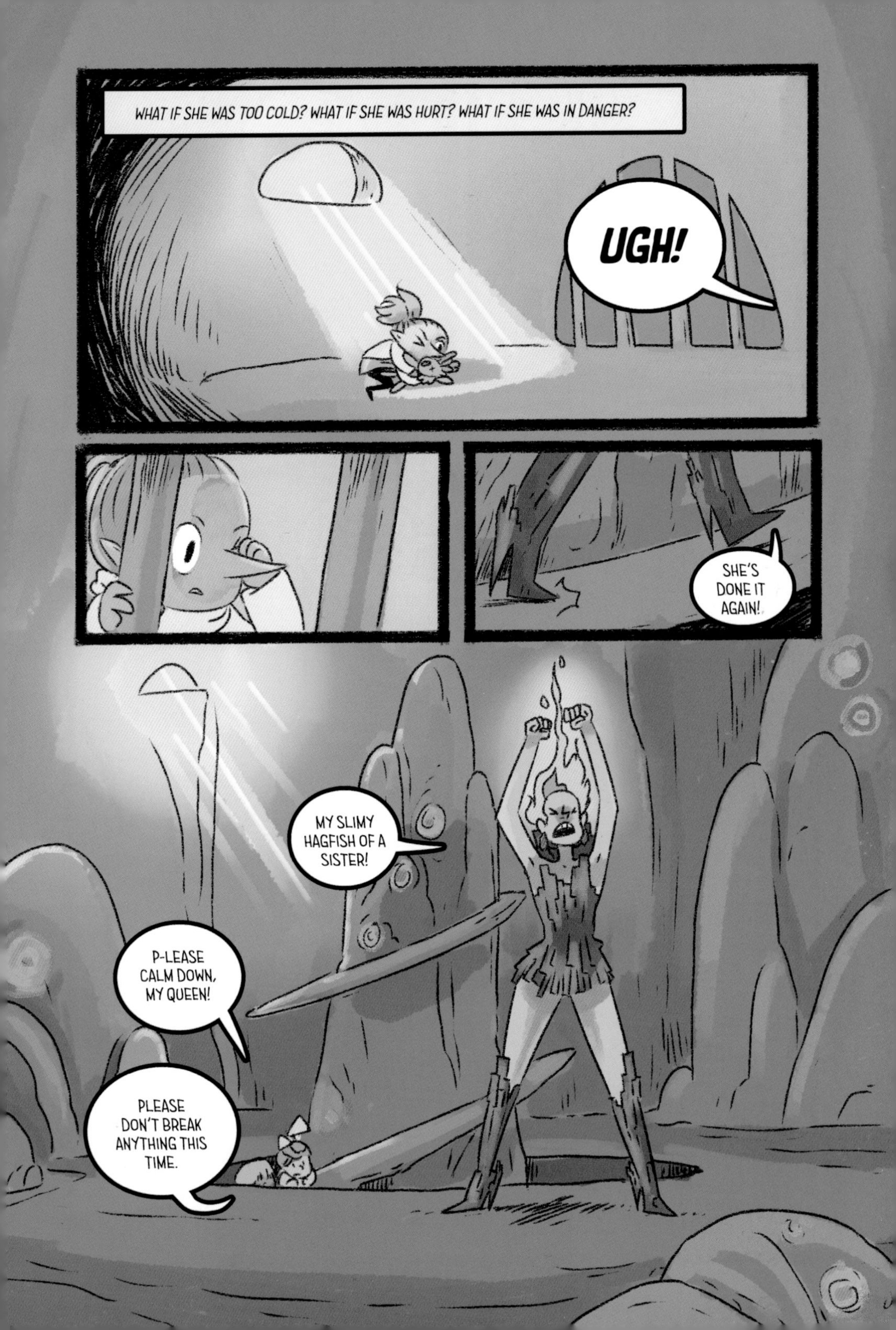
WHAT IF SHE WAS TOO COLD? WHAT IF SHE WAS HURT? WHAT IF SHE WAS IN DANGER?
UGH!
SHE'S DONE IT AGAIN!
MY SLIMY HAGFISH OF A SISTER!
P-LEASE CALM DOWN, MY QUEEN!
PLEASE DON'T BREAK ANYTHING THIS TIME.

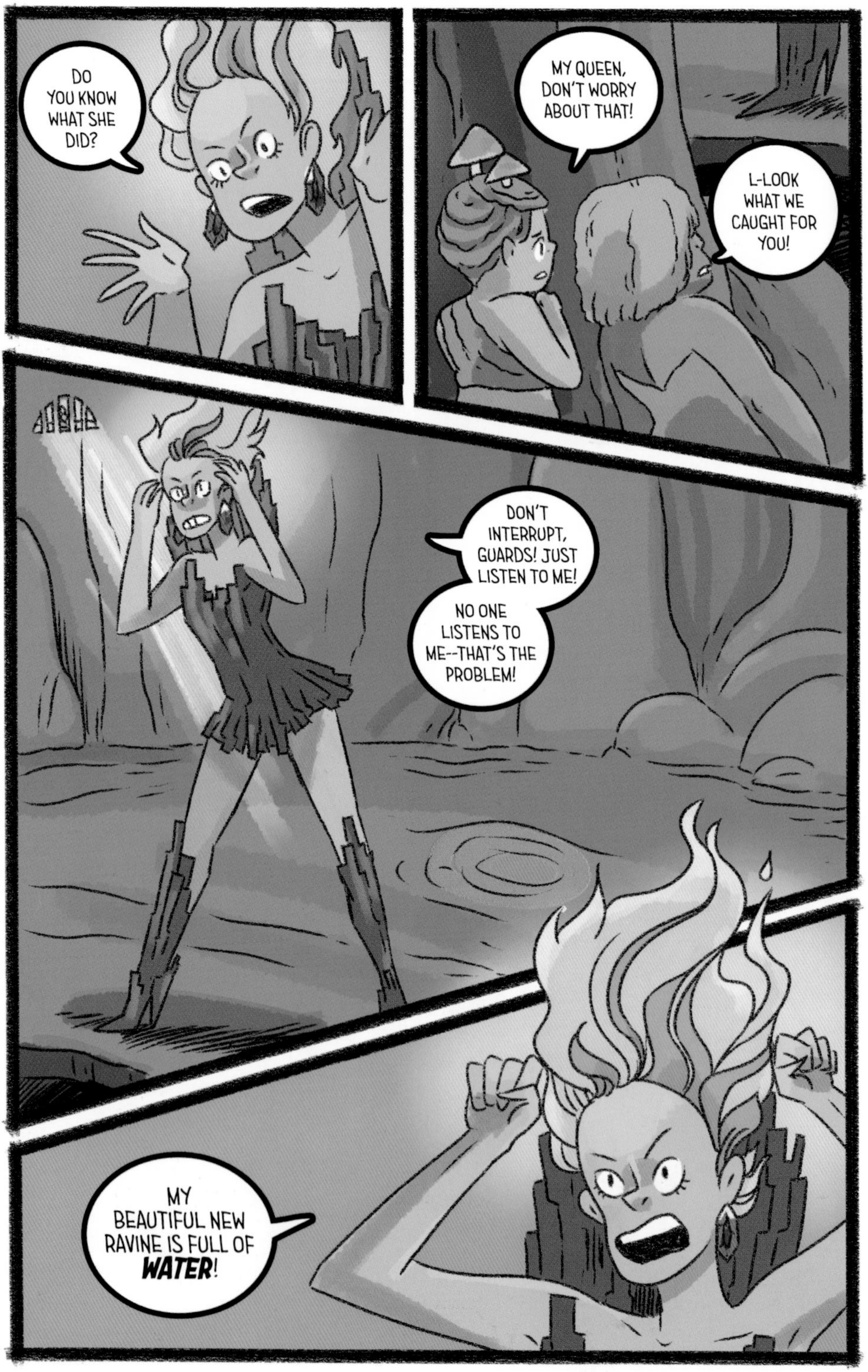
DO YOU KNOW WHAT SHE DID?
MY QUEEN, DON'T WORRY ABOUT THAT!
L-LOOK WHAT WE CAUGHT FOR YOU!
DON'T INTERRUPT, GUARDS! JUST LISTEN TO ME!
NO ONE LISTENS TO ME--THAT'S THE PROBLEM!
MY BEAUTIFUL NEW RAVINE IS FULL OF **WATER**!

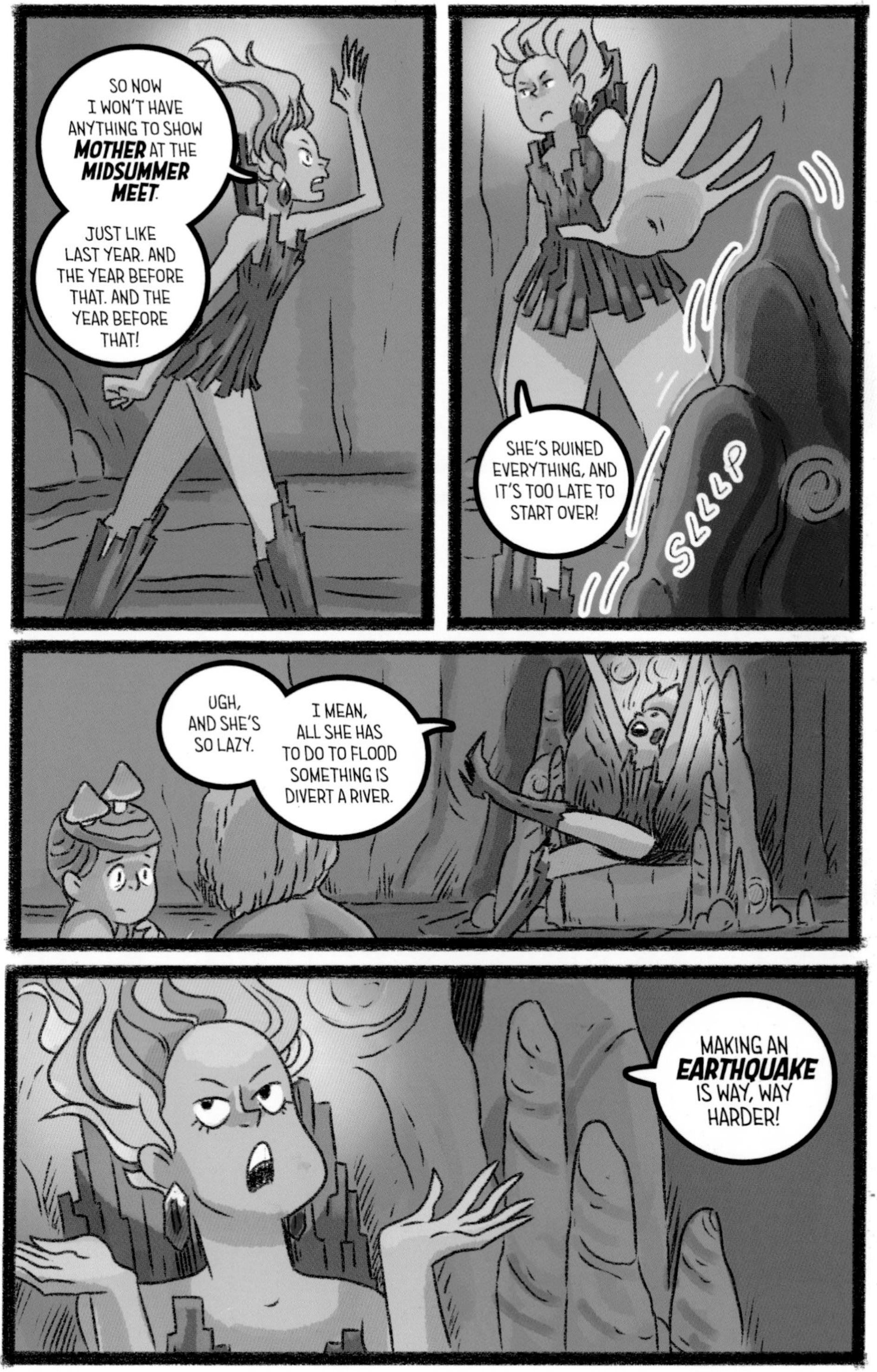
SO NOW I WON'T HAVE ANYTHING TO SHOW **MOTHER** AT THE **MIDSUMMER MEET**.
JUST LIKE LAST YEAR. AND THE YEAR BEFORE THAT. AND THE YEAR BEFORE THAT!
SHE'S RUINED EVERYTHING, AND IT'S TOO LATE TO START OVER!
SLLLP
UGH, AND SHE'S SO LAZY.
I MEAN, ALL SHE HAS TO DO TO FLOOD SOMETHING IS DIVERT A RIVER.
MAKING AN **EARTHQUAKE** IS WAY, WAY HARDER!

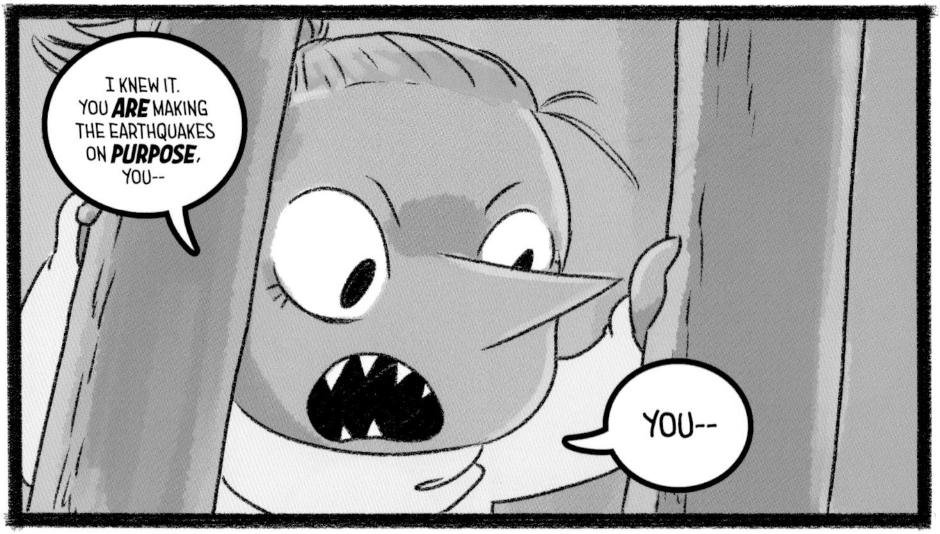
I KNEW IT. YOU **ARE** MAKING THE EARTHQUAKES ON **PURPOSE**, YOU--
YOU--

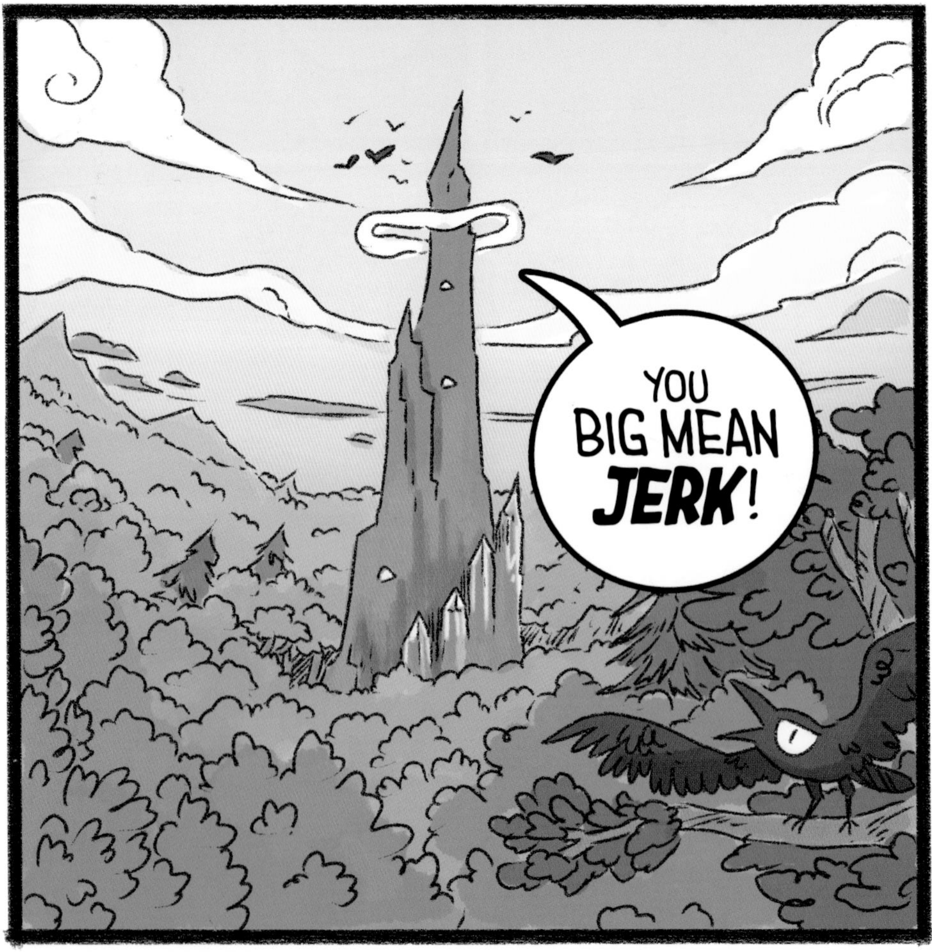
YOU BIG MEAN **JERK**!

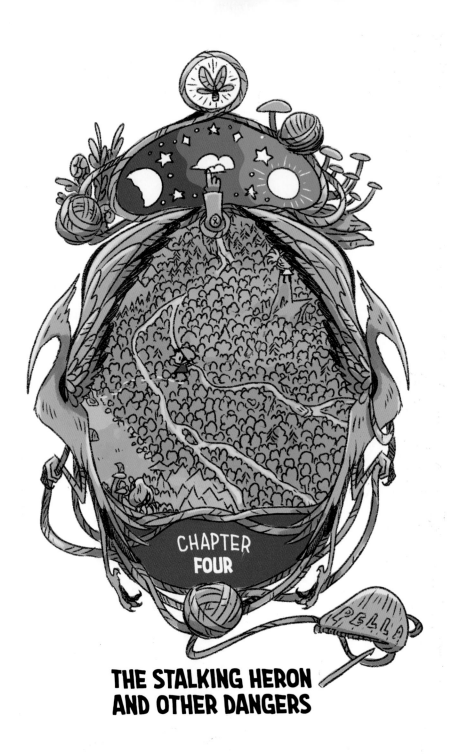

CHAPTER
FOUR

**THE STALKING HERON
AND OTHER DANGERS**

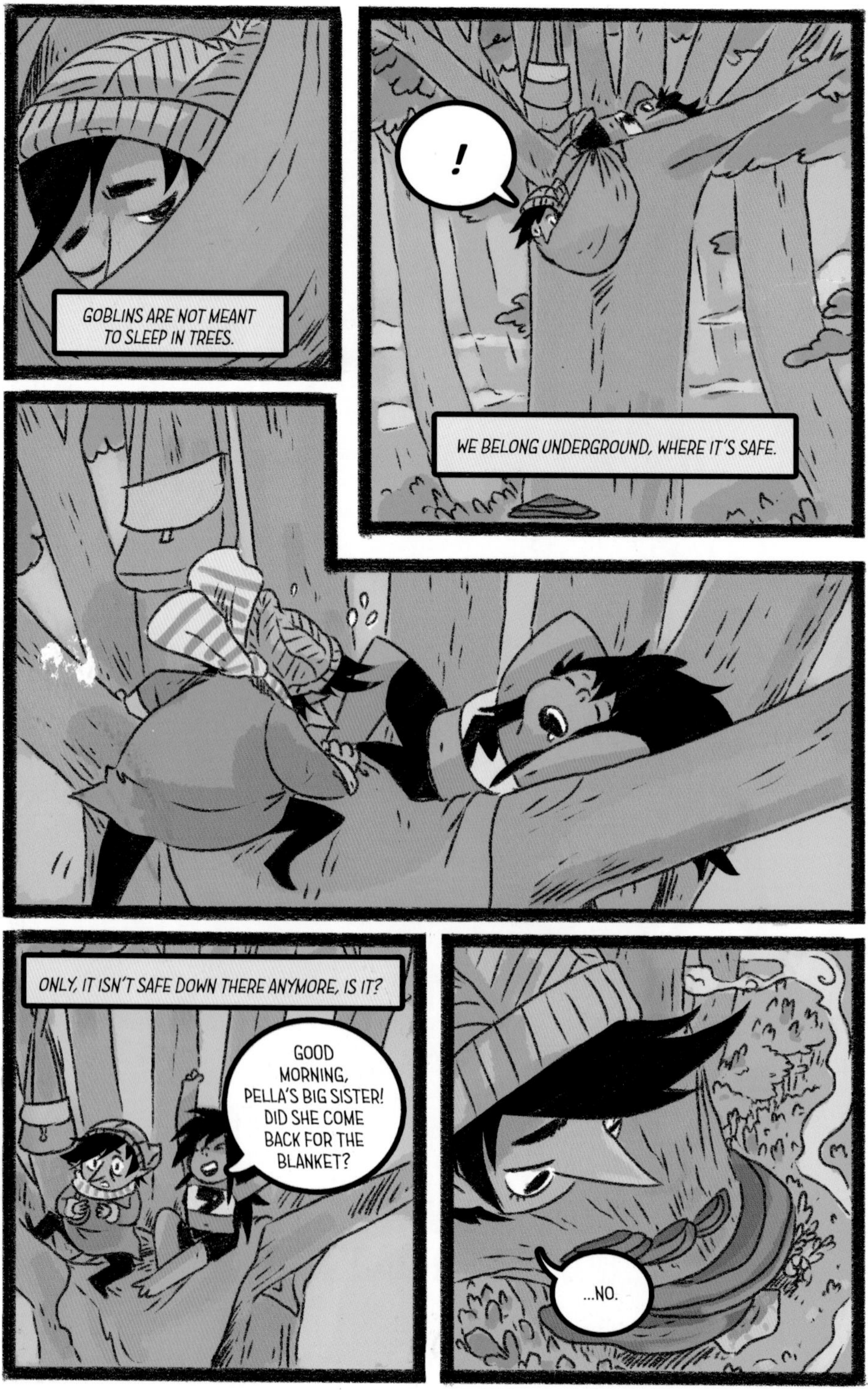
GOBLINS ARE NOT MEANT TO SLEEP IN TREES.
!
WE BELONG UNDERGROUND, WHERE IT'S SAFE.
ONLY, IT ISN'T SAFE DOWN THERE ANYMORE, IS IT?
GOOD MORNING, PELLA'S BIG SISTER! DID SHE COME BACK FOR THE BLANKET?
...NO.

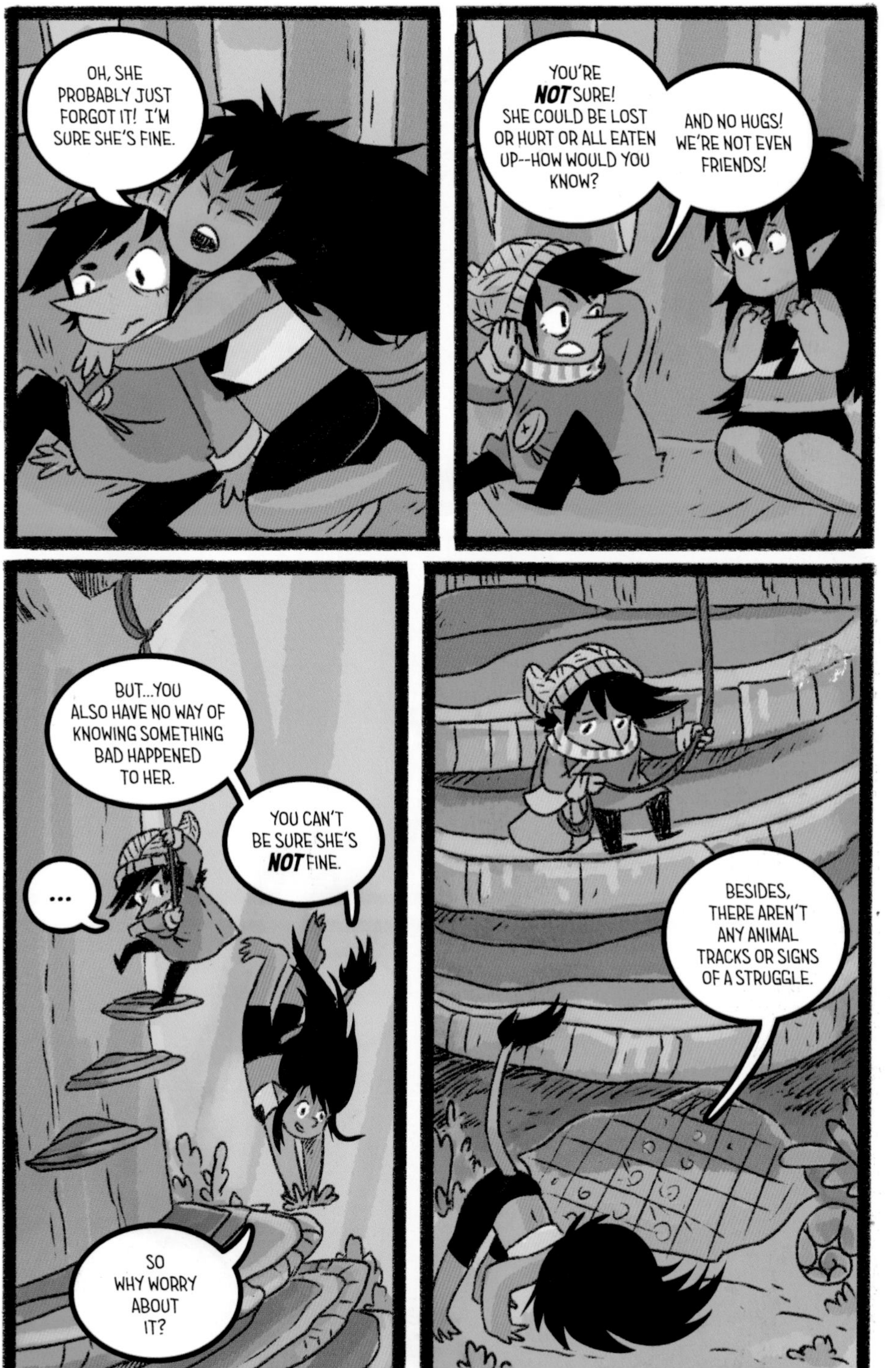
OH, SHE PROBABLY JUST FORGOT IT! I'M SURE SHE'S FINE.
YOU'RE **NOT** SURE! SHE COULD BE LOST OR HURT OR ALL EATEN UP--HOW WOULD YOU KNOW?
AND NO HUGS! WE'RE NOT EVEN FRIENDS!
BUT...YOU ALSO HAVE NO WAY OF KNOWING SOMETHING BAD HAPPENED TO HER.
YOU CAN'T BE SURE SHE'S **NOT** FINE.
...
SO WHY WORRY ABOUT IT?
BESIDES, THERE AREN'T ANY ANIMAL TRACKS OR SIGNS OF A STRUGGLE.

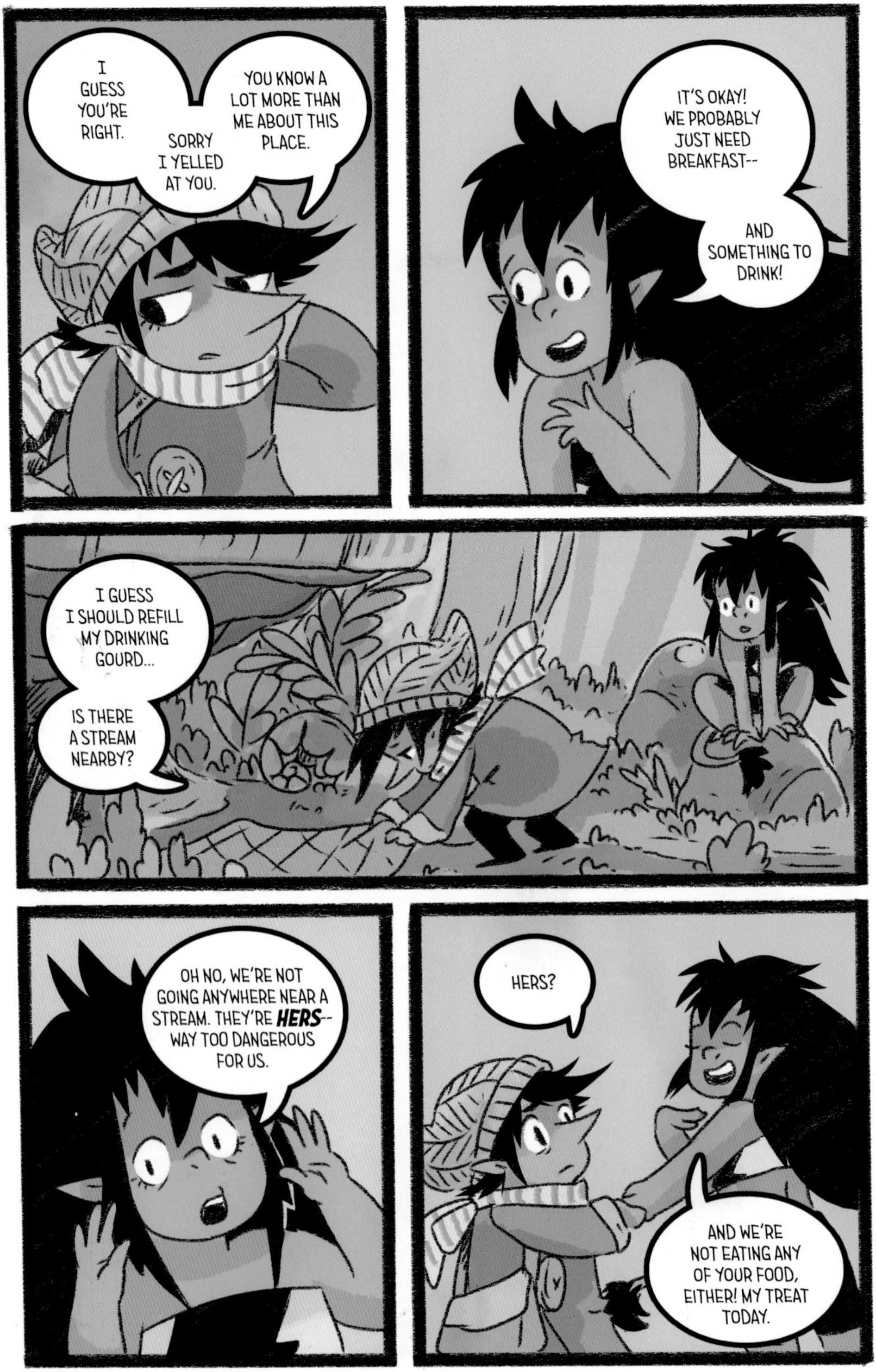
I GUESS YOU'RE RIGHT.
SORRY I YELLED AT YOU.
YOU KNOW A LOT MORE THAN ME ABOUT THIS PLACE.
IT'S OKAY! WE PROBABLY JUST NEED BREAKFAST--
AND SOMETHING TO DRINK!
I GUESS I SHOULD REFILL MY DRINKING GOURD...
IS THERE A STREAM NEARBY?
OH NO, WE'RE NOT GOING ANYWHERE NEAR A STREAM. THEY'RE **HERS**-- WAY TOO DANGEROUS FOR US.
HERS?
AND WE'RE NOT EATING ANY OF YOUR FOOD, EITHER! MY TREAT TODAY.

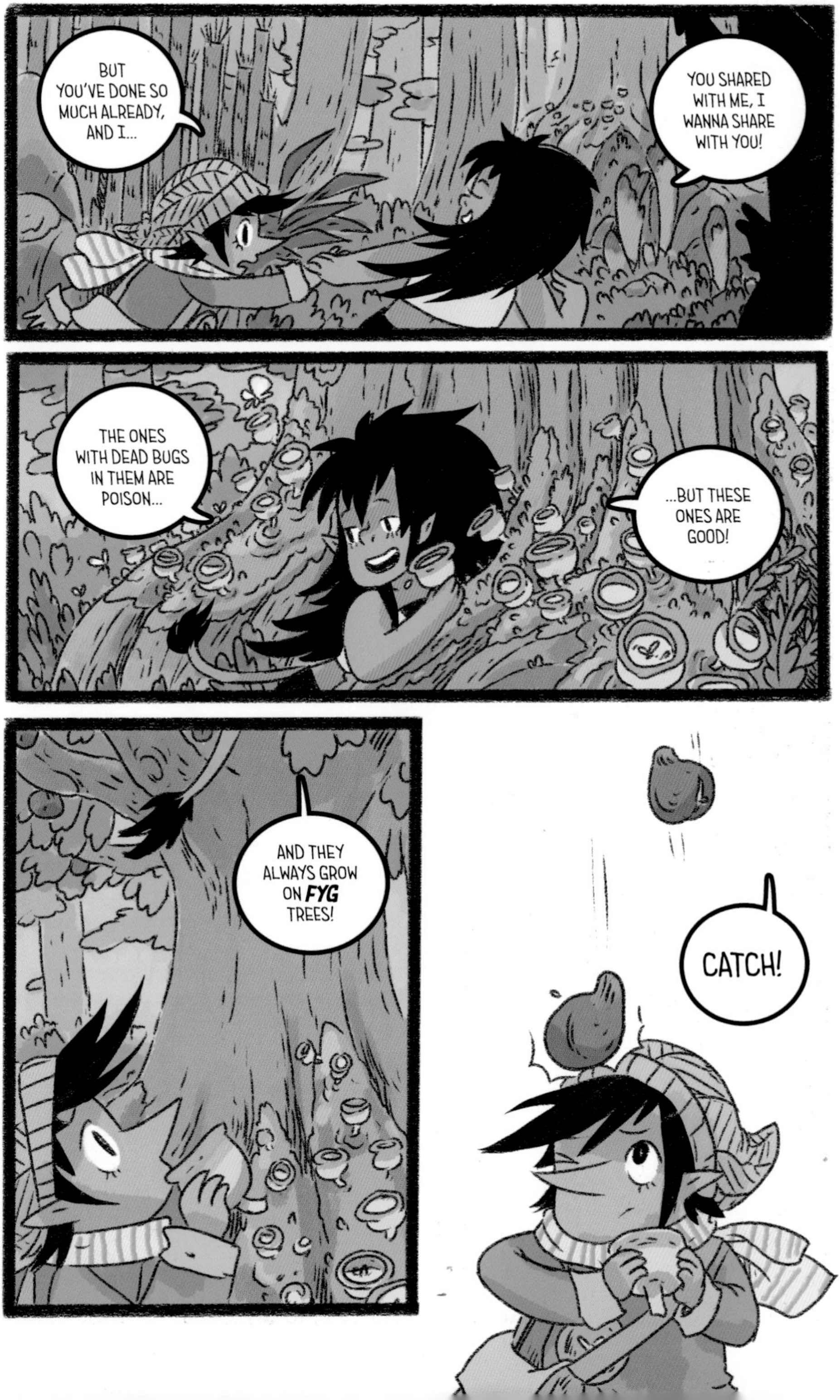
BUT YOU'VE DONE SO MUCH ALREADY, AND I...
YOU SHARED WITH ME, I WANNA SHARE WITH YOU!
THE ONES WITH DEAD BUGS IN THEM ARE POISON...
...BUT THESE ONES ARE GOOD!
AND THEY ALWAYS GROW ON FYG TREES!
CATCH!

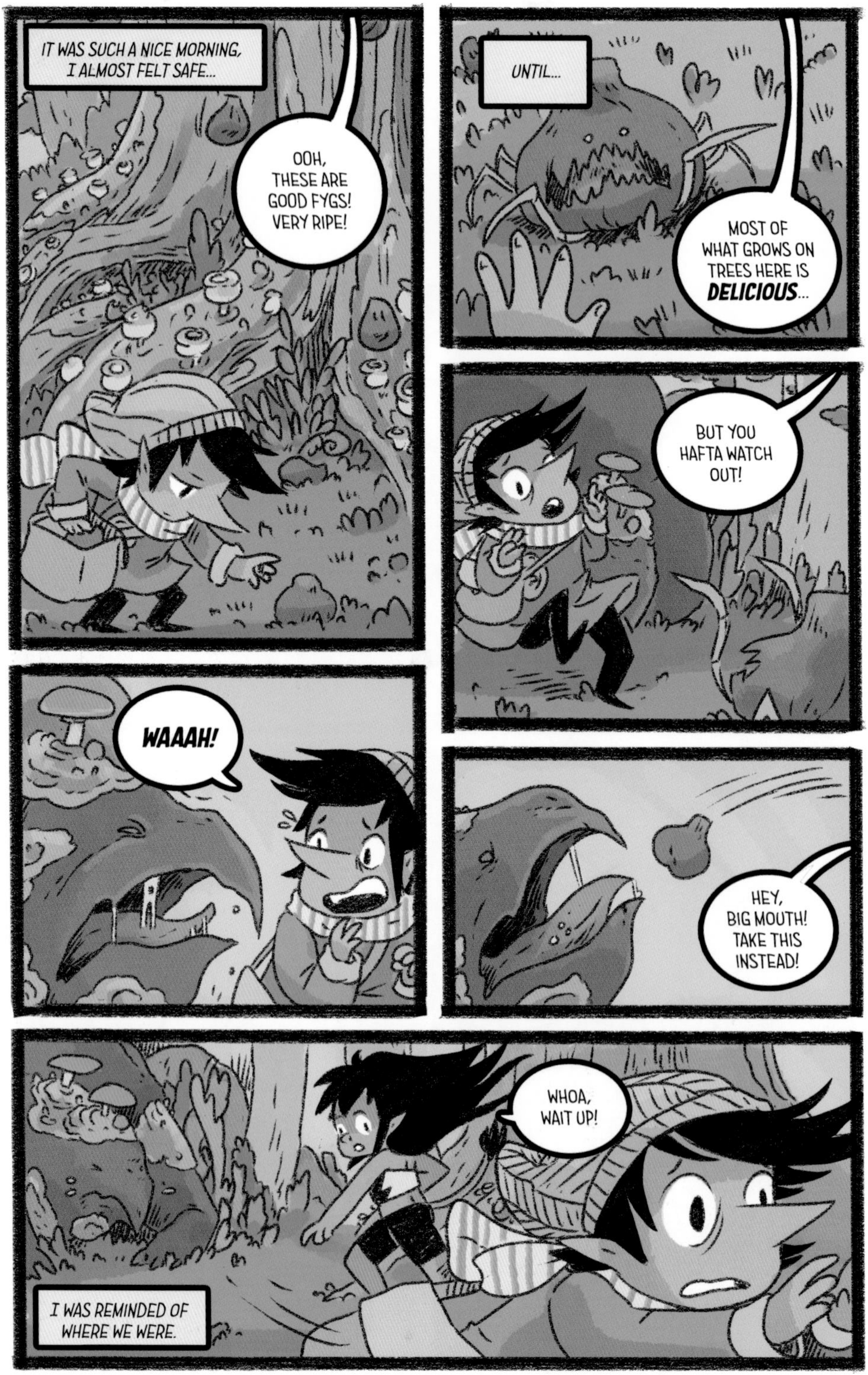
IT WAS SUCH A NICE MORNING, I ALMOST FELT SAFE...
OOH, THESE ARE GOOD FYGS! VERY RIPE!
UNTIL...
MOST OF WHAT GROWS ON TREES HERE IS DELICIOUS...
BUT YOU HAFTA WATCH OUT!
WAAAH!
HEY, BIG MOUTH! TAKE THIS INSTEAD!
WHOA, WAIT UP!
I WAS REMINDED OF WHERE WE WERE.

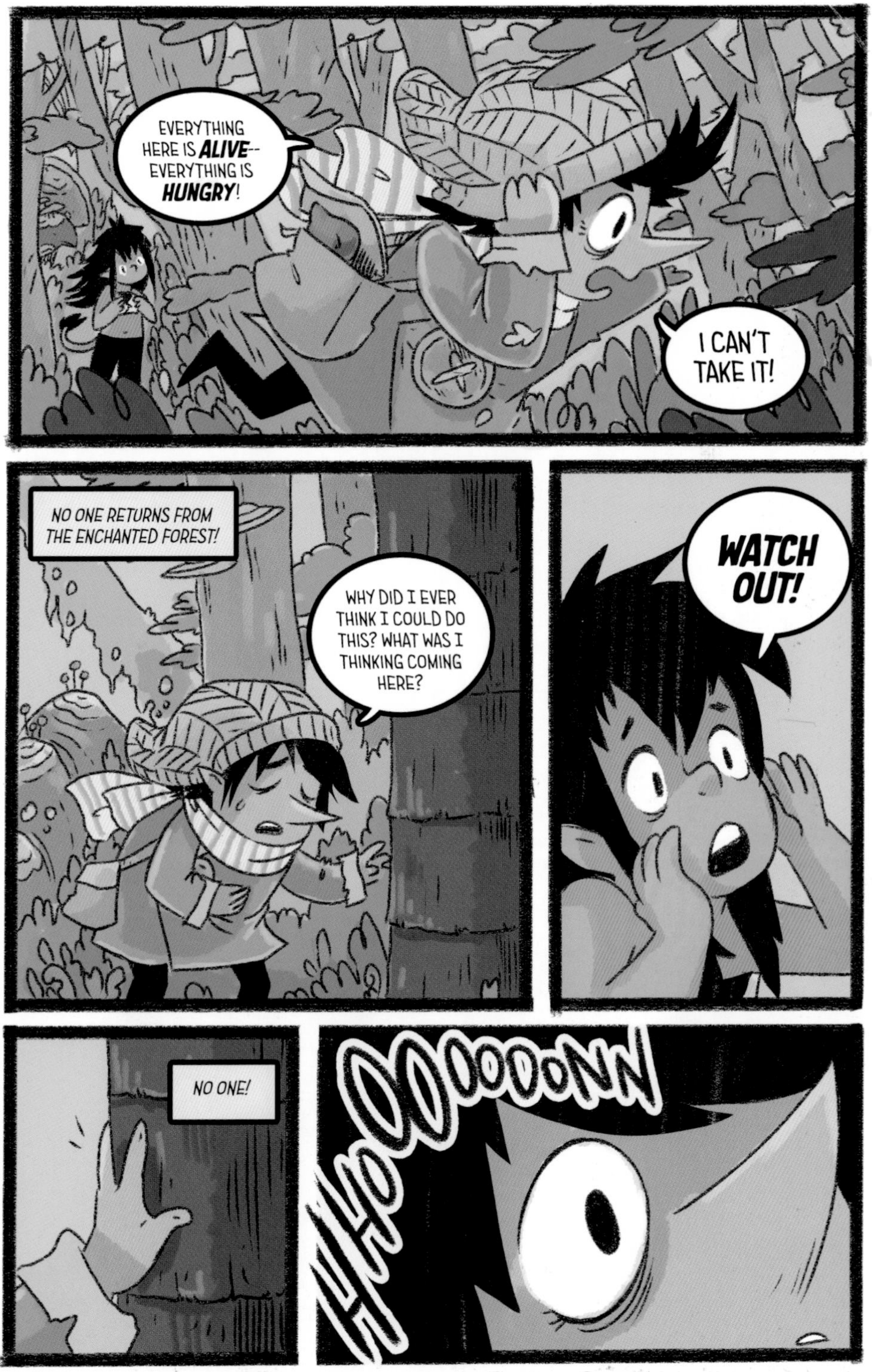
EVERYTHING HERE IS **ALIVE**-- EVERYTHING IS **HUNGRY**!
I CAN'T TAKE IT!
NO ONE RETURNS FROM THE ENCHANTED FOREST!
WHY DID I EVER THINK I COULD DO THIS? WHAT WAS I THINKING COMING HERE?
WATCH OUT!
NO ONE!

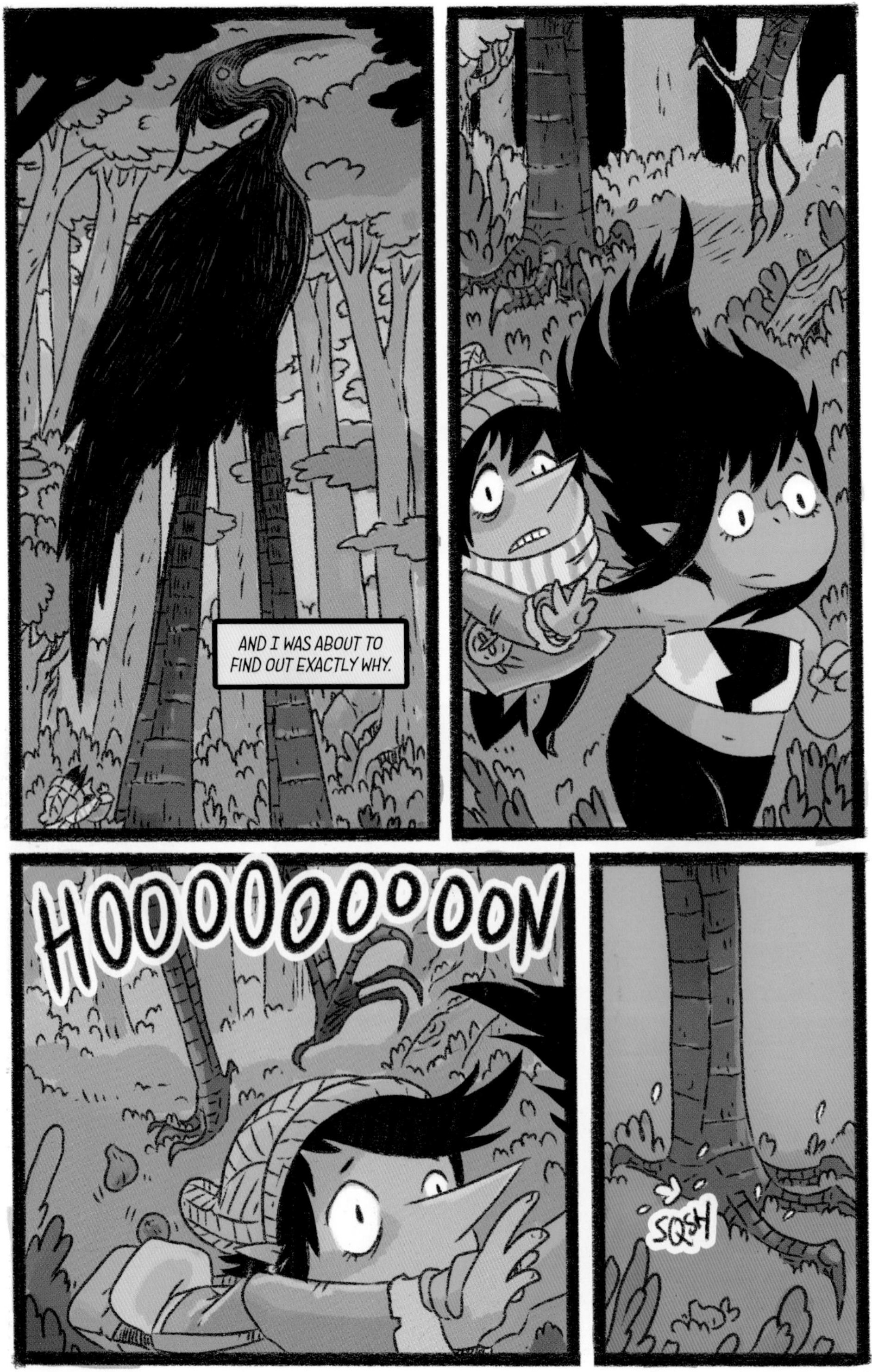
AND I WAS ABOUT TO FIND OUT EXACTLY WHY.
HOOOOOOOOON
SQSH

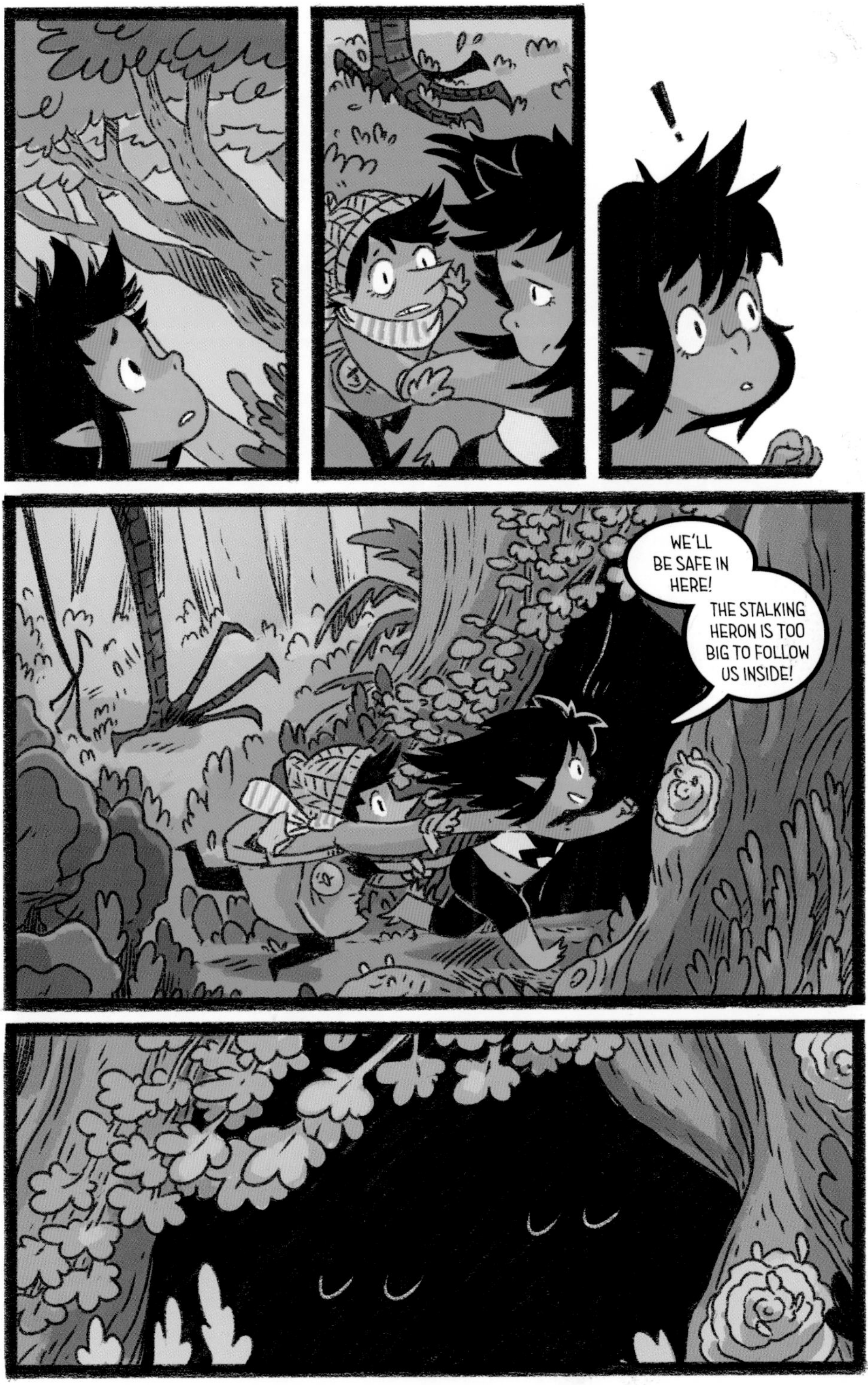
!
WE'LL BE SAFE IN HERE!
THE STALKING HERON IS TOO BIG TO FOLLOW US INSIDE!

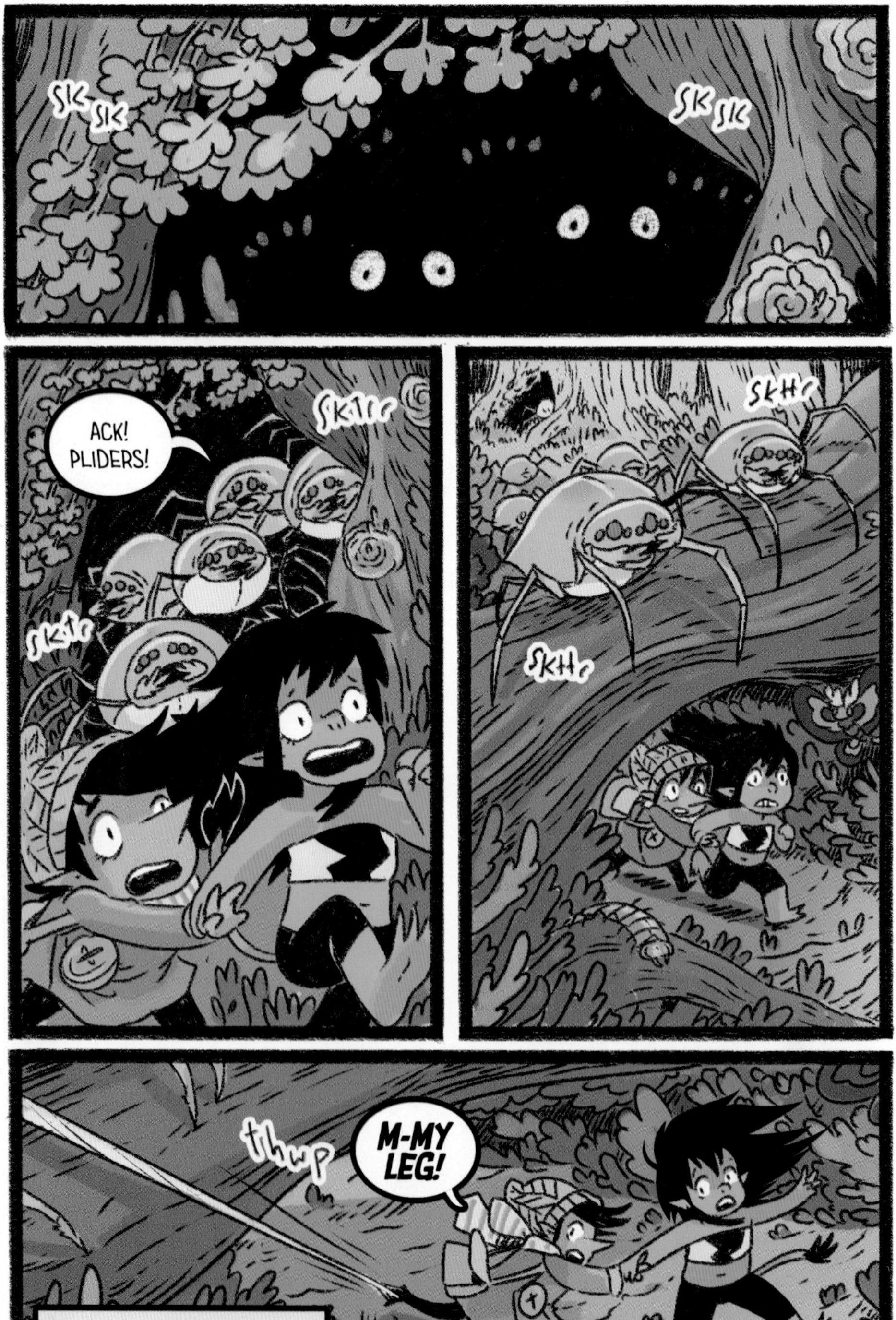
SK SK
SK SK
ACK! PLIDERS!
SKTTr
SKTTr
SKHr
SKHr
thwp
M-MY LEG!
EVEN MY WILDEST WORRIES COULDN'T COME UP WITH THIS SCENARIO!

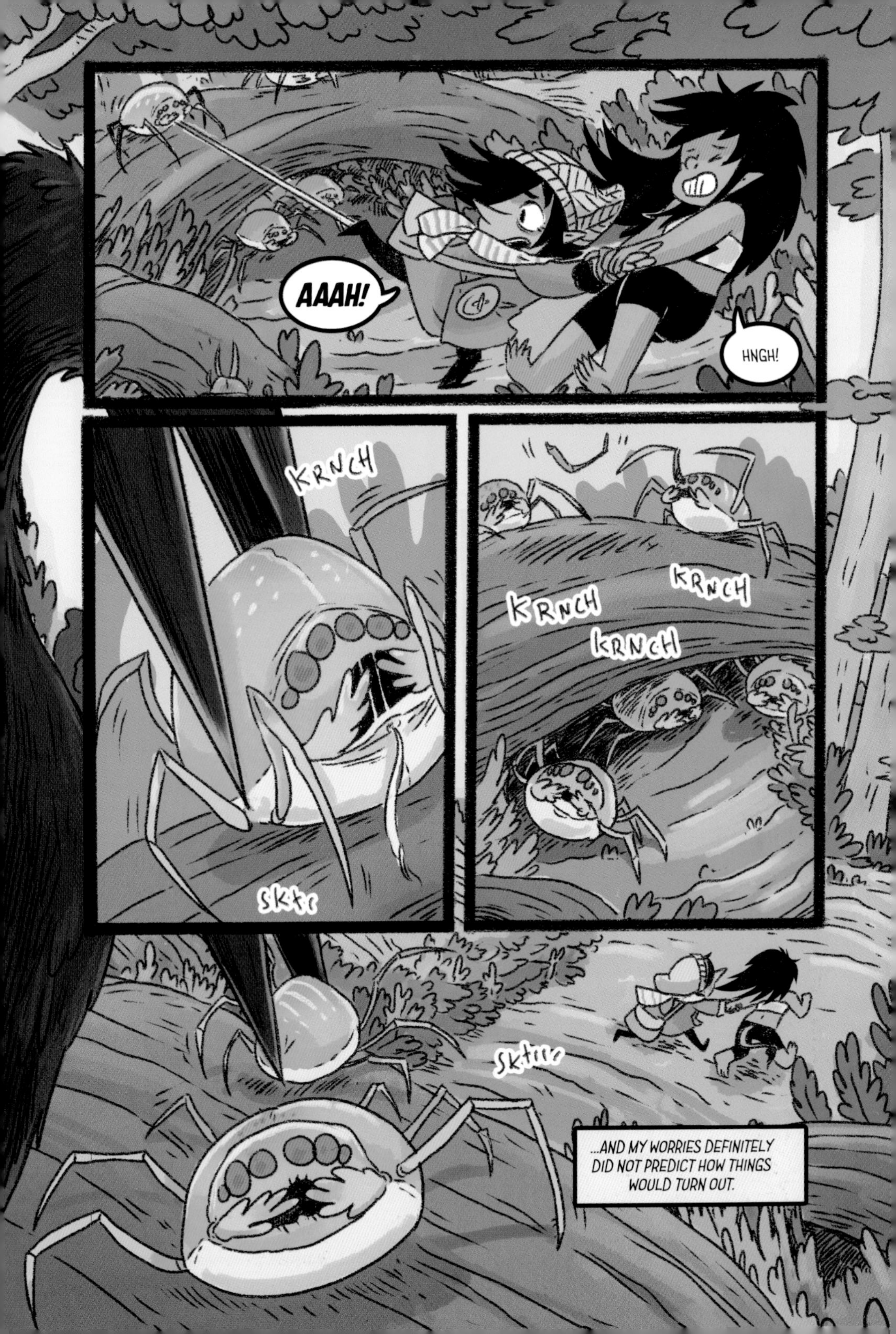
AAAH!
HNGH!
KRNCH
SKTR
KRNCH
KRNCH
KRNCH
SKTRR
...AND MY WORRIES DEFINITELY DID NOT PREDICT HOW THINGS WOULD TURN OUT.

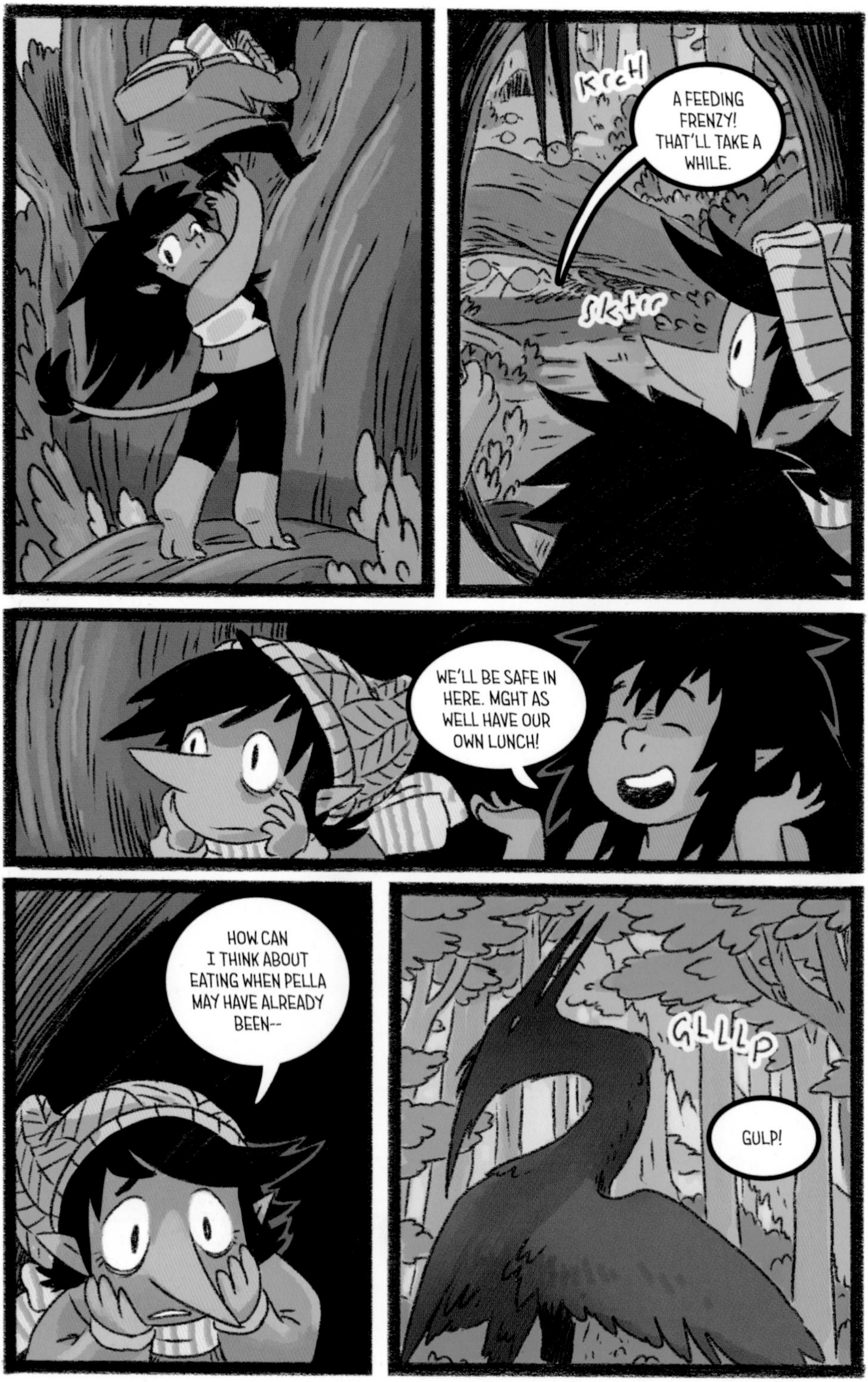
KRCH
A FEEDING FRENZY! THAT'LL TAKE A WHILE.
SKTRR
WE'LL BE SAFE IN HERE. MGHT AS WELL HAVE OUR OWN LUNCH!
HOW CAN I THINK ABOUT EATING WHEN PELLA MAY HAVE ALREADY BEEN--
GLLLP
GULP!

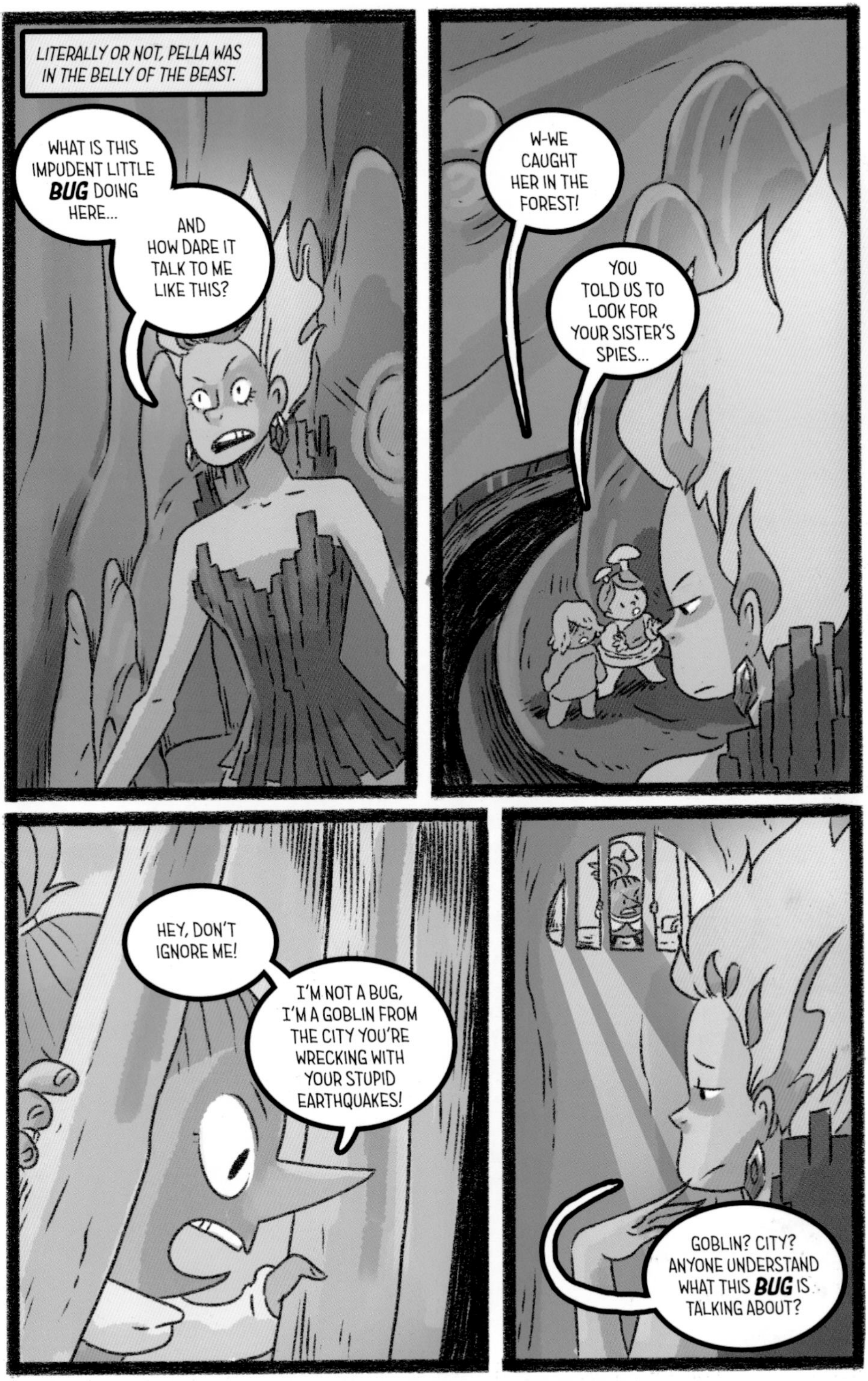
LITERALLY OR NOT, PELLA WAS IN THE BELLY OF THE BEAST.
WHAT IS THIS IMPUDENT LITTLE **BUG** DOING HERE...
AND HOW DARE IT TALK TO ME LIKE THIS?
W-WE CAUGHT HER IN THE FOREST!
YOU TOLD US TO LOOK FOR YOUR SISTER'S SPIES...
HEY, DON'T IGNORE ME!
I'M NOT A BUG, I'M A GOBLIN FROM THE CITY YOU'RE WRECKING WITH YOUR STUPID EARTHQUAKES!
GOBLIN? CITY? ANYONE UNDERSTAND WHAT THIS **BUG** IS TALKING ABOUT?

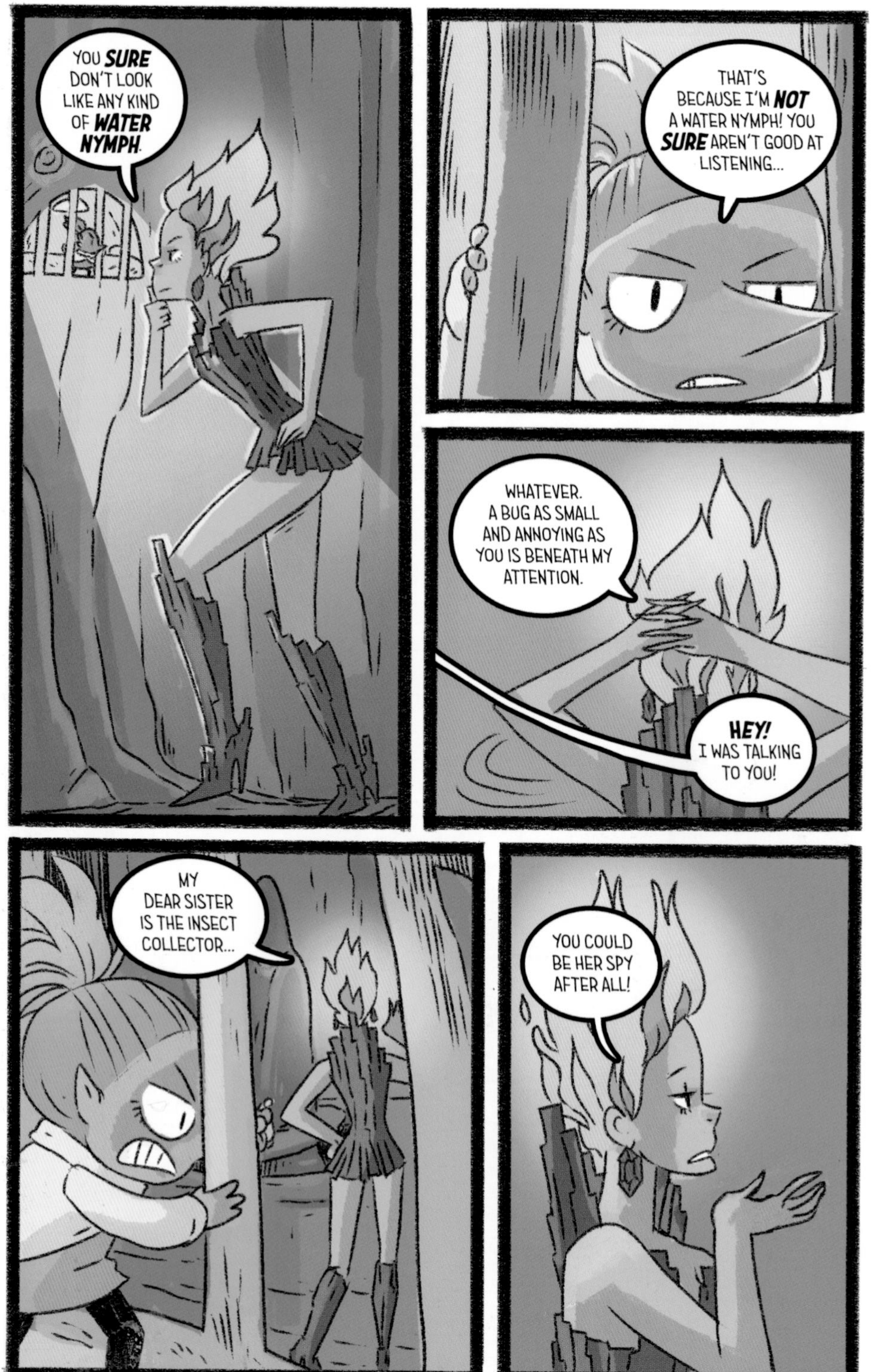
YOU **SURE** DON'T LOOK LIKE ANY KIND OF **WATER NYMPH**.
THAT'S BECAUSE I'M **NOT** A WATER NYMPH! YOU **SURE** AREN'T GOOD AT LISTENING...
WHATEVER. A BUG AS SMALL AND ANNOYING AS YOU IS BENEATH MY ATTENTION.
HEY! I WAS TALKING TO YOU!
MY DEAR SISTER IS THE INSECT COLLECTOR...
YOU COULD BE HER SPY AFTER ALL!

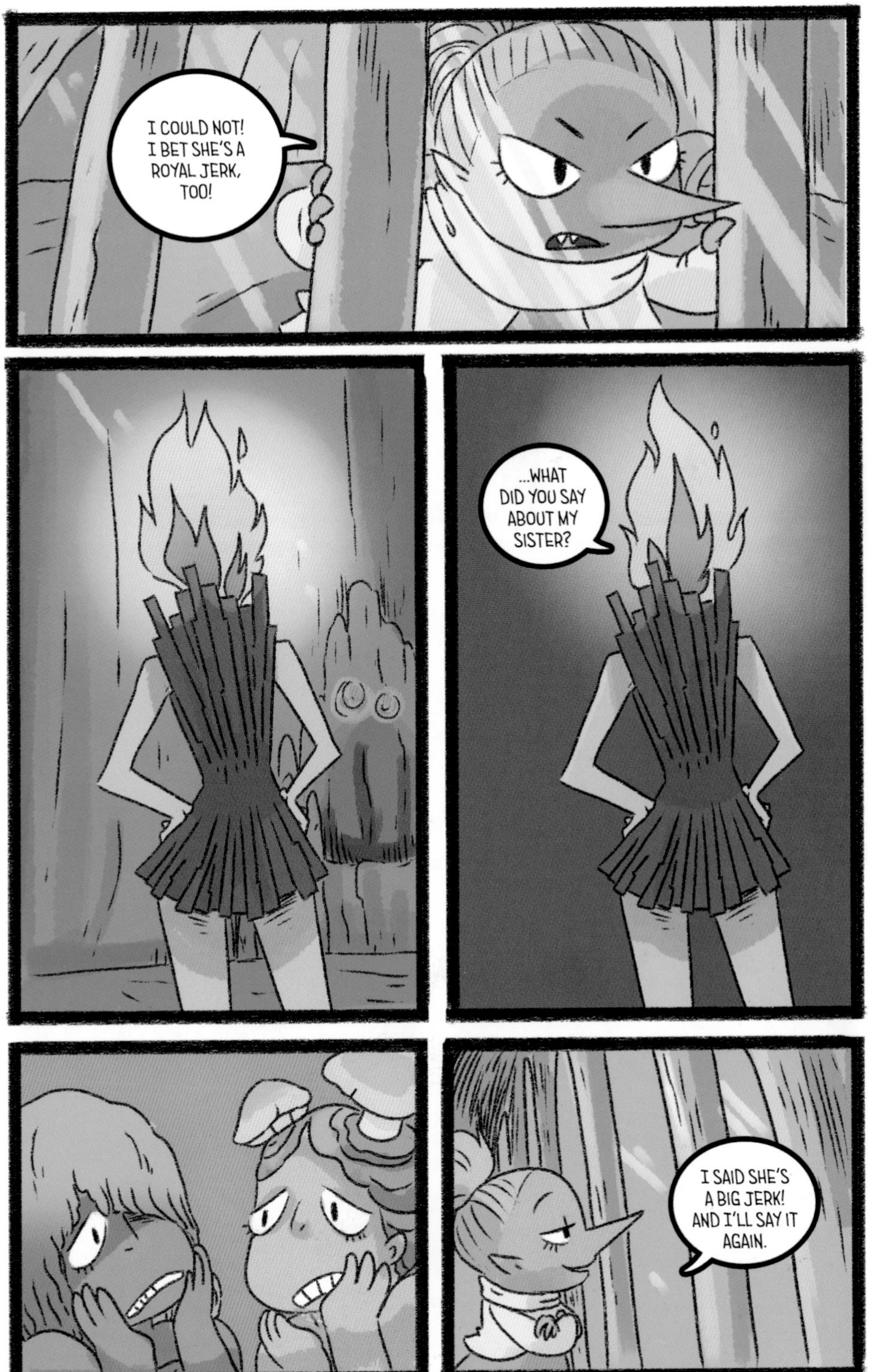
I COULD NOT! I BET SHE'S A ROYAL JERK, TOO!
...WHAT DID YOU SAY ABOUT MY SISTER?
I SAID SHE'S A BIG JERK! AND I'LL SAY IT AGAIN.

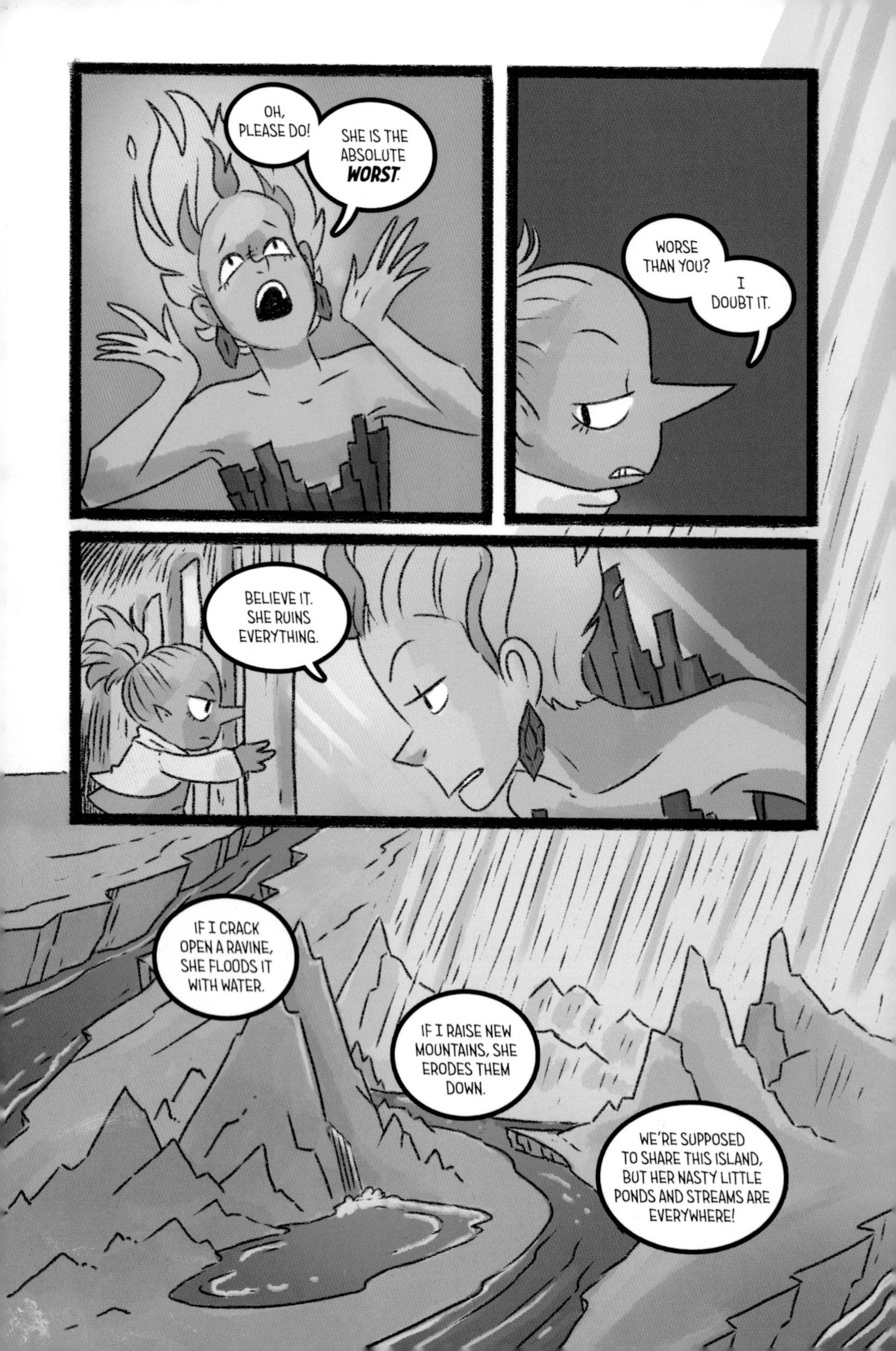
OH, PLEASE DO!
SHE IS THE ABSOLUTE **WORST**.
WORSE THAN YOU?
I DOUBT IT.
BELIEVE IT. SHE RUINS EVERYTHING.
IF I CRACK OPEN A RAVINE, SHE FLOODS IT WITH WATER.
IF I RAISE NEW MOUNTAINS, SHE ERODES THEM DOWN.
WE'RE SUPPOSED TO SHARE THIS ISLAND, BUT HER NASTY LITTLE PONDS AND STREAMS ARE EVERYWHERE!

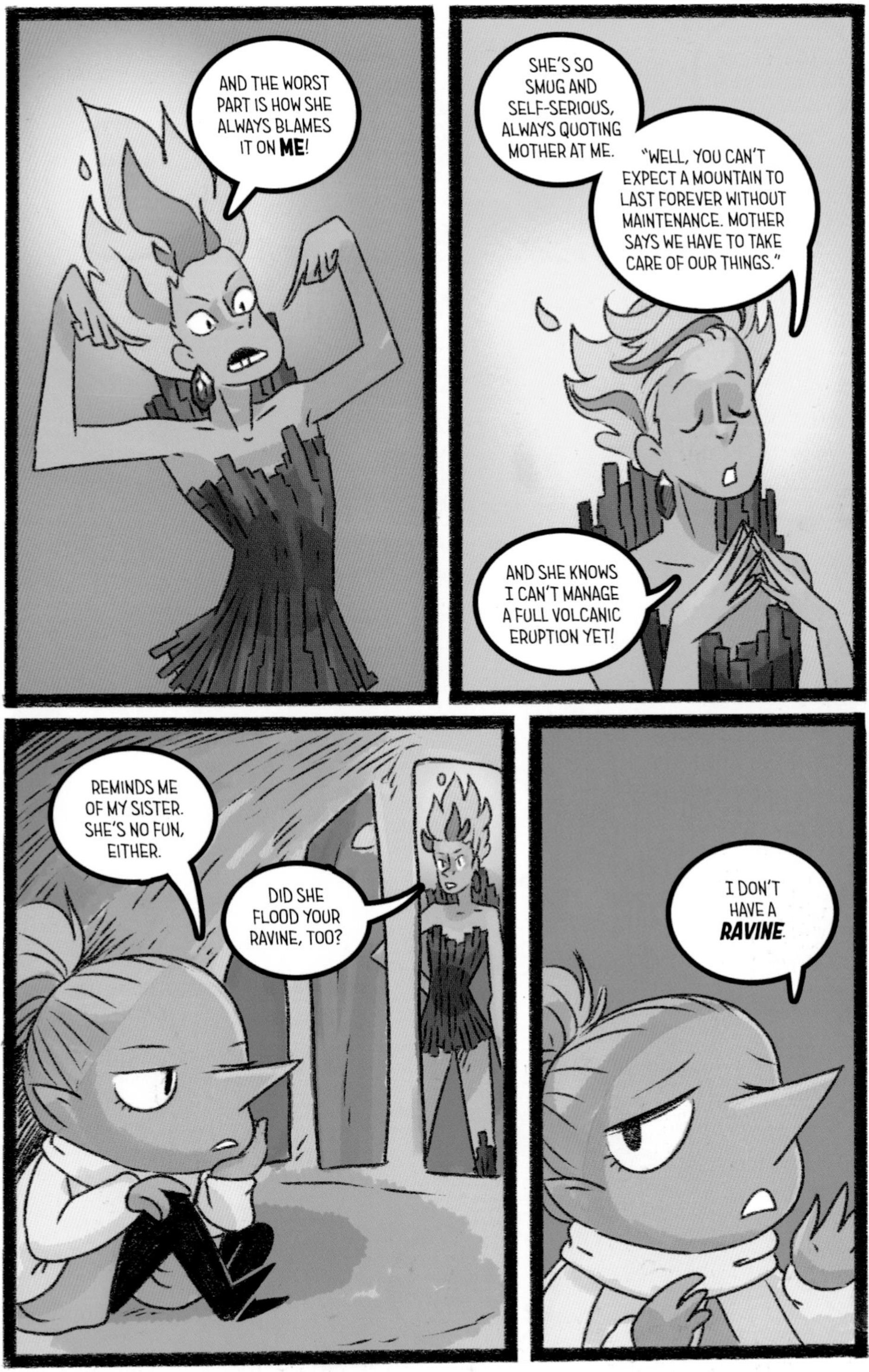
AND THE WORST PART IS HOW SHE ALWAYS BLAMES IT ON **ME**!
SHE'S SO SMUG AND SELF-SERIOUS, ALWAYS QUOTING MOTHER AT ME.
"WELL, YOU CAN'T EXPECT A MOUNTAIN TO LAST FOREVER WITHOUT MAINTENANCE. MOTHER SAYS WE HAVE TO TAKE CARE OF OUR THINGS."
AND SHE KNOWS I CAN'T MANAGE A FULL VOLCANIC ERUPTION YET!
REMINDS ME OF MY SISTER. SHE'S NO FUN, EITHER.
DID SHE FLOOD YOUR RAVINE, TOO?
I DON'T HAVE A ***RAVINE***.

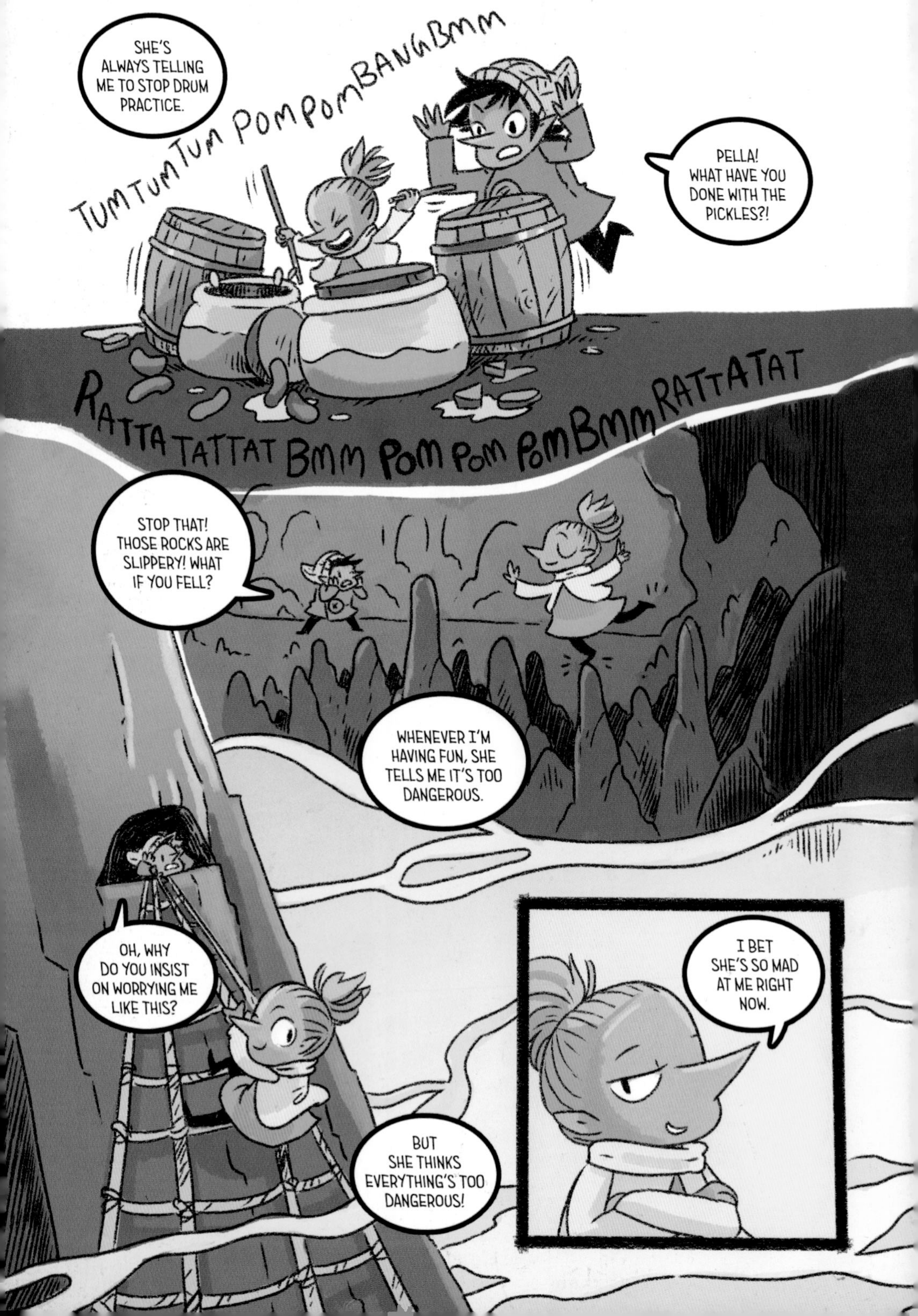
SHE'S ALWAYS TELLING ME TO STOP DRUM PRACTICE.
TUM TUM TUM POM POM BANG BMM
PELLA! WHAT HAVE YOU DONE WITH THE PICKLES?!
RATTATATTAT BMM POM POM POM BMM RATTATAT
STOP THAT! THOSE ROCKS ARE SLIPPERY! WHAT IF YOU FELL?
WHENEVER I'M HAVING FUN, SHE TELLS ME IT'S TOO DANGEROUS.
OH, WHY DO YOU INSIST ON WORRYING ME LIKE THIS?
BUT SHE THINKS EVERYTHING'S TOO DANGEROUS!
I BET SHE'S SO MAD AT ME RIGHT NOW.

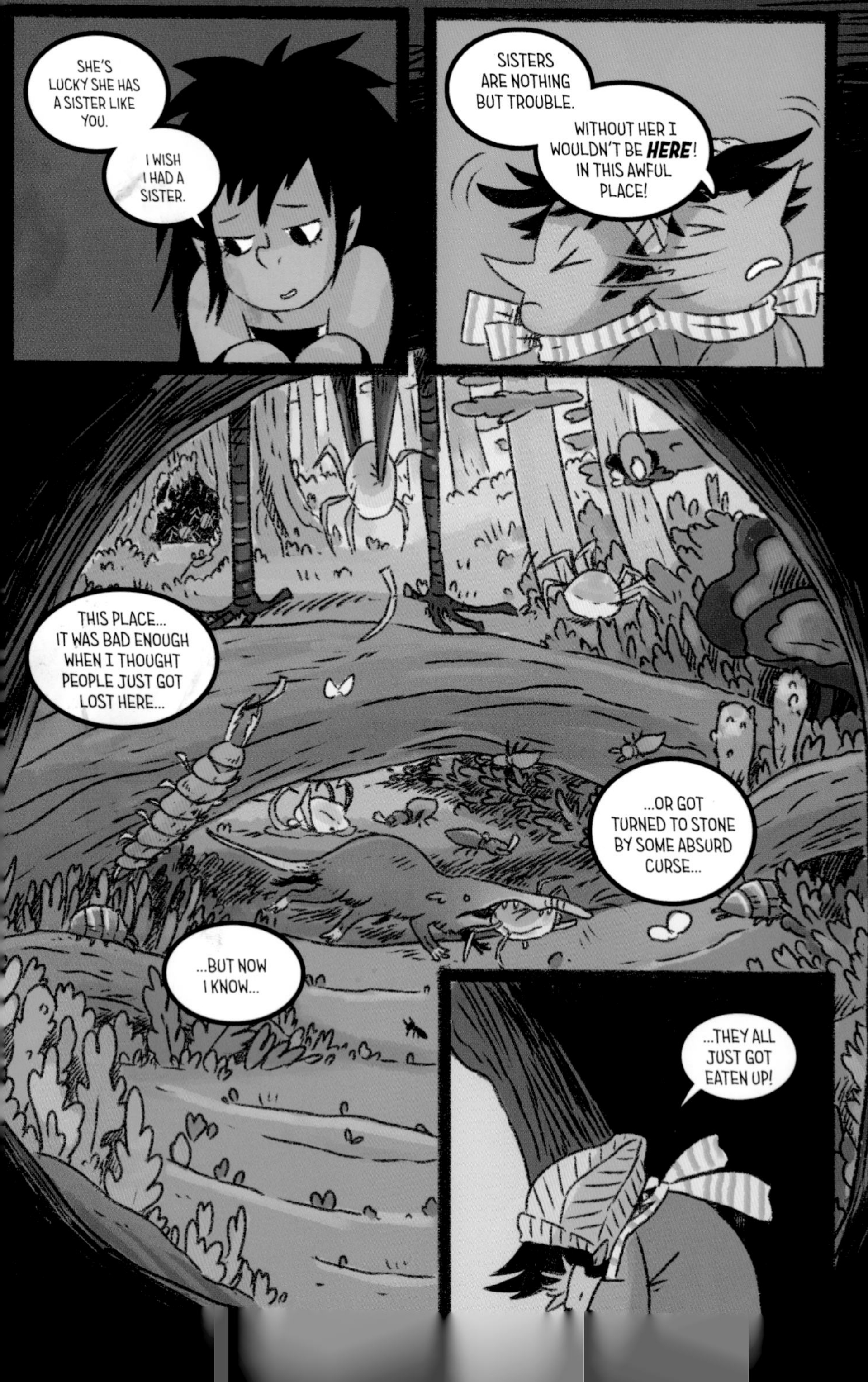
SHE'S LUCKY SHE HAS A SISTER LIKE YOU.
I WISH I HAD A SISTER.
SISTERS ARE NOTHING BUT TROUBLE.
WITHOUT HER I WOULDN'T BE **HERE**! IN THIS AWFUL PLACE!
THIS PLACE... IT WAS BAD ENOUGH WHEN I THOUGHT PEOPLE JUST GOT LOST HERE...
...OR GOT TURNED TO STONE BY SOME ABSURD CURSE...
...BUT NOW I KNOW...
...THEY ALL JUST GOT EATEN UP!

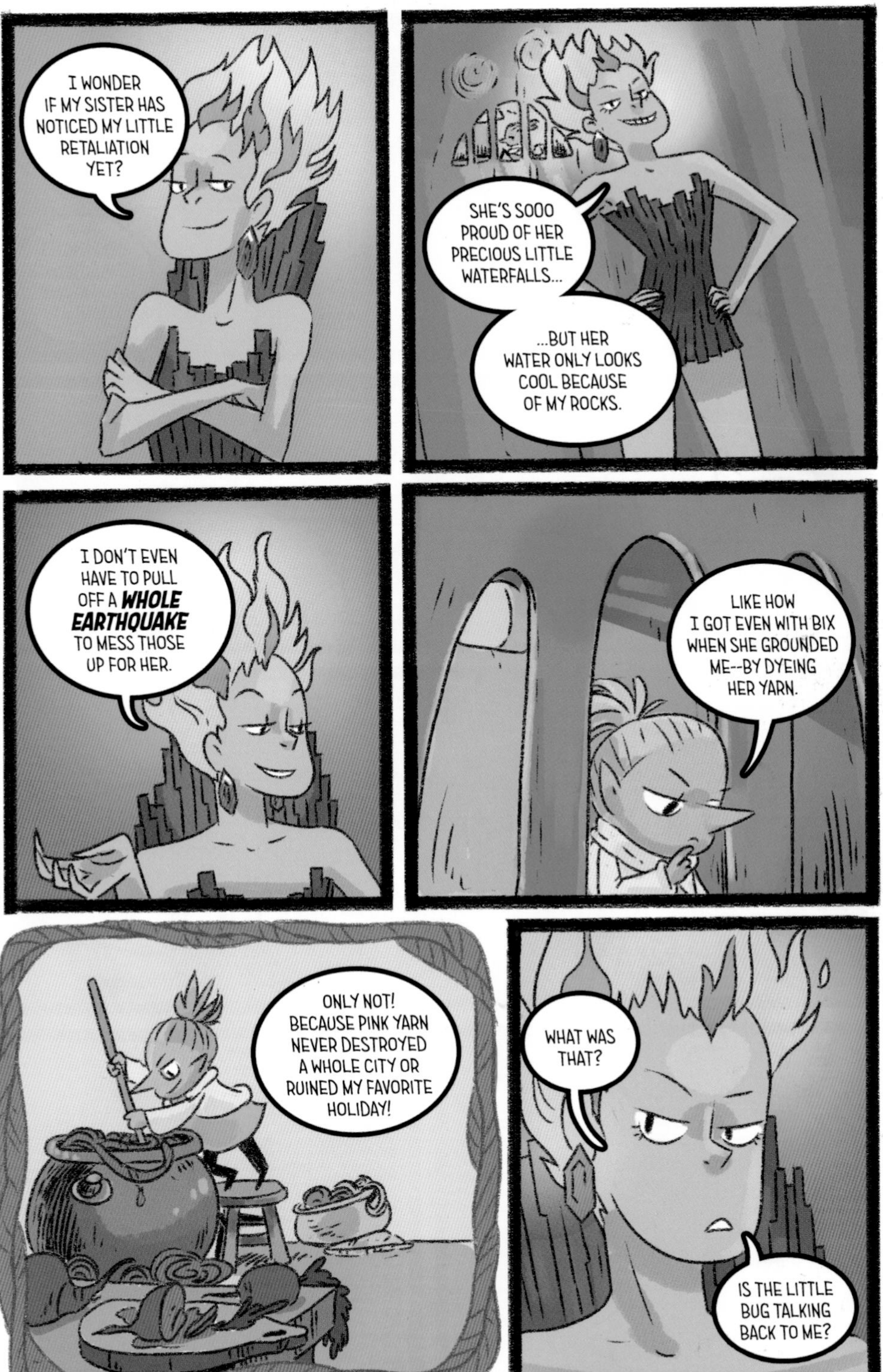
I WONDER IF MY SISTER HAS NOTICED MY LITTLE RETALIATION YET?
SHE'S SOOO PROUD OF HER PRECIOUS LITTLE WATERFALLS...
...BUT HER WATER ONLY LOOKS COOL BECAUSE OF MY ROCKS.
I DON'T EVEN HAVE TO PULL OFF A **WHOLE EARTHQUAKE** TO MESS THOSE UP FOR HER.
LIKE HOW I GOT EVEN WITH BIX WHEN SHE GROUNDED ME--BY DYEING HER YARN.
ONLY NOT! BECAUSE PINK YARN NEVER DESTROYED A WHOLE CITY OR RUINED MY FAVORITE HOLIDAY!
WHAT WAS THAT?
IS THE LITTLE BUG TALKING BACK TO ME?

86

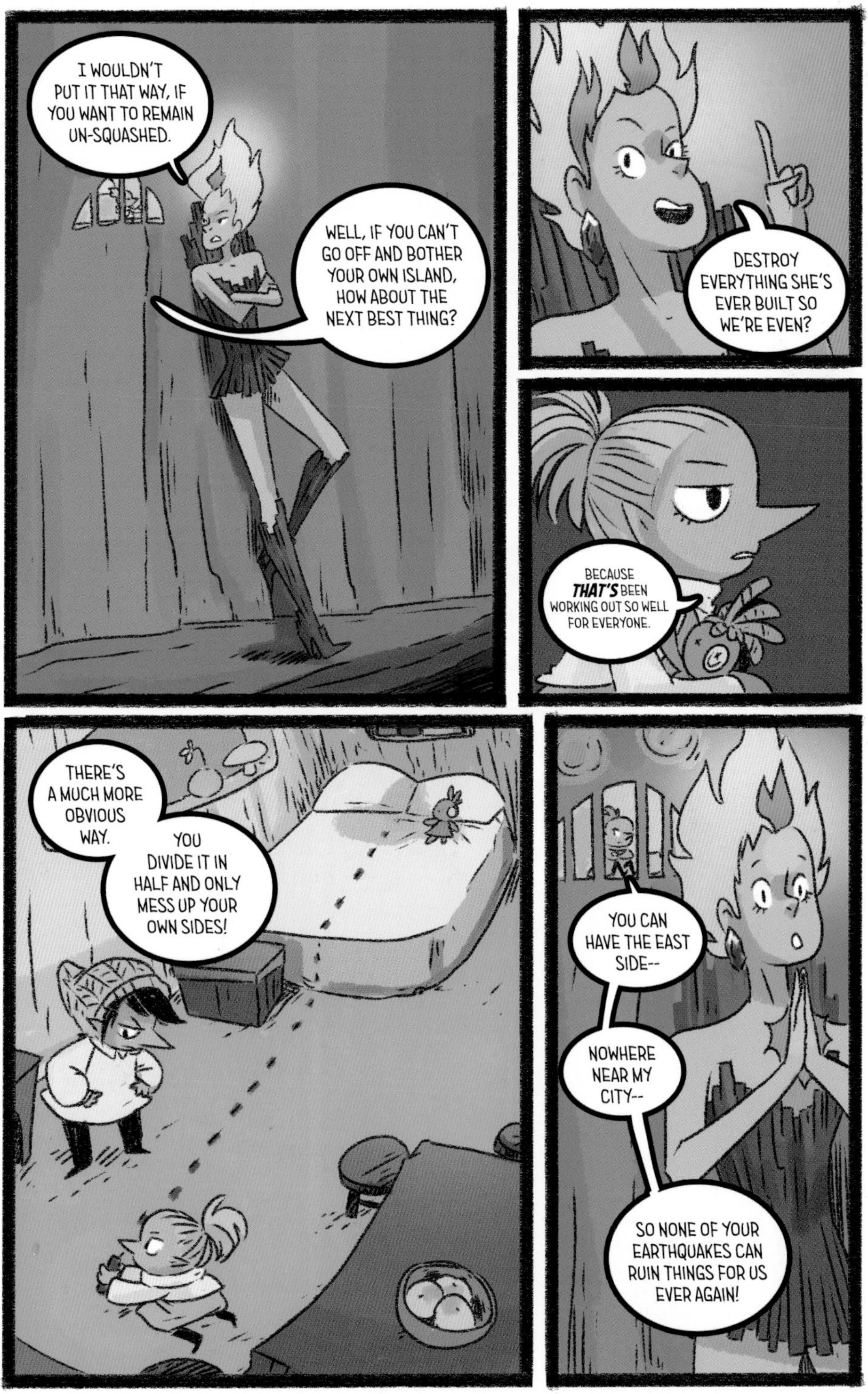
I WOULDN'T PUT IT THAT WAY, IF YOU WANT TO REMAIN UN-SQUASHED.
WELL, IF YOU CAN'T GO OFF AND BOTHER YOUR OWN ISLAND, HOW ABOUT THE NEXT BEST THING?
DESTROY EVERYTHING SHE'S EVER BUILT SO WE'RE EVEN?
BECAUSE ***THAT'S*** BEEN WORKING OUT SO WELL FOR EVERYONE.
THERE'S A MUCH MORE OBVIOUS WAY.
YOU DIVIDE IT IN HALF AND ONLY MESS UP YOUR OWN SIDES!
YOU CAN HAVE THE EAST SIDE--
NOWHERE NEAR MY CITY--
SO NONE OF YOUR EARTHQUAKES CAN RUIN THINGS FOR US EVER AGAIN!

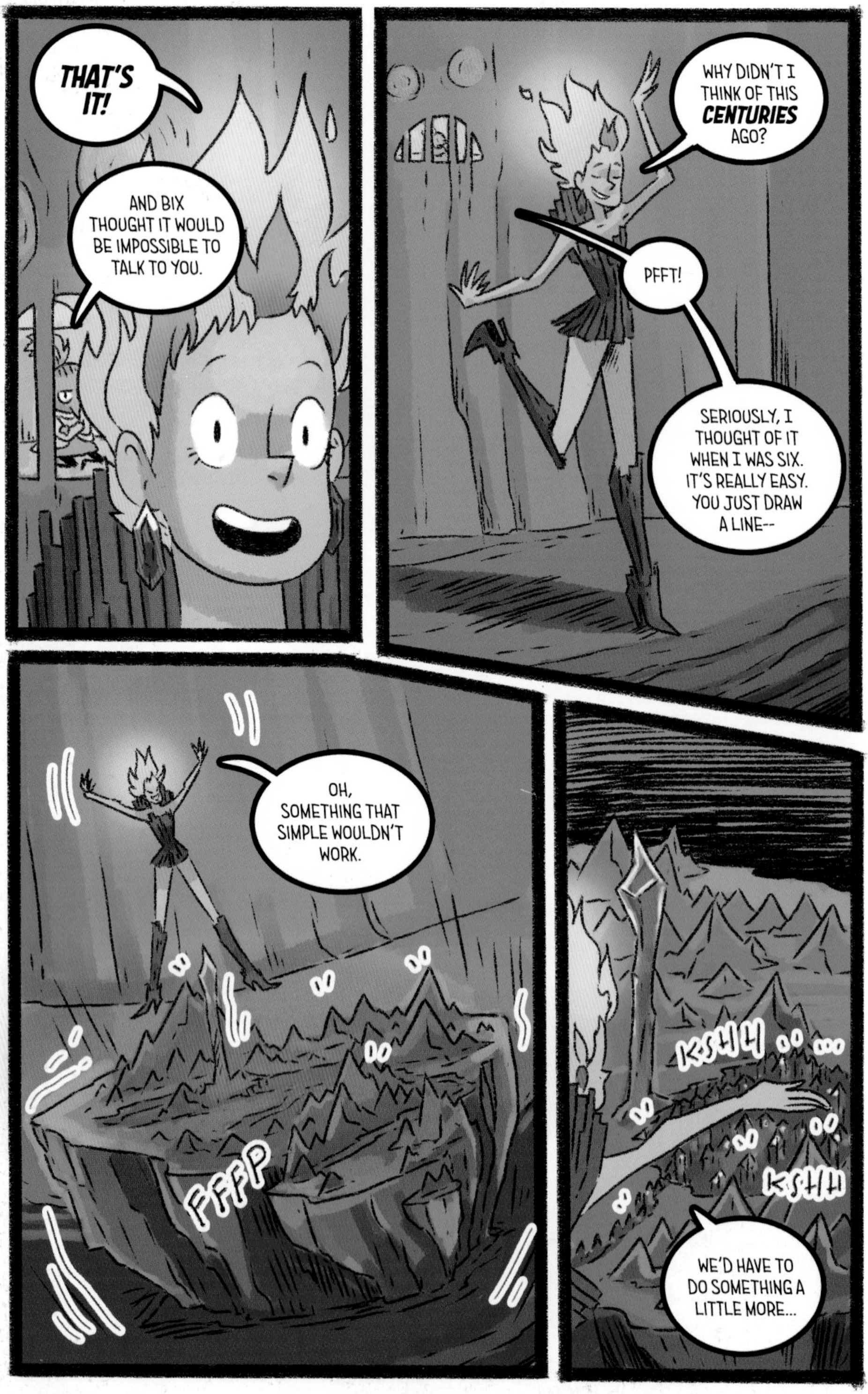
THAT'S IT!
AND BIX THOUGHT IT WOULD BE IMPOSSIBLE TO TALK TO YOU.
WHY DIDN'T I THINK OF THIS **CENTURIES** AGO?
PFFT!
SERIOUSLY, I THOUGHT OF IT WHEN I WAS SIX. IT'S REALLY EASY. YOU JUST DRAW A LINE--
OH, SOMETHING THAT SIMPLE WOULDN'T WORK.
FFFP
KSHH
KSHH
WE'D HAVE TO DO SOMETHING A LITTLE MORE...

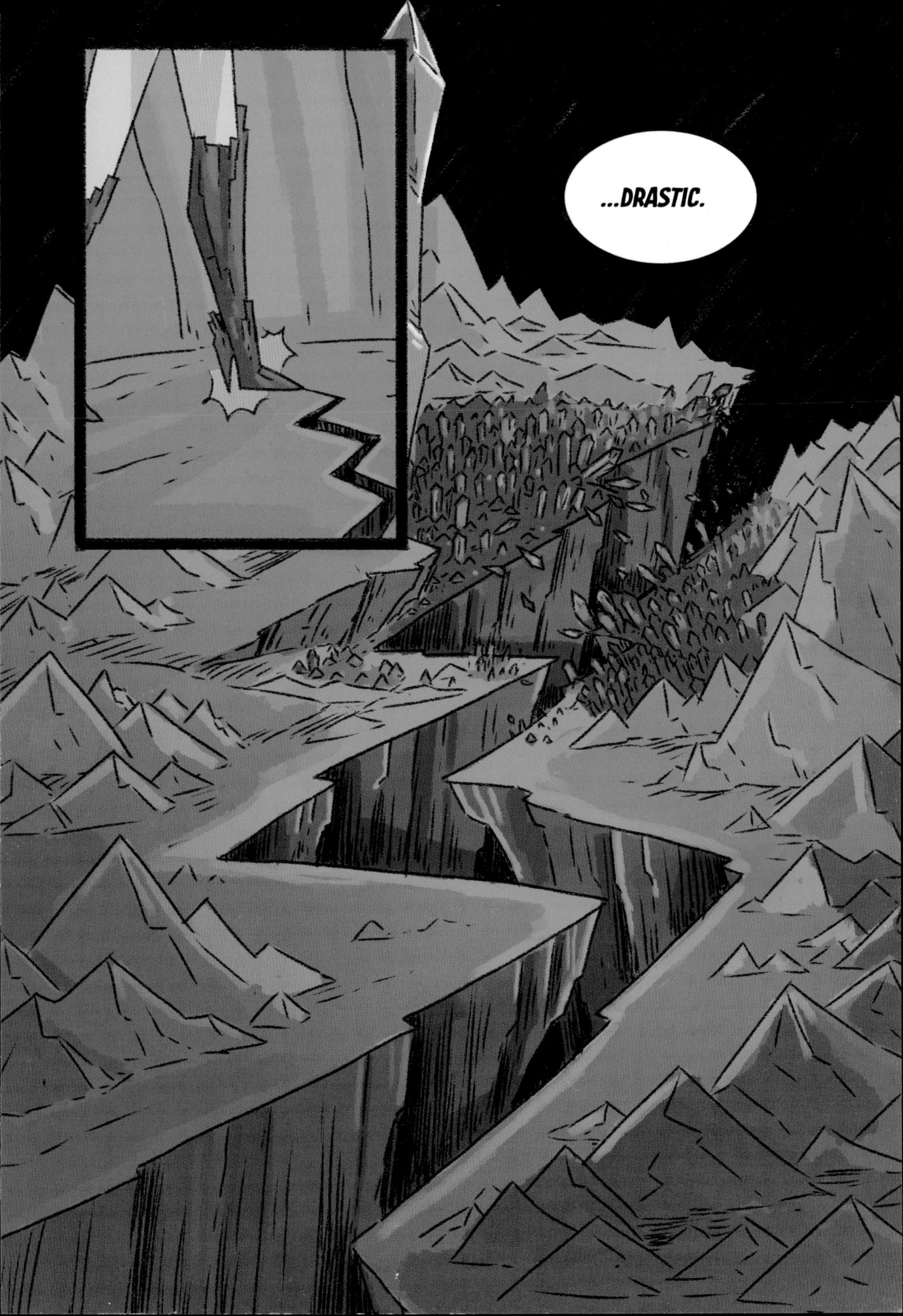
...DRASTIC.

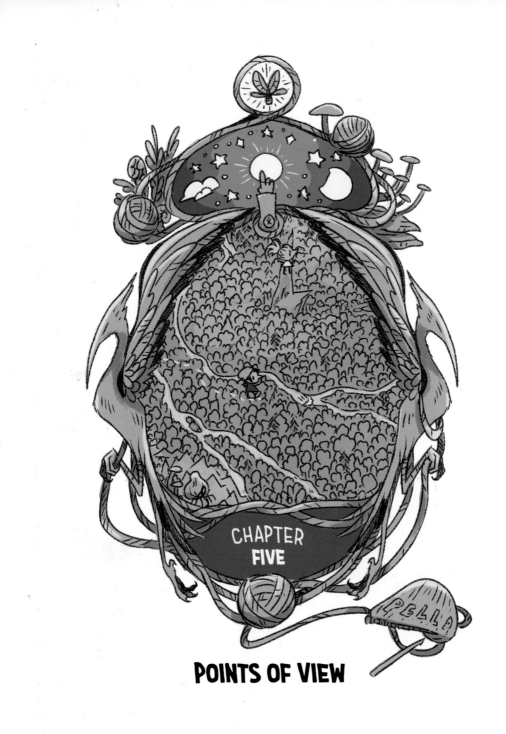

CHAPTER FIVE

POINTS OF VIEW

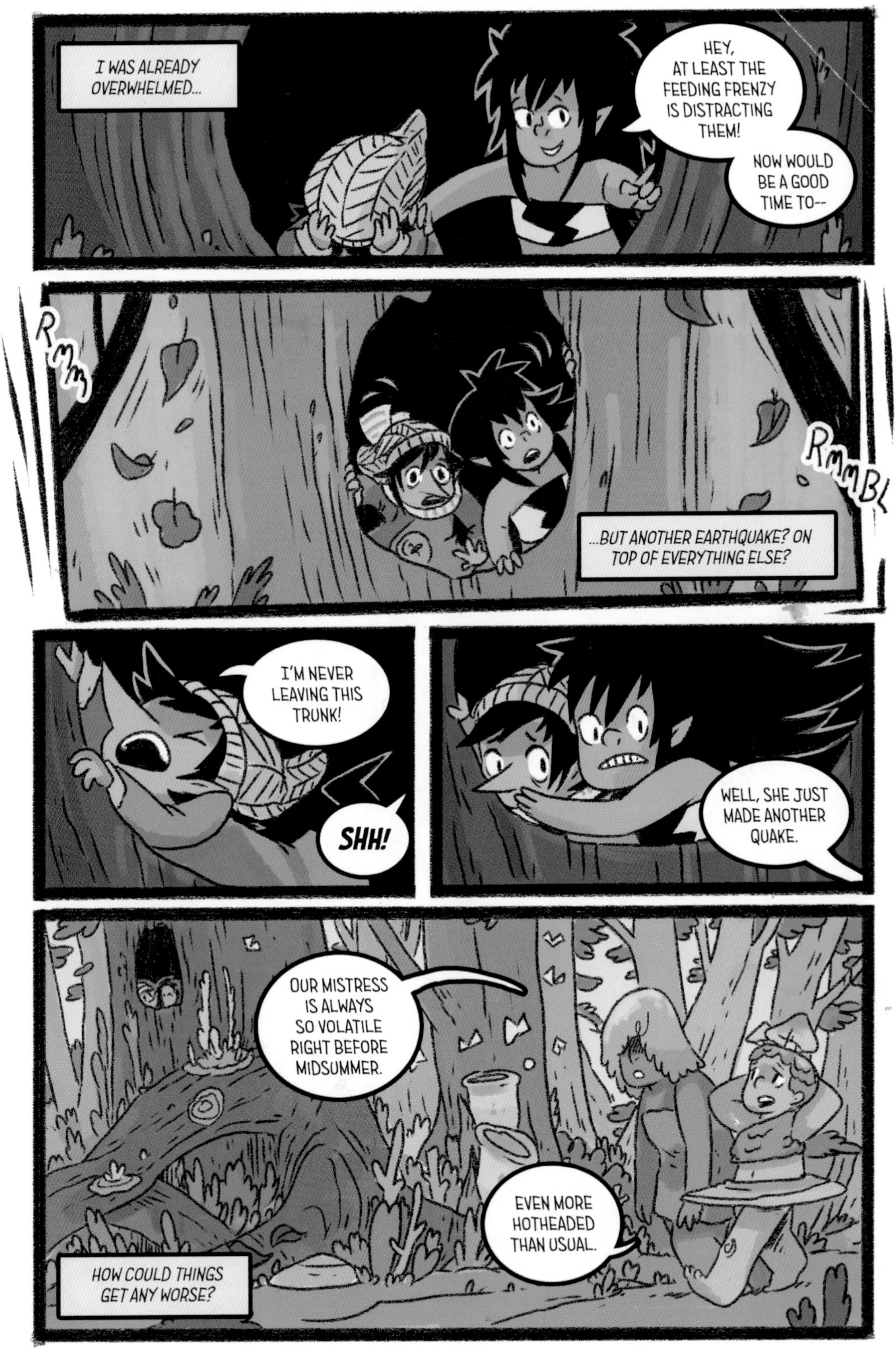
I WAS ALREADY OVERWHELMED...
HEY, AT LEAST THE FEEDING FRENZY IS DISTRACTING THEM!
NOW WOULD BE A GOOD TIME TO--
RMM
RMMBL
...BUT ANOTHER EARTHQUAKE? ON TOP OF EVERYTHING ELSE?
I'M NEVER LEAVING THIS TRUNK!
SHH!
WELL, SHE JUST MADE ANOTHER QUAKE.
OUR MISTRESS IS ALWAYS SO VOLATILE RIGHT BEFORE MIDSUMMER.
EVEN MORE HOTHEADED THAN USUAL.
HOW COULD THINGS GET ANY WORSE?

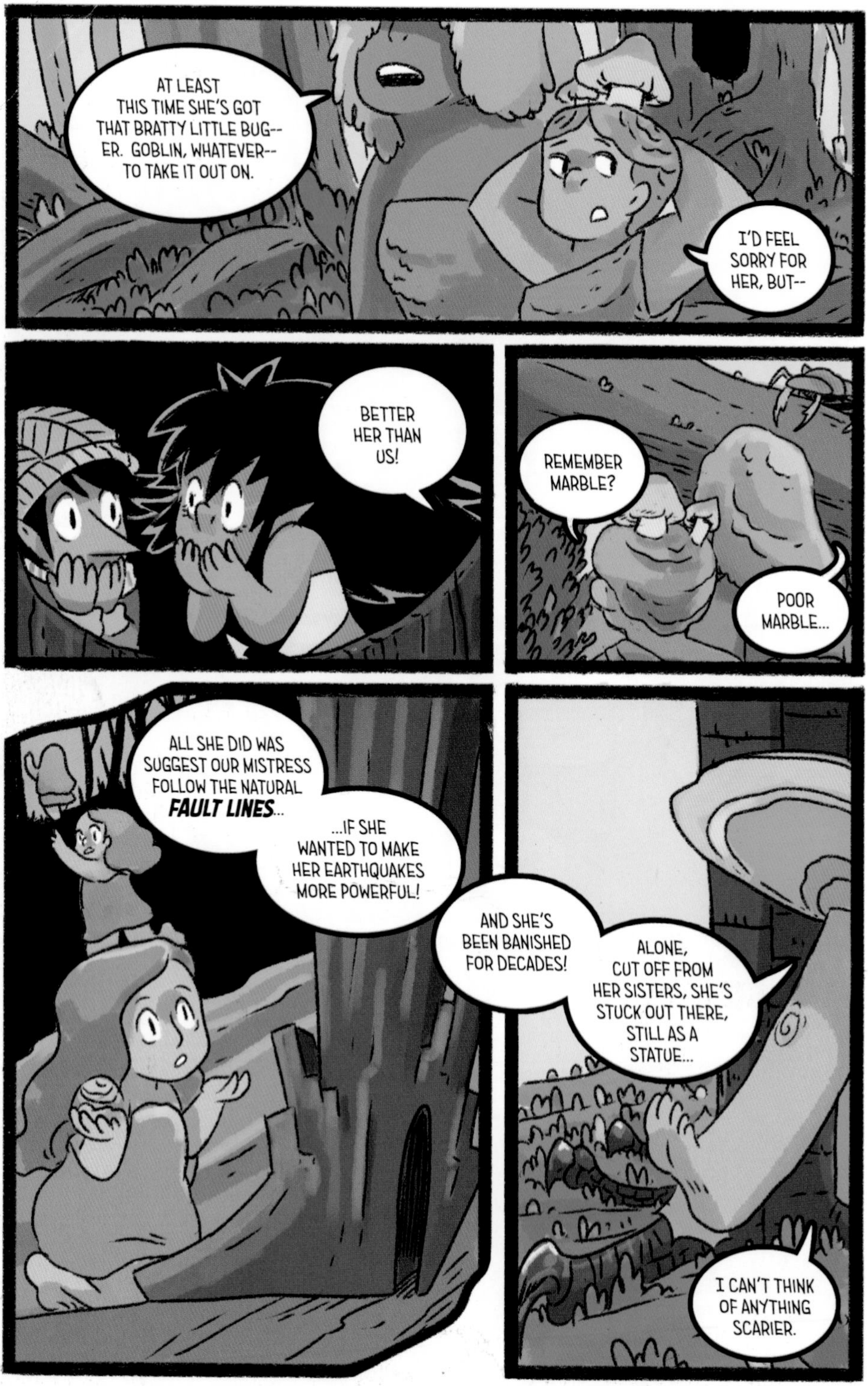
AT LEAST THIS TIME SHE'S GOT THAT BRATTY LITTLE BUG-- ER. GOBLIN, WHATEVER-- TO TAKE IT OUT ON.
I'D FEEL SORRY FOR HER, BUT--
BETTER HER THAN US!
REMEMBER MARBLE?
POOR MARBLE...
ALL SHE DID WAS SUGGEST OUR MISTRESS FOLLOW THE NATURAL **FAULT LINES**...
...IF SHE WANTED TO MAKE HER EARTHQUAKES MORE POWERFUL!
AND SHE'S BEEN BANISHED FOR DECADES!
ALONE, CUT OFF FROM HER SISTERS, SHE'S STUCK OUT THERE, STILL AS A STATUE...
I CAN'T THINK OF ANYTHING SCARIER.

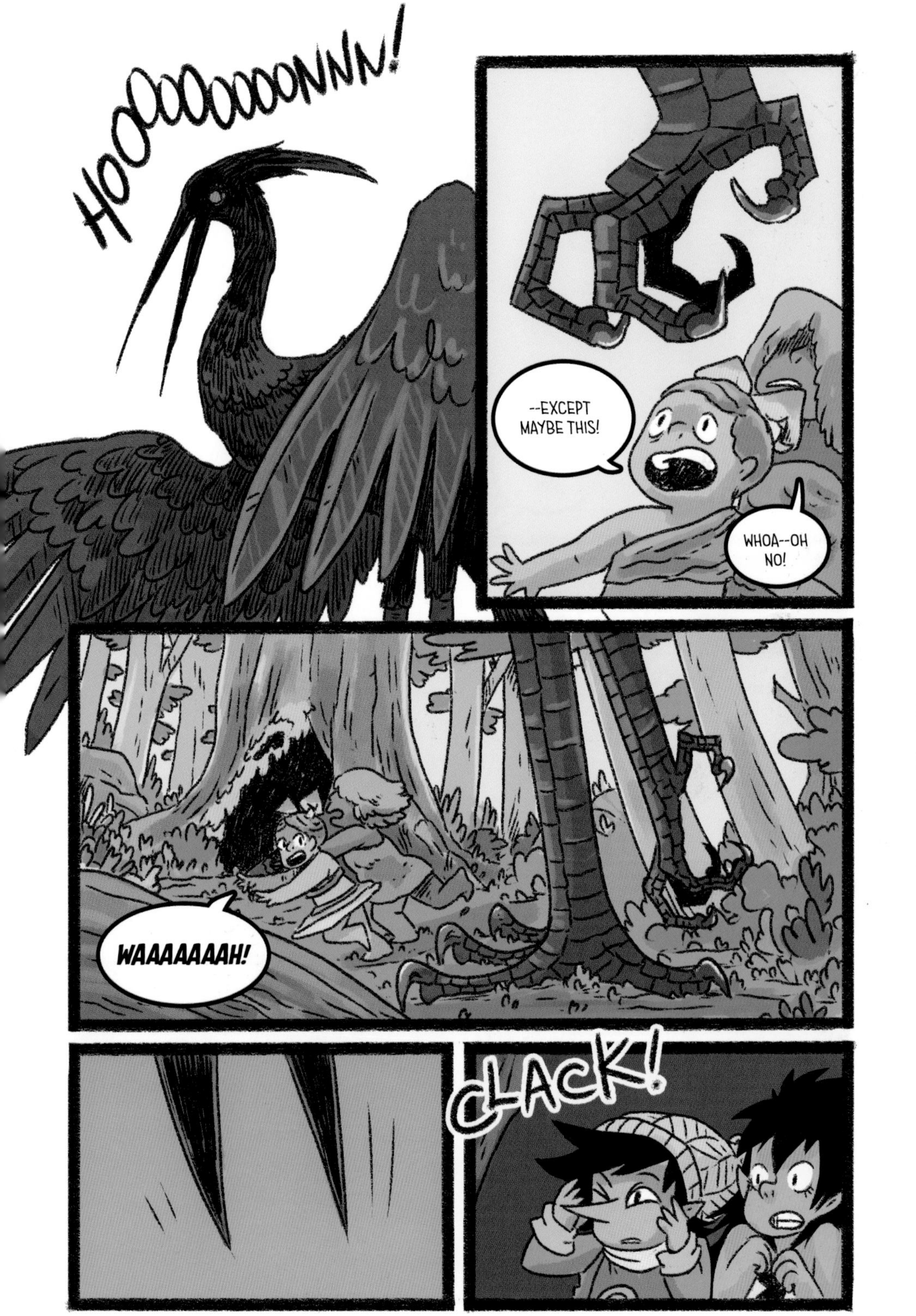
HOOOOOOOONNN!
--EXCEPT MAYBE THIS!
WHOA--OH NO!
WAAAAAAAH!
CLACK!

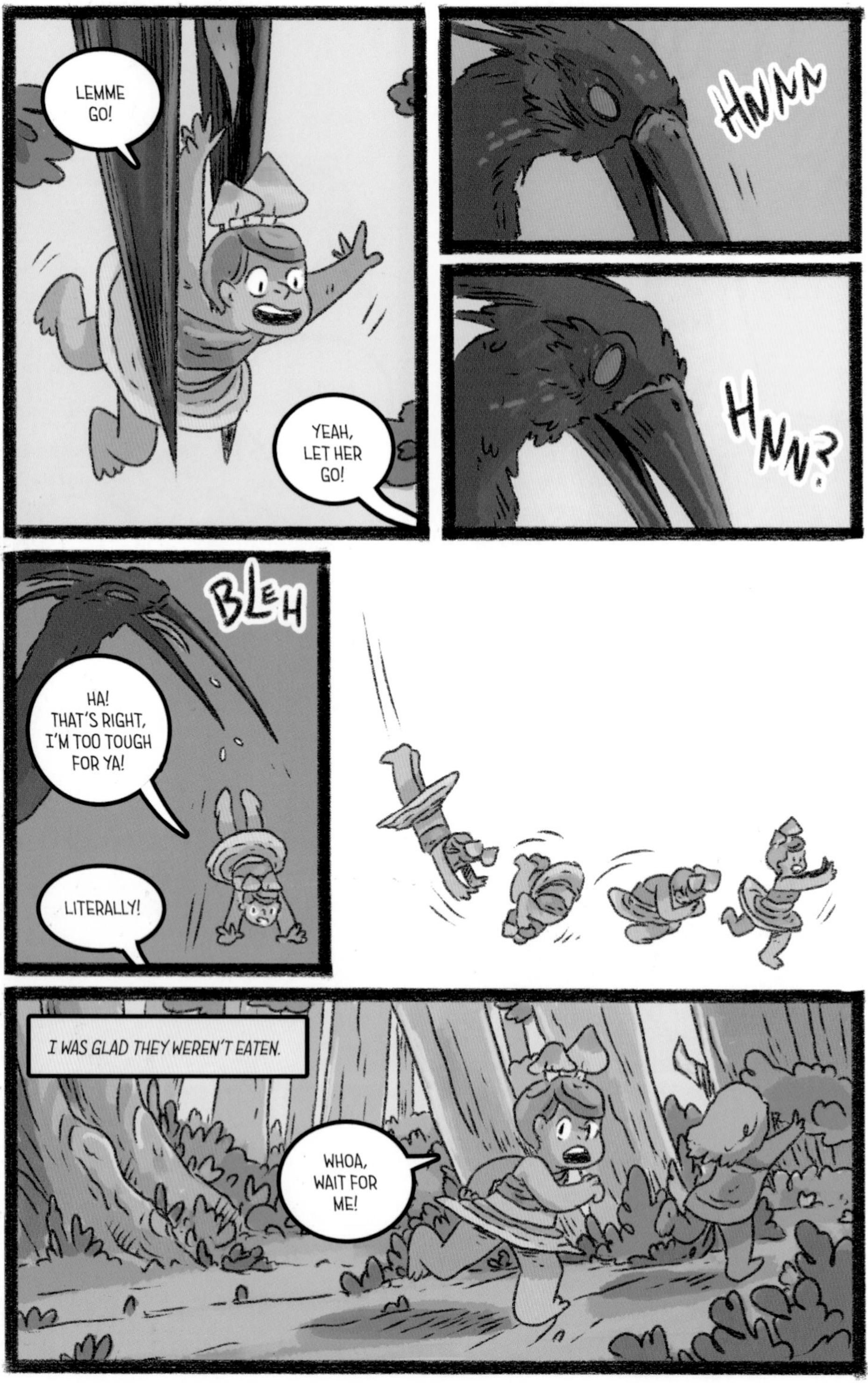

LEMME GO!
YEAH, LET HER GO!
HNNN
HNN?
BLEH
HA! THAT'S RIGHT, I'M TOO TOUGH FOR YA!
LITERALLY!
I WAS GLAD THEY WEREN'T EATEN.
WHOA, WAIT FOR ME!

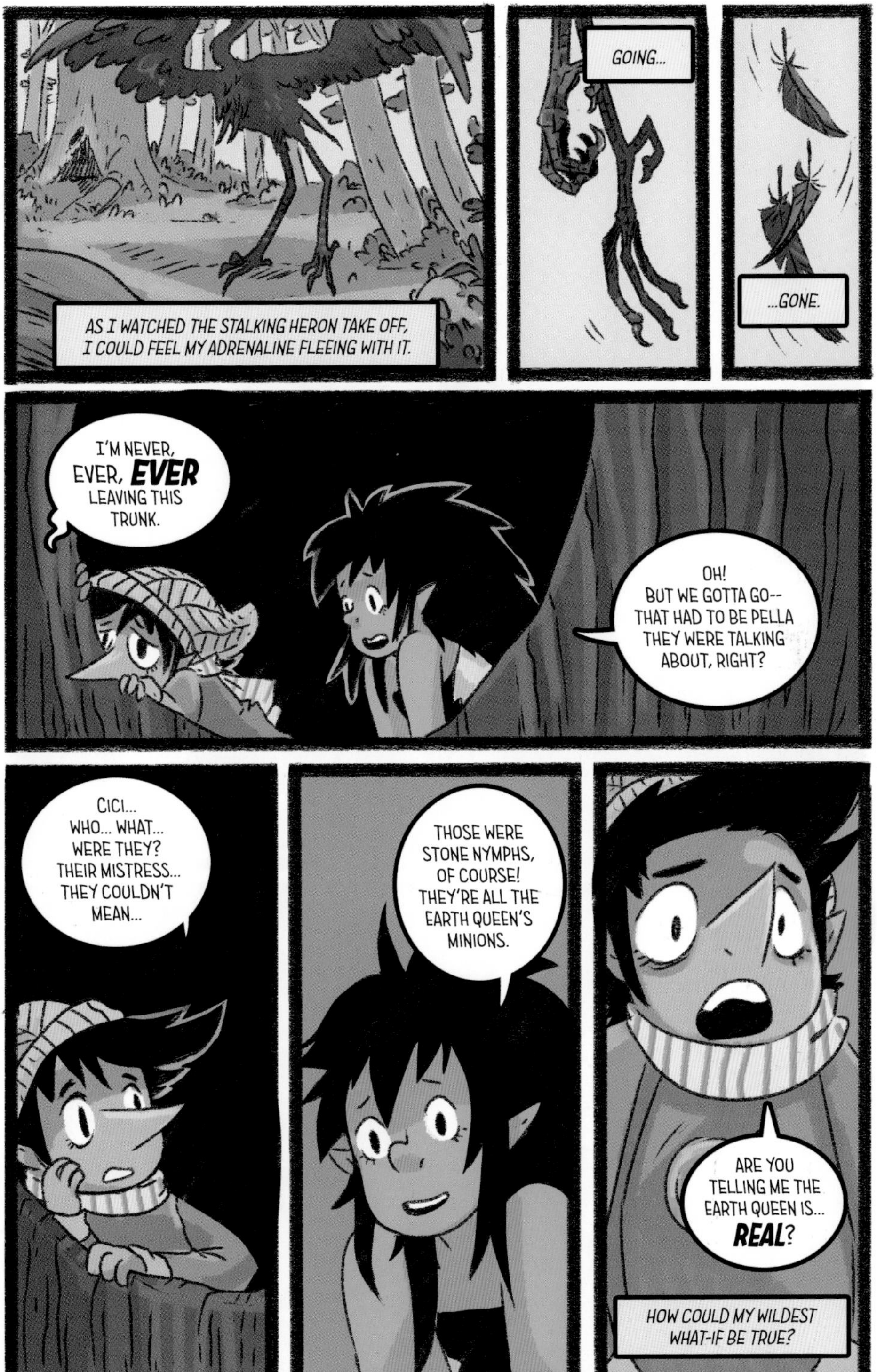
AS I WATCHED THE STALKING HERON TAKE OFF, I COULD FEEL MY ADRENALINE FLEEING WITH IT.
GOING...
...GONE.
I'M NEVER, EVER, **EVER** LEAVING THIS TRUNK.
OH! BUT WE GOTTA GO-- THAT HAD TO BE PELLA THEY WERE TALKING ABOUT, RIGHT?
CICI... WHO... WHAT... WERE THEY? THEIR MISTRESS... THEY COULDN'T MEAN...
THOSE WERE STONE NYMPHS, OF COURSE! THEY'RE ALL THE EARTH QUEEN'S MINIONS.
ARE YOU TELLING ME THE EARTH QUEEN IS... **REAL**?
HOW COULD MY WILDEST WHAT-IF BE TRUE?

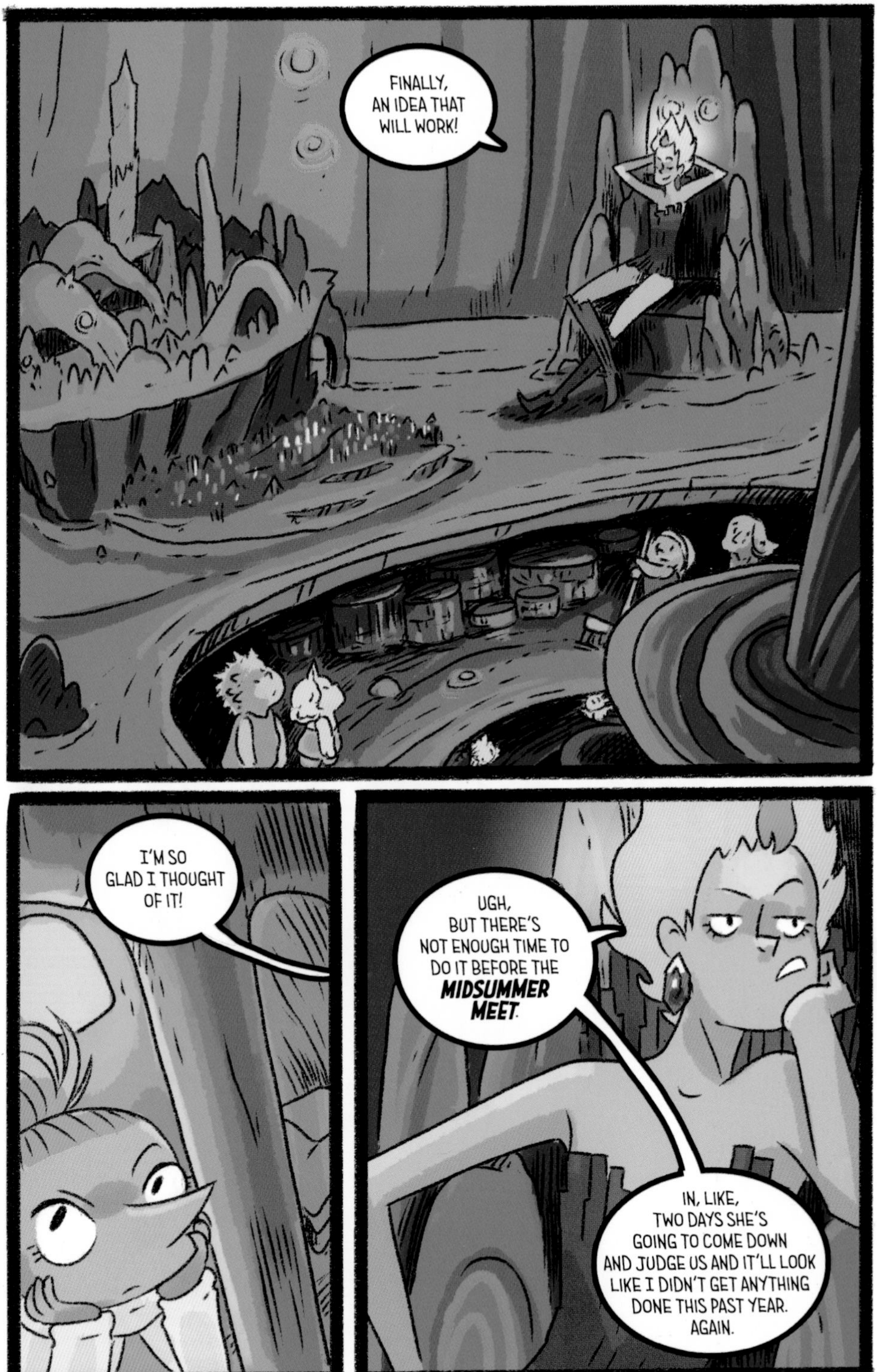
FINALLY, AN IDEA THAT WILL WORK!
I'M SO GLAD I THOUGHT OF IT!
UGH, BUT THERE'S NOT ENOUGH TIME TO DO IT BEFORE THE **MIDSUMMER MEET**.
IN, LIKE, TWO DAYS SHE'S GOING TO COME DOWN AND JUDGE US AND IT'LL LOOK LIKE I DIDN'T GET ANYTHING DONE THIS PAST YEAR. AGAIN.

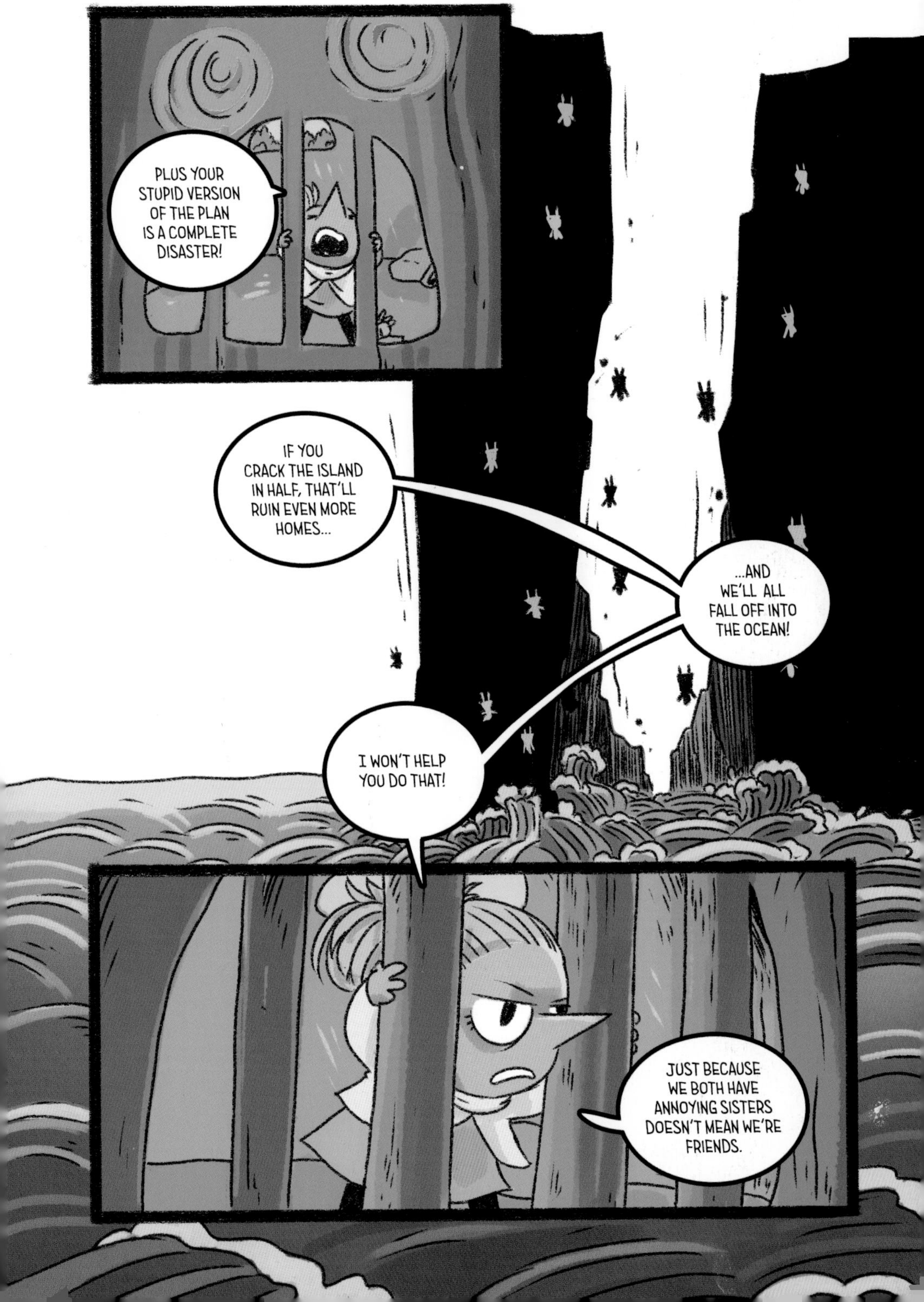
PLUS YOUR STUPID VERSION OF THE PLAN IS A COMPLETE DISASTER!
IF YOU CRACK THE ISLAND IN HALF, THAT'LL RUIN EVEN MORE HOMES...
...AND WE'LL ALL FALL OFF INTO THE OCEAN!
I WON'T HELP YOU DO THAT!
JUST BECAUSE WE BOTH HAVE ANNOYING SISTERS DOESN'T MEAN WE'RE FRIENDS.

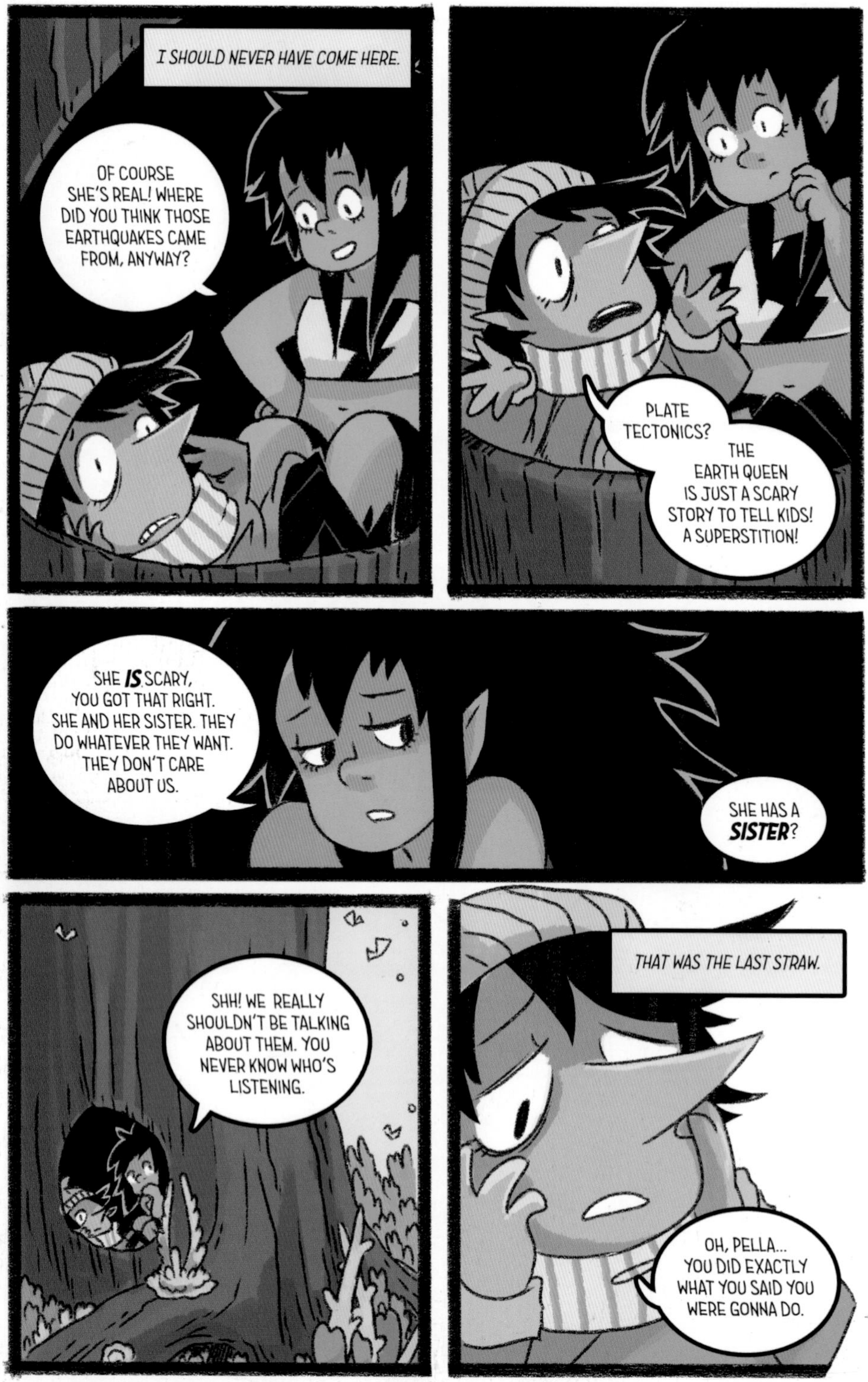
I SHOULD NEVER HAVE COME HERE.
OF COURSE SHE'S REAL! WHERE DID YOU THINK THOSE EARTHQUAKES CAME FROM, ANYWAY?
PLATE TECTONICS?
THE EARTH QUEEN IS JUST A SCARY STORY TO TELL KIDS! A SUPERSTITION!
SHE ***IS*** SCARY, YOU GOT THAT RIGHT. SHE AND HER SISTER. THEY DO WHATEVER THEY WANT. THEY DON'T CARE ABOUT US.
SHE HAS A ***SISTER***?
SHH! WE REALLY SHOULDN'T BE TALKING ABOUT THEM. YOU NEVER KNOW WHO'S LISTENING.
THAT WAS THE LAST STRAW.
OH, PELLA... YOU DID EXACTLY WHAT YOU SAID YOU WERE GONNA DO.

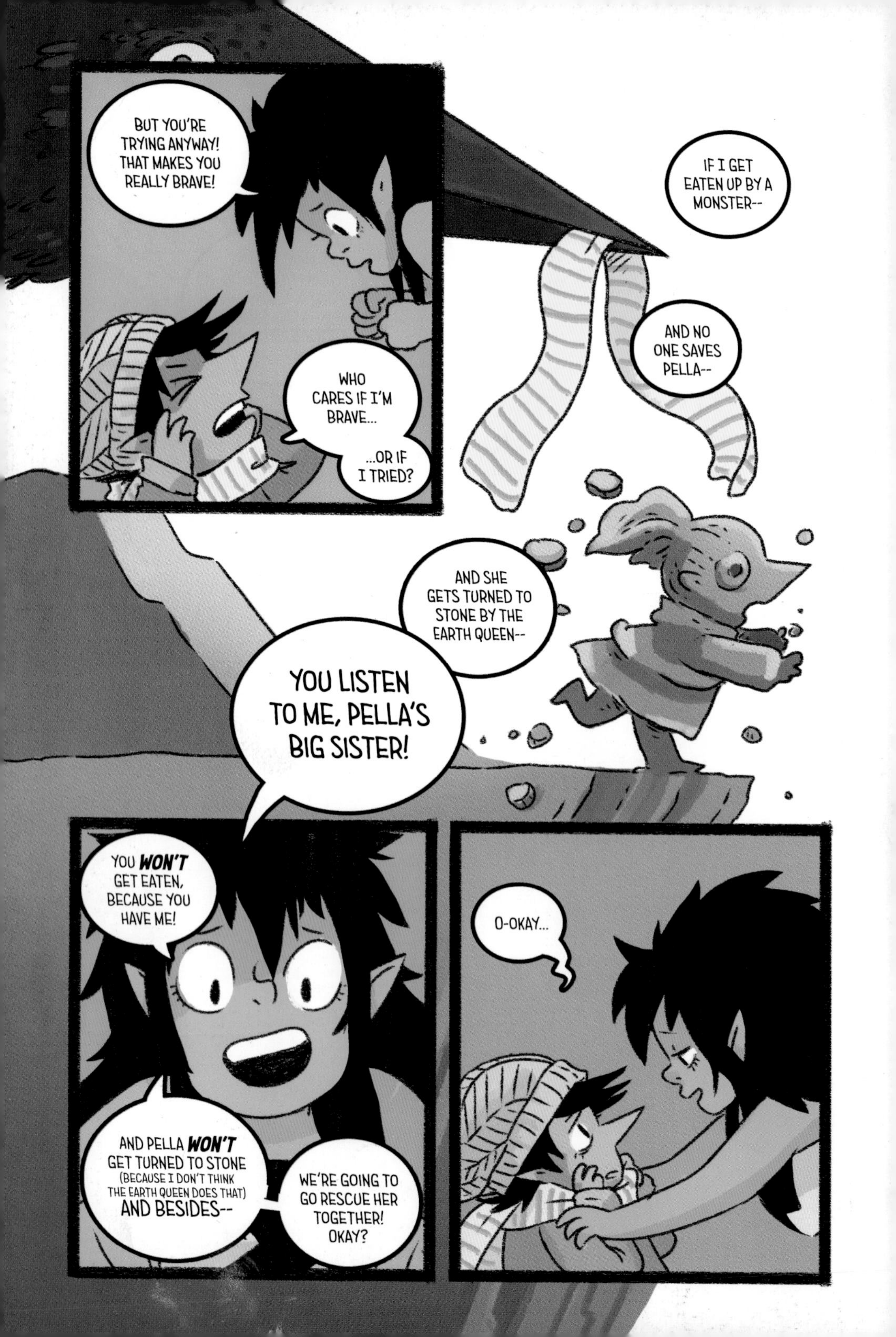
BUT YOU'RE TRYING ANYWAY! THAT MAKES YOU REALLY BRAVE!
WHO CARES IF I'M BRAVE...
...OR IF I TRIED?
IF I GET EATEN UP BY A MONSTER--
AND NO ONE SAVES PELLA--
AND SHE GETS TURNED TO STONE BY THE EARTH QUEEN--
YOU LISTEN TO ME, PELLA'S BIG SISTER!
YOU **WON'T** GET EATEN, BECAUSE YOU HAVE ME!
AND PELLA **WON'T** GET TURNED TO STONE (BECAUSE I DON'T THINK THE EARTH QUEEN DOES THAT) AND BESIDES--
WE'RE GOING TO GO RESCUE HER TOGETHER! OKAY?
O-OKAY...

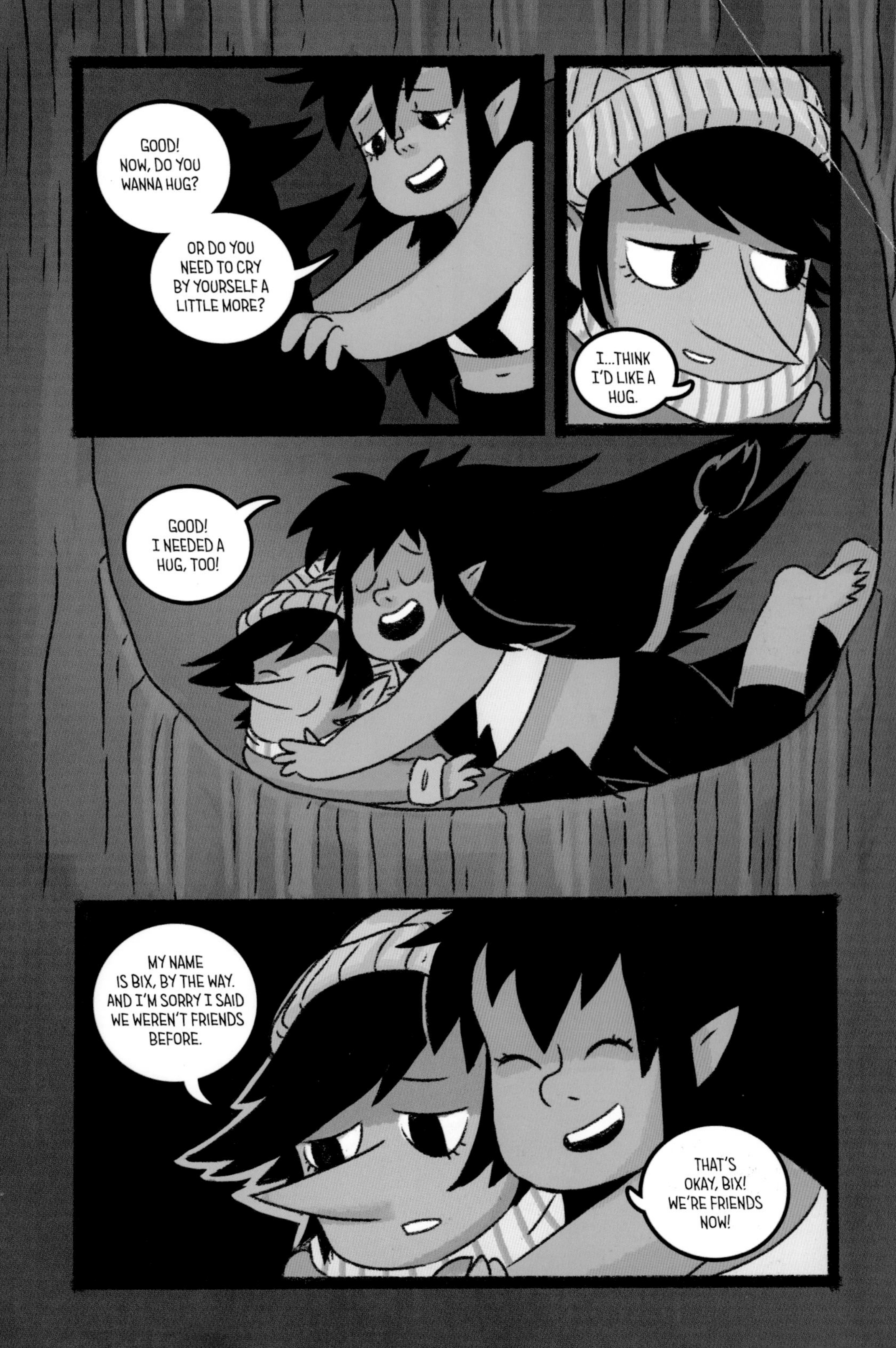
GOOD! NOW, DO YOU WANNA HUG?
OR DO YOU NEED TO CRY BY YOURSELF A LITTLE MORE?
I...THINK I'D LIKE A HUG.
GOOD! I NEEDED A HUG, TOO!
MY NAME IS BIX, BY THE WAY. AND I'M SORRY I SAID WE WEREN'T FRIENDS BEFORE.
THAT'S OKAY, BIX! WE'RE FRIENDS NOW!

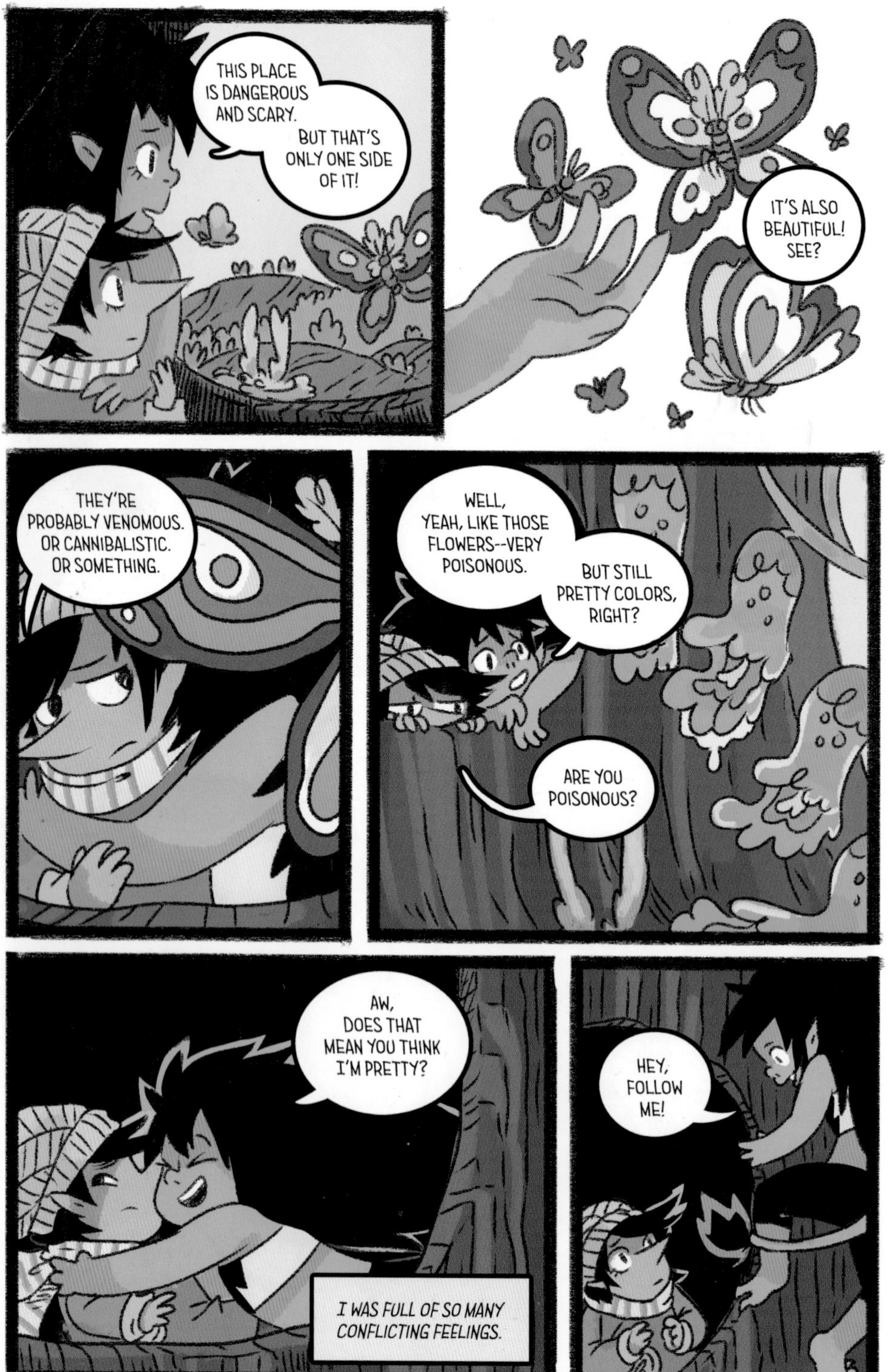
THIS PLACE IS DANGEROUS AND SCARY.
BUT THAT'S ONLY ONE SIDE OF IT!
IT'S ALSO BEAUTIFUL! SEE?
THEY'RE PROBABLY VENOMOUS. OR CANNIBALISTIC. OR SOMETHING.
WELL, YEAH, LIKE THOSE FLOWERS--VERY POISONOUS.
BUT STILL PRETTY COLORS, RIGHT?
ARE YOU POISONOUS?
AW, DOES THAT MEAN YOU THINK I'M PRETTY?
I WAS FULL OF SO MANY CONFLICTING FEELINGS.
HEY, FOLLOW ME!

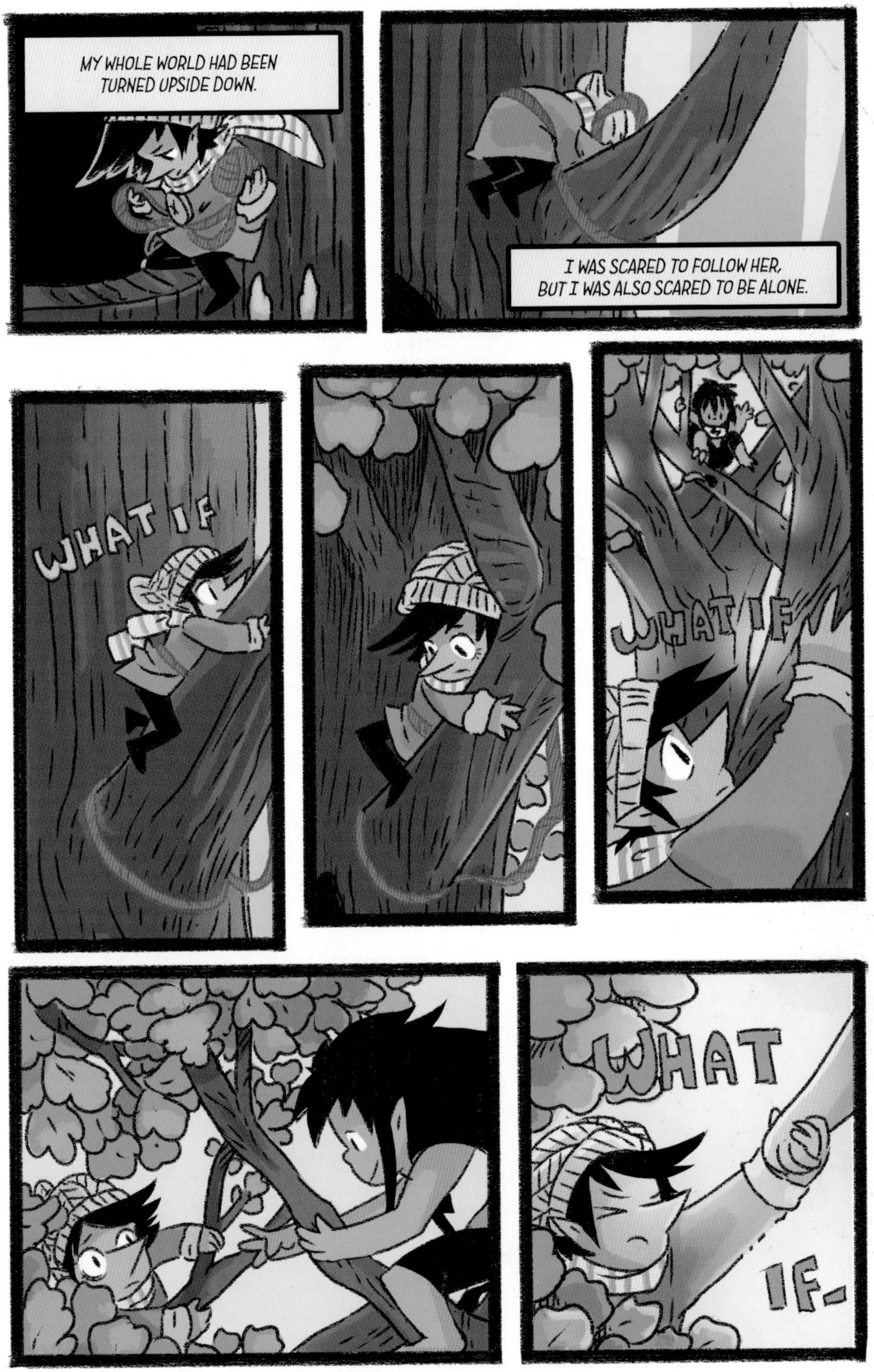
MY WHOLE WORLD HAD BEEN TURNED UPSIDE DOWN.
I WAS SCARED TO FOLLOW HER, BUT I WAS ALSO SCARED TO BE ALONE.
WHAT IF
WHAT IF
WHAT
IF-

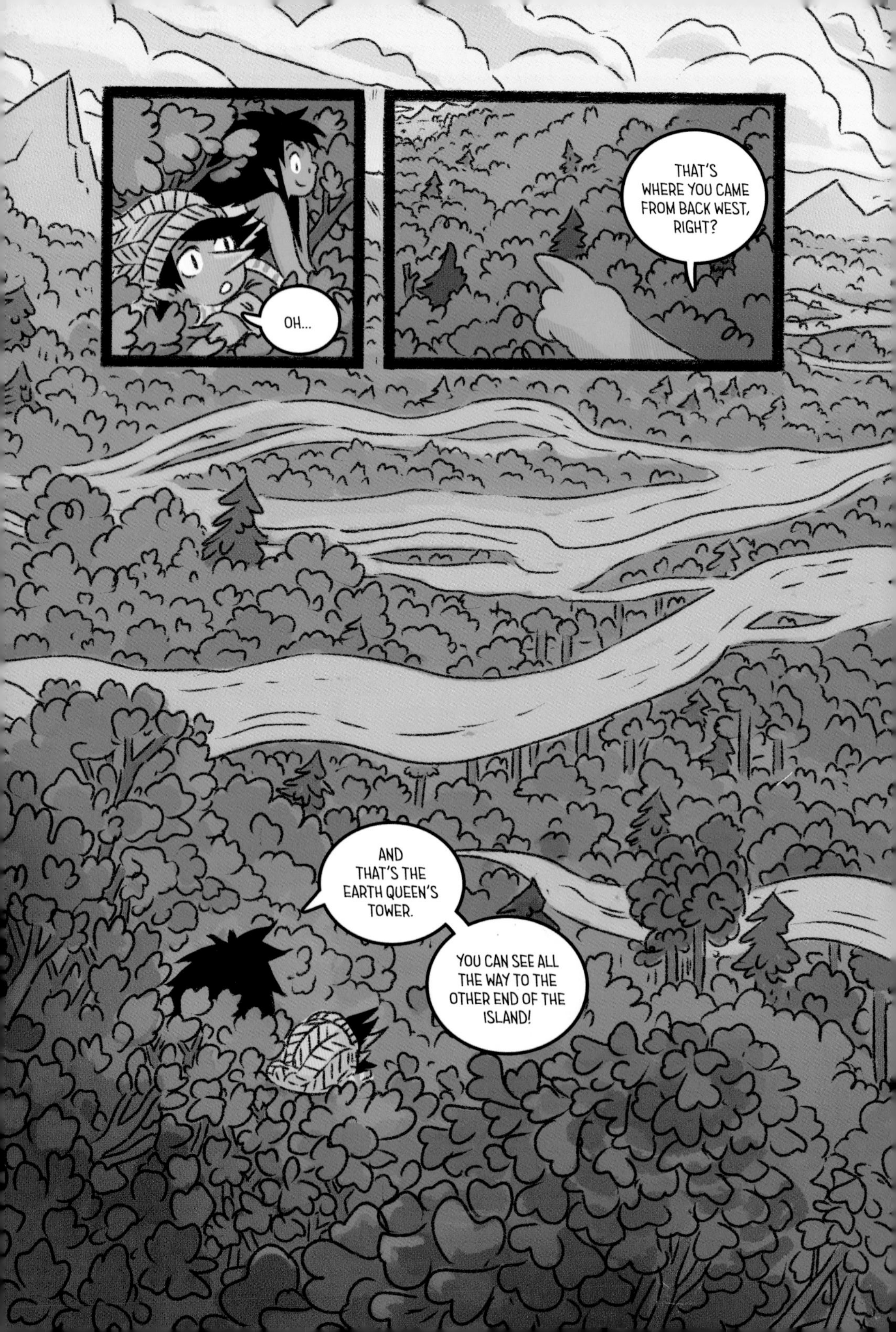
OH...
THAT'S WHERE YOU CAME FROM BACK WEST, RIGHT?
AND THAT'S THE EARTH QUEEN'S TOWER.
YOU CAN SEE ALL THE WAY TO THE OTHER END OF THE ISLAND!

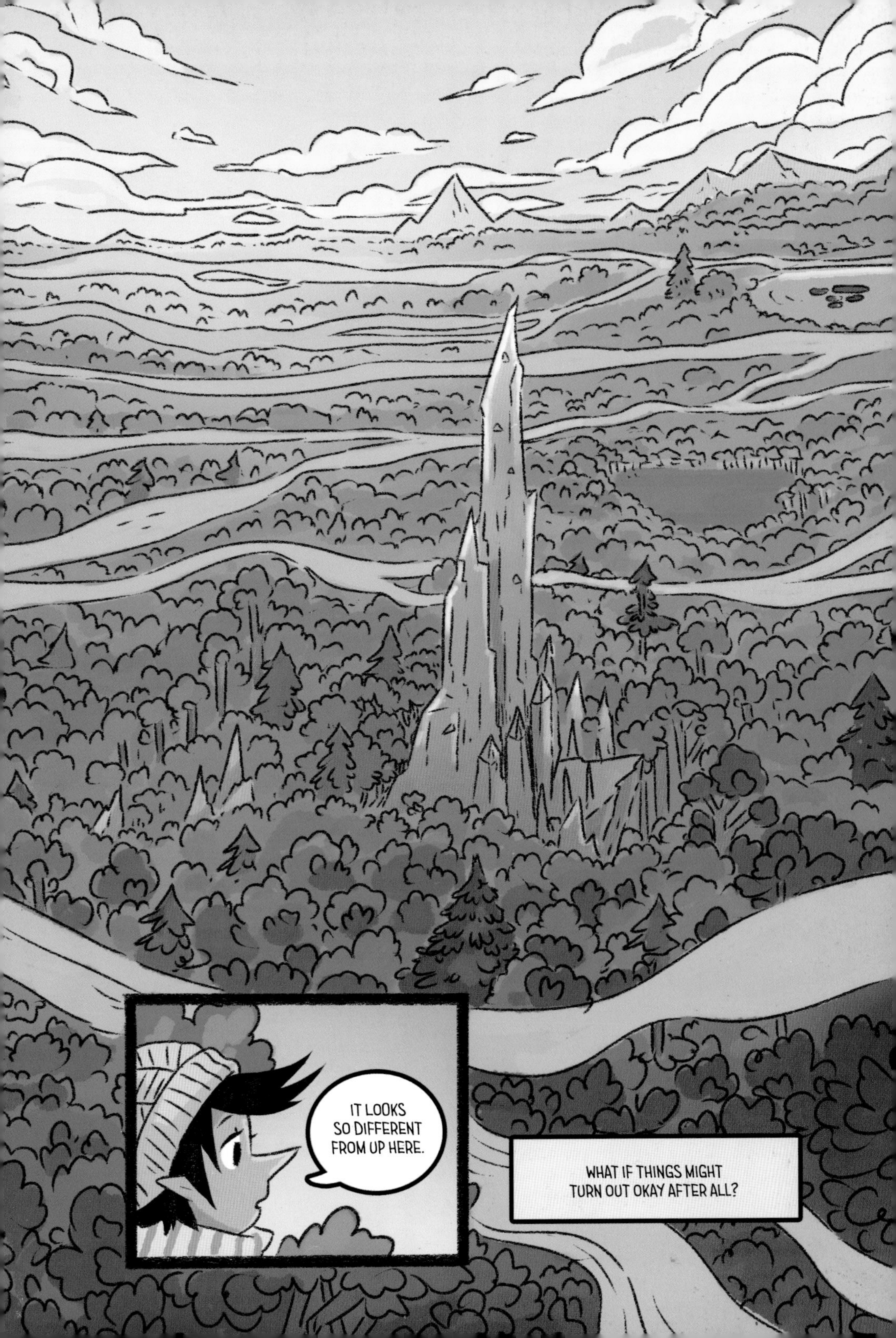
IT LOOKS SO DIFFERENT FROM UP HERE.
WHAT IF THINGS MIGHT TURN OUT OKAY AFTER ALL?

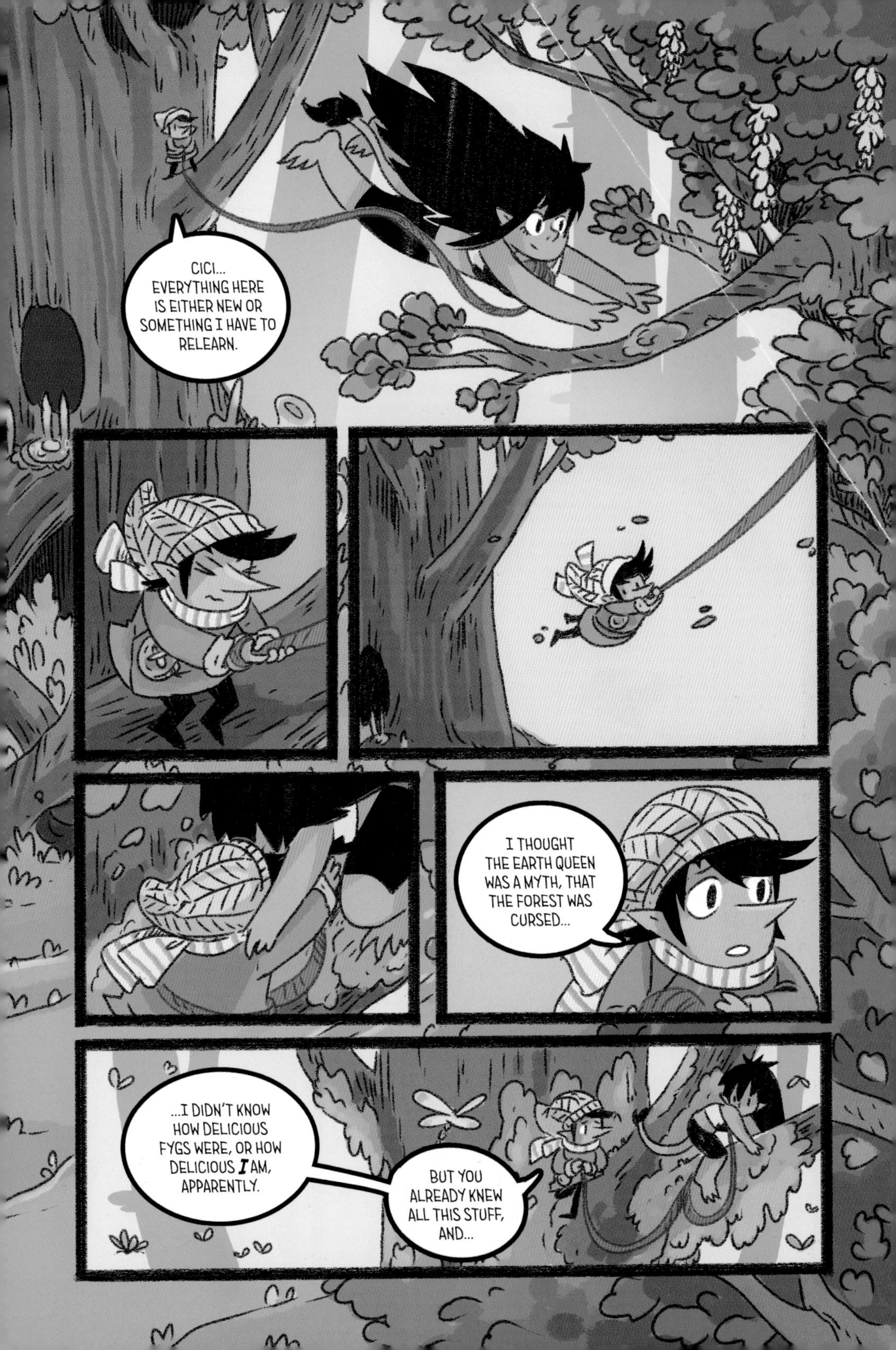

CICI... EVERYTHING HERE IS EITHER NEW OR SOMETHING I HAVE TO RELEARN.
I THOUGHT THE EARTH QUEEN WAS A MYTH, THAT THE FOREST WAS CURSED...
...I DIDN'T KNOW HOW DELICIOUS FYGS WERE, OR HOW DELICIOUS *I* AM, APPARENTLY.
BUT YOU ALREADY KNEW ALL THIS STUFF, AND...

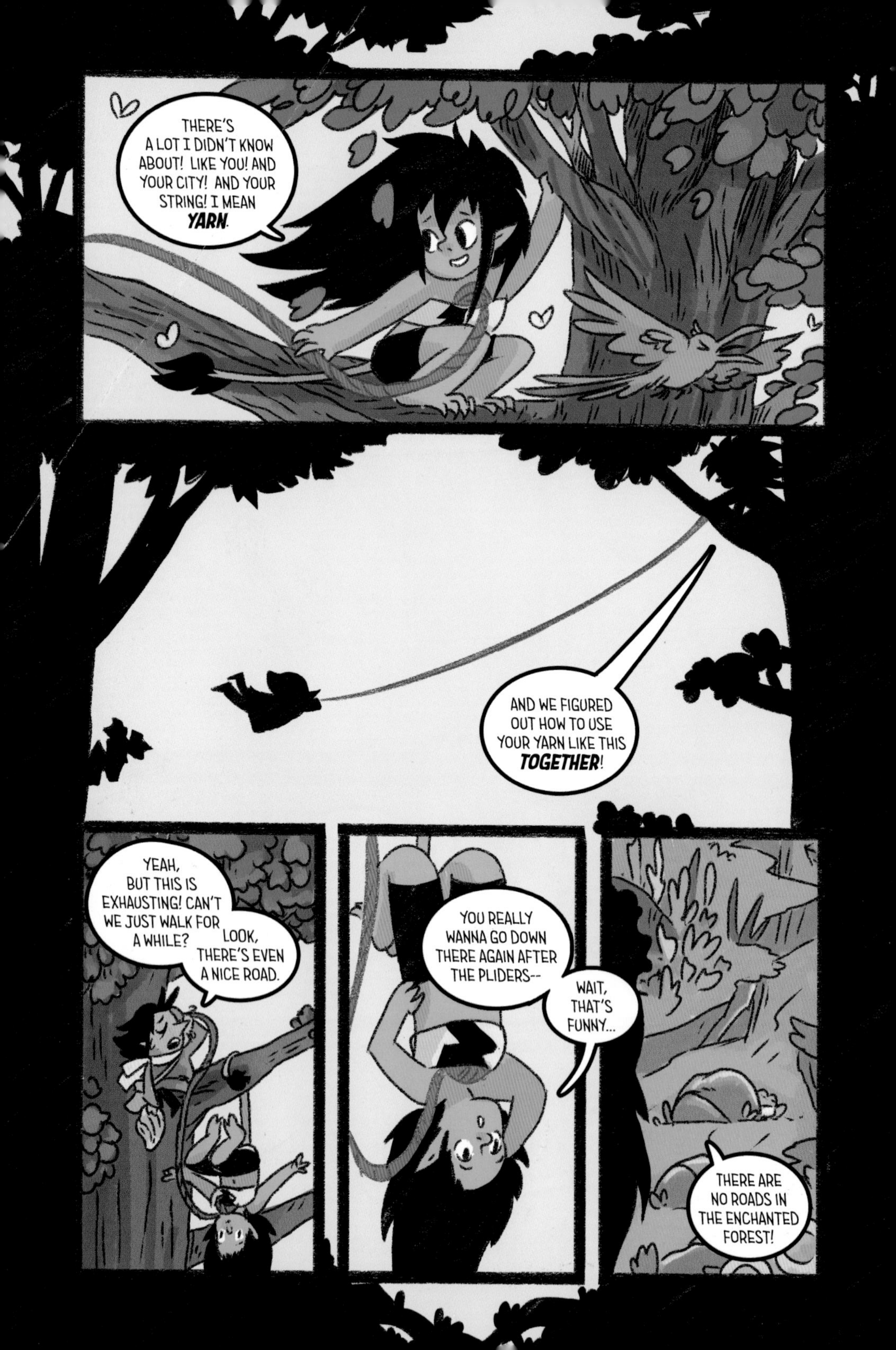
THERE'S A LOT I DIDN'T KNOW ABOUT! LIKE YOU! AND YOUR CITY! AND YOUR STRING! I MEAN YARN.
AND WE FIGURED OUT HOW TO USE YOUR YARN LIKE THIS TOGETHER!
YEAH, BUT THIS IS EXHAUSTING! CAN'T WE JUST WALK FOR A WHILE?
LOOK, THERE'S EVEN A NICE ROAD.
YOU REALLY WANNA GO DOWN THERE AGAIN AFTER THE PLIDERS--
WAIT, THAT'S FUNNY...
THERE ARE NO ROADS IN THE ENCHANTED FOREST!

114

CHAPTER
SIX
PELLA

WISHES

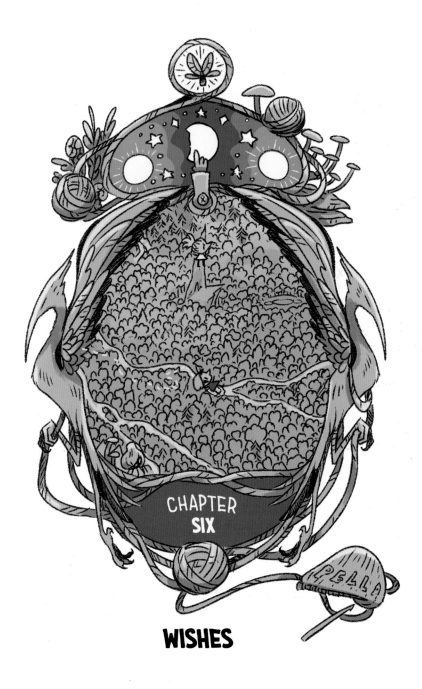

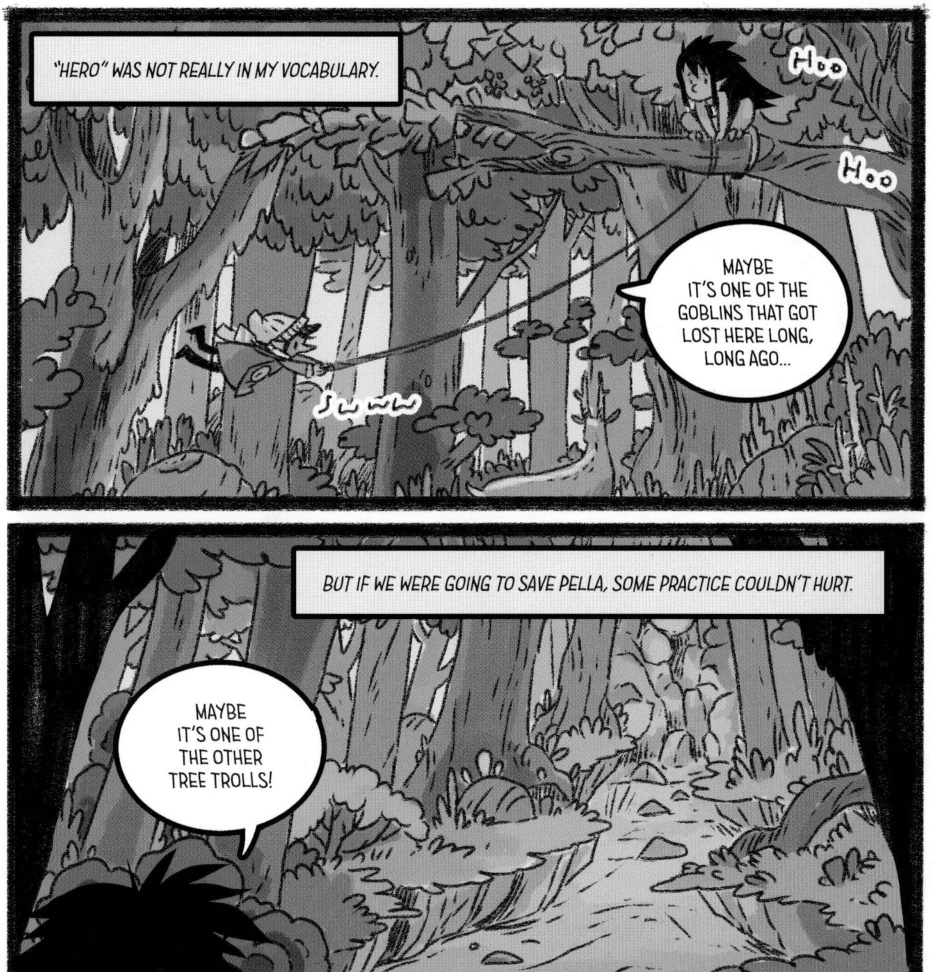
"HERO" WAS NOT REALLY IN MY VOCABULARY.
Hoo
Hoo
MAYBE IT'S ONE OF THE GOBLINS THAT GOT LOST HERE LONG, LONG AGO...
BUT IF WE WERE GOING TO SAVE PELLA, SOME PRACTICE COULDN'T HURT.
MAYBE IT'S ONE OF THE OTHER TREE TROLLS!
AND BESIDES, I COULDN'T JUST IGNORE THAT SOBBING. IT SOUNDED LIKE HOW I FELT.
THERE ARE OTHER TREE TROLLS? WHOA--WHO'S **THAT**?

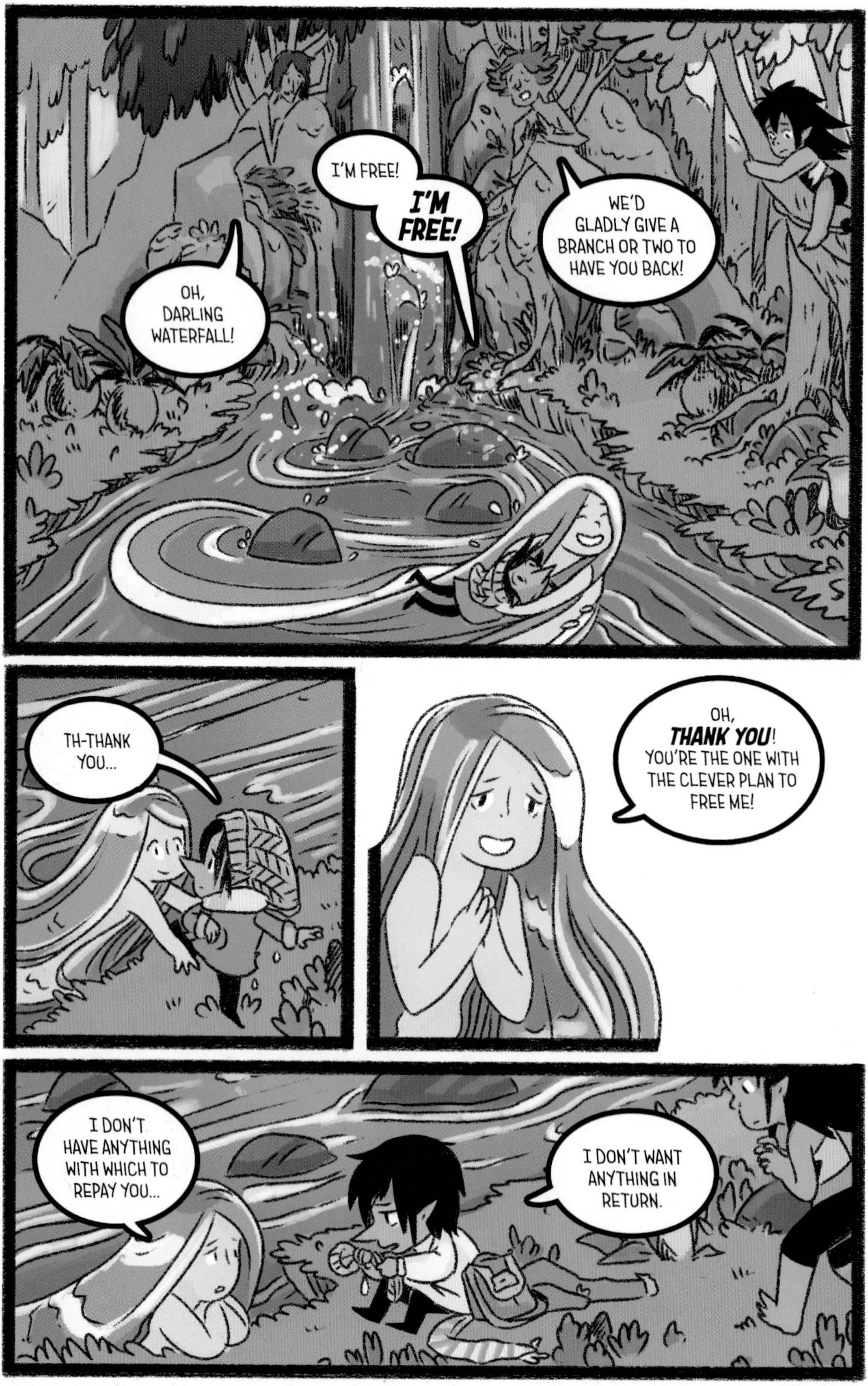
I'M FREE!
I'M FREE!
WE'D GLADLY GIVE A BRANCH OR TWO TO HAVE YOU BACK!
OH, DARLING WATERFALL!
TH-THANK YOU...
OH, THANK YOU! YOU'RE THE ONE WITH THE CLEVER PLAN TO FREE ME!
I DON'T HAVE ANYTHING WITH WHICH TO REPAY YOU...
I DON'T WANT ANYTHING IN RETURN.

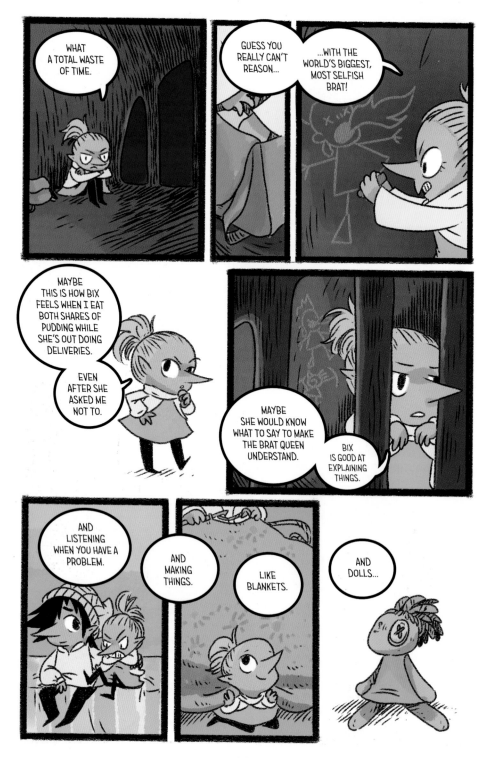

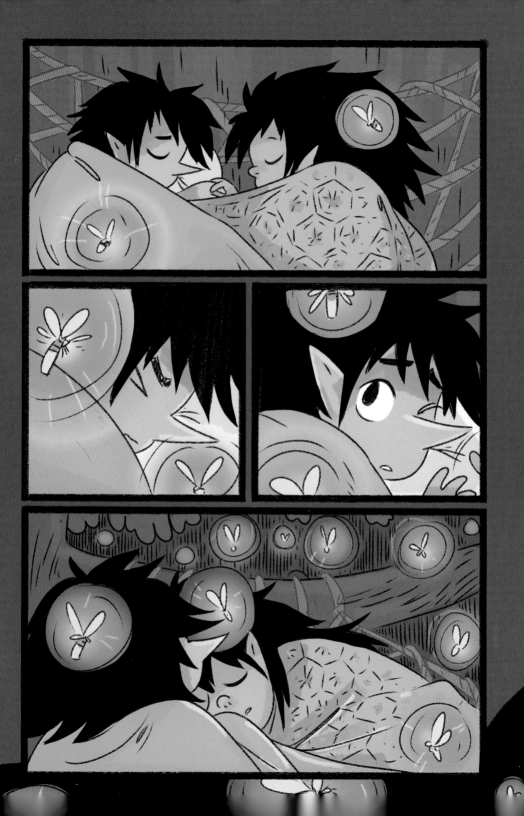

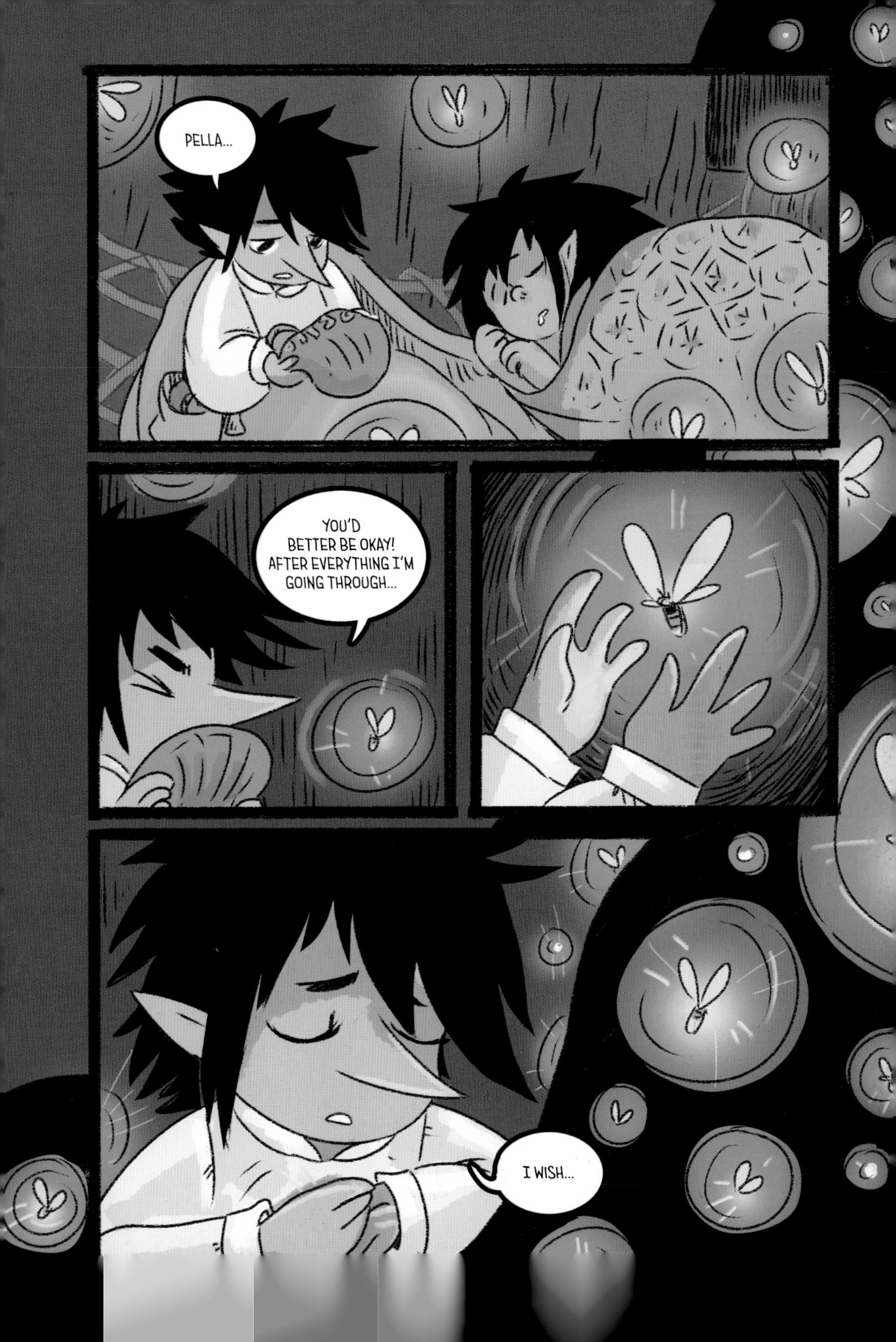
PELLA...
YOU'D BETTER BE OKAY! AFTER EVERYTHING I'M GOING THROUGH...
I WISH...

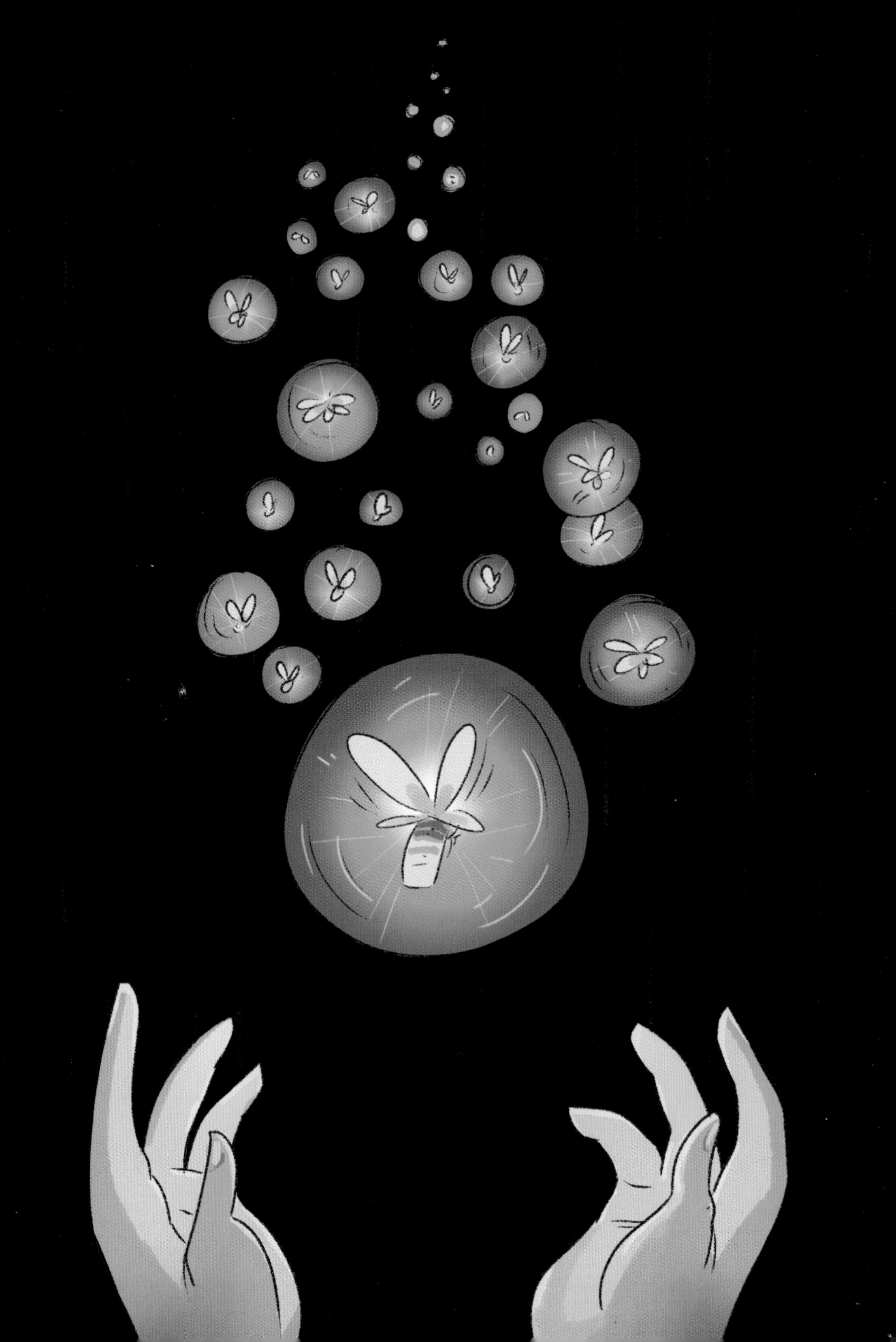

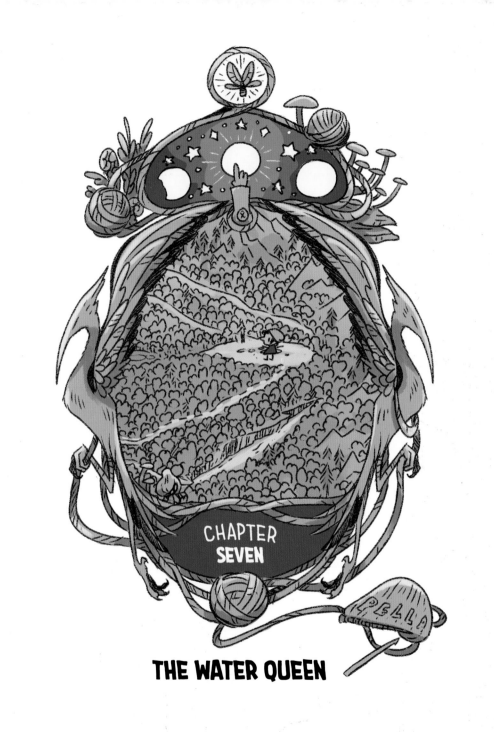

CHAPTER
SEVEN

THE WATER QUEEN

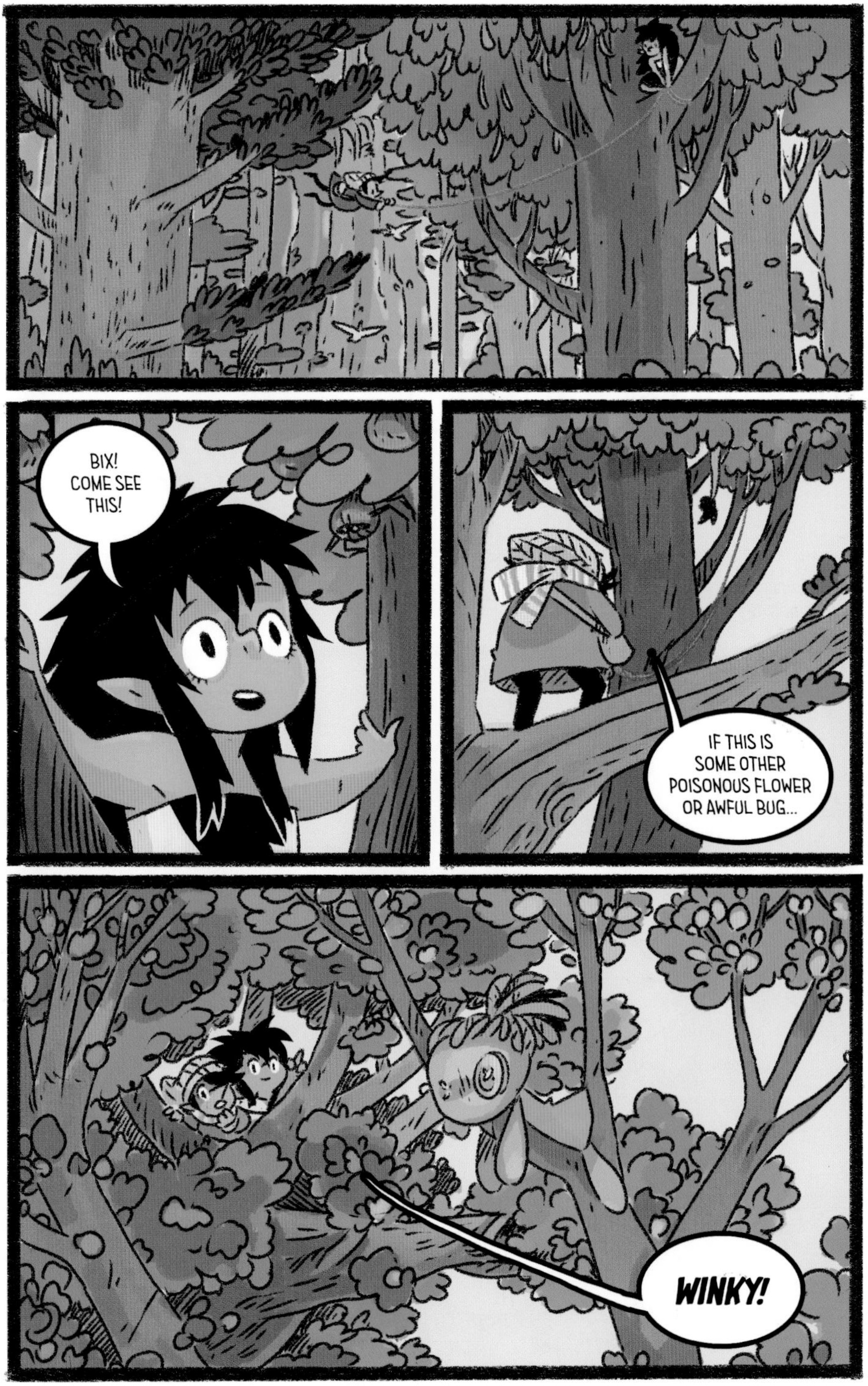
BIX! COME SEE THIS!
IF THIS IS SOME OTHER POISONOUS FLOWER OR AWFUL BUG...
WINKY!

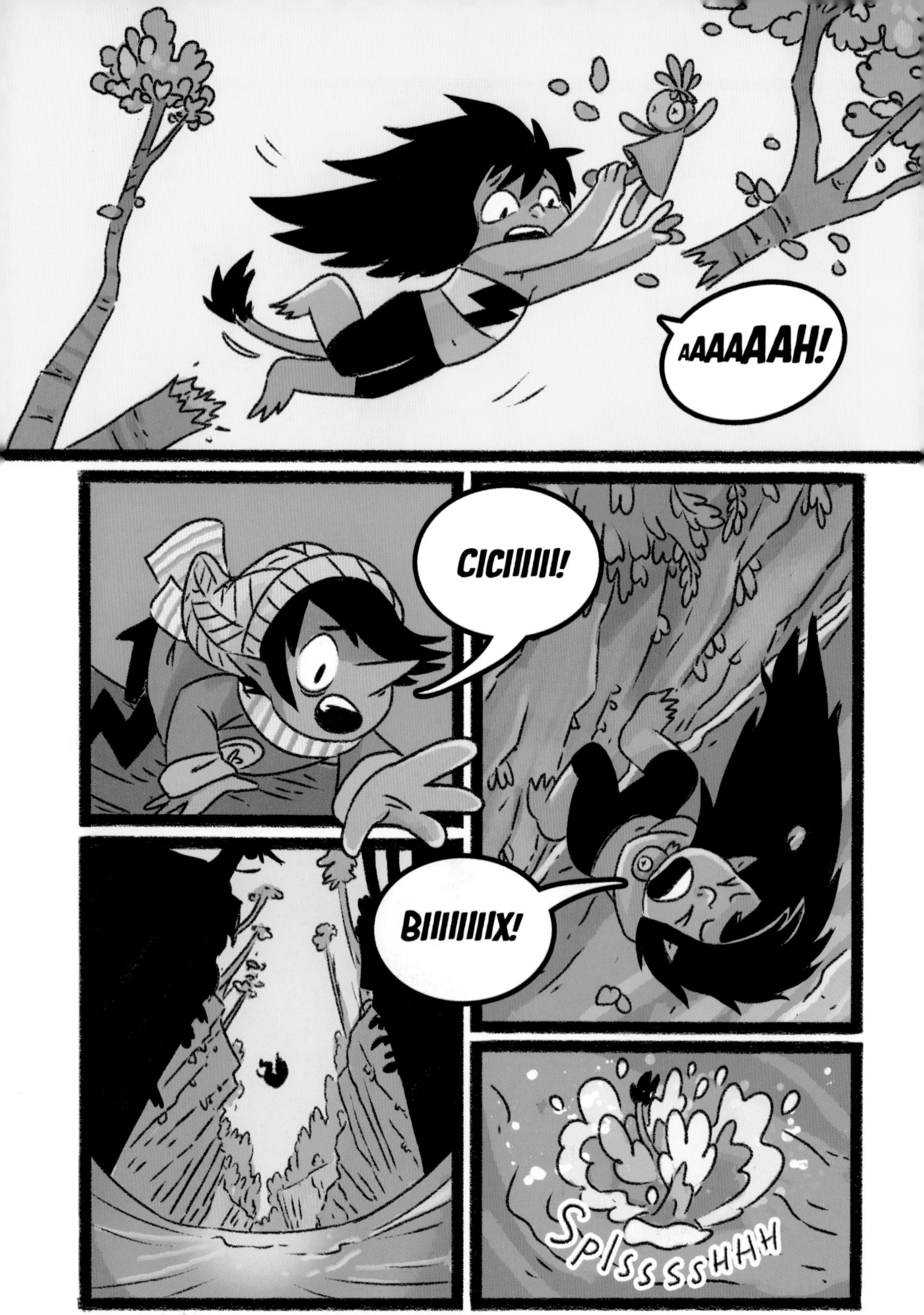
AAAAAAH!
CICIIIIII!
BIIIIIIIX!
SPLSSSSSHHH

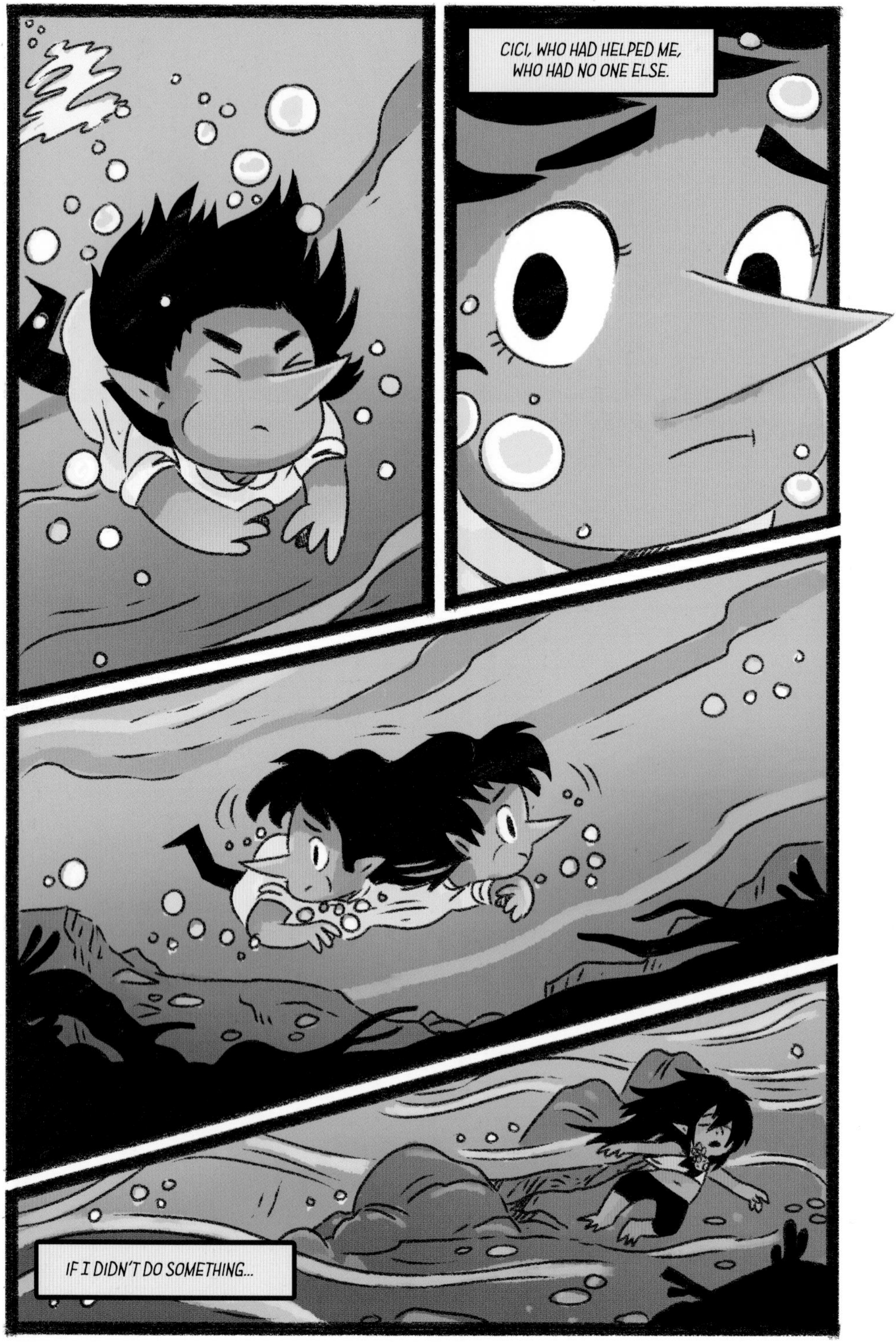
CICI, WHO HAD HELPED ME,
WHO HAD NO ONE ELSE.
IF I DIDN'T DO SOMETHING...

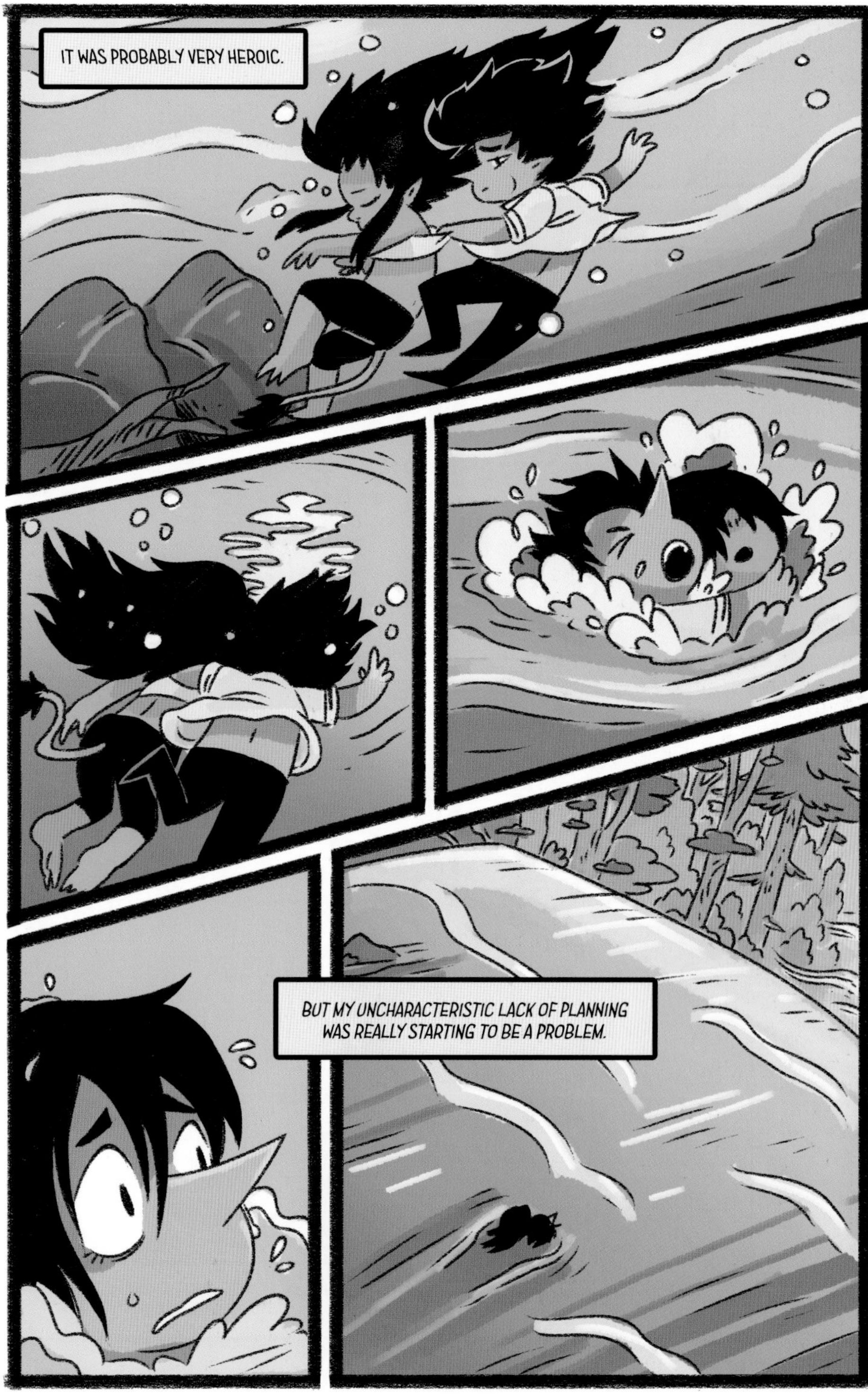
IT WAS PROBABLY VERY HEROIC.
BUT MY UNCHARACTERISTIC LACK OF PLANNING WAS REALLY STARTING TO BE A PROBLEM.

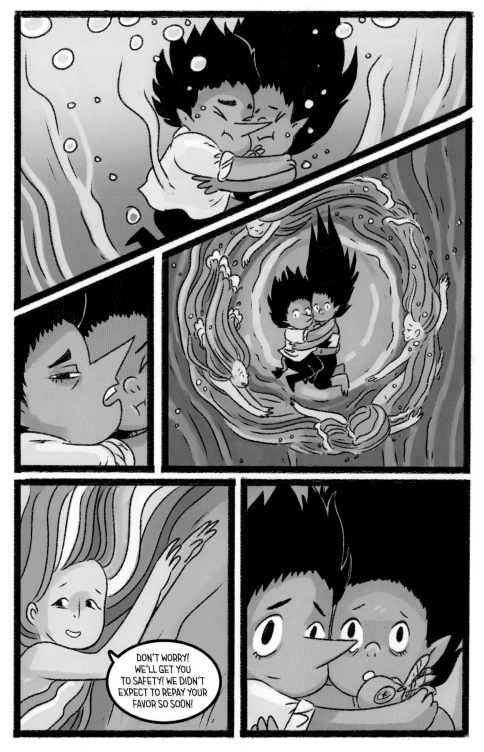

DON'T WORRY!
WE'LL GET YOU
TO SAFETY! WE DIDN'T
EXPECT TO REPAY YOUR
FAVOR SO SOON!

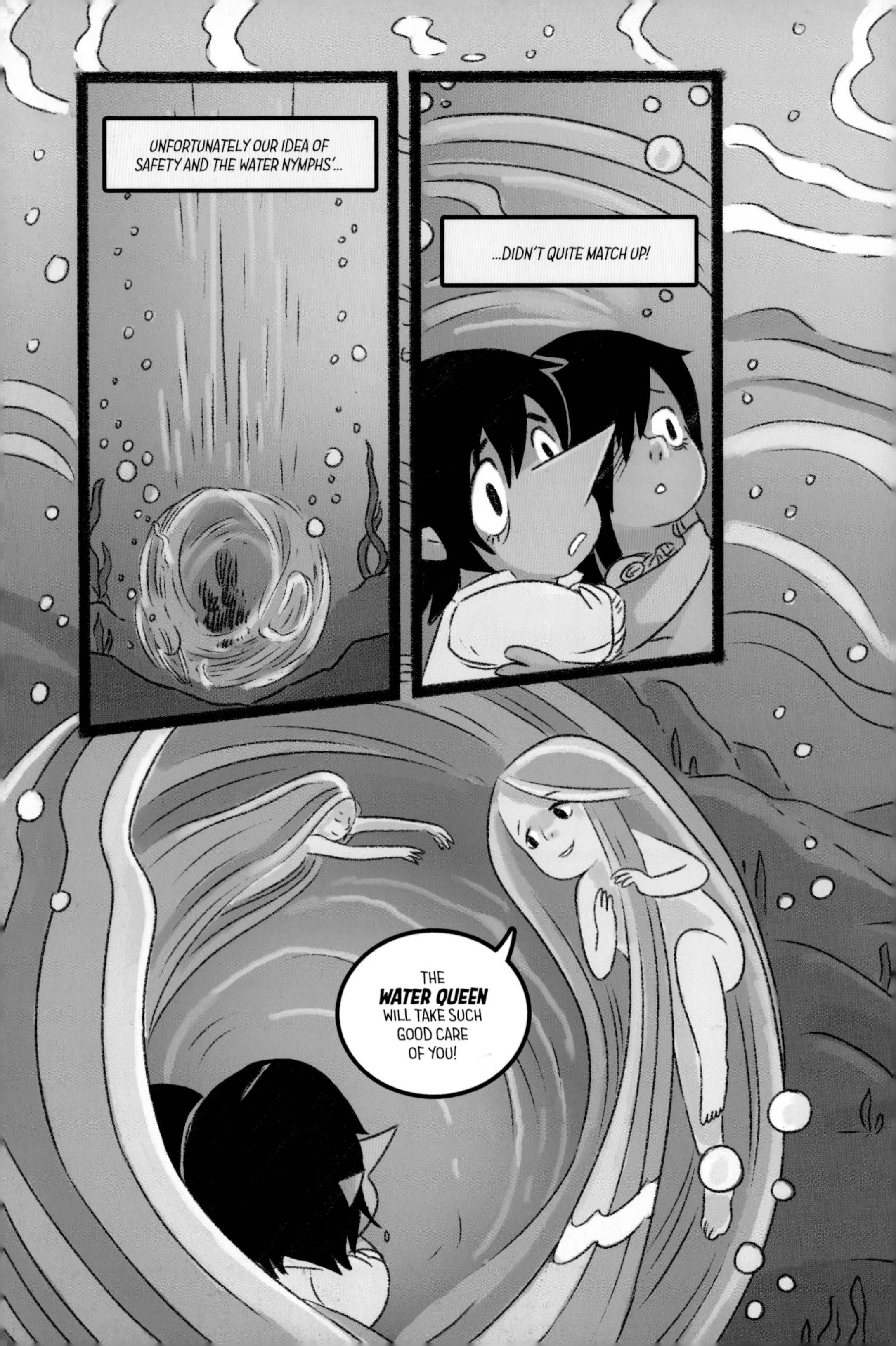

UNFORTUNATELY OUR IDEA OF SAFETY AND THE WATER NYMPHS'...
...DIDN'T QUITE MATCH UP!
THE **WATER QUEEN** WILL TAKE SUCH GOOD CARE OF YOU!

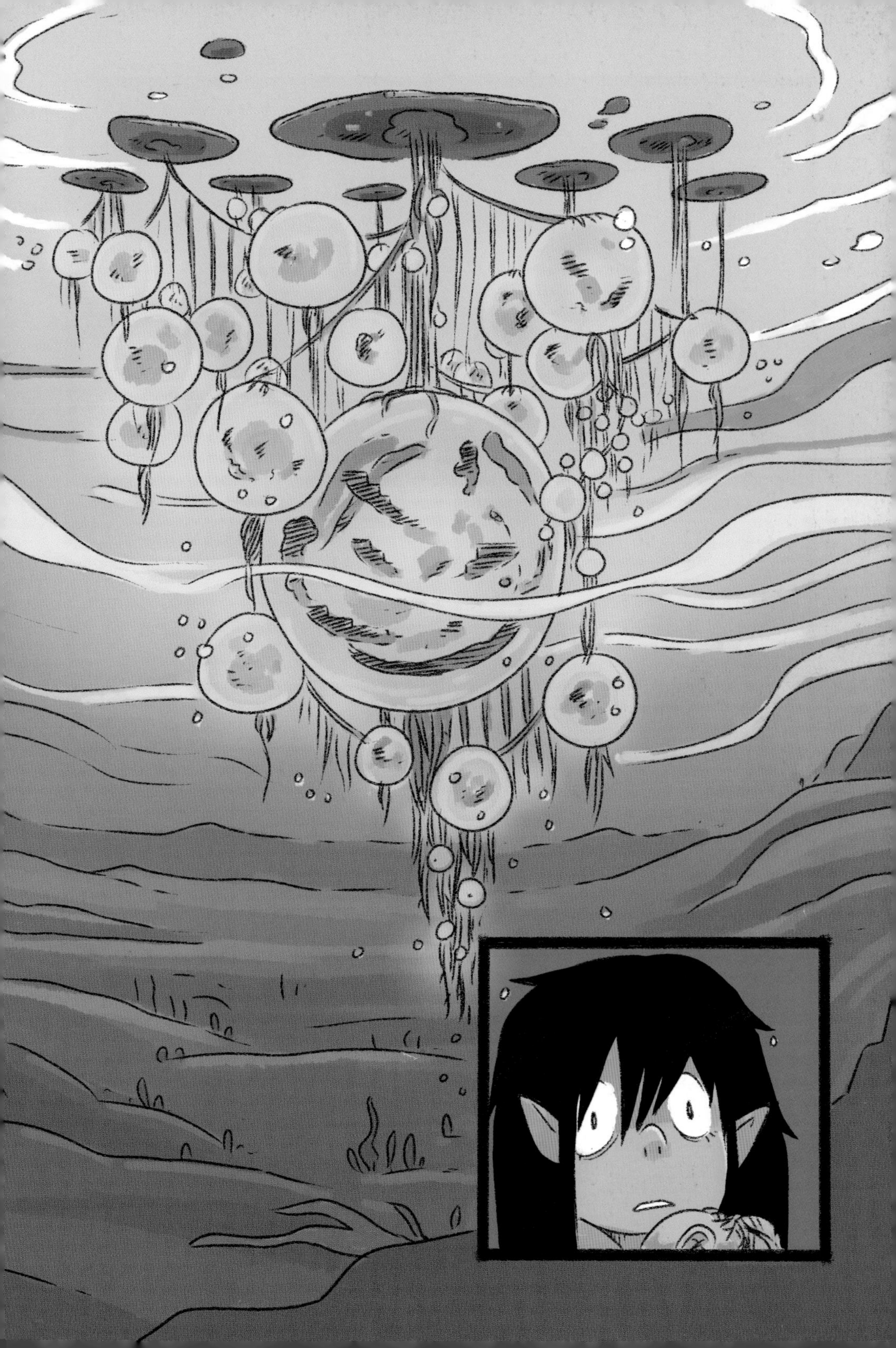

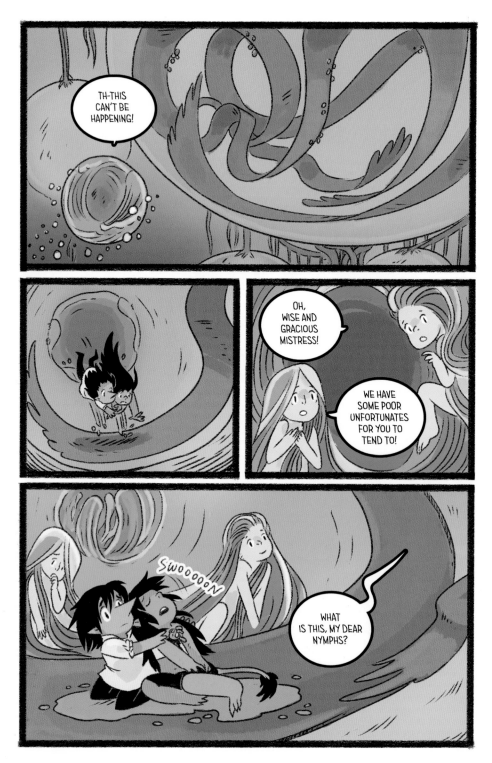

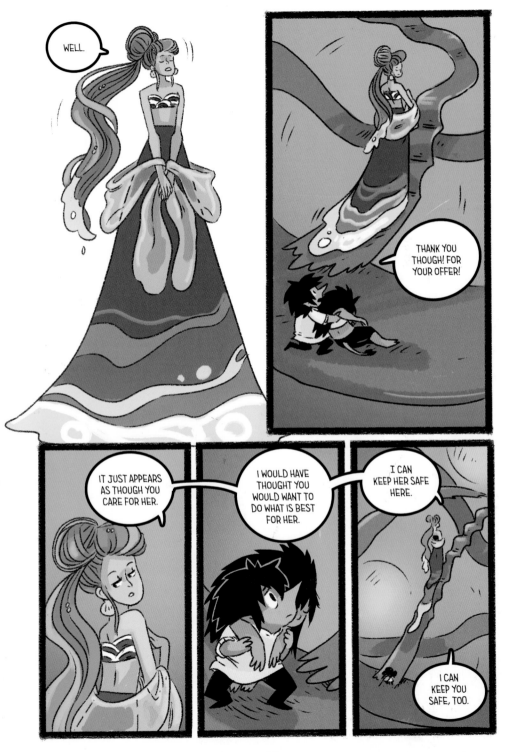

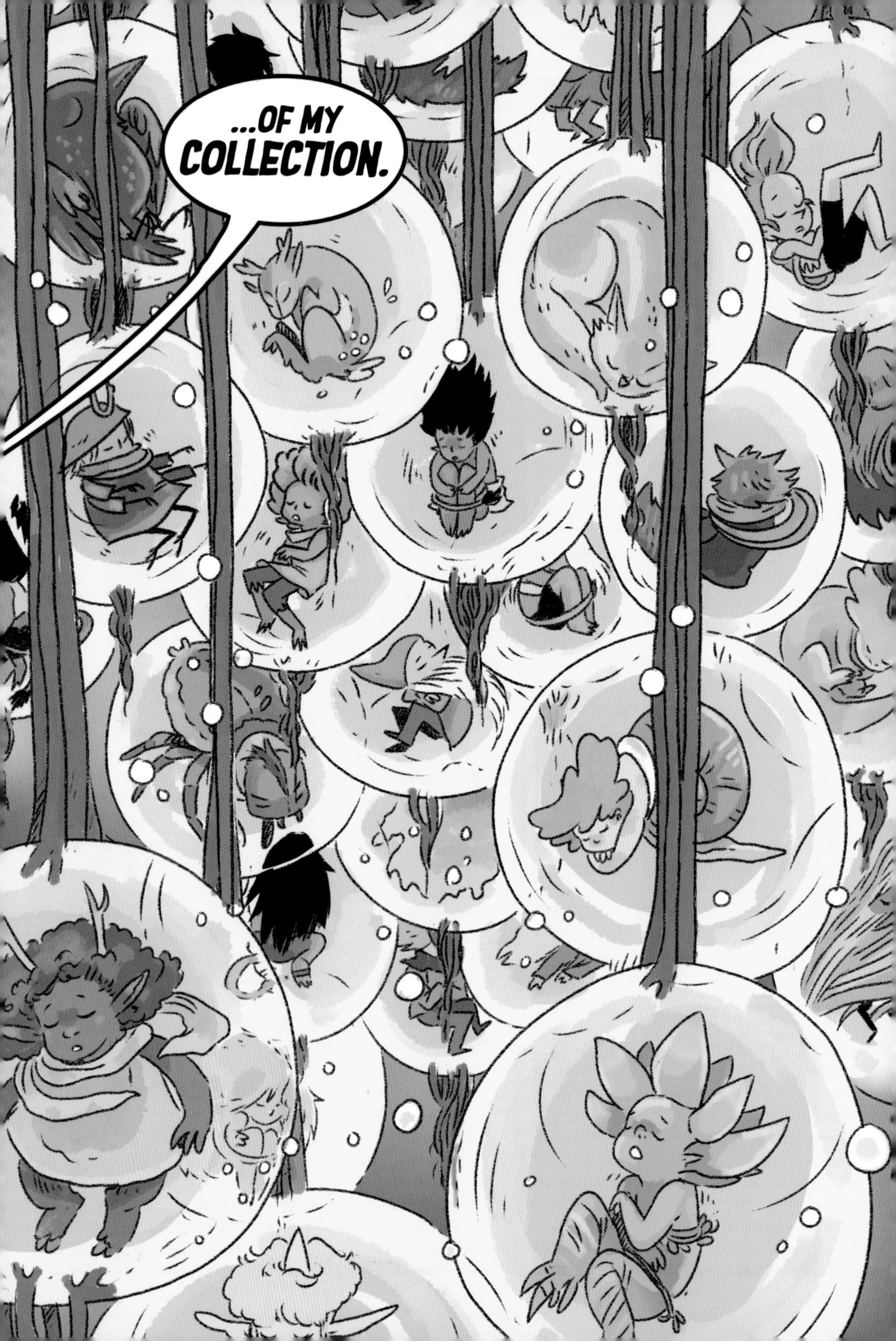
...OF MY COLLECTION.

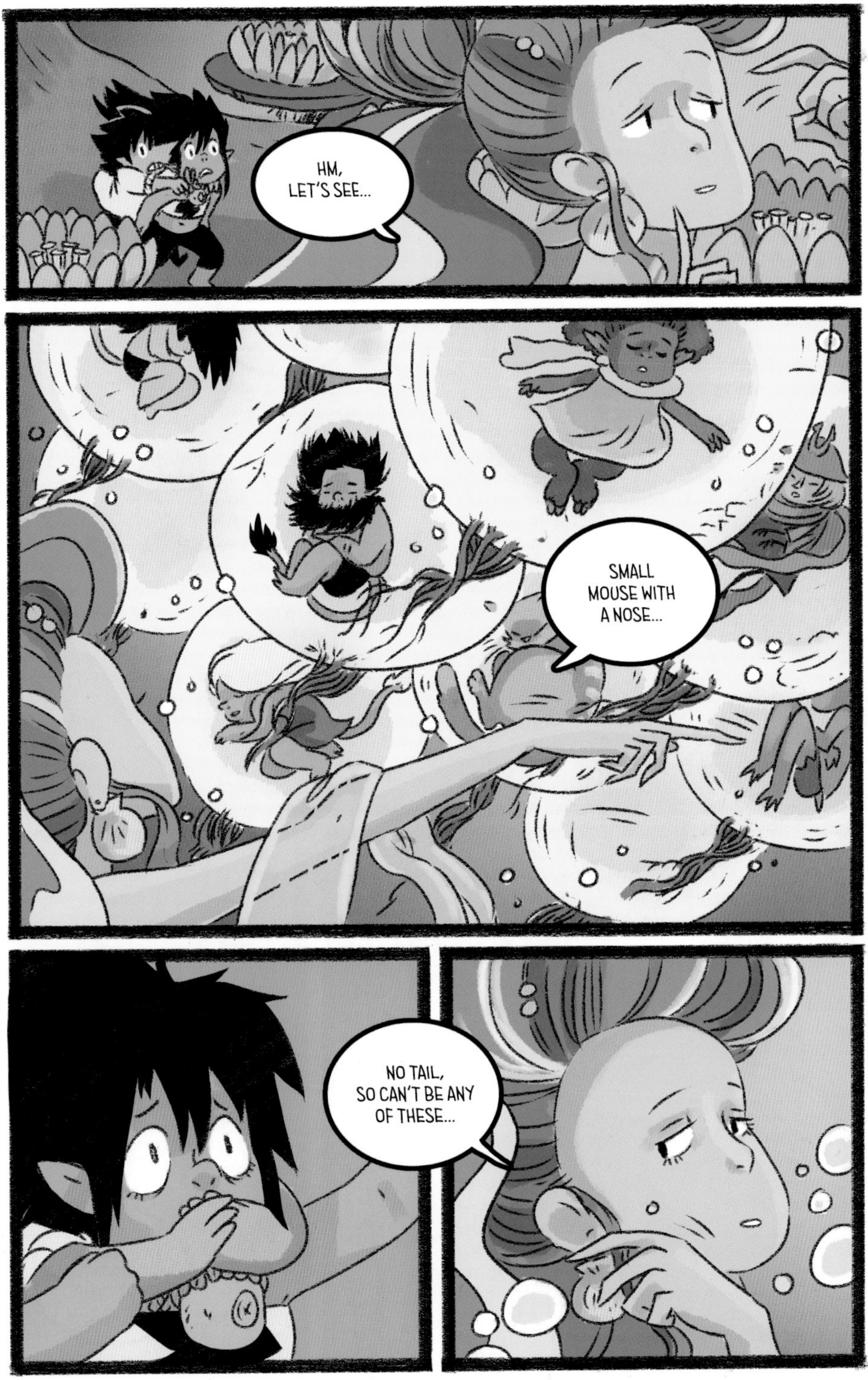
HM, LET'S SEE...
SMALL MOUSE WITH A NOSE...
NO TAIL, SO CAN'T BE ANY OF THESE...

...WAS HOW MUCH I WANTED TO SEE PELLA AGAIN.
ARE YOU GOING TO SLEEP ALL DAY, LITTLE BUG?
WHATEVER. BE LIKE THAT. YOU SHOULD BE THINKING ABOUT WHAT YOU'RE GOING TO SAY TONIGHT...
TO HELP ME CONVINCE THE **QUEEN MOTHER**--
HEY, ARE YOU LISTENING TO ME?

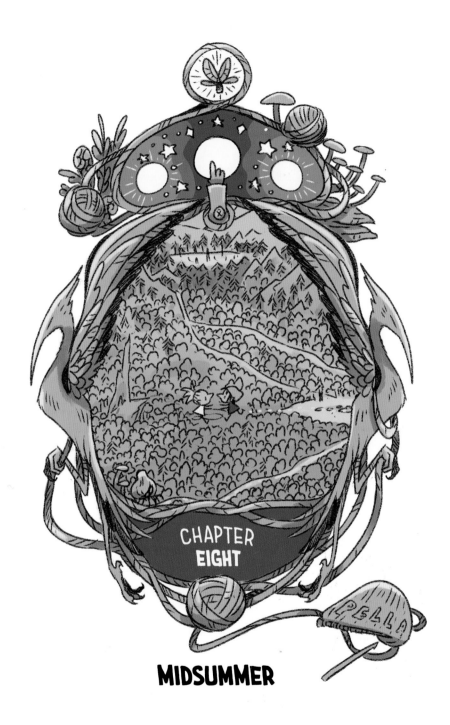

CHAPTER
EIGHT

MIDSUMMER

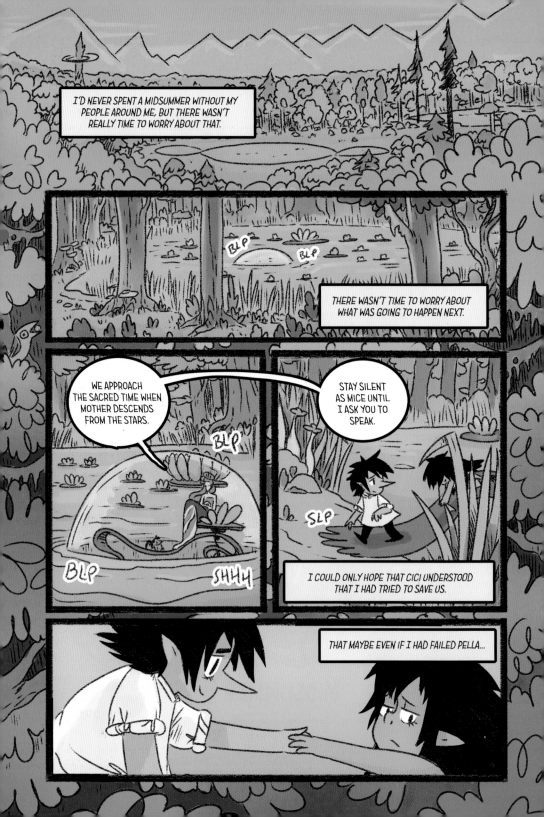

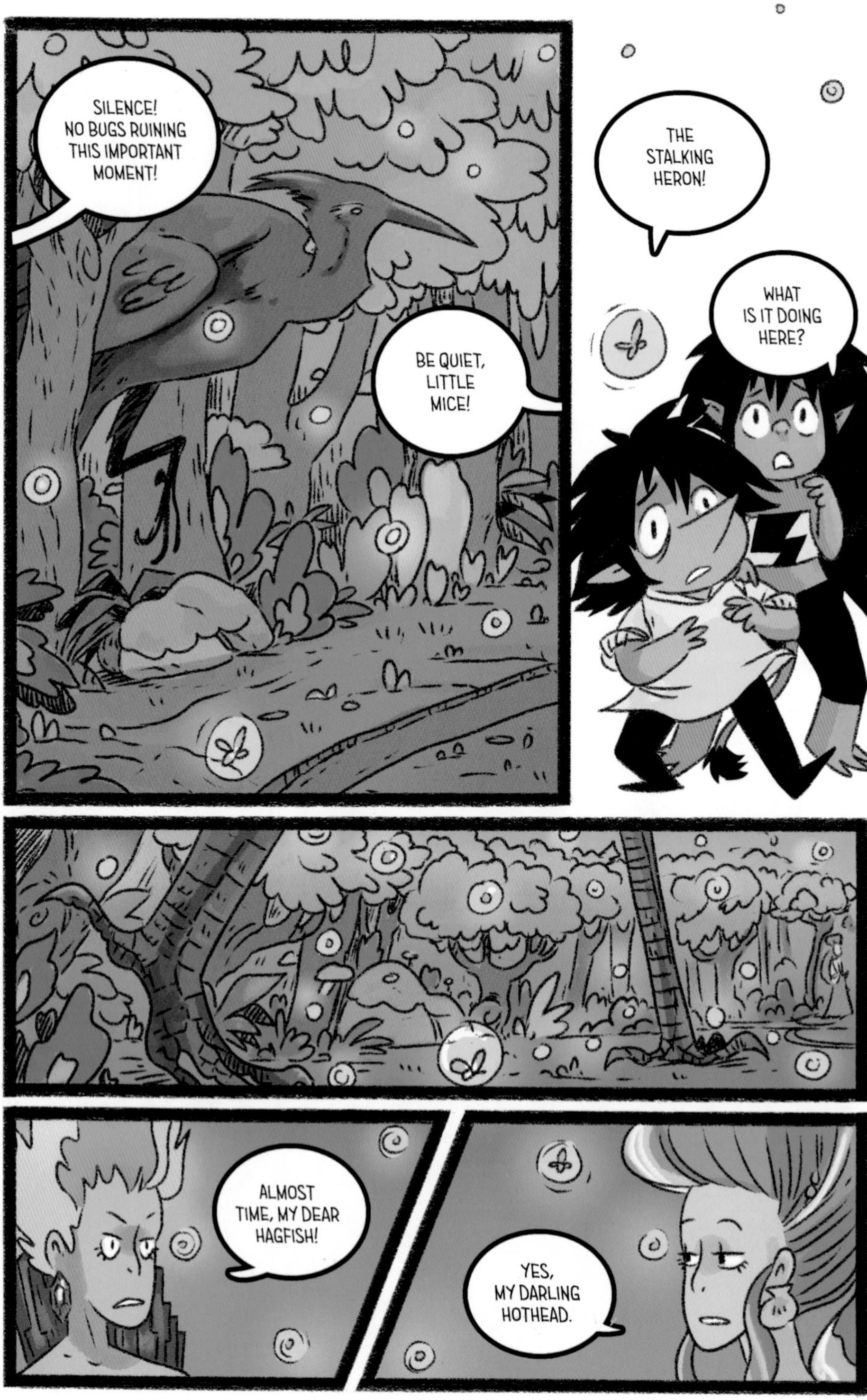
SILENCE! NO BUGS RUINING THIS IMPORTANT MOMENT!
BE QUIET, LITTLE MICE!
THE STALKING HERON!
WHAT IS IT DOING HERE?
ALMOST TIME, MY DEAR HAGFISH!
YES, MY DARLING HOTHEAD.

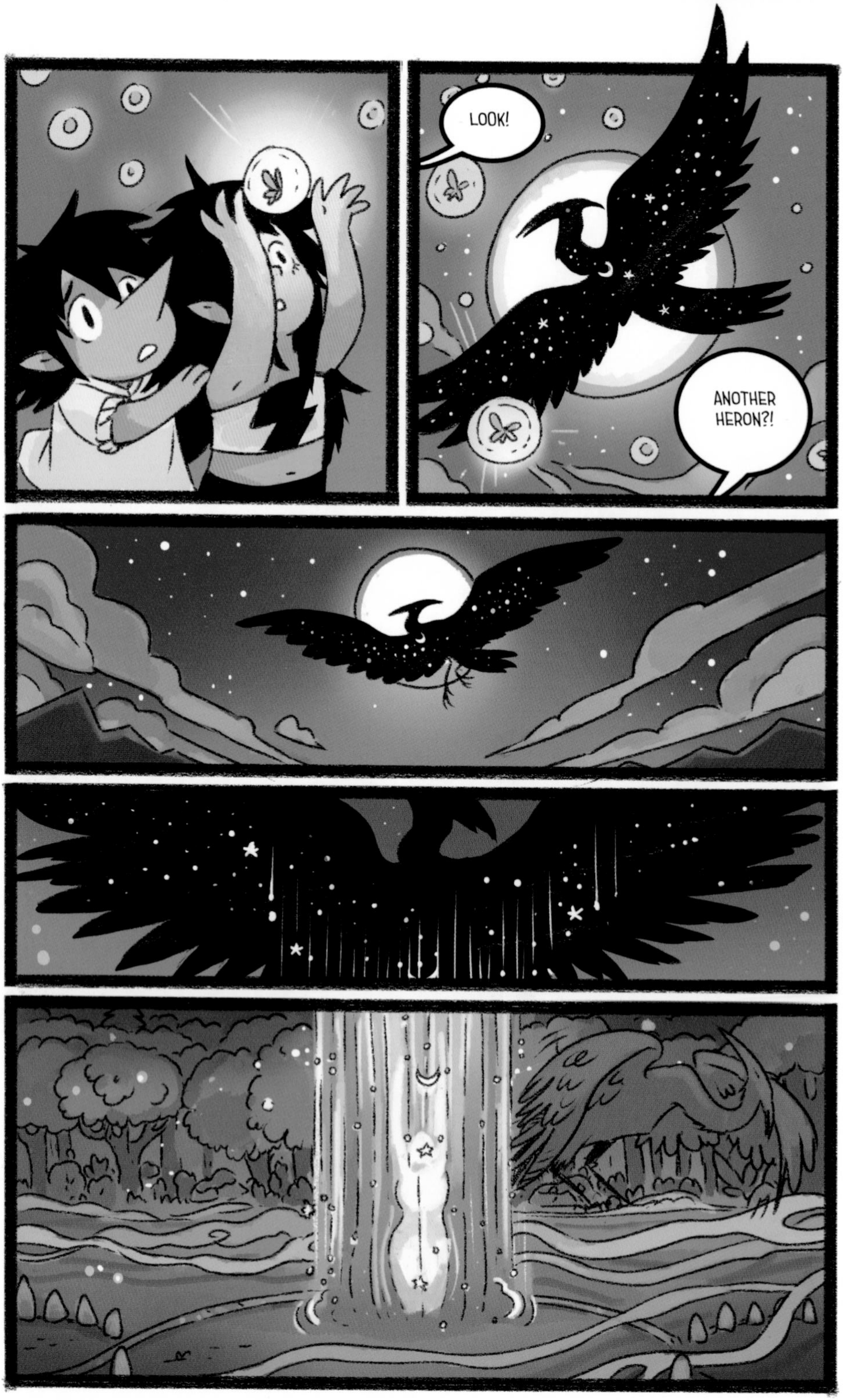
LOOK!
ANOTHER HERON?!

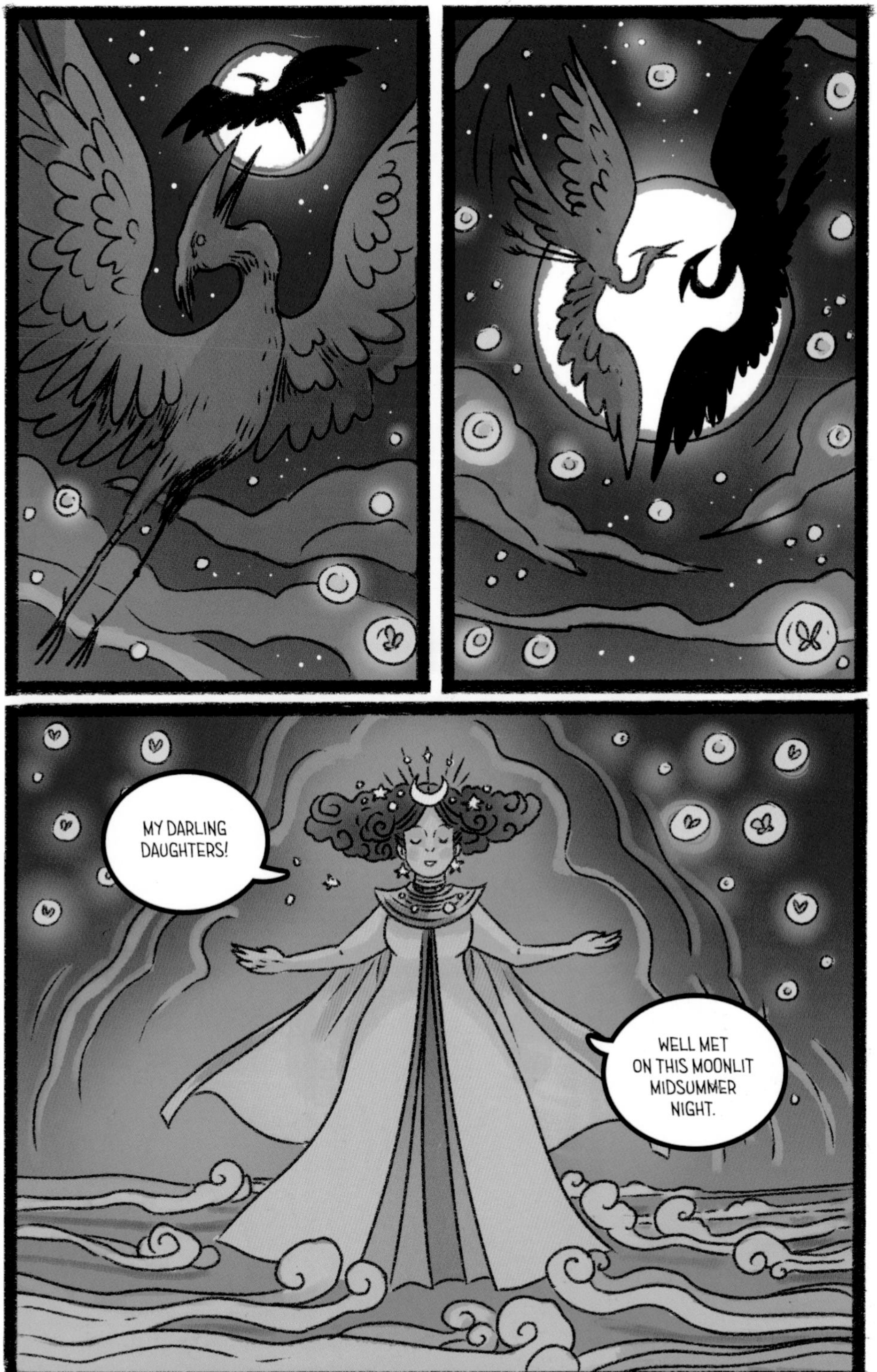
MY DARLING DAUGHTERS!
WELL MET ON THIS MOONLIT MIDSUMMER NIGHT.

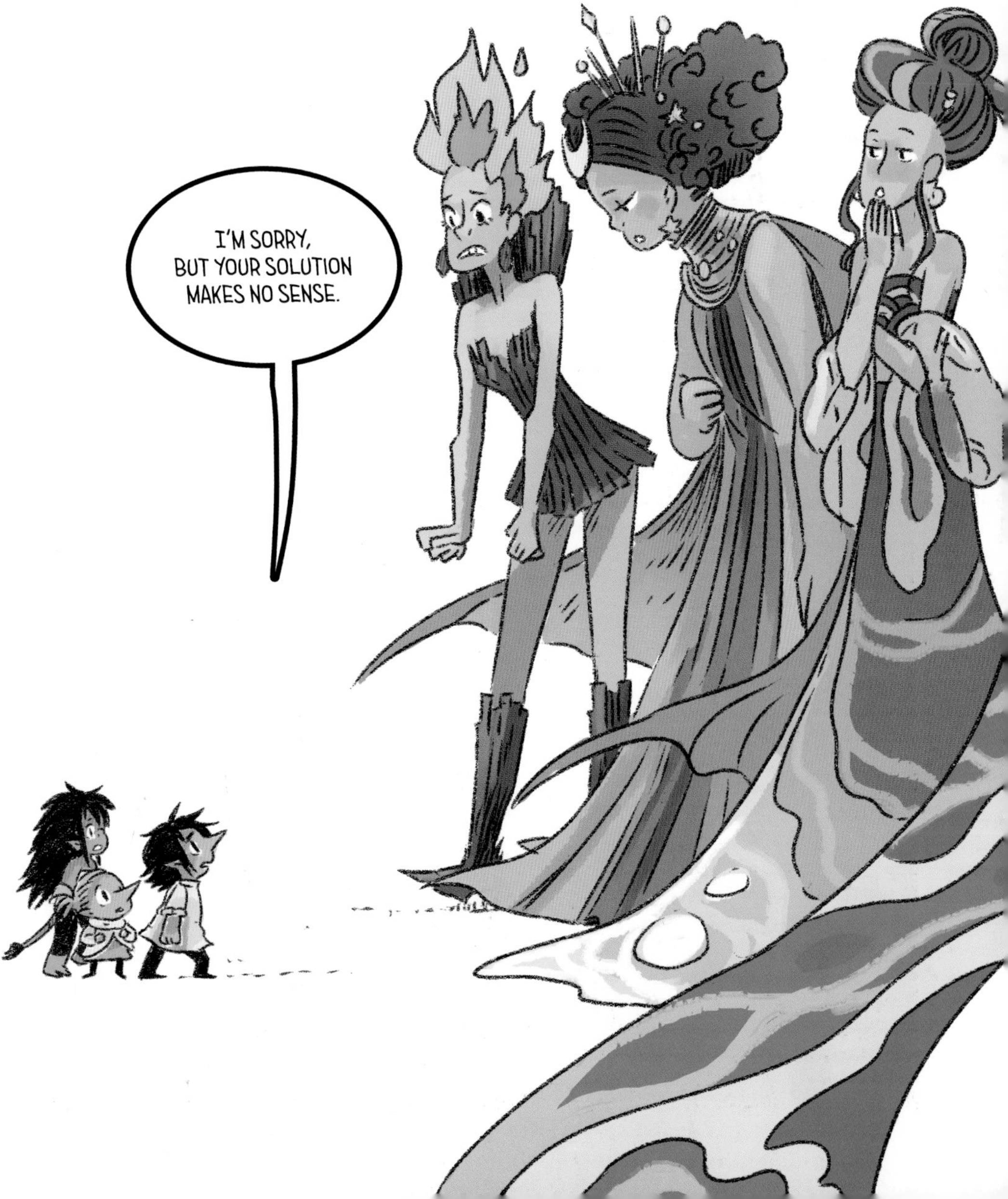
I'M SORRY, BUT YOUR SOLUTION MAKES NO SENSE.

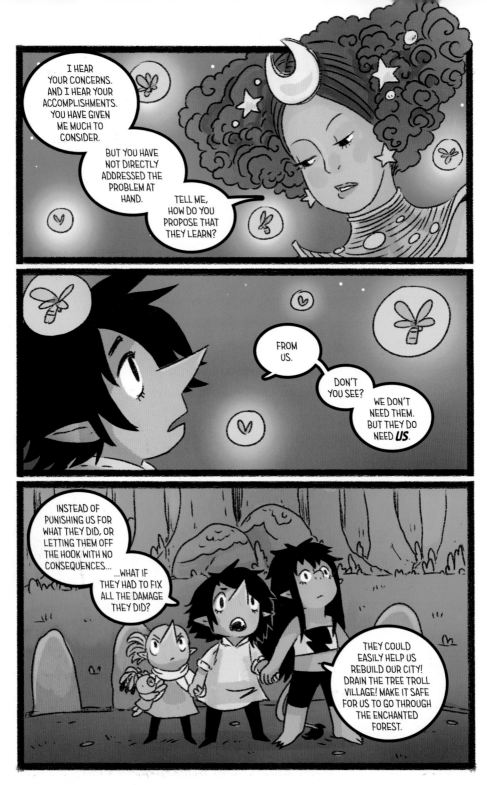

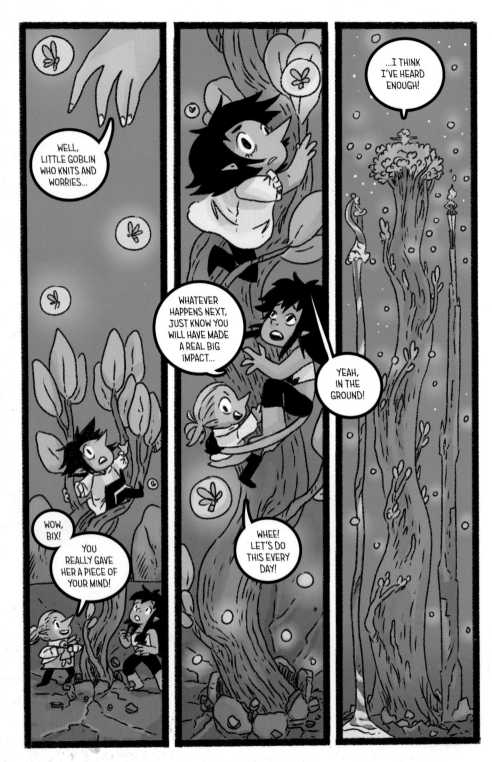

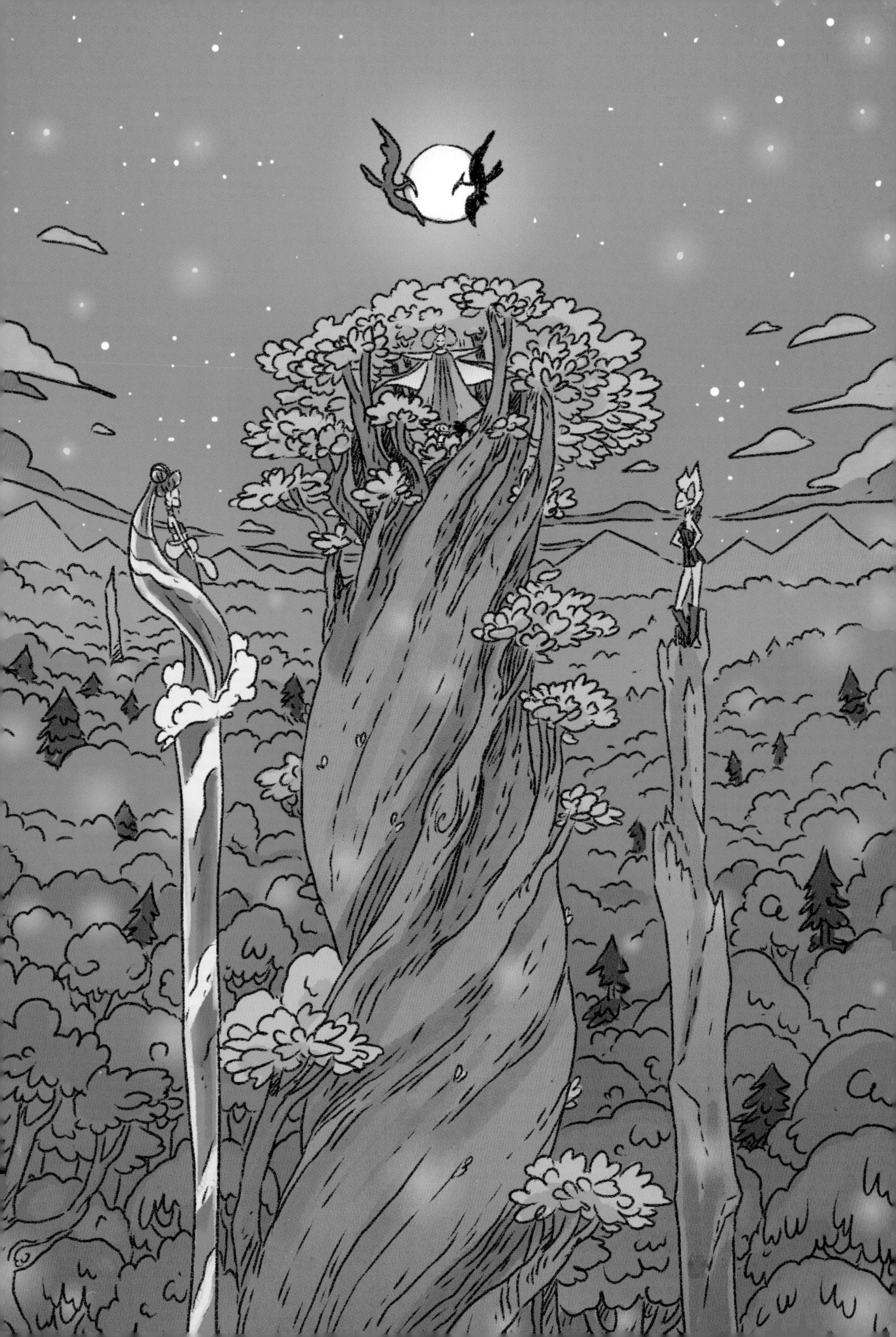

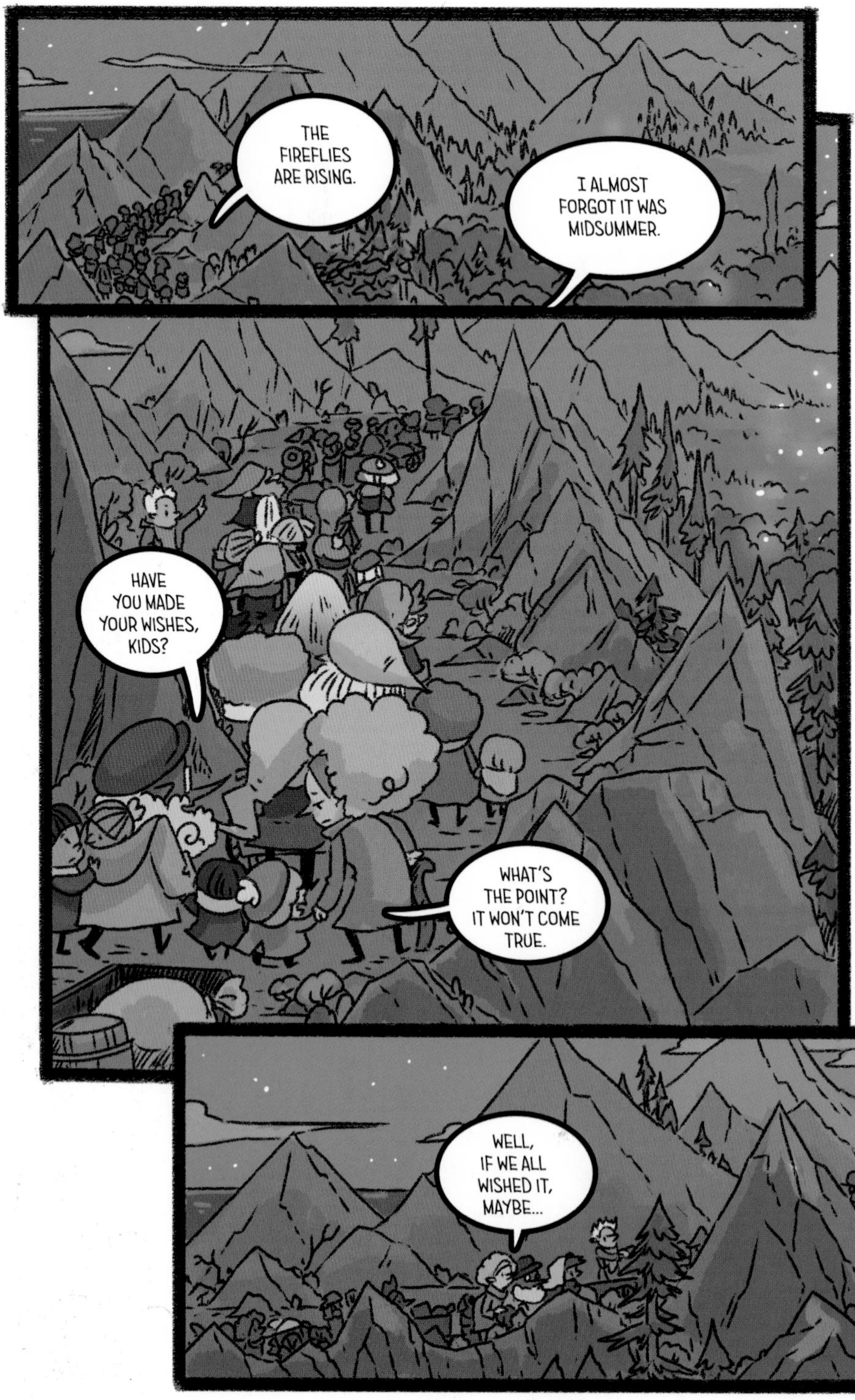
THE FIREFLIES ARE RISING.
I ALMOST FORGOT IT WAS MIDSUMMER.
HAVE YOU MADE YOUR WISHES, KIDS?
WHAT'S THE POINT? IT WON'T COME TRUE.
WELL, IF WE ALL WISHED IT, MAYBE...

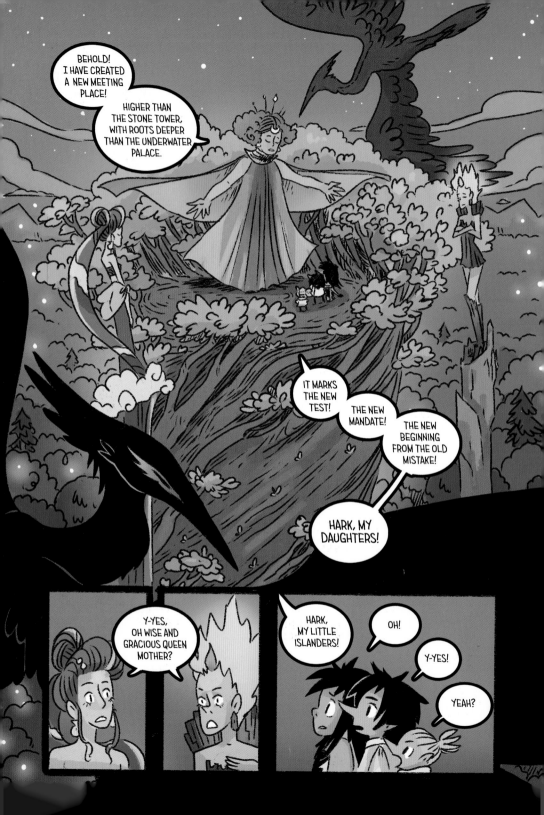

218

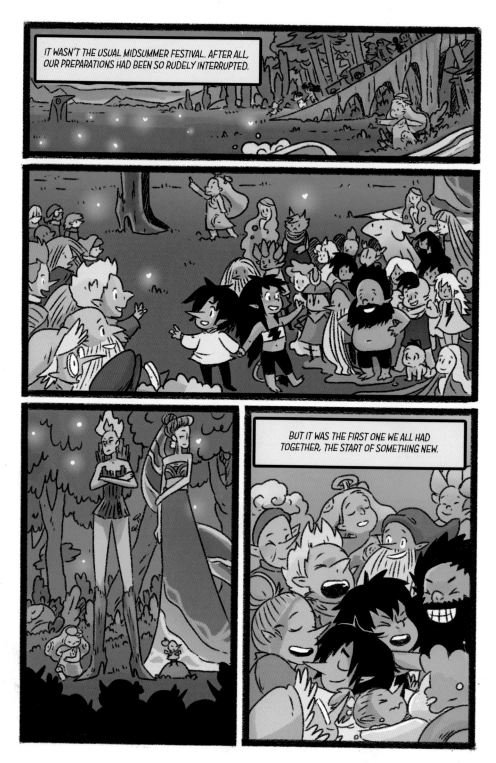

IT WASN'T THE USUAL MIDSUMMER FESTIVAL. AFTER ALL, OUR PREPARATIONS HAD BEEN SO RUDELY INTERRUPTED.

BUT IT WAS THE FIRST ONE WE ALL HAD TOGETHER, THE START OF SOMETHING NEW.

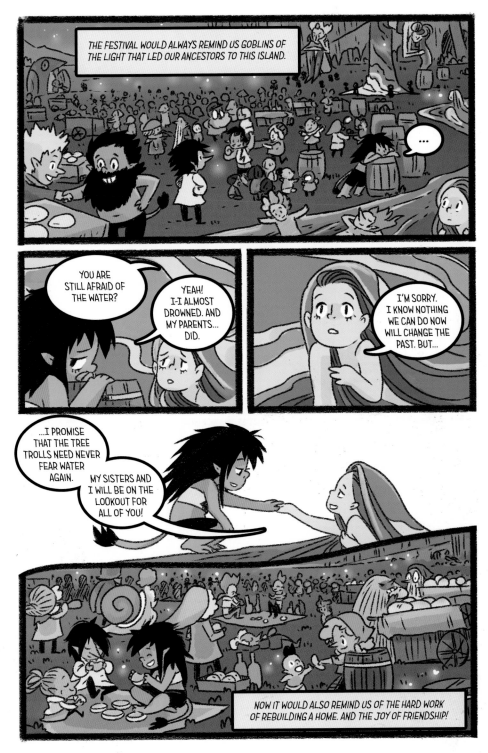

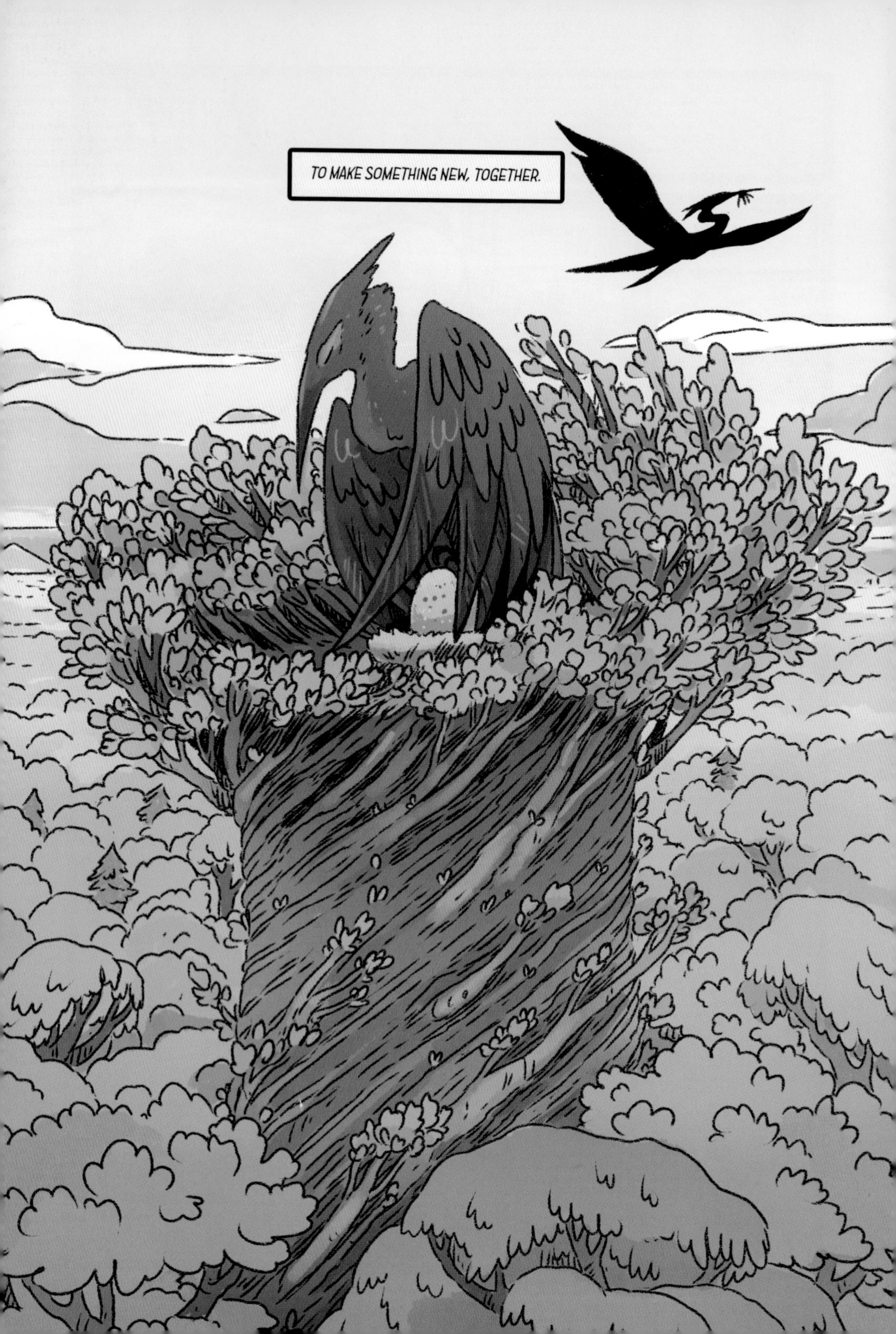
TO MAKE SOMETHING NEW, TOGETHER.

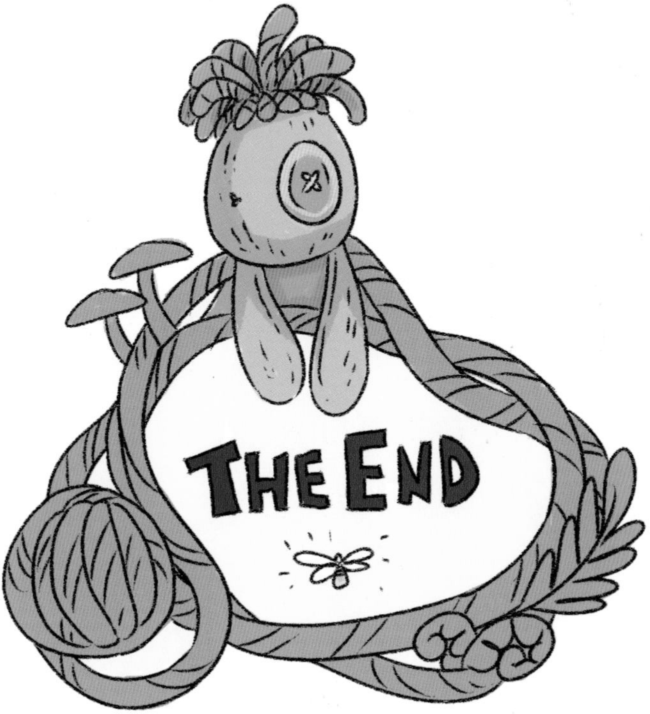
THE END

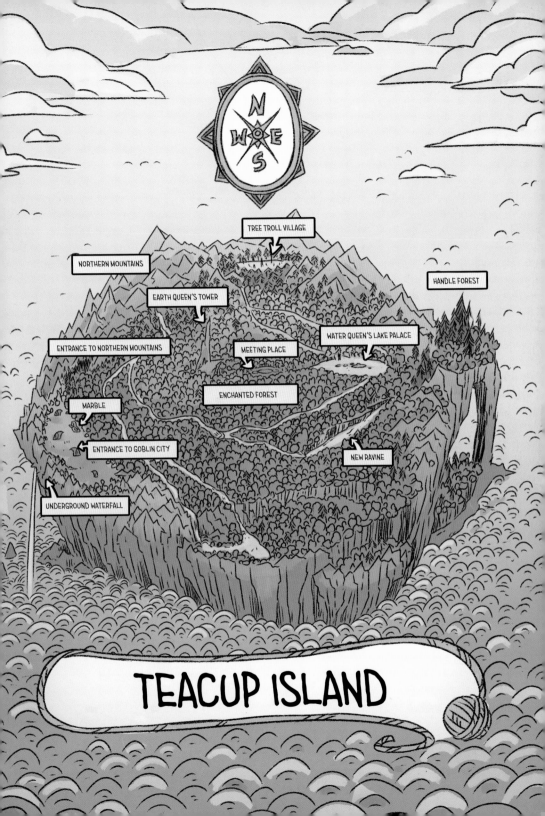

BESTIARY

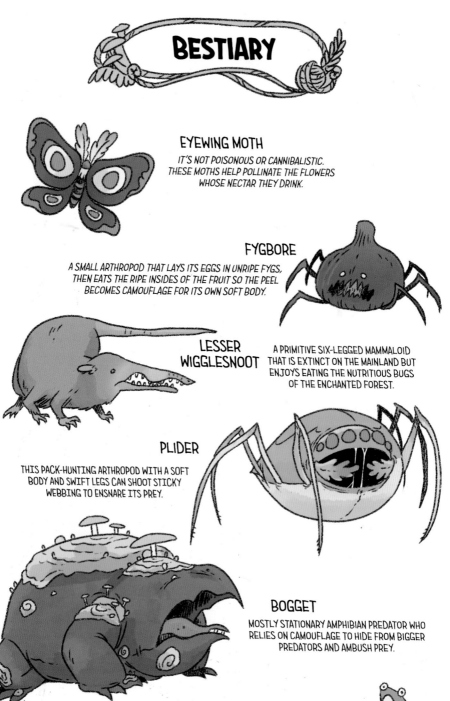

EYEWING MOTH

*IT'S NOT POISONOUS OR CANNIBALISTIC.
THESE MOTHS HELP POLLINATE THE FLOWERS
WHOSE NECTAR THEY DRINK.*

FYGBORE

*A SMALL ARTHROPOD THAT LAYS ITS EGGS IN UNRIPE FYGS,
THEN EATS THE RIPE INSIDES OF THE FRUIT SO THE PEEL
BECOMES CAMOUFLAGE FOR ITS OWN SOFT BODY.*

LESSER WIGGLESNOOT

*A PRIMITIVE SIX-LEGGED MAMMALOID
THAT IS EXTINCT ON THE MAINLAND BUT
ENJOYS EATING THE NUTRITIOUS BUGS
OF THE ENCHANTED FOREST.*

PLIDER

*THIS PACK-HUNTING ARTHROPOD WITH A SOFT
BODY AND SWIFT LEGS CAN SHOOT STICKY
WEBBING TO ENSNARE ITS PREY.*

BOGGET

*MOSTLY STATIONARY AMPHIBIAN PREDATOR WHO
RELIES ON CAMOUFLAGE TO HIDE FROM BIGGER
PREDATORS AND AMBUSH PREY.*

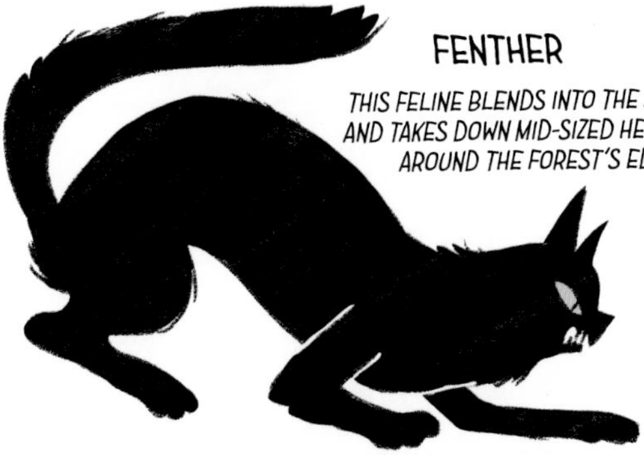

FENTHER

THIS FELINE BLENDS INTO THE SHADOWS AND TAKES DOWN MID-SIZED HERBIVORES AROUND THE FOREST'S EDGE.

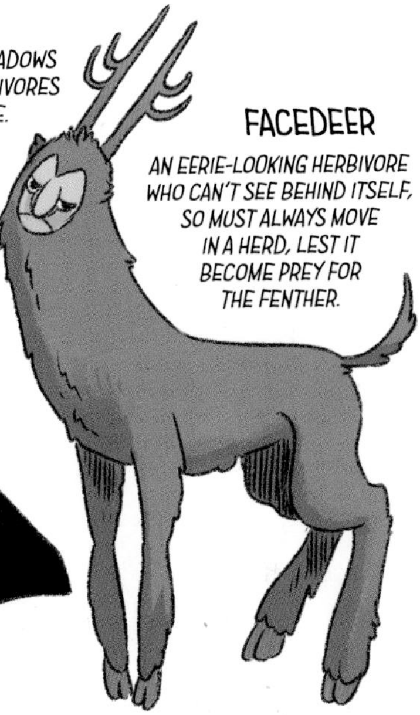

FACEDEER

AN EERIE-LOOKING HERBIVORE WHO CAN'T SEE BEHIND ITSELF, SO MUST ALWAYS MOVE IN A HERD, LEST IT BECOME PREY FOR THE FENTHER.

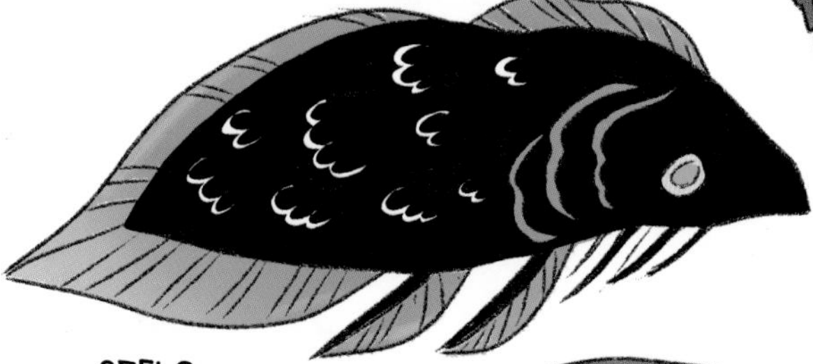

SEELO

A LARGE AND MYSTERIOUS FRESHWATER FISH THAT FEEDS ON THE SMALLER FISH ATTRACTED TO THE GLOWING PODS OF THE WATER QUEEN'S PALACE.

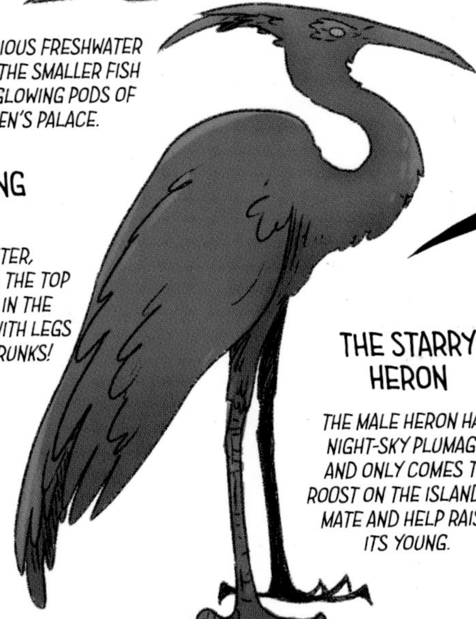

THE STALKING HERON

A VORACIOUS HUNTER, THE FEMALE HERON IS THE TOP OF THE FOOD CHAIN IN THE ENCHANTED FOREST, WITH LEGS THE SIZE OF TREE TRUNKS!

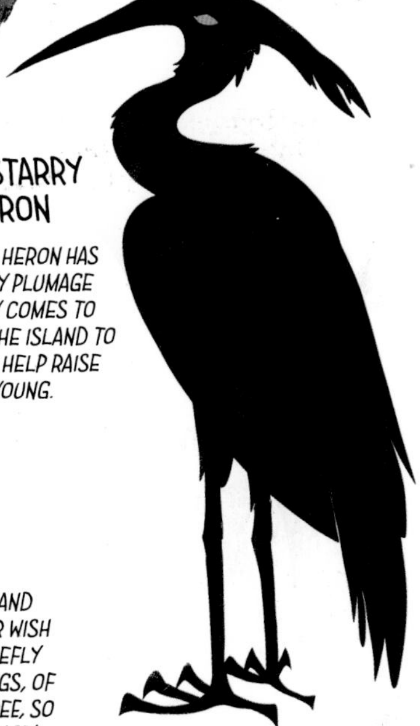

THE STARRY HERON

THE MALE HERON HAS NIGHT-SKY PLUMAGE AND ONLY COMES TO ROOST ON THE ISLAND TO MATE AND HELP RAISE ITS YOUNG.

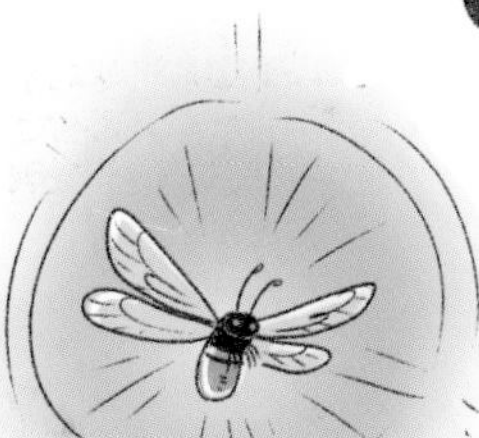

THE WISHING FIREFLY

IT IS SAID THAT IF YOU CATCH A FIREFLY AND MAKE A WISH, WHEN YOU RELEASE IT, YOUR WISH WILL RISE UP TO THE STARS WITH THE FIREFLY AND SOMEDAY IT WILL COME TRUE. THE BUGS, OF COURSE, ALWAYS JUST WISH TO BE SET FREE, SO THE LEGEND HELPS ENSURE THAT, AT LEAST!

THE LOCALS

GOBLINS

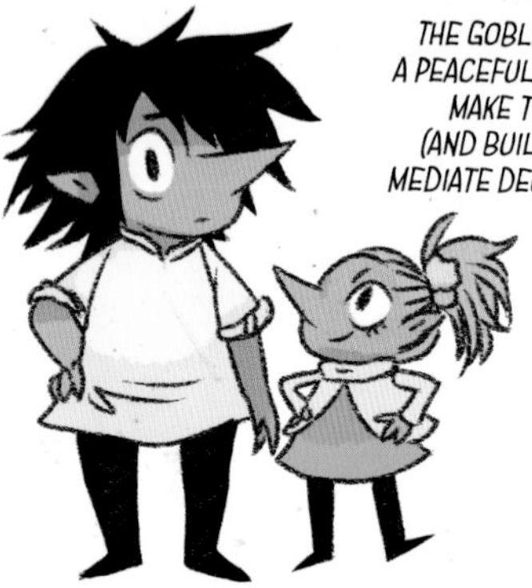

THE GOBLINS OF TEACUP ISLAND ESCAPED WAR ON THE MAINLAND TO SET UP A PEACEFUL CITY ON THE ISLAND. THEY LOVE TO BUILD AND DESIGN THINGS THAT MAKE THEIR LIVES EASIER AND GIVE THEM MORE TIME TO TELL STORIES (AND BUILD AND DESIGN NEW THINGS!). THEIR THREE COUNCIL ELDERS HELP MEDIATE DECISIONS THAT THE PEOPLE BRING TO REGULAR MEETINGS IN THE CITY CIRCLE, AS WELL AS TEACH CLASSES FOR ALL AGES.

TREE TROLLS

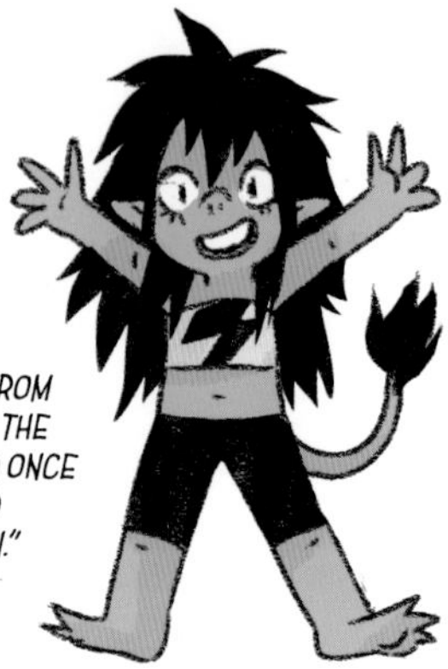

THE TREE TROLLS ALSO CAME FROM THE MAINLAND, DESCENDED FROM A SHIPWRECKED PIRATE CREW. THEY USED THEIR SKILLS CLIMBING THE MASTS OF SHIPS TO MOVE INTO THE TREES AS THEIR ANCESTORS HAD ONCE DONE, AND A FEW GENERATIONS LATER, THEY BECAME SKILLED ARCHITECTS. THEY STILL CALL THEIR ELECTED LEADER "CAPTAIN."

STONE NYMPHS

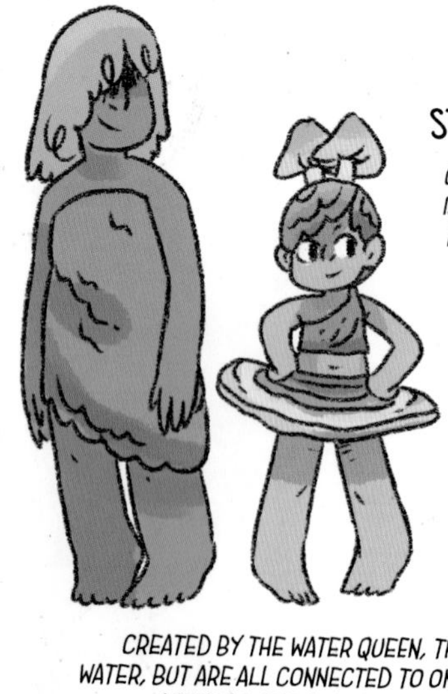

CREATED BY THE EARTH QUEEN OUT OF THE NATIVE STONE OF TEACUP ISLAND. IF THEY STRAY TOO FAR FROM HER THEY LOSE THE ABILITY TO MOVE UNTIL SHE COMES CLOSER. THEY ARE TOUGH AND STRONG AND DURABLE ENOUGH TO DEAL WITH HER TEMPER TANTRUMS, BUT THEY NEED A BREAK!

WATER NYMPHS

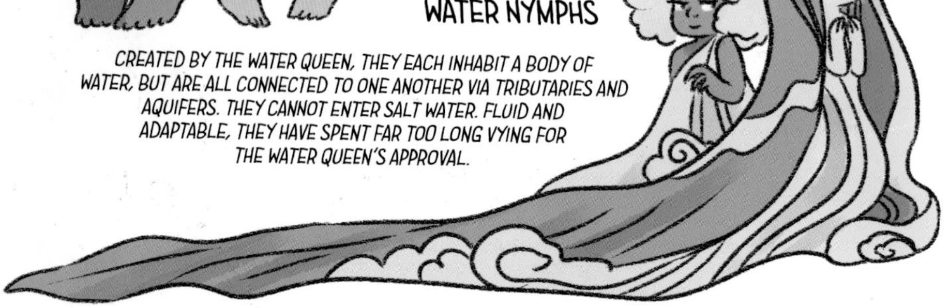

CREATED BY THE WATER QUEEN, THEY EACH INHABIT A BODY OF WATER, BUT ARE ALL CONNECTED TO ONE ANOTHER VIA TRIBUTARIES AND AQUIFERS. THEY CANNOT ENTER SALT WATER. FLUID AND ADAPTABLE, THEY HAVE SPENT FAR TOO LONG VYING FOR THE WATER QUEEN'S APPROVAL.

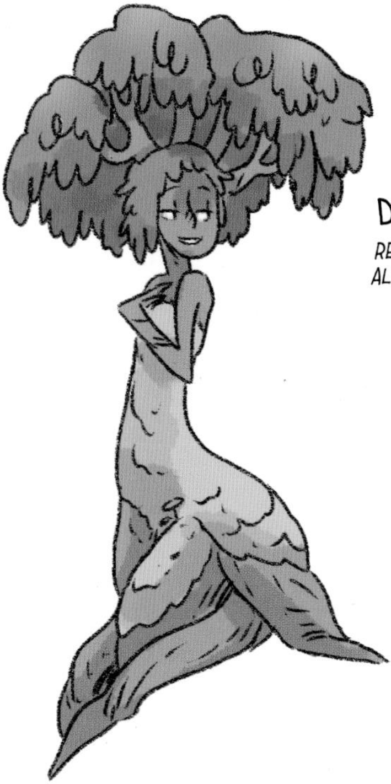

DRYADS

RELYING ON BOTH EARTH AND WATER, BUT OWING ALLEGIANCE TO NEITHER QUEEN, THE DRYADS ALL GREW FROM SEEDS THAT WASHED ASHORE FROM THE MAINLAND.

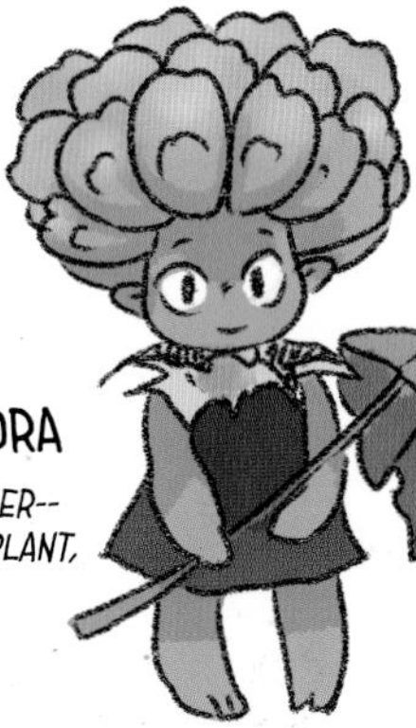

MANDRAGORA

MORE MOBILE THAN DRYADS--AND MUCH SMALLER-- THESE FOLKS ARE A SYMBIOTE OF MAMMAL AND PLANT, AND PHOTOSYNTHESIZE!

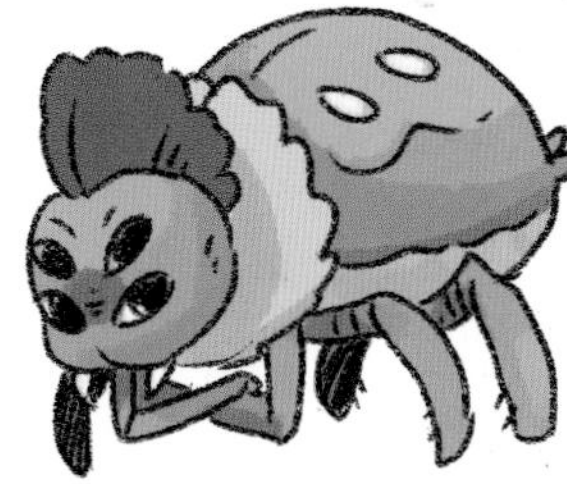

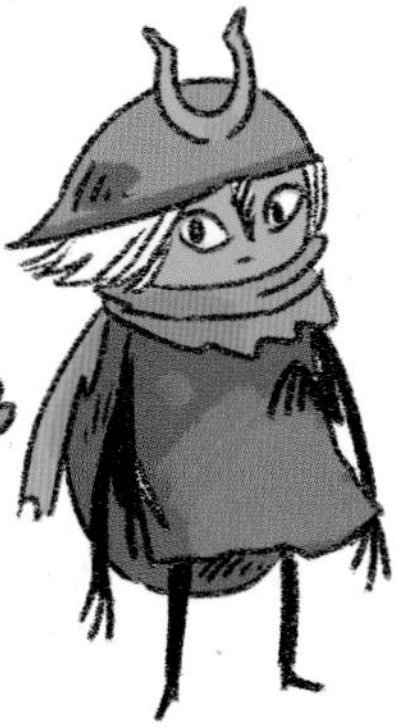

BUGLETS

A WIDE VARIETY OF BUGLETS EXIST. THEY TEND TO LIVE IN THE SOUTHERN REACHES OF THE ISLAND WHERE IT IS WARMER, BUT MANY HAVE VENTURED INTO THE ENCHANTED FOREST ONLY TO BE CAPTURED BY THE WATER QUEEN.

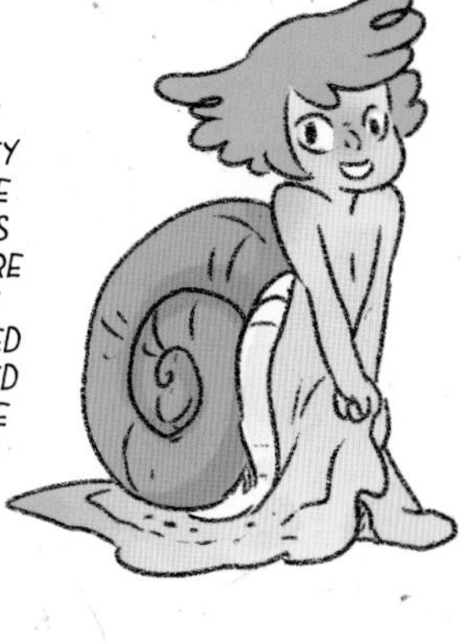

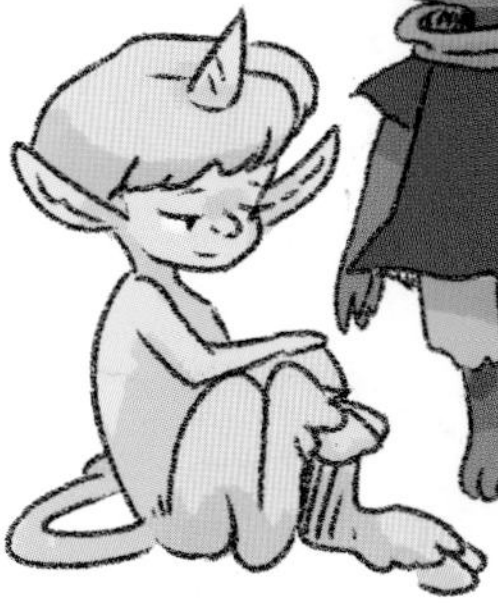

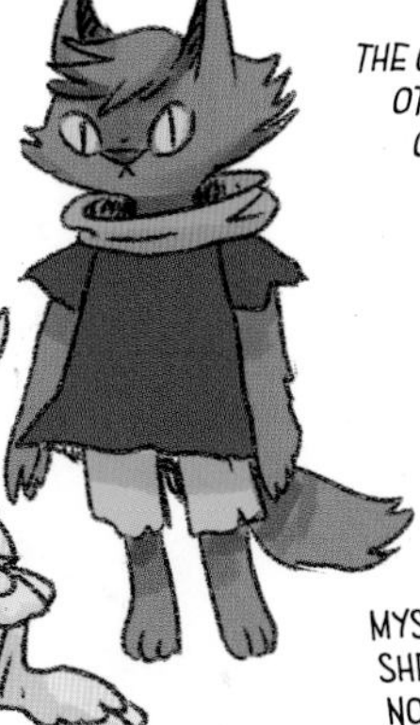

OTHERS...

THE UNICORN, THE JOURNEYCAT, AND MANY OTHER INTERESTING INDIVIDUALS LIVE ON THE ISLAND. SOME HAVE HOMES ELSEWHERE, SOME ARE EXILES, ALL HAVE THEIR OWN STORIES TO TELL.

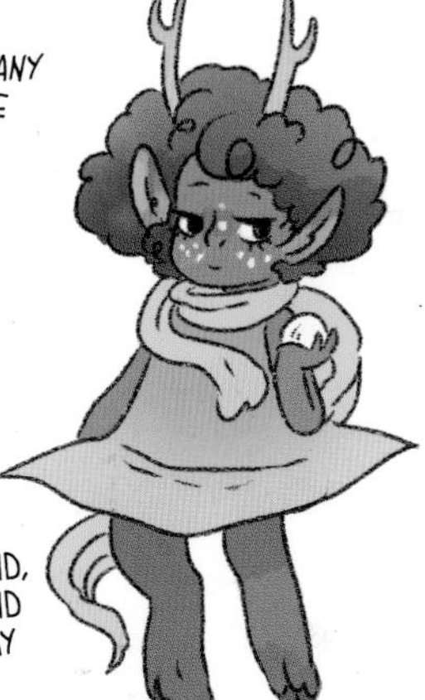

THE DEW FAIRY

THE MOST BEAUTIFUL AND MYSTERIOUS INHABITANT OF THE ISLAND, SHE'S UNIQUE AMONG THE LOCALS, AND NOW THAT SHE'S FREE, NEW MAGIC MAY BEGIN TO WORK ON THE ISLAND...

TIME FOR A THANK-YOU PILE!

This is my first author-illustrator book to roam the wild, and while it was a very personal
achievement, it also took so much help from other people to make it happen.
You can't do something this big alone!

Thank you to the team at First Second for all your hard work,
and thanks to my agent, Amy Stern, for everything behind the scenes.
Without the kindness and generosity of my friends and family,
I could never have completed this book, let alone to my satisfaction.
Elle, you counseled me through many bouts of impostor syndrome.
Steph, you inspire me to write better so I can catch up with you!
Rachel, you make me feel like a star.
Jamie, you make me want to work hard!
Caitlin, thank you for luring me out of hermitage with bubble tea.
Hannako, you challenged me to grow and helped me do it.
Stephie and Nike, you believed in me when we were just artist alley kids!
Lucy and MaryEllen, you brightened every week!
Betsey, I will never capture the energy you have, but I'll try!
CJ, you keep me going.
Nathan worked hard to color every character in this book,
and Will fed me breakfast that powered me through dozens of pages.
And of course I owe a special debt to Alan and Jesse,
who taught me how to be a big sister.
Also, Alan taught me how to letter comics, and encouraged me to make better
comics than I knew I could, so that's a lot of lessons from one little brother.
Thank you both for the musical inspiration as well. You are incredible.
There's room in this world for every person to be themselves and make an impact.
Never forget that.